PORTALS, PASSAGES & PATHWAYS

✳ ✳ ✳

PART I
IN THE LAND OF MAGNANTHIA

B . R . MAUL

ISBN-13: 9781493703821
ISBN-10: 149370382X
Library of Congress Control Number: 2013920491
CreateSpace Independent Publishing Platform
North Charleston, South Carolina

TABLE OF CONTENTS

1

A LONELY PLACE

The guardian knew what he had to do. He had trained and prepared for moments like these. He had spent months trying to identify and reveal the rogue wizard, a madman with no scruples. Bad luck had kept him a step behind...until now. Now he was a full step ahead of the betrayer.

The guardian had received word from a trusted source that the wizard was bringing the princess to this abandoned cabin near the top of Cold Hinge Mountain to deliver her to the overlord. The guardian knew this wizard trusted no one, so he would do the dirty work himself.

The guardian waited, watching the front door, the only way in or out. The cabin was nothing more than a single room with two small windows. Years of standing in high winds at the peak of the mountain had taken its toll on the cabin. The floorboards were loose and the walls were bowed in. The cabin moaned and its ripped curtains flapped nervously in the howling wind. It was a wonder this place hadn't been blown over the mountain's edge long ago.

Moonlight shone through the hole-riddled roof. The guardian stood still in the darkness, exhausted and sore from battle. Blood trickled from several cuts on his arms and face, and the gash in his side still burned despite the healing potion he recently drank. He channeled what little energy he could spare and healed several more wounds to avoid passing out. Then he rested his right hand upon his sword's hilt.

The sword was a gift from Boullengard, the Ward Wizard of the North. Boullengard was a grandmaster wizard and the guardian's dearest friend.

On his left hand, the guardian's thumb rubbed the ring on his finger. It gave him comfort knowing it was there. The ring was like an old friend, a friend to whom he owed his life. He had lost count years ago how many fights and battles the ring aided him, even lead him through, and how many enemies he defeated because of its powers.

He shivered. Not from the chill in the night, but knowing his choices, or lack thereof, put him in this predicament. He had already lost two of his closest friends to the enemy this night. Even worse, he had failed as a guardian. The princess was his sole responsibility. Because he let down his guard and trusted the wrong people, he had to do the unthinkable; he had to do what was best for the kingdom. The king and queen were going to hate him, curse the day he became a guardian, but he had to do it. No matter how many times he ran the recent events through his mind, he could think of no other way to end it. It was risky, but the kingdom he had called home would surely fall, leaving the land he loved and swore to protect in the hands of the enemy. If he failed to make the right choice, Magnanthia would be no more.

The winds increased and clouds began blanketing the moonlit sky. A lightning storm was threatening to emerge over the solemn hilltop. Heavy shadows danced about.

The guardian remained still, watching the door. Eventually he heard a familiar sound, a small, methodical thunderclap, and it wasn't from lightning. A passage had opened. The wizard he was waiting for finally arrived.

A gust shook the cabin. The oncoming lightning revealed a hooded figure swaying awkwardly back and forth. Through one of the cabin's windows the guardian watched the figure looking around at his surroundings, pausing here and there, looking for someone, or perhaps avoiding them. When the hooded figure turned and walked up to the door, it started drizzling.

The guardian drew his sword and readied himself. He would strike without warning. The door slowly opened. The figure paused, swayed, and then fell to the ground half way into the cabin. It started to pour. Rain slapped down upon the hooded figure's boots.

The guardian waited a moment before moving closer. He cautiously looked outside in the storm and then quickly around the dark cabin. Seeing no one else, he approached the figure. The guardian was confident it was not the wizard, who was taller than the person lying before him.

Ready to thrust the sword into the hooded cloak, he kicked the hood off of the body. His heart jumped up into his throat and he gasped for air. Even in the sporadic flashes of lightning he recognized the long, brunette hair of his princess.

He dropped to his knees, turned her over, and held the young woman's head in his hand. "Your highness, can you hear me?" he asked. She didn't respond. Her skin was pale and marred; her eyes were swollen as if she had been crying. He could barely look at her. Tears welled up in his eyes. How could this have happened? How did they ever fool him, the guardian whose sole purpose was to protect her?

The guardian was going to check her pulse when he heard another thunderclap behind him, different from the peals of thunder from the storm. In one, fluid motion he picked up his sword, jumped to his feet, and swung the blade out into the rain. The tip of his sword was within a foot of another hooded figure.

The figure was lean, tall, and stood confidently, holding a decorated staff at his side. His voice was equally as confident as his stance, with just a hint of surprise. "What are you doing here Peter?" asked the wizard.

"I should ask you the same thing," said Peter, keeping his sword pointed at the cloaked man in front of him. Peter stood between the wizard and the princess, who remained lying over the cabin's threshold. Now that he had the princess he wasn't letting anything or anyone between them.

The rain was relentless, blowing into Peter's face. But Peter didn't blink. He stared into the eyes under the hood, eyes he had seen and trusted for years, eyes belonging to one of the oldest and most powerful wizards in Magnanthia. Warwick Darken, one of only a handful of grandmaster wizards, was the Ward Wizard of the West. He protected the western boarder and managed the affairs in western Magnanthia for the royal family. Nothing ever happened in the west without Warwick knowing about it. In the west he was second only to the king, and he was a stern ruler that many feared. The fear that Peter was feeling, however, was for the princess's life, not his own.

Warwick took his eyes off of Peter just long enough to glance down at the princess, "She's badly hurt Peter," said Warwick, "Step aside so I can see to her wounds."

"Not a chance!" said Peter, choking back his tears and moving his sword an inch closer to the wizard.

In a controlled, calm voice Warwick asked, "Why did you bring her here?"

The wizard's question caught Peter by surprise. "What are you talking about? She arrived with you!"

Warwick's eyes narrowed and his upper lip curled up like he smelled something rank; Peter recognized this glare. The wizard grew angry. "Peter, I just arrived, *alone*. It's not possible she came with me. Now put down your sword, guardian." Warwick's voice rose above the pouring rain, but he didn't move a step closer. He just stood holding his staff, staring.

Peter's head ached. This had to be a trick! "She arrived just moments before you, through a passage, half dead," Peter said, keeping his stance and his advantage on the wizard, "We both know the princess possesses no magic of her own. She could not have come through the passage without the help of a wizard!" Peter yelled through the ever-growing thunder.

"Or a guardian," hissed Warwick. "You have the same capabilities as do I to open passages and portals."

"But I was here before she arrived!"

"You two are the only ones here, Peter! And as you just pointed out, she could not have come through the passage without the help of a magic-user! ANY magic-user!"

Warwick was growing angrier. He was renowned for his short fuse. Peter considered attacking the wizard before being attacked. It may be his only chance to buy some time, or even survive.

"Guardian, if you do not lower your sword and back away from the princess you will feel my wrath, one you have witnessed but never experienced!" The wizard took a step closer to Peter's blade.

Peter's head hurt. None of this made sense. Why would Warwick send the princess through a magic passage alone and then come through another passage?

Was he trying to cover his tracks in case Peter made it out of here alive? Then he could just claim he was trying to save the princess from Peter.

Peter stood his ground, "If you want the princess you'll have to kill me!"

"That," barked Warwick, "I can do!"

Warwick raised his staff and then froze at the echo of another recognizable thunderclap. This time it came from within the cabin. Another wizard had just joined them.

Peter quickly adjusted his stance so he was directly over the princess with one foot in the cabin and the other foot in the pouring rain. He wanted to be able to see both inside and outside the cabin.

The arrival of the other wizard brought Peter mixed emotions. He felt both hope and sorrow. In the center of the cabin stood the Ward Wizard of the North, Boullengard.

Boullengard protected the northern border and watched over northern Magnanthia for the royal family. He ruled by the book, seeking justice and order.

But Boullengard's arrival perplexed Peter. How did he know they were here? Was Boullengard also betraying the king? Had he been with Warwick from the beginning? Or was he here to protect them from Warwick? Peter's mind was full of unanswered questions, but he was running out of time.

"Boullengard? What are you doing here?" asked Peter, trying not to sound defensive, but he could hear the tremor in his own voice.

"Boullengard! The guardian is trying to kill the princess!" snapped Warwick. "He has succumbed to the power of greed like the other pathetic guardians!"

Peter turned a glare on Warwick. How could he say such a thing? "That's not true and you know it Warwick!" Peter's voice trembled. "I know you're behind the whole thing. There's no way the overlord could have gotten as close to the king as he did without inside help!"

The rain and thunder intensified with Peter's anger. Lightning struck a boulder near the edge of the cliff sending dust and small pieces of rock down the steep edge into the rolling sea below. Warwick, still standing outside in the storm, glanced up to the flickering sky and then to Peter. Peter sensed that Warwick was considering his options.

"Put down your sword and step aside," said Warwick glancing around. "It's over, Peter! The queen is dead! The king disbanded the Order of Guardians! Every member is either dead, or scattered, including your company."

Peter fought to hold his tears back by embracing his anger.

Boullengard finally spoke, "What are your intentions Peter?" His voice was powerful and sincere.

Peter, still glaring at Warwick, didn't seem to hear Boullengard.

"No need to look for him. He's dead! Your precious overlord didn't put up much of a fight," Peter mocked bitterly.

"The overlord is dead?" asked Warwick.

"Disappointed?" Peter blurted out.

"On the contrary. But why take the princess if you killed the overlord?" inquired Warwick.

"Are you taunting me?" An anger Peter hadn't felt in years boiled up from deep in his soul. He wanted to scream and thrust the cold steel blade into the warm blood pumping in Warwick's wretched heart, but his training and honor wouldn't allow it.

Then he heard Boullengard calling to him.

"Peter … Peter." The warm, familiar voice sedated Peter's anger for a moment. Keeping his sword raised in Warwick's direction he turned and looked at Boullengard. He saw compassion and sorrow in the old wizard's eyes.

"Peter. What are your intentions with Princess Elleanor?" asked Boullengard like a concerned father asking the whereabouts of his lost child.

Peter couldn't take it. He hurt from the disappointed tone in Boullengard's voice and the sad look in his eyes. He didn't want to hurt Boullengard. He was like a father to Peter, and had taught him so much. But he knew Boullengard didn't believe him. Boullengard didn't seem threatened by Warwick; instead he focused on Peter, and for good reason.

The only magic-users wizards fear, are guardians. Guardians have the strength and skills of a master swordsman, are as cunning as a master ranger, and have the magical abilities of both a master cleric and a master wizard. If other wizards were standing on either side of Peter at this moment he wouldn't be so worried. But with not one, but two grandmaster wizards against him he knew his chances were poor. To make matters worse, he was hurting and very weak from the recent battle. Time was the only thing he could buy.

More tears welled up in Peter's eyes and they rolled down his cheeks as he looked at Boullengard. In a quivering whisper Peter answered, "I'm doing what's best for her and the kingdom."

"Boullengard," snapped Warwick, "he's going to kill her!"

This was it; time had run out. Before it was too late Peter cast a protective shield around himself and the princess, who lay motionless under his stance. The shield, a transparent blue orb, deflected the heavy rain that, moments ago, was blowing through the doorway. The bitter wind could no longer touch Peter and the princess inside the protected barrier.

"You see!" yelled Warwick to Boullengard, "Why would the guardian feel the need to protect himself if he had nothing to hide?"

Peter looked down at the princess. She looked as if she could be in a restful sleep she was so peaceful. Once a little girl who would beg Peter to give her rides on his back, giggling as he twirled in circles and she pretended to fly, now she was a young lady who bloomed into every aspect of beauty.

Was he doing the right thing? After all, his sworn duty was to protect her at all costs. Evil had found its way into the heart of Magnanthia, within the walls of her home, Castle Kincape. The queen was dead, murdered by hands that once protected her; corruption was spreading, and the king's heart had hardened with hatred.

Who was going to take care of her? The princess was like no other he had ever known. He would not allow evil to get its ugly talons on her, no matter what the cost. He saw no other way.

One of these wizards wanted her dead and would be more than willing to take Peter down in the process. The other wizard thought him a betrayer. Even his beloved ring wouldn't be enough to fight his way through two grandmaster wizards...and protect the princess from harm.

Tears full of regret fell from Peter's eyes and landed on the princess. He choked back more tears and struggled to take deep breaths. What he would give to undo the events that lead to this moment.

Taking the hilt of his sword in both hands, Peter raised it high above his head. The blade of the majestic sword pointed straight down.

What followed would be Peter's last sentient moments. Horrific yells echoed around him; raging lightning and thunder threatened to tear the heavens wide open above him. At the same time Peter thrust his sword down, Warwick's conjured fireball illuminated the night; he cast the inferno upon Peter.

The thin, blue orb absorbed the blunt of the blow, but dissipated along with the frail cottage door and parts of the threshold. Splinters of wood blew into the cabin. Peter had sent the sword through the dark cloak the princess wore and six inches into the earthy floor before the fiery heat from the fireball's after-effect knocked Peter to the ground. Grabbing the hilt of the sword, Peter knelt over her. He was convinced it would hold her.

The cold rain gave little comfort to his burned face and hands, but he didn't give them a second thought.

Warwick gazed at the sword standing erect near the princess's upper abdomen. "What have you done?" he shouted, horrified at what he saw.

The prevalent flashes of lightning revealed just their silhouettes. Warwick was still standing outside in the rain with his hood over his head. Boullengard stood inside the house with a better view of Peter and the princess.

Peter reached down and touched her cheek.

"I will do whatever it takes to keep the princess from you and your monstrous army!" It looked like he was yelling at the princess, for he didn't take his eyes off of her.

"You are a bigger fool than I thought!" Warwick yelled through the enraged thunder. "You and all the other guardians have gone mad!" He started conjuring another fireball.

"Warwick! Don't!" Boullengard protested. He too began conjuring a spell. Green mist began swirling from his staff and a large green hand protruded from the eerie mist.

Boullengard cast his spell before Warwick could hurl his fireball. The large green hand sailed toward Warwick, passing behind Peter's back and leaving a green contrail in its wake. Warwick slung the fireball toward Peter, sending an inferno toward the cabin. Neither spell reached their targets.

In the heat of the moment both wizards failed to notice that as Peter was touching the princess's face with one hand, he was casting a spell above the small crystal ball on his sword's hilt with his other. The crystal turned purple before blowing up into thousands of tiny particles and sending a burst of bright gold energy into the night. Its power broke both wizards' spells, dissipating the fireball and the green hand. The impact of the explosion from the tiny crystal blew the remaining doorway, along with half of the cabin, into wood splinters. Both wizards were blown onto their backs.

A second explosion emanating from the hilt of Peter's sword sent thousands of brilliant purple and gold particles, like tiny stars, swirling around Peter and the princess. The small, purple and gold tornado began to expand, as if to encompass the remains of the cabin and the two wizards. But then, in a matter of seconds, the twinkling particles imploded for a moment before exploding and disintegrated the guardian and princess into small particles of glimmering dust.

"No!" both wizards yelled as they watched the glowing dust scatter to the winds. Where the cabin's doorway once stood laid a small pile of ashes, which the wind quickly picked up and tossed amidst the burning chunks of wood and embers hissing in the rain. There was no sign of the princess, Peter, or his sword.

2

AN UNEXPECTED FRIEND

Somewhere hidden among the rolling hills of the upper-Midwest, and shadowed by a vast forest of tall, dark pines and lush maple trees lies the quaint, quiet town of Riverside. Not much happened in this sleepy community unless the locals made it happen.

Today the little town was filled with hustle and bustle. There was excitement and energy in the air. Some of the old-timers continued their annual grumbling over having too much activity as residents of Riverside prepared for their annual Fall Festival.

There isn't a better time of year than autumn to gather around the dining room table with neighbors and friends, sipping roasted coffee and swapping who-said-what-to-whom, or in the case of adventuresome children, huddling behind closed doors telling tall tales until the tales grew even taller.

During autumn, the nights grow longer and the weather becomes frigid. As the leaves turned several shades of red and orange, and the trees prepared to go dormant for another season, the small town of Riverside was coming to life with the preparations of Fall Festival. But for one local teen, an event much larger than a small town festival would forever turn his world upside down… or perhaps throw him into a whole different world altogether.

Simon Whittaker was on his way to choir practice. With Fall Festival just around the corner, the choir director scheduled several evening rehearsals in addition to the extended after school choir practices. Riverside High School choir was performing in the Fall Festival opening ceremonies as it has for many years. Simon left the house right after dinner.

"I'll do dishes tonight since you have to head back to school," said his father. He then cracked a grin as he proceeded to toss crumpled napkins and their paper plates into the empty pizza box.

"Great. Thanks Dad," said Simon rolling his eyes. Then he chugged the rest of his Coke, picked up his backpack with his choir music in it, and headed out the front door.

No one really understood Simon except his dad. He more than understood Simon, he accepted him, appreciated him, and loved him. His dad wasn't at all like some of the other local fathers who were physically present at the house, but unavailable for anything outside of sports, fishing, and hunting. No, his dad was always available for him. Maybe it had something to do with being a single parent. Simon's mother died when he was a toddler. Maybe it had something to do with how much they were alike. He and his father both preferred a quiet afternoon at home, reading a book over going downtown to the who-knows-what-for celebration of the week in the community center. Ultimately it didn't matter why. Simon's dad was his best friend...and for a while his only friend.

A picturesque fall evening, the air was crisp, but wasn't cold. Simon left his fall jacket unzipped as he continued toward school. It still felt weird walking to the high school and not the junior high. He was a freshman now. He was starting to see himself differently, more as an adult than a kid.

That brought on a mix of emotions. He was eager for the future, but he was also sad and afraid at the same time. All the other kids at school seemed to be either enjoying childhood, or embracing young adulthood. But Simon felt lost. So much was changing. On the inside his emotions were more intense, sad was sadder, mad was madder, and his curiosity about...everything just kept growing. He wanted to know all there was to know. On the outside...well, that was changing too. He just felt awkward.

He paused at the foot of the cement steps leading up to the main entrance. He looked up at the stern building. High school, the place where the transition from childhood to adulthood is completed. It's the last stop before entering the real world.

For a moment he felt a little emotional. Maybe it was just the magic hour. The sun was just below the horizon, casting a cascade of orange, red, and purple clouds in the sky. The smell of evening dinners wafted in the air, and the sound of children giggling and playing came from somewhere in the distance.

He took a breath of the cool air and ascended the steps, wondering how many students took these steps before him, anxiously anticipating their future. How many others were afraid?

Making his way through the quiet hallways of the old school, Simon couldn't help feel that the past was watching him. The students looking back at him in the photos, displayed alongside trophies and ribbons of years gone by, had walked these halls, touched the dark oak banister as they trotted up and down the stairs, and passed under the thick, oak archways carrying with them their hopes and dreams. How many of them followed their dreams? How many never tried? How many of them are still alive to tell?

He snapped out of his nostalgic moment when he heard the harmonic tones of the choir echoing down the corridors. They must have started warming up already.

Mr. Rodenberg, the choir director, glared over his spectacles at Simon as he struck the notes on the grand piano. He watched Simon as he found his assigned seat and joined in the warm-up exercises. Mr. Rodenberg looked up at the clock and then back at Simon with a disgusted expression, pounding the piano keys even harder. Without looking at the clock, Simon knew he wasn't more than two minutes late. On the other hand, Simon knew that he was twelve minutes too late according to Mr. Rodenberg.

The choir director's wild hair, which Simon always thought made him look like Albert Einstein, along with his compelling gestures and booming voice, intimidated most students. Mr. Rodenberg was a perfectionist. He paced in front of the choir, grabbing his hair like a mad scientist when he couldn't get what he wanted out of his students, which tended to be most of the time. Although the choir director was renowned for his musical talents, and praised by the school and community alike for his grand choir concerts, he seldom was satisfied with the results of his choirs' performances. And yet, he always sincerely praised the students for giving it their best.

Simon was hoping he had dodged a bullet after five minutes of nonstop vocal exercises, especially since the choir director hadn't looked up from the piano after glaring at him. But when the final note of their exercises finally trailed off leaving a thick silence, Simon's face flushed. Still looking down at the piano's keys as he stood, the choir director spoke in a controlled, hoarse tone, as if he were addressing the grand piano itself. "If you are going to be late, for whatEVER REASON, be it your beloved pet died, or you just don't find rehearsal to be important enough to make time in your busy little schedules, then I suggest you don't come at ALL!" He paused for a dramatic moment. "Do I make myself *clear*?"

Murmurs from the choir followed.

"Yes Sir."

"Yes Mr. Rodenberg."

"Yes choir director."

A girl in the soprano section turned her head and shot Simon a look of disapproval followed by a colorful grin, and then rolled her eyes. Simon's face went from pink to red. Jessica Wells seemed to wait for moments like these, moments for which she could needle him. Her long, wavy hair bounced playfully when she flicked her head forward upon hearing the choir director speak.

"Is that going to be okay with YOU Mr. Whittaker?" hissed the choir director while still looking down at the piano.

"Yes Sir," answered Simon. "I'm really sorry, I ..." but his mouth froze shut when the choir director slowly lifted his head and glared at him.

"I suggest you ALL take out the first piece, 'Remember.' It's time to see who has been practicing this week and who hasn't." Simon was suddenly thankful he and Jessica had practiced several times together this week, something they have done for several years now.

Music was how Simon and Jessica met, or at least the reason they ended up becoming best friends. They grew up across the street from one another, so he knew *of* her and saw her regularly playing outside in the yard with her friends. Simon was envious of how easily Jessica made friends. He was shy and went out of his way to keep his distance from others, including her...until one warm afternoon.

✳ ✳ ✳

Simon was nine years old. He was sitting on the steps of his front porch, watching Jessica's older brother, Randal

Wells, and one of his buddies wrestle in the front yard. Simon had given up long ago trying to play with Randal. Randal was three years older than Simon, and made it clear he wanted nothing to do with him. The last time Simon crossed the street and asked Randal if he could play with him and his friends it didn't go well.

"You've got to be kid'n!" Randal scoffed, looking like he had just bit into something sour.

Three of Randal's buddies were sitting on the front steps. One of them, a boy with long, greasy hair, and smacking annoyingly on a wad of gum jumped down next to Randal.

"Maybe we should give the shrimp a chance," said the boy tossing a football back and forth in his hands. His sarcastic tone made Simon feel self-conscious and worried.

"Hmm. Maybe you got a point Chuck," Randal replied. "We were just thinking about playing football. We could use another player," he said rather sincerely, perhaps too sincerely. "But you have to try out first. Can you do that?" A toothy smile covered Randal's face.

"What do you mean?" asked Simon.

"Like trying out for a football team," Randal explained. "We have to see if you can even catch the ball."

Randal looked at Chuck and then back to the other boys. "What do you think guys? Should we see if little Simon is up to it?"

"Yeah, let's do it!" answered the skinniest one.

"I say we give him the chance he deserves," said Chuck as he handed Randal the football.

"Alright. You got one chance," said Randal. Simon wasn't sure, but he thought Randal sneered as he turned facing the length of the yard, holding the ball like the quarterbacks in the NFL.

"Go deep!" Randal shouted.

Something wasn't right, but like a dog's initial instinct to run when he hears "fetch," Simon took off running down the side of the yard. Randal overthrew it and Simon ran as fast as he could to reach the spiraling football. He leaped as far as he could with both arms extended.

Simon landed hard on his right shoulder, which knocked the air from his lungs. However, he could feel the ball's tough leather in his grasp. He caught it! He couldn't believe it! Gasping for air, Simon slowly stood up to show Randal.

For a moment he didn't understand what was going on. The four boys, with Randal in the lead, were yelling and running full stride at him.

"Wait," Simon managed in a forced whisper between gasps.

Randal didn't slow down. He lowered his head and wrapped his arms around Simon. Simon's feet left the ground as he flew backward. Randal, almost twice Simon's size, slammed down atop of him with all his weight, knocking what little air he had out of his lungs.

Then one of the boys yelled, "Dog pile!" and the three of them flopped down upon Randal and Simon.

Simon's lungs burned and he couldn't breathe. He wiggled and jostled frantically under the pile of boys fighting for air...and then it was over. The boys rolled off of him and he was choking on air that smelled of grass, earth, and pungent body odor.

When he could breathe again, Simon sat up. Randal had retrieved the football and the other three boys were laughing and pointing at him.

Laughing hysterically, Chuck said, "Something tells me...you didn't make...the team!"

"Now beat it!" Randal barked. He glared at Simon as he slowly stood up.

Still trying to control his breathing, Simon turned and started toward his house. He felt a lump in his burning throat and hot tears filled his eyes, but he didn't want to give them the satisfaction. He fought to hold his tears back as Randal and his buddies chuckled and teased him.

"And when I say stay away I mean it!" Randal shouted. "It's bad enough I have to see your ugly mug from across the street. I don't want it in my yard!"

Simon continued walking, his head hanging low. He didn't turn around because he didn't want them to see the tears.

"Hey! You hear me?"

Something hard hit him in the back. The pain caused him to reach back, but he lost his balance and fell in the street. Sharp pain shot up from his knee when he landed on it. He turned to see what, or who, hit him. The football was rolling awkwardly near his feet.

"Nice hit!" yelled one of the other boys.

They laughed as Simon scrambled back into his house. He slammed the front door shut, but he could still hear the laughing and jeering outside.

That was just a few months ago.

So there he sat on his front porch, watching Randal wrestle his buddy to the ground with ease since he outweighed him by at least twenty-five pounds. He recognized Chuck, the kid gasping for air under Randal. Chuck was one that had joined in on the football incident. That's how Simon referred to it, the football incident. He still felt foolish about it.

What Simon didn't understand was the lack of interest Randal showed toward him. Randal made it clear he didn't like him, but he didn't go out of his way to track him down and pick on him.

Simon witnessed Randal and his buddies on several occasions make a point of demonstrating their dominance upon some unlucky child minding his own business. But only when Simon crossed paths with Randal did Randal give him any notice. It was like Jessica's older brother was avoiding him.

Movement inside the big picture window of the Wells' house caught Simon's attention. Jessica had poked her head through the curtains and was looking over at Simon's house. At least he thought she was, or maybe it was something in his yard or perhaps on the front porch. He looked around on either side of him and saw nothing of interest. Then he realized it *was* something on the front porch she was looking at...him.

She wouldn't take her eyes off him, like she was studying him, trying to draw a conclusion from what she saw. He was very uncomfortable and resorted to looking down at the sidewalk as if he had seen something interesting. He studied the cracks and rocks that lie forever frozen in the cement.

When he finally dared a glance at the large window again, the curtains were drawn and there was no sign of

Jessica. It was just Randal and Chuck battling in the front yard. Simon was both relieved and disappointed.

He was just going to get up to see what his father was up to when the Wells' front door swung wide open with a bang, making enough noise to stop the two boys in mid battle. Jessica pranced down the front steps holding something by its handle in the palm of her fist, looking directly into Simon's eyes. She walked with as much authority as a nine-year-old girl can; she seemed determined. Randal turned around and watched his little sister, but didn't say anything.

She crossed the street with only slight glances to each side checking for traffic, but didn't miss a beat as she walked up to the end of the steps where Simon sat wide-eyed and perplexed. Even though he was three steps above her, Simon couldn't help but lean back a little when she extended her arm in a rapid, methodical gesture holding a Creamsicle. After a period of silence it appeared she wasn't going to say anything or do anything, but stand there.

Embarrassed, Simon asked, "Is that for me?"

She opened her mouth to speak, but thinking twice about it snapped shut her mouth and instead gave him a half grin and a half role of her eyes and replied, "Yes," in an are-you-going-to-take-this-or-not tone.

"Umm...thank you," he replied. He jumped up like an ant had just bit him and went down to her. They stood facing each other for another moment before Simon reached for the Creamsicle. Jessica gently handed the icy treat to him.

"I'm Simon."

"I know."

This is the closest Simon had ever been to her. He hadn't noticed until now that she had small, faint freckles on her nose and upper cheeks, and dark brown eyes full of wonder that seemed to be studying him. Her long, sandy blonde hair floated in the warm breeze.

"What's this for?" asked Simon.

"We should be friends," she said. And smiled.

This must be some practical joke Randal schemed up. But then something happened that convinced him she was sincere. The look in her eyes went from curiosity to a warm sparkle, and she said, "I'll call you soon." And with that she turned and walked straight back to her house.

Randal had been watching them the whole time. He looked disgusted. He began to say something to her as she walked up to their house, but Jessica stopped, gave her brother a stern look and said something that shut him up. Randal looked confused and a little concerned as Jessica went into the house without looking back. Simon stood holding the Creamsicle when Randal shot him a glance. Was it frustration, or apprehension in his eyes?

A couple of days had passed since Simon received the unexpected treat from an unsuspecting neighbor. He was in his bedroom watching the rain. The day seemed determined to keep the sun away...far away. But Simon didn't mind. He had just finished reading a story and was daydreaming about it. There was nothing like a fantastic adventure found within the pages of a book. Real life was full of routines and void of close friends, so he spent a lot of time thinking about how life could be. He was almost in a trance from the rain tapping at the window and watching it fall like tears down the windowpane when his father's voice came from a distant place.

"Simon!" his father yelled from downstairs. "Telephone!"

"Coming!" Simon couldn't remember the last time he received a phone call. He ran out of his bedroom and down the stairs with his newly found energy.

His father was waiting for him at the bottom of the stairs holding the cordless phone in one hand and cupping the receiver in the other.

"It's for you, son," he said with a warm smile.

Who could it be? Simon wondered. He was so excited he forgot to ask his dad who it was.

"Hello?" he said tentatively.

"Hi Simon," came a tender voice on the other end. "This is Jessica."

Her voice was synonymous with her brown eyes, sweet and determined.

He was searching in his jumbled mind what to say to her, but all he came up with was a simple, "Hi."

"Would you like to come over and bake cookies with my mom and me?" she asked. "Your dad told my mom it's okay with him if it's okay with you."

He wasn't sure what to say. He was nervous and excited. His initial thought was to think of an excuse not to go. But before he could come up with the perfect reason, or any reason, she quickly added, "I would really like to see you."

She was so sincere he couldn't say no.

"Sure," he said.

"Great! How does three o'clock sound?"

"Okay." He felt compelled to say something, actually anything that was more than one word long. But he was in a floating silence that just hovered. His ears suddenly felt hot and the phone started sticking to his ear from sweat.

Jessica broke the silence, "See you soon then?" she asked.

"Uh…yeah," he said.

As soon as she hung up Simon couldn't put the phone down quick enough. He sighed with relief and then looked at his father, who must have been standing there during the entire conversation.

"You have fifty minutes to get ready," his father said tapping his watch and smiling…still. Simon must have looked worried because his father paused, sat down on the steps, and gestured to Simon to take a seat next to him. "It's okay to be a little nervous," his father said. "You've been hanging around the house a lot lately. I think this will do you some good to get out, make a few friends."

What did he mean *a few friends*? Was he referring to Randal too? Randal! He had forgotten about him. This was a big mistake! Randal will kill him if he sets foot in that house! He wanted to tell his father about his encounter with Randal, but didn't know how. Perhaps he should cancel. He couldn't tell his dad he was feeling sick. Then he thought of a good excuse. "Dad. She's a girl," he said. "What will everyone think?"

"First of all," his father asked, "who is everyone?"

"Everyone at school." Simon felt sheepish after he said it. He didn't even sound convincing to himself. He was sure his dad wasn't going to buy it.

"Second, since when do you hold what everyone else thinks in high regard?" asked his father.

Simon couldn't answer that, at least truthfully. He just shrugged his shoulders. His father knew him well... sometimes too well.

"We can't live our lives trying to please everyone," his father said in a low and caring tone. "We can only do the best we can for those we love, including ourselves." His dad gave him a little nudge and said, "But you already knew that."

Simon felt even more sheepish because his father was right...again.

His father put his arm around Simon. "How about some helpful advice?" He said rhetorically. "Don't overstay your welcome. If they don't invite you to stay for dinner come home by five-thirty," he said. "If they invite you to stay for dinner, don't ask what they're having. Tell them that would be nice, and then ask to use their phone to call me."

I might have to stay for dinner? Simon thought.

He began feeling more nervous and might actually become sick.

His father must have sensed his discomfort. He gently rubbed Simon's shoulder. "I tell you what son, if they ask you to stay for dinner and you're uncomfortable with it, ask to use their phone to call and ask me. I'll tell you I would like you to come home. On the other hand, if you would like to stay you can tell them I already gave you permission to stay, if you're asked." His dad pulled him in tight. "How does that sound?"

It was actually a pretty good plan. "Okay," he said taking in a deep breath.

"All right then. Now go get ready." His dad stood up. "I have a book with my name on it. I'll be here if you need me." He turned and headed toward the study.

"Thanks Dad."

His dad looked back and winked before disappearing into the study.

At three o'clock it was time to go. It took Simon a whole five minutes to get ready, so he poked around his bedroom waiting for three o'clock, for what seemed to be all afternoon. He even straightened out his junk drawer, desperate to pass the time and help him not think about Randal and what might happen when he saw Simon in his house. There was no mistaking that if Randal didn't want Simon in his yard, he definitely did not want him in his house. On top of that, Simon was also a little reluctant about making friends with a girl. After all, how much could they have in common? The girls at school seemed to talk a lot and play games that weren't appealing, like hopscotch and tag, which was nothing more than running around chasing each other.

With a sigh he realized he didn't spend much time with the boys at school either. Many of them played baseball or soccer, neither of which he was good at, or was even interested in. He tried, but he couldn't kick a soccer ball straight to save his life and as for baseball, he was so afraid of getting pelted in the face with the ball that he couldn't "keep his eye on the ball" as he was told to do so many times.

After giving up on sports he tried hanging around the tech-heads, or computer jocks as they liked to be called. The videogames they talked about sounded fun, but that's all they wanted to do. Simon didn't mind playing for three to five hours a week, but when he got together with them they spent that amount of time gaming in a day.

His father made it clear that sitting around watching television or staring at a videogame day after day would do the mind an injustice and that it was best to exercise his imagination and feed his mind with knowledge. Instead, he encouraged Simon to spend more time on conventional activities, like reading, building models, or playing board games, which the two of them often did together.

This wasn't what bothered Simon. What bothered him was the feeling he was missing out on something. It wasn't soccer, baseball, videogames, or even television. In fact, he found the things he and his father did together more exciting than what the majority of kids his age were doing.

It was something else. Somewhere deep in an unexplored crevice of his spirit there was a tug. Often it was subtle. But at times it shook his entire being. In those moments he knew, without a doubt, there was something he was supposed to be doing. But what was it? He needed to know.

Simon eventually accepted the reality that he wasn't going to fit in with everyone else; he would have to find things to do on his own. And that is precisely what Simon had been doing for a long while, spending time alone. Until now.

There was no sign of Randal outside, but Simon cautiously approached the house. The rain had become a slight drizzle; the air was cool and damp. Simon felt he was doing something forbidden stepping onto Randal's front porch. He was expecting Randal to jump out of nowhere and drag him off, never to be seen again.

He stood at their front door. The beveled glass refracted the light from within. The sound of soft, tranquil piano music gave purpose to the gray, melancholy afternoon. A melody played from the keys of a piano accompanied a delicate, yet trained voice that sang in perfect harmony with the piano notes.

Realizing he probably looked stupid gazing at their front door, he rang the doorbell. The music stopped in mid-chord and within a few moments Jessica was standing in the doorway.

"Hi Simon," she said. She seemed pleased to see him. "I have to finish my voice lesson, but I will only be a minute. You're welcome to come in and listen."

Jessica had a formal presence about her that he hadn't seen before, or at least noticed anyway. And he was thankful she was nothing like her brother. Her kindness and sincerity instantly put Simon at ease.

Jessica led Simon into a formal, yet cozy room, a black, shiny grand piano at its center. Jessica's mother, Mrs. Wells, was sitting on the piano bench.

"It's good to see you Simon," said her mother. "We'll wrap this lesson up and get going on those cookies."

A wonderfully sweet and lemony aroma wafted through the already comfortable room. And when Simon took a seat in the nearest chair, he was not surprised to find it was very comfortable. Simon wondered how such a warm and well-mannered household could be home to a loud and unpleasant bully like Randal.

"I thought I would heat up the stove by baking a lemon poppy-seed cake. Do you like lemon-flavored desserts?" Mrs. Wells asked.

"I love them!"

"Good, because I'll be icing it with lemon frosting soon." Simon could see where Jessica inherited her kind and sincere smile.

Mrs. Wells paused for a moment. She seemed to be admiring him. Simon could feel he was blushing. Mrs. Wells turned around on the piano bench, cued Jessica, and began playing their rehearsed song.

The sound was beautiful. Both piano and singer seemed to be one. Simon couldn't believe it was Jessica singing. He had seen her often at school, outside her house, and around the neighborhood, but she had always seemed like just another girl. But as he sat and listened while the music engulfed him, she suddenly seemed like a completely different person. She, in no way, seemed ordinary. She sang with poise and confidence. She had a well-trained voice. As her voice drifted off and the final note hung in the air, Simon found himself wanting to hear more.

"Thanks for waiting," said Jessica. "How about those cookies?"

Simon was speechless. He just nodded and followed her and her mother into the kitchen, which was as unique as it was amazing. It was the epitome of a kitchen from a medieval castle. Stepping into the room was like stepping back in time. Mrs. Wells took the lemon poppy-seed cake out of the oven.

The baking supplies were already laid out on large timber counter tops beneath a hanging rack filled with large brass pots, pans, and kettles. This was the coolest kitchen Simon had ever seen.

Amidst the scent of the lemon cake, the loving guidance from mother to daughter as they prepared the ingredients together, and the light patter of cold raindrops against the window, Simon felt a pinch of sadness.

Is this what he had been missing out on all these years without a mother? His father never told Simon what caused her death, but he did tell him she had passed away shortly after he was born. Simon was only a few months old when he lost his mother. He never had the opportunity to create memories with her. He never had moments like these to spend time with her, baking treats or making a meal together. He had a sudden desire to know more about his mom. He was sure they would have enjoyed baking cookies together on a cool, rainy day.

"Simon?" Jessica was standing in front of him looking concerned. He didn't notice when she walked over to him. "Are you alright?" she asked gently.

"Umm...yeah," said Simon a little choked up. He was embarrassed to look her in the eyes. Then she reached out and took hold of his hand, and just like that his sadness melted away. She led him to the counter and paused to smile at him, still holding his hand. Without saying a word he knew she was telling him, "*You're in good hands.*"

They spent the remainder of the afternoon baking cookies, telling jokes, and listening to Mrs. Wells tell some interesting stories about a faraway land. They even sang a couple of songs, although Jessica and her mom did most of the singing.

They invited Simon to stay for dinner. Not wanting this day to end, Simon quickly blurted out that his father already told him he could stay.

It was just the three of them having dinner. Jessica's father, Dr. Wells, was out on business and Randal was staying at a friend's house. That was okay with Simon. He didn't tell them how glad he was that Randal wasn't home.

As they ate cookies and waited for the homemade pizza to finish baking in the stone hearth oven, Simon mustered up the courage and asked, "Mrs. Wells, could you teach me how to sing like that?"

"Of course I can," she said. And after taking another bite of her cookie said, "It will be an honor."

From that day on Simon and Jessica were best friends.

✳ ✳ ✳

Mr. Rodenberg dismissed the choir and then retired to his office mumbling something about needing more time to practice. Jessica shook her head as she walked up to Simon. "Are you trying to make things hard on us all?" she asked playfully. "You know how much he hates it when people are late, especially one of his star students," she mocked. But Simon knew there was truth to that, even though she was equally coveted by the choir director as he was.

From the first day Simon and Jessica auditioned together to join the choir, Mr. Rodenberg knew he had not one, but two gems. By the end of their duet, "The Music of the Night," Mr. Rodenberg had an open smile from ear to ear and gave them a standing ovation, followed by everyone else in the room. Both of them were immediately assigned lead chair in their sections. Jessica was lead soprano and Simon was lead tenor. So out of character was his reaction that to this day the only ones who believe it are the students who were in the choir room when it happened.

"You really should go and say something to him," Jessica said gesturing to Mr. Rodenberg's office. Simon knew she was right. She always seemed to be right. He tapped on Mr. Rodenberg's office door. Even though it was open he didn't step in.

"Come in," Mr. Rodenberg replied from behind his desk. He didn't look up from the sheet music he was studying. He also didn't sound angry like he had just moments ago in class. He simply sounded tired.

"Hi," said Simon as he slowly approached Mr. Rodenberg's desk, "Can I have a word?"

"You may have as many as you like," he replied still focusing on the music.

"I just wanted to apologize for coming in late," said Simon.

There was such a long pause Simon didn't know if Mr. Rodenberg heard him. He just kept looking at the music. Simon looked back at Jessica, who was standing just outside the office door, and shrugged his shoulders. She gestured back, sweeping her fingers in the air to say, "*Keep going.*"

"Sir," said Simon.

"Go on," said Mr. Rodenberg into the sheet music.

"Go on?" Simon asked.

"Go on. Say your apology."

Simon was confused. Didn't he just say it?

"Oh..." it occurred to him what Mr. Rodenberg meant. "I'm really sorry for coming in late. Forgive me?"

Mr. Rodenberg finally looked up at Simon. For a moment Simon thought, this is it. I'm going to receive a lecture now on common courtesy and responsibility. But instead Mr. Rodenberg smirked and said, "Yes Simon, you're forgiven."

Simon was relieved. "Okay. See you later, sir."

Mr. Rodenberg looked back down at the music. "Simon."

"Yes?"

"Great music comes from the heart," he peered at Simon over his reading glasses. "You have a great voice... don't ever lose it." And he returned to his work.

3

STRANGERS IN RIVERSIDE

Simon and Jessica left Riverside High as quickly as they could. Most days they stayed after choir practice to visit with Mr. Rodenberg. But he was a little more moody than usual, and Jessica was anxious to get downtown to The Village Corner Café. During lunch a rumor started floating around, and by the time the last bell dismissed school for the weekend, the gossip had spread like wildfire. There was no way of knowing what was true and what was hearsay, and Jessica wanted to find out what was going on. The Village Corner Café was a great place to start. After that, Simon and Jessica were going to a movie.

Their footsteps echoed in the empty halls as they raced to their lockers. Simon ran as fast as he could, his sneakers squeaking every time he rounded a corner. But it was no surprise when Jessica reached the school's main doors before he did. Somehow she always beat him when they were racing.

Twilight had come and gone and the stars had taken to the sky while they were in choir rehearsal. It was warmer than normal for this time of year. It almost felt like a cool summer's night. As they made their way down the street Simon noticed something. It wasn't something he saw, but rather something he felt. The air was electric.

His heart beat faster as they neared downtown. Jessica must have felt the same thing because Simon had to pick up the pace to keep up with her.

The Village Corner Café was Riverside's most popular hangout any night of the week. It was well known for its fresh baked pies and towering milkshakes; people from all around the county frequented the small diner. It was also the best place to go for the latest news and gossip. From the county sheriff to the mayor of Riverside, anyone who was someone swung through the old café on the corner of Main Street and Center Avenue.

As they crossed the street to the café, Simon's stomach growled from the aroma of greasy burgers hot on the grill. Apparently the pizza he had earlier wasn't enough.

Sara Nygard was near the café's entrance with two others, waiting for Simon and Jessica. Sara was thin with long dark hair. And even though she was shorter than average, she stood tall. Simon had a crush on her in seventh grade, but never told anyone. As he got to know her he learned that her father had left Sara and her mother when she was only five, and her mother had been spending every day since then taking it out on Sara. Despite her rough upbringing, Sara had a kind heart and loved life. She also had a wholesome laugh. She was easy to spot because she had a favorite denim jacket she wore every chance she could. Simon enjoyed making her laugh because it was so genuine. Her laugh was the reason for his crush.

Sara was talking with Brian Laney and Scott Lundeen. Simon didn't know much about Brian, other than he was the envy of every other boy in school. His good looks and charm made him popular with the girls, and he was so innocent about his popularity that as much as his peers would love to hate him, he was easy to like. Brian's father was the principal of Riverside High.

Scott was just a big teddy bear...that could bite. He had always been the biggest in the class with a soft sense of humor. He joked around a lot, but at his own expense. He didn't like to see people get their feelings hurt. Simon saw Scott take on three juniors one time because they were teasing a freshman, Francis Carlson, who had a bad stutter. Scott was so worked up it took three men to restrain him until he calmed down. That was two years ago when Scott was in seventh grade. Ever since then other kids tended to watch their P's and Q's around Scott. No one had ever dared to mention, or even acknowledge, Francis Carlson's stutter since.

Sara, Brian, and Scott had been friends with Jessica since preschool. Simon got to know them over the years because of Jessica, but he wasn't close to them. He felt like the outsider since the four of them had been friends for so long.

"Where have you two been?" asked Sara impatiently as soon as she saw them.

"We had choir rehearsal tonight," said Jessica. "We got here as soon as we could!"

"Well, you've been missing out," said Sara.

"On what?" asked Jessica.

"Someone moved into the mansion on Tuttle Point," said Sara as if this was the most shocking news of the decade.

"That's it?" asked Simon. "Someone moved into the mansion?" Simon had been excited all afternoon ever since he heard the gossip about something big going on. This was a let-down. "Is it someone famous?" he asked hopefully.

"No. It's no one famous," said Sara, "But you're missing the point. These people moved in overnight. The mansion has been vacant now for how many years?"

Although it was a rhetorical question, Scott blurted out, "Twelve!"

"Thanks Scott," said Sara kindly under her breath, and continued, "And then, just overnight, an entire entourage appeared."

"What do you mean, appeared?" asked Jessica. She seemed concerned.

"I mean…no one has set foot in that place for years. The township put in a proposal to buy the place, but the Tuttle family refused to sell for any price. They insisted the land and the manor be left alone. And now, just like that," Sara snapped her fingers, "someone moved in under the cover of darkness and no one knows who they are. The only thing anyone has seen all day are trucks coming and going from Tuttle Point…like those," she said and pointed at two oncoming trucks.

Two shiny, jet-black eighteen-wheelers, trimmed with dark blue sidelights, pulled up to the four-way stop at the intersection just outside the doors to The Village Corner Café. Their dark, tinted windows fit well with the semis' ominous sleek and high tech design. Simon was waiting for them to suddenly transform into a humanoid robot and launch into outer space.

"They're unmarked," said Brian more to himself than the group.

"That's what I noticed," said Sara. "Not one mark on 'em."

One in front of the other, the two semis turned onto Main Street and disappeared into the night.

"How do you know the township wanted to buy the mansion?" asked Jessica.

"My mom was on the committee that put the proposal together," said Sara. They all looked at her with dumbfounded expressions. "What...I listen," she said, embarrassed. "I remember my mom having a fit about it at the time. She was telling someone over the phone she thought the Tuttle family was being selfish and stubborn for no reason."

Suddenly the wind picked up, bringing with it a surprisingly bitter chill. The tall pine trees down the road starting swaying. Simon zipped up his jacket.

"Maybe we should go inside," said Scott flicking his head toward the café.

But Brian hesitated. "I may know who they are."

Sara turned and almost bumped into Simon. "What!" she said. "Why didn't you say something earlier?"

"It just dawned on me," said Brian in deep thought.

"You think it could be that Jak kid?" asked Scott.

Brian shot a glare at Scott, who was oblivious to what he did wrong. "Yeah...but I wasn't supposed to tell anyone," said Brian aggravatingly.

"Come on," said Jessica and Sara at the same time, "We won't say anything."

Sara was giving Brian her you-can't-resist-me smile. Simon was a little jealous; he had wanted to be at the receiving end of that smile before, but he was too afraid to ask her out.

"Okay" said Brian, "but you can't tell anyone."

Brian hesitated for a moment. Then he looked at Simon.

Simon put his hands up in the air like Brian was pointing an invisible pistol at him. "I won't say thing," he said. "Promise!"

As Brian began to speak they all huddled to keep warm and to make sure no one overheard.

"My father received a call the other night. At first I thought it was just a parent asking questions about our school and town, you know, someone looking at moving into the area. But then my dad got really quiet and signaled me to leave the room. I did, but I stayed within earshot. Whoever was on the other line did most of the talking because my dad didn't say much. I got the gist of the phone call afterward when he spoke to my mom.

"Get this," said Brian and leaned into the center of their circle. "The guy told my dad he wants the teachers to come teach his nephew at a private facility until their replacements arrive, his private tutors. No one is to ask his nephew any questions about his family, his past, or even their home. This guy is going to pay the teachers triple their salary as long as they are teaching his nephew, but made it clear that if they violate any of his rules they will be terminated on the spot and released immediately."

"How do you know it was a guy?" asked Jessica.

"Because I heard my dad refer to him as Mr. Jakobsin. He even spelled out their name, J-A-K-O-B-S-I-N, because it sounds like 'Jacobson,' but he wanted my dad to 'know the family name properly,'" said Brian.

"Where do the teachers have to go?" asked Sara.

"That's the weird part. He wouldn't tell my dad. He told him he would call him at home and let him know when the time was right," said Brian. "I could tell my dad was uncomfortable with the whole conversation."

"Has he called back?" asked Sara buttoning her top button on her jean jacket and putting up the collar.

"Not that I know of."

"That *is* rather bizarre," said Jessica.

"Bizarre is only the beginning," said Brian. "I didn't find out what the first name of Mr. Jakobsin is, heck, my dad probably doesn't even know, but my dad did get the name of his nephew." Everyone was silent for a moment. Somewhere in the distance a dog barked. "Jak. Jak Jakobsin," he said, "J-A-K, instead of J-A-C-K."

Sara asked, "Why is the spelling of his name so important?"

"I don't know," said Brian, brushing away the question, "but for some reason he was adamant that my father get their name right. But that's not what's so bizarre. I did a little online research...you won't believe what I found. Someone wrote a poem about Jak. It says he's the most evil creature on earth, or anywhere else for that matter, and that there is no way he has a soul. It was crazy."

Jessica dived into her backpack.

"What are you doing?" asked Brian.

Jessica retrieved her smart phone and rapidly poked the screen with excitement.

"I'm looking up this poem you're talking about. I want to see it," replied Jessica as she navigated the Internet.

Jessica's parents had recently given her a smart phone for doing so well in school; she was short by a single A- from obtaining a perfect 4.0. Simon wanted one, but his father believed cell phones were another way to be consumed into the busy lifestyle many families are trapped in. He appreciated his father's old-fashioned ways most of the time, but this was different. Simon didn't feel like he was missing out on video games, cable television, or even computer pads. Reading books and going to the movie theater was enough for him. But everyone had a smart phone. He felt out of the loop not having one, not even a "stupid" phone.

"Found it!" exclaimed Jessica as if she had just found the lost treasure of the Knights Templar. She began reading something from the little screen to herself.

Sara was almost beside herself. "Well…read it aloud!"

"It's more of a riddle than a poem," said Jessica still staring into her phone. Her face was aglow. Jessica loved a good mystery; she had a knack for figuring things out. "OK! Listen to this," she said. She read,

"In the eye of the storm lies the reason
Waiting amidst turmoil, despair, and treason.
Unattainable and unforgivable it'll remain

Stained in his father's blood and forever insane.
He's the most vile creature in our world, or beyond,
His secret – at the bottom of Sin's pond.
He either has no soul or it has fell
To the darkest depths of the worst imaginable hell. "

She read the last three words slowly.

"But it doesn't mention his name anywhere," said Sara.

"Oh…I forgot," Jessica cleared her throat. "It's titled 'Jak Jakob'sin'."

Sensing an ominous presence, Simon looked over his shoulder. The night had grown cold. The others must have sensed the same thing because they all looked out into the night and spoke not a word.

Scott broke the silence. "How do we know that's the Jak Jakobsin that moved here?"

"Because how many J-A-K J-A-K-O-B-S-I-Ns do you know?" said Brian caustically.

"Scott has a point," said Sara. "How do we know it's not about a Jak Jakob… and his sin?" No one answered. "And besides, it's probably fictitious," she said unconvincingly.

"Hey guys, let's go inside and discuss this," Simon suggested. He noticed Jessica was starting to shiver, and like the air, the atmosphere had become chilly. Everyone agreed and started toward the café's entrance, but Sara paused and said quietly, "Wait! Look at that!"

They were stunned. A shiny, jet-black Rolls Royce limousine rolled slowly through the stop sign at the intersection and without a sound rolled to a stop next to them. The Rolls Royce shared the same ominous ambiance as the semis that passed moments ago; it had dark tinted windows and a dark blue glow around and under it. Sitting motionless and silent it looked more like a prowler waiting for its prey. Even the headlights were a piercing blue, casting foreboding shadows along the street.

The engine was so quiet Simon didn't know if it was still idling. The car showed no sign of life hidden behind its tinted windows. No movement and no sound, until... someone screamed. Dulled and muffled behind the black glass, it was still intense. The car didn't shake or jostle as if someone were trying to get out; it just sat there, still.

Jessica grabbed Simon's wrist. The screaming didn't stop. It grew louder, more agonizing. Then, just as abruptly as it had started, the screaming stopped.

Simon took a step toward the car, but Jessica kept her grip on his wrist.

He looked at her and whispered, "It's okay. I'm just gonna see if they're alright."

Jessica looked reluctant, but then let him go. Simon stepped onto the road. He came within ten feet of the majestic Rolls Royce before it took off like a phantom into the night, toward Tuttle Point.

Simon, still standing in the middle of the road, turned and looked back at Jessica, Sara, Brian, and Scott; they looked as baffled as he felt.

"That was nothing short of weird and freaky," said Brian, "and not necessarily in that order. Let's get our butts into the café!" Brian wasn't one to scare easily, but Simon could tell he wasn't joking around.

Simon paused in the doorway and looked back toward Tuttle Point. He could barely see the distant pine trees shivering in the chilly night air. It had become dark so quickly. And Simon couldn't help feel that the darkness itself was trying to push him into the warmth and brightness of The Village Corner Café.

They tucked into a corner booth. Very little was said beyond trivial comments about what to order. It wasn't until their food came that the talking picked up. Munching on burgers and fries, and slurping on malts they rehashed the encounter with the Rolls Royce, the information they saw on the Internet, and some of the gossip they heard during school about the Jakobsin family. Simon took the gossip with a grain of salt.

At one point Brian called the sheriff's office from his cell phone after the group agreed it was the best thing to do. However, Sara's suspicion that there wasn't anything the local law enforcement could or would do was confirmed when Deputy Brady politely explained to Brian that they can't go around arresting people regardless of how weird or freaky the sounds coming from their vehicle may be. "Unless you saw something suggesting someone's in danger, there's nothing we can do son," said the deputy. That ended that.

By the time they each polished off their piece of pie, except Scott, who had two pieces because he couldn't decide between apple and pecan, they concluded there was nothing they could do for now. Jessica was the only one who wanted to go to Tuttle Point to see if they could meet the family, but no one else wanted to go. Tuttle Point was on a peninsula so there was only one way in and one way out, which meant to get to the mansion they would either have to obtain the Jakobsin's permission or trespass. Neither option seemed like a good idea.

Especially since the Jakobsins didn't seem to want anyone coming around.

Eventually Jessica conceded. So after Scott finished licking all the pie crumbs from his plate, and Sara stopped laughing at the site of Scott's face covered in pie crumbs, they left.

Simon and Jessica headed toward the movie theater. Simon loved going there. Since he didn't have cable television, the theater was Simon's second home. He loved watching movies as much as he enjoyed getting lost in a good book. He craved adventure, but he wasn't quick to search for it unless it was on the pages of a storybook or between the credits of a movie. Usually Jessica was as excited as Simon about going to a good movie, but she seemed preoccupied with her own thoughts.

He was going to ask her if she wanted to cancel the movie, but he didn't want her to say yes. So, he took a different approach. "You seem fascinated with the Jakobsins," he said.

"Not fascinated, just curious," she said.

"Why?" he asked. "They seem to be just another quirky family that just wants to be left alone."

"But that's just it," said Jessica, "They don't seem to be just another family. There's something…off about them…. Something isn't right."

"You don't even know them. What makes you think something isn't right about them?" asked Simon.

Jessica thought about it. "It's just a feeling I get, that's all."

Simon wanted to ask her what kind of feeling she gets, but it was obvious she didn't want to talk about it anymore when she quickly changed the subject.

"I don't want to miss the previews," she said. "Want to split a popcorn?" she asked as they entered the theater. She didn't have to ask him twice. Popcorn always makes a movie more enjoyable.

About twenty minutes into the movie something odd happened. The double doors at the back of the theater burst open with a loud thud and then someone slammed them several times against the wall.

Simon and Jessica, along with half of the theater, turned around to see what the commotion was about.

"Stupid, cheap doors!" A teenage boy was madly kicking the doors until they stuck open. This resulted in a wide ray of light stemming down the center aisle. He was cradling a very large bucket of popcorn in one arm while holding a large pop.

"This sucks! I've missed the beginning!" said the stranger loudly as if he were the only person in the theater. He seemed oblivious to the glaring onlookers as he made his way toward the center of the theater, making racket and cursing the ones he was stepping over to get to a seat.

"Move it fat stuff," the stranger said aloud to a large boy who couldn't have been more than ten years old.

"OUCH! That was my toe," a girl cried out.

"Don't start bawl'n!" said the stranger.

"Cool it kid!" a guy a few rows up snapped.

"Yeah, yeah," said the stranger plopping into an empty seat.

"Jerk!" someone yelled.

Simon got a good look at the boisterous stranger who had taken a seat four rows back from him. He looked a few years older, but it was difficult to tell because his disheveled, dark hair covered part of his face. He was lanky and looked disgusted as he slumped down into the chair. He looked more annoyed than everyone else.

Jessica leaned in to Simon. "Can you believe that guy?" she whispered.

Simon shook his head.

Simon soon lost himself in the movie again and forgot about the earlier disruption. However, the movie's engrossing plot was disrupted again and again. Simon was pulled back to reality several different times as the stranger roared with laughter long after the funny scenes were over.

Moviegoers protested openly when the stranger roared with phony laughter during more serious scenes and shouted obscenities at the screen every time the villain failed to overcome the hero.

Several people left the theater, but the stranger took no notice of them. He shoveled handfuls of popcorn into his mouth and yelled at the movie screen, spraying popcorn on the irritated moviegoers in front of him.

"That's not real! He couldn't do that!" he yelled followed by more menacing comments and phony laughing.

The more the people in the theater became disgruntled, the louder and more vexing the stranger became. Soon their insults and gestures toward the stranger became hostile, and a few people even started arguing with others.

The movie was turning into a disaster. Simon was sure a fight was going to break out if something wasn't done soon.

And then, as if Simon's thoughts had triggered it, the guy who told the teenager to "cool it" earlier stood up with his hands balled into fists. "That's it! I've had enough of you, you little twerp!"

To everyone's surprise, the obnoxious stranger leaped out of his seat, sending the rest of his popcorn spewing into the audience, and frantically charged toward his challenger when the houselights suddenly came on, momentarily blinding everyone.

"Jak!"

Two large men in black suits came stomping down the aisle. For the first time in a while, the theater was silent. The movie was still rolling on the silver screen, but there was no sound.

Jak stopped short of his challenger and turned to the two men coming down the aisle.

"Whadda you two think you're doing here?" Jak belted out in disgust.

Neither of them answered.

There was no way these two were theater security. For starters, Simon knew the theater didn't have security. And with their well-tailored suits and rigid walk these guys weren't from anywhere around here.

The two men strode down the aisle toward Jak. One look at the two large men, and the local angry man unclenched his fists and obligingly stepped out of their way.

Jak didn't move. The men stopped three paces from him. Jak looked furious, but the two large men maintained their serious disposition.

Nobody in the theater moved. The silence thickened. Simon saw the theater manager, who had graduated from high school three years earlier, standing behind the double doors.

"Jak, you can do this your way, or you can do this our way, but either way you're coming with us." The man in the black suit spoke with cool authority.

"Your way is fine with me," said the other man in black. He seemed to be jeering Jak.

Breathing heavily, Jak stood erect, staring at the two men. After what felt like half of eternity, Jak yelled, "FINE! Just keep your grubby hands off me!"

The men in suits escorted Jak up the aisle. As they passed the young theater manager, Jak slammed his fist into the door the manager was holding open for them and continued to stomp out of the theater. The audience applauded Jak's departure.

"Well, I think it's safe to assume that this Jak is the one referenced in the riddle," said Jessica over the applause.

Simon didn't applaud. He couldn't comprehend how someone could be filled with so much animosity; it weighed on his mind. What causes a person to become so hostile?

The manager apologized for the disruption. He started the film over for those who could stay later and gave a free pass to each of those who couldn't. Simon and Jessica elected for a free pass.

On their way out Simon and Jessica overheard some girls talking. Jak and his escorts got into a Rolls Royce limo. The girls couldn't stop talking about how cool the limo was and how Jak was cute in his own eccentric way.

"I have a feeling we'll be seeing more of Jak," said Jessica.

"Why do you think that?" asked Simon.

"Because that's what he seems to want. To be seen."

He didn't say it, but he thought it. *She's probably right.*

4

JUST PLAIN OLD MEAN

There was no way Jak was getting out again tonight. His uncle sent two of his brutes into town to bring him back to the mansion. One of them was sitting outside his bedroom door, which was electronically locked. His uncle was a control freak, so every window and every door was secured by a remote he alone carried.

The fat goon who plopped down outside his bedroom was nasty and smelly. Such a waste of money dressing him up, but his uncle insisted his men wear black suits. May as well strap a tuxedo on a hog. If Jak were running the show, he wouldn't waste time or money on a sloth like Mickey. Sure he was strong, and even obedient, but he had a bad temper and made the family look bad every time he spoke because he was the epitome of a dumb bodyguard. Maybe his uncle sent men like Mickey out to find him just to annoy him.

Thinking of his uncle always made Jak a little nauseous, but getting embarrassed in front of a crowd by his henchmen was making Jak's blood boil. His face was getting hot; he didn't have to look in the mirror to know it was turning red. It always turned red when he was angry. He hated his uncle, so he was angry often.

And since the goon outside his bedroom door didn't allow him to take out some of his anger earlier in the movie theater, Jak felt like a steam whistle with a broken chain. He needed a release. Besides, this wasn't right! He's Jak Jakobsin! It was *his* father that took over the family business. His uncle was just around for the ride as his father and grandfather did all the work. He, Jak, should be running the show, not his good-for-noth'n, conniving uncle…that scrawny bastard.

Jak ran his hand through his long, dark bangs and paced back and forth in his solitude. Although most families didn't have living rooms the size of his bedroom, Jak felt like the walls were closing in on him. His uncle had no right locking him up like this!

Jak ripped off the bedding and threw it on the ground. Since that didn't seem to help, he picked up three statuettes from an African safari set and threw one at the door. The lion hit the door with a thud, but only his nose was chipped. The pitiful result made Jak even angrier so the rhino followed close behind, shattering into shards that rattled on the wooden floor. He let out a cry and then flung the mountain gorilla at the bedroom door, whooping and hollering as it burst into tiny, white pieces that scattered across the glossy floor.

He stood still and listened, but he didn't hear a thing. He was hoping Mickey would get revved up, but the lazy bum either didn't care or the other brute, whose name he forgot and didn't care to remember, was there instead. Either way, no one came in.

Unfortunately, there was no way he was going out the window. Not only was he on the third floor, but his uncle had this place sealed like Fort Knox before they moved in.

"Damn it!" he yelled and kicked the door. He didn't want to come to this stupid town anyway. Riverside...what kind of name is that?

Then something dawned on him. It was the driver's fault that he was locked up in his room. That's right! He wouldn't let Jak out of the car when they were driving down Main Street. If he had, Jak wouldn't have taken one of his uncle's cars and gone back to town.

***

"Stop here!" said Jak. The limo had just crossed an intersection, but the driver instinctively brought the car to a rolling stop upon command. Two girls standing in front of a café had caught Jak's eye; he wanted to make an impression. The two girls were hanging around three local guys that all looked like losers, so making an impression shouldn't be too hard in a Rolls Royce limo.

Jak tried the power window, but it wouldn't go down. He grabbed the door handle, but despite yanking it a half a dozen times the door wouldn't budge. His first thought was the door must be broken or jammed, so he slid over to the other side and tried that door. No luck.

"What the...," he muttered to himself. He looked up to tell the driver, Wiersbe, to try the window, but Wiersbe was watching him through the rearview mirror. He could tell by the look in his eyes Wiersbe had been watching him the whole time.

"Unlock the doors Wiersbe," said Jak attempting to keep his temper at bay.

"Sorry Master Jak," said Wiersbe in his nonchalant, controlled English tone, "orders from your uncle."

"What orders?" he yelled. Forget holding back.

"I am to bring you straight to Tuttle Point. No stops. No excuses," he replied calmly.

"I don't CARE!" He looked at the group of kids standing outside the little café on the corner. All five of them looked impressed and curious. Unfortunately they couldn't see him through these windows. This car was built for privacy, and for transporting unwanted or unnecessary guests when needed. The driver could over-ride all outlets if he needed to. Wiersbe was exercising that ability this very moment.

"What are you gawking at!" he snapped at the five teenagers at the corner.

"Sir, you will have to *speak up* so they can hear you," said Wiersbe politely.

"I KNOW THAT, WIERSBE! DON'T BE STUPID!"

Jak's face was warm and sweat began beading on his forehead. He just wanted to make an impression! He thought for a moment and realized there was no way he was getting out of this car. It may look extravagant, but it was built like a tank. With no other plan and feeling defeated he clutched the black leather seat he sat upon and screamed at the top of his lungs. He screamed until his lungs started burning and then he screamed even harder. Wiersbe raised the clear, soundproof partition between them. Jak kept screaming until nothing more than a faint, hoarse squeak came out.

Then he noticed Wiersbe concentrating on the side view mirror on the passenger side. Jak turned to see what had Wiersbe's attention. One of the boys, wearing a concerned look, had stepped out onto the street and was walking slowly toward the limo. The boy was probably a couple years younger than Jak.

Jak wondered if the pretty girl who had been holding that boy's hand was his girlfriend. As Jak was speculating, Wiersbe drove off before the boy got any closer.

✳ ✳ ✳

Jak woke to the sound of mechanical clicking coming from his bedroom door. He couldn't make out who came into his room because his eyes were adjusting to the bright, morning sun. He squinted and held up his hand to block the sunshine. He recognized the voice even before his eyes focused on his visitor.

"Your mother was worried about you last night," said his uncle. Most people heard sincerity and empathy when Roy Jakobsin spoke, but Jak knew his uncle better than that. His uncle was condescending and wasn't capable of empathy. "You need to start showing a little more respect. After all, you're the reason we had to move here, in case you had forgotten." His uncle took a moment and straightened his tie.

Jak rolled his eyes. *Only a pompous idiot wears a suit every day!* He thought.

"The poor thing is already burdened with a heavy heart. Don't make things harder than they already are for your dear mother." His uncle was also witty; his words often had either a double or a hidden meaning. Either way, he trusted his uncle as much as he liked looking at him. Not at all.

"Did you tell her I was safely locked up in my bedroom all night like a prisoner?" asked Jak caustically.

"Oh no...I wouldn't do that," said his uncle acting concerned. "I wouldn't want her to worry about her poor baby."

There was movement outside his bedroom door. As usual, his uncle had his bodyguards waiting for him like well-trained attack hounds.

"I told her you went for a walk and wanted to be left alone...again." He walked up to Jak's bedside. Instinctively, Jak sat up.

"Jak, my boy, you have nothing to worry about. I'm not going to hurt you," said his uncle as if he were talking to a five-year-old. "I just wanted to inform you that I have some important work to attend to tonight, and I don't want *any* interruptions from you. Your mother is going out tonight with some old friends of hers that are flying in to see her. She is in much need of consoling these days...as you know." A grotesque grin grew on his uncle's face. "Your father's untimely death haunts her...and she still cannot look at you for what you did."

Those words stung Jak in the heart. Since his father's death, over four months ago, his uncle was the only one who verbalized what so many were thinking; Jak was to blame for his father's death. This made Jak an outcast. Even Danielle, his little sister who used to pester him for attention or just a moment of his time, wanted nothing to do with Jak.

The thought of his mother's sorrow pained him; the hurt was deep and he did whatever he could to keep from thinking about it.

Jak couldn't think of anything to say. He had no fight in him.

"You, on the other hand, will remain in the mansion with Mickey attached to your hip. Think of him as your best friend for the next twenty-four hours," his uncle continued on. "I don't care where in the mansion you go, just as long as you stay away from me. You have all the video games you could possibly ever play in a lifetime and all the movies you could ever watch. Just keep yourself busy...and out of trouble." His uncle turned and started walking away, paying no attention to the broken pieces of ceramic crunching under each step.

Then Jak thought of something. "How did you know where I was last night? There's no way your goons saw me leave!"

His tall, scrawny uncle stopped and paused. Jak couldn't see his face because he didn't turn around, but he knew his uncle was grinning.

"I have my ways, Jak." Even his voice had a grin.

As soon as his uncle left the room a black-suited arm reached in and closed the door. Jak was once again alone. He usually preferred it that way, but he didn't particularly want to be left to his own thoughts right now.

✳ ✳ ✳

Jak missed New York already; there was always something fun going on in the city. He was sure he was going to die of boredom in this wretched place. It was easy to see why the Tuttles eventually left Riverside.

As for Tuttle Point...it was too secluded. Jak felt he was cut off from the rest of the world. The entire property was on a peninsula that overlooked Lake Superior. The spot where the mansion stood was the only open space. The rest all gave way to a thick forest of very tall pine trees standing like ancient sentries.

Currently Jak was sitting in one of the studies just off the library, where he had spent the latter part of the day. Mickey was sitting on the other side of the room playing a video game on a computer pad, which wasn't available to the public yet; it was top-of-the-line-technology. Of course, everything his family had was top-of-the-line, or higher.

When Jak was younger, his father had him take an IQ test. Afterward, his father explained to Jak that knowledge is power, and it was important he never forget it.

Ever since, Jak had been empowering himself. With an IQ of 139, knowledge came easy to Jak. His favorite area of study was science, quantum physics being his most recent passion. The more he read about energy and power, the more he wanted to learn how to control it.

He slammed the book, *Quantum Physics: Theories and Practices,* shut and threw it on the table. Why was he wasting his time? He knew he was destined for greatness. Jakobsins were better than everyone else. His father was a brilliant man who took a company and made it into an empire. Jak would have the money and resources he needed someday. The problem was that 'someday' was two years away. Eighteen was the magic number to gain access to his trust fund. And his uncle spent all his time in the labs spending Jak's inheritance. Jak would eventually have to take care of that problem.

What exactly did his father do in the labs? It had something to do with power and energy, specifically what, Jak had no clue. When they lived in New York there were mysterious people coming and going all hours of the night and day. The movers hadn't even unpacked their suitcases in their latest home in Riverside, and it was already the same routine. Company trucks brought in equipment no one was allowed to see.

Jak walked over to the tall windows. It was dusk but there was still enough light to see the tall pines on the other side of the courtyard. They looked forlorn, as if they knew the darkness of night was almost upon them.

Jak shivered. The thought of the massive lake on the other side of the mansion brought on a chill.

✳ ✳ ✳

Jak was five years old when he and another little boy fell off a sailboat. Jak was wearing a life preserver, but the other boy was not.

"He'll be fine," said the boy's mother. "We've been sailing for years my dear. Don't worry."

Jak's mother put the life preserver on him anyway.

He can't remember many of the details, other than the big boat jerked to one side and tossed Jak and the other boy over the edge. They both screamed as they tried staying above water, but the other boy was flailing about, pulling Jak under with him. Jak kept swallowing water and then he panicked. He punched and kicked the other boy off him until the last thing he felt was the boy clawing at his legs before sinking beneath the surface.

Waiting for the sailboat to come back felt like years. He was half expecting the boy to come back from the deep and pull him under, or for a shark to bite his legs off.

✳ ✳ ✳

Ever since then Jak was terrified of the water. He could almost feel the great waves pounding at the foot of Tuttle Point, trying desperately to bring the entire mansion tumbling down into the dark waters below to be swallowed whole from the hungry waves.

Maybe I should call for dinner, he thought trying to shake the images out of his head.

He was about to turn away from the windows and call the butler when a loud boom, like thunder, shook the room. The floor vibrated beneath them for a few moments and then faded along with the rolling thunder boom.

"Is there a storm out there?" asked Mickey temporarily looking up from his video game.

Jak got as close to the window as he could trying to look straight up for any thunder clouds, but the few clouds there were offered no threat of a storm of any kind.

"No. I don't see..." and then off in the distance in the thick of the pine trees he saw dazzling blue lightning that sustained itself for about seven seconds without a cloud anywhere near it.

"Whaaat? What is it?" asked Mickey engrossed in the video game.

"Um...nothing," said Jak.

He was trying to think of something to say, or do, so he could get away from Mickey and check out the phenomenon. And then, just after the distant lightning disappeared the power went out. It killed the power to the entire grounds. All the outside and inside lights were out, including the backup lights. Even the tablet computer Mickey was playing was dead. The only sound was the echo of metallic snaps throughout the entire mansion as the electronic locks on every door and window were released.

Jak knew that meant the security system was completely down. The same system was installed in their mansion in New York. The security system was designed to stay fully functional on its own power backup for up to seventy-two hours.

Jak took this moment to make his escape. Dusk was quickly turning into night so there was only a weak amount of light, casting very large shadows across the study. He stayed close to the walls and away from Mickey's voice, which was easy because he kept calling out for Jak.

"Where are you Jak? Come on, this ain't a joke."

Jak made his way through the library. He picked up the pace when he heard Mickey stumble into something and crash to the floor, cussing in pain.

The entire mansion was blacked out. Whatever it was, it also took out the emergency backup power. Jak was anxious to see for himself what was out there, what caused the unnatural lightning and complete blackout. After fumbling around for a jacket in the closet he found a flashlight. It wasn't working but he took it anyway, and left through a side door before he ended up bumping into a servant or bodyguard. No one was allowed to let Jak leave the mansion without his uncle's permission.

He was walking briskly through the courtyard he just moments ago was observing from the library, when the lights around the courtyard and mansion all flickered back to life. He took off running as fast as he could, hoping no one saw him disappear into the darkness of the trees.

He tried the flashlight again and this time it worked. Once he felt he was at a safe distance, he stopped and looked back to see if he was being followed. He turned around and headed in the direction he had seen the cryptic lightning.

The air was static beneath the lofty pines. The unusual silence made Jak uneasy. It felt like the pine trees were looking down at him and knew he didn't belong there. When he couldn't see the lights from the mansion behind him, he used the moon that was slowly making its way higher in the sky as his guide. He was lucky it was a full moon. Even the towering timbers couldn't fully block the moonlight. And if he lost the moon he would lose his way because every direction looked the same.

Jak wasn't sure how far he had traveled, but according to his watch he had been walking for almost twenty-five minutes. He was already tired of tripping over fallen branches and tree roots. What was he thinking coming out here? He hated the smell of bark and dirt. And if one more branch scraped his face he was going to lose it and burn down the entire forest. He started snapping branches off and throwing them to the ground while murmuring obscenities.

He decided to give it ten more minutes before turning around and going back to the mansion, when he heard something. He stopped and clicked the flashlight off. He waited and listened. A stiff breeze carried with it the scent of charred wood, the obvious result of lightning dancing in a forest. After seconds turned in to what had to have been minutes he began to believe he may not have heard anything, but then he heard it again. A faint cry.

Jak walked slowly and didn't turn on the flashlight. Soon he saw a faint, orange glow about forty yards away flickering high in the trees. He cautiously moved closer until he saw that the orange glow came from flames lapping at the bark of a few pines.

I hope the whole forest burns, he thought.

Then he heard a voice, plead.

"Please. Why won't you help me?"

Jak crouched down.

"I know you can hear me. I need help." A dry, choking cough followed.

Why was someone else out here? The closest place, other than the mansion, was Riverside, about eight miles away. No other structures were on the peninsula.

Jak cautiously made his way toward the dark orange glow from the charred trees and dying flames trying desperately to stay alive on them. The smoke burned his nose and stung his eyes.

Then a breeze suddenly swirled through the trees. Thick smoke and hot ashes overtook Jak. He couldn't see more than five feet in front of him, but he kept walking slowly. The ash looked like snow blowing around, and he felt a strange sensation. It felt like he stepped through an unseen barrier. The chilly night air was quickly replaced by warm air, as if he had walked into a room, a room with no walls. But a room it was not. It was an area clear of any trees and debris; he was standing in an opening in the forest, a perfect circle. The ash on the ground went up to his ankles.

"I need you to warn the others what has happened here," the voice cried, but Jak still couldn't see anyone.

Every tree around the opening was damaged. The breeze let up and the ash started to settle again. Each of his steps gently stirred the deep ash like ripples of pond water. He looked up toward the moon and then all around him. It was like the trees that once stood tall and proud in this empty circle were vaporized.

Ashes to ashes, Jak thought. Then he clicked on the flashlight.

He slowly pivoted until the flashlight revealed a man standing nearby; his back was to Jak.

"Can *you* help me?" the stranger asked in desperation.

Jak was trying to get a look at who the man was talking to, but he could only see trees.

"I don't under-st-stand," the stranger cried between coughs and sniffles, "why will you not speak?"

Jak couldn't see anyone else. There were only trees in every direction.

"Who are talking to?" said Jak, trying to sound as big and intimidating as he could, but felt his voice may have revealed a bit more than he lead on. However, it did have the desired effect Jak had hoped. The stranger, startled, whipped around, almost falling back against the tree he was facing just moments ago.

The man was covered in ash, dirt, and something wet. His dark, dim eyes stared at Jak, or perhaps through him. A stench lingered around the man, despite the smoldering trees surrounding them. The man stumbled forward and reached for Jak.

"Help me, please," the man pleaded wearily.

Jak backed away and shown the light in the man's face. The man groaned and put up a hand to block the bright light.

Jak finally got a good look at the stranger. He wore clothes made mostly of wool and leather. His hide-leather boots were tide tight with thick laces. Chain mail covered both of his knees and both arms. An empty quiver hung on his back, but there was no sign of a bow.

The man stumbled toward Jak again, reaching out with one arm. That's when Jak noticed the man's other arm was pulled tight against his body, pieces of motley flesh dangled from it. One side of the stranger's face was mangled, and much like his clothes, the skin ripped and tattered. The dark, wet trails running down the man's body were blood.

Repulsed, Jak stepped backward, but the man kept stumbling after him.

"What do you want!" yelled Jak still backing away from the man's feeble reach. The man tried to say something, but pain overcame him, he groaned and losing balance gripped a nearby tree with his unscathed arm.

"Stay away from me you freak!" Jak yelled. Panic-stricken, Jak tripped over a large branch and dropped the flashlight. He fell backward, hitting the ground hard, knocking the air out of him. He gasped, but little air came. His lungs began to burn. Reaching behind him in an attempt to find the flashlight he peered into the darkness trying to see the stranger. He gasped again for fresh air. In the moonlight Jak saw the tattered man limping through the smoke toward him.

"Please," the stranger cried, "I need your help."

Jak fumbled faster for the heavy Mag flashlight and finally grasped it as the bloodied stranger fell to the ground and grabbed Jak's ankle.

"Help." The bloody man could barely get the word out.

Jak sat up and swung the flashlight, hitting the wounded man on the head. Then he kicked him several times.

"No...please..." the man cried in agony.

Jak stood up; his face was hot and he could feel his temples pulsing. This freak had no right being here and no right coming after him.

"Don't touch me!" Jak yelled, "Don't ever touch me, you freak!"

Jak fell on the stranger and drove a knee into his side causing the wounded man to choke.

I can say it was in self-defense. But that was Jak's last thought.

When he raised the flashlight in the air, he felt a sharp pain on the back of his head, and then everything went black.

5

LAST-MINUTE PLANS

The view was serene and majestic. Simon was overlooking a mighty forest. Towering mountains hid behind a heavy mist. The trees were tall and strong. Great waterfalls rumbled quite some distance away, yet their refreshing, misty presence reached Simon and beyond. Multiple rainbows crisscrossed over the waterfalls and reached high above the forest's canopy. He sensed more trees standing behind him like faithful guardians. He felt safe and so alive. He was joyful. It was as if he had been dead inside until now.

"Simon." Her soothing voice came from afar.

He wanted to answer her, but when he opened his mouth no words came out.

Who is she? he wondered.

"Simon?"

I hear you, but where are you? Oh no...Maybe she's looking for me and can't find me! Simon's heart began beating faster.

"Simon," her soft voice called out again.

He tried to say hello. He felt his tongue and lips form the word, but he had no voice. The more he tried, the harder it became to move his mouth. It was as if he had forgotten how to speak...or his voice was taken to keep him from answering her.

"Simon?" Her voice sounded familiar; he knew her. "Simon...come with me," she said politely, beckoning him.

Mom? Is that you? He waited for an eternity. *Maybe she left me.*

The joy he felt moments ago was melting from his memory.

"Mom?" This time the word came out. With little effort, his thought formed into letters and he spoke the word again, "Mom?"

She touched his arm, but he still couldn't see her. Her touch was gentle. He wanted to cry. He wanted to know it was okay to cry.

"Don't leave," he said.

"I'm not going anywhere," she said, but her voice changed. It was still gentle and kind, but she sounded... younger.

He squeezed his eyes closed, but just as if his eyelids were transparent he could still see the trees and waterfall.

I don't understand. What's happening?

Her touch left his arm; someone started tapping his shoulder. An invisible force tugged on him, pulling him from this serene place.

Don't…I want to stay…Mom! As he yelled the invisible force pulled him up into the sky, but before the land below him drew out of his sight all went dark.

His first attempt to open his eyes was much like his first attempt to speak. The more he tried the heavier his eyelids became…until they flew open and the bright light blinded him.

"Simon? Are you okay?"

"Jessica? Is that you?" Simon was lying on his bed with his blanket and sheet twisted tightly around him, and his pillow and T-shirt were wet and cold. He felt disoriented…and disheartened as reality drew itself around him, suffocating the memory of the dream.

"Are you okay?" asked Jessica, concerned.

He looked around, making sure he was actually in his bedroom. The window was cracked open letting in a crisp breeze. The sky was pink, orange, and blue; the sun wasn't too high in the horizon. It was dawn. It was Saturday morning.

"I just had the most amazing dream…it was so real," he said as he sat up on the side of his bed.

"Must've been. I thought you were awake at first because you were talking, but then I realized you were talking in your sleep," she said still looking concerned.

"What was I saying?" asked Simon, but wasn't sure he wanted to know.

Her look of concern turned awkward. "I...can't really remember...you were more muttering than talking," she said, looking down at her shoes.

He was hoping she didn't hear him say "Mom" aloud. The thought embarrassed him.

"Was it scary?" she asked. "Because you started rolling and kicking."

He didn't know what to say.

"I hope I didn't frighten you when I tried waking you," said Jessica apologetically.

"No. It wasn't you," Simon said trying to erase her uneasiness. "But it really was an amazing and vivid dream. It was so beautiful...and comforting. I didn't want to leave."

"Now I feel bad for waking you up," she said in a subtle, yet acknowledgeable pout. Jessica was proud in having a well-held composure, so when she did let slip a glimpse of her tender side it stood out like a beacon. She tossed her long hair over her shoulder, its silky sheen brilliant in the sunrise.

"No...don't, it was just a dream," he said ruffling his hair. He wanted to ask her what she was doing here so early on a Saturday, but he didn't want to be rude. "Want to have breakfast?" he asked getting up and rummaging through his dresser for a clean shirt.

He felt awkward and wanted to get out of his room as soon as possible. He was embarrassed she had heard him talk in his sleep and he probably looked like he felt... disheveled.

Jessica must have detected his unease for her demeanor began to mimic his. She moved indecisively about the room trying to stay out of his way. Several times they almost ran into each other.

"Look, I was just coming over to surprise you," she said awkwardly.

Simon stopped in the middle of the room. He was holding a sneaker in one hand and a slipper in the other and realized he didn't even know what he was looking for. He was searching aimlessly for nothing. It was like he had forgotten where everything was in his room.

"It worked," he said looking down at his boxer shorts and then the sneaker and slipper.

"I didn't mean...." She stopped to regain her composure.

There was a moment of silence. Then Simon looked at her and shrugged his shoulders. He realized how ridiculous he must look and smiled.

Jessica took a folded pair of jeans off the top of his dresser. "Looking for these?" she said and handed them to him.

He snatched the pair of jeans from her and then they both laughed.

"What I meant was I wanted to surprise you with a gift," she said with a big smile.

"A gift?" asked Simon. "What's the occasion?"

"No occasion. I just asked my parents and they thought it was a good idea, too." She seemed delighted with herself.

"You asked your parents?" He was feeling borderline concerned. How important was this gift?

Simon enjoyed giving gifts to others. He often went out of his way to give someone a gift once he was set on it.

One summer he mowed thirty-two yards, washed twenty-three cars, and helped a neighbor, Mr. Conan, lay rock around his house, to save enough money to buy a 1950 edition of *The Lion, The Witch and the Wardrobe* for his dad's birthday.

His dad read that story many times to Simon before bedtime when he was little. Each time his dad read the ending he would pause for a moment or two in speculation, close the book, pat the cover like it was an old friend, and kiss Simon on the forehead. Then he would turn out the lights and leave the bedroom, without saying a word.

So when Simon found the first edition on display at The Bay's Best Bookstore in downtown Riverside, it was only fitting that his father be the owner of such a precious commodity.

But Simon didn't feel the same about receiving gifts. When someone gave him something he felt self-conscious. He always wanted to give something back in return. But he believed that wasn't an appropriate response.

"Yeah," said Jessica matter-of-factly. "We're taking a trip to Itasca State Park and renting a cabin for a couple of nights. My parents thought it was a great idea when I suggested you come along too."

Simon didn't know what to say. He didn't even know the Wells were leaving town. His first thought was that being stuck with Randal in a vehicle for hours was not his idea of a fun time.

"When did you guys plan this?" he asked aware he didn't sound as excited as he intended. "I mean…I didn't know you were leaving town this weekend."

Jessica shifted her stance. "Well…my parents decided last minute it would be fun to get out of the house before winter is upon us and it's too late…." She didn't seem to know what else to say. "Come on," she said, almost pleading. "I know you and Randal don't get along much, but we don't have to hang around him."

Much? That was a major understatement.

"Plus," she continued, "there's a really cool place I want to show you. We can hike around the headwaters and then I'll show you what I mean. You've been talking about going to the headwaters for years."

Simon did want to see the headwaters, but hadn't had the opportunity, until now. The headwaters of the great Mississippi River started in the placid and peaceful water of Lake Itasca. Itasca is one of the crown jewels of Minnesota. Simon enjoyed the outdoors, and seeing the headwaters has been on Simon's to-do list for some time. Jessica knew this. This really was a surprise.

"Well…I'll have to ask my dad, but…"

"We already asked him," she blurted out in excitement, "and he said it's fine with him, but up to you." She gazed into his eyes, again almost pleading. He couldn't get a read on her. She looked excited, but a little worried or concerned too.

A last minute trip was odd for the Wells family. Her parents, like Jessica, liked to have a plan and a reason for everything. This was way out there for them.

"Sure," he found himself saying. "A hike sounds like a great idea!"

Jessica was relieved. She smiled and then hugged him tight. "Great!" she said practically sashaying to the door.

"Wait! What do you want me to bring?" he asked.

"Yourself of course," she said caustically. "We're only staying a couple of nights so you don't need to bring much."

"When are we leaving?"

"Oh yeah," she said, holding onto the bedroom door handle, "my parents want us to leave right away. As soon as you're packed."

Simon looked out his bedroom window. Across the street their van was backed into the driveway and Dr. Wells was loading stuff into the back.

"You guys are ready to go now!" Simon said in astonishment.

"Yep! So you better get a move on!" she said, then shrugged her shoulders and closed the door as she left.

Simon watched from his window as Jessica darted out his front door and up her driveway.

"Okay! He's coming!" Her anxious voice rang from across the street.

Simon closed the window, and just then Dr. Wells looked up at him. He looked anxious, but managed a courteous smile. Dr. Wells said something to Jessica as she walked up to him. She looked surprised and then hurried into their house.

What's the rush? thought Simon.

Simon grabbed his duffle bag and threw in some clothes including his hiking boots, sweatshirt, and base-ball cap. For good measure he tossed in a book, in case he needed a good excuse to spend time alone.

He made his way down to the kitchen to grab a snack.

"Simon, I want you to be careful," said his father in a low tone.

"Of course I will Dad," Simon said into the cabinet as he pushed his way around cereal boxes to the breakfast bars, "I'll be with the Wells family, how much safer could I be?" he said playfully.

He turned around with several breakfast bars in his hand. His father was standing in the doorway wearing a look of serious concern. "Dad...what's wrong?"

"Just promise me you'll be careful," said his father. He looked tired and worried.

"Alright...I promise."

"Stay close to the Wells family and don't wonder off."

"Dad, I'm almost fifteen I don't wonder off anymore," Simon said trying to lighten the mood.

"I know," said his father. "It's not you, it's the others."

"The others?" Simon was confused. "Dad, if you don't want me to go I won't. It's not a big deal."

"Never mind...I mean, they'll take good care of you...." His father leaned heavily against the doorway.

"Dad...what is it?"

His father's face tightened and his jaw clenched. It looked like he was going to cry, but his demeanor quickly changed. Lifting a smile to his face he walked over and gave Simon a big hug. "Son, I love you so much. You know that, right?"

"Dad, you're starting to scare me."

"No, no, don't be scared. I just haven't said it in a while and a father should always let his son know he loves him. That's all."

There came a knock at the front door and then someone entered.

"Simon! Are you ready?" Jessica called out from the living room.

Simon and his father walked into the living room.

"Hi Mr. Whittaker," she said.

"Hi Jessica," he said politely.

"Dad," said Simon, "I love you too." He gave his father another hug, feeling a little guilty he was leaving his father in this mood. He wanted to talk to his father and find out what was on his mind, but there was no time. "A son should always let his father know he loves him," he said and smiled. Simon felt better when his father smiled back.

"We'll take good care of him Mr. Whittaker," said Jessica sincerely, "I promise."

"I know you will, Jessica," said his father. "Now you two go. Explore and be adventurous."

Simon and Jessica started to leave.

"Simon…I'll see you soon," said his father and then glanced at Jessica.

"Come on Simon," she said grabbing his hand, "we really need to get going." And then she led Simon from his house…and from his life as he knew it.

6

SLEEP WELL MR. GOODY TWO SHOES

The trip to Itasca was a blur, literally. Simon woke from a deep sleep. He was in the back seat of the Wells' van parked near a cabin. He was alone. He looked around for any sign of Jessica and her family, but all was quiet.

He tried recollecting the events from when he left his house to arriving at the cabin, but his thoughts were hazy and he had to fight the urge to fall back to sleep. He assumed he was in Itasca since that was the game plan.

After leaving his father, Simon and Jessica ran across the street. Dr. Wells, a prominent medical doctor who was as kind as he was brilliant, took Simon's bag and placed it with the rest of their belongings. The entire family was moving like they were running late to catch the downtown train.

"Is there anything I can do to help?" he asked Dr. Wells who was surveying the back of the van. The van was packed with duffle bags, suitcases, coolers, and grocery bags. They had enough supplies to last a solid week.

"No. I think we're good," said Dr. Wells more to himself than to Simon. "Go ahead and get in," he said motioning to the van. Jessica led him to the back seat and sat beside him.

Randal didn't say anything. He just took one of the captain seats for himself leaving the back seat to Jessica and Simon. Simon felt awkward being in the same vehicle with Randal, considering their history. Simon wouldn't consider Randal an enemy, per se, but he also wouldn't consider him a friend, either.

In fact, Simon wasn't sure what to consider Randal. Their relationship had become rather unorthodox. Simon couldn't take his mind off the fact Randal had developed a quirky ability to both loath and look out for Simon at the same time. There seemed to have been a growing number of incidences over the years to support this reasoning.

The first incident happened when Simon was nine years old, three weeks after Simon had spent the day baking cookies with Jessica and her mom. For a whole week after that day Simon neither saw nor heard a sign of Randal, or his buddies. There was no whooping and yelping from the belligerent group as they wrestled each other, yelled insults at younger kids, or insults toward Simon. There wasn't a peep. The neighborhood was quiet and peaceful that week.

Even school was quieter. With Randal gone, Chuck and the other two hooligans didn't make near the fuss they usually did. They were like a great white shark with no teeth, intimidating to look at, but no real threat.

Simon didn't ask Jessica about Randal's whereabouts because he didn't want to broach the subject. Simon wasn't sure how she would feel if he admitted to the fact he didn't like her older brother.

Unfortunately, the following week Simon saw Randal leaving his house with his football tucked under his arm. This shattered Simon's fantasy about Randal being shipped off to a faraway boarding school, perhaps in the tundra.

However, there was something different about Randal. There was a change in the way he walked and talked. Even the expression on his face had changed. Instead of a chronic scowl, Randal displayed contemplation. This was unlike Randal. He usually didn't think. He reacted.

It took all of a week to realize the biggest difference. Randal wasn't bullying much and when he did it was at a lesser caliber than before. He also hung around Chuck and his other two buddies less.

Randal's walk was different because he seemed sure of where he was going. His face looked different because he wasn't constantly bitter. Simon even saw Randal smile for the first time. He didn't smile at Simon, it was while he was talking with another boy at school, but he smiled nonetheless. And even though Randal was back from wherever it was he went, the neighborhood remained quiet and peaceful.

Simon stepped onto the front porch to read on this particular day. The day was calm and temperate. Two chapters into his book, Simon realized the repetitive sound of a football being caught and two familiar voices from across the street. Glancing up he saw Randal and Chuck. This was the first time in three weeks one of Randal's buddies was at the Wells' house. He was afraid to look up again in case he made eye contact with one of them. He tried focusing on the book, but found their bantering back and forth too distracting.

Simon was thinking about going back in the house when suddenly one of the familiar voices across the street, which had been yelling insults and obscenities at him for years, echoed once more across the two yards.

"Hey brainiac!"

Simon knew he was waiting for a response, but maybe it wasn't directed at him. Maybe he was talking to someone else.

"Hey! I'm talking to you!"

The sound of the football being caught had ceased. He was definitely waiting for Simon to respond. Reluctantly, Simon looked up. Randal and Chuck were standing in the Wells' front yard. Randal was holding onto the football, whereas Chuck was moving a few paces closer toward the street, awaiting Simon's reply.

"Are you going deaf nerd boy?" Chuck heckled and then stopped a few feet into the street.

Simon's heart jumped several beats. The familiar knot returned in the pit of his stomach. Although he didn't look around, Simon was sure the entire neighborhood was watching, judging his every move. His throat was dry and sore.

"No," Simon said, trying to hide the quiver in his voice, "I didn't know you were talking to me."

"Well I am!" yelled Chuck.

Simon was anticipating a sarcastic comment from Randal, but none followed. Randal remained in his yard, holding the football.

"Sorry," said Simon, but didn't know what else to say.

"Sorry?" said Chuck sarcastically and throwing Randal a look, a cue to join in. Getting no response from Randal he redirected his attention to Simon. "Are you mocking me kid?" Chuck's voice went up a whole octave.

"No," said Simon.

Chuck stepped into the middle of the street, his gangly hair swaying on the sides of his head from shaking it in disapproval.

"Come over here!" he said pointing down at the street.

Simon looked up and down the street hoping to see someone, anyone. Maybe one of the neighborhood adults would say something to stop this, or his dad would return from the store.

"I said get down here Sigh-Man!" he demanded. The more Chuck played angry, the angrier he became.

Simon, ever so slightly, shook his head. Chuck stomped across the street and down the sidewalk leading up to Simon's porch. Simon stood up.

"Okay," said Simon, and made his way down the porch. The last thing he wanted was Chuck coming after him in his house where no one would be able to see what was going on. At least this way he was in public.

Simon stopped on the bottom step. Chuck stopped midway down the sidewalk. About twenty feet separated the two.

"Get over here you runt!" Chuck growled. "When I tell you to do something you do it!"

Simon's eyes began swelling with tears.

"Don't start crying you big baby!" Chuck barked. "Now get over here," and he pointed to the ground again with his long, scrawny finger.

Simon slowly took the last step onto the sidewalk and slowly walked toward Chuck, who displayed a triumphant grin.

Chuck was two years older and more than a foot taller than Simon. Even worse he had a mean spirit and a point to prove to anyone watching. Simon anticipated a terrible beating.

Simon weighed his options. He could run, but Chuck would eventually catch him, or catch up to him. He could try talking to Chuck, but he didn't think he would get too far with that either.

Then it happened. Randal, who had been watching from afar, threw the football just as Chuck said, "Listen to me you little…AAAHH!" Chuck's head jolted unnaturally to the left as the spiraling football connected. From his head it bounced back into the street.

"What the…!" Chuck turned around holding his hand over his right ear. Randal was making a beeline to Chuck. "Whatcha think you're do'n dude?" Chuck yelled. His face was turning violet with pain, or anger, or both. Red rings encircled his eyes as they swelled with tears, which Chuck tried to hide.

Simon's feet were frozen to the ground; he watched as Randal grabbed fistfuls of Chuck's shirt and pushed him back a good ten paces. Chuck's eyeballs doubled in size and he lost footing, but Randal held him up.

"What did I tell ya about him?" Randal growled. Their faces were just inches apart. Chuck was lost for words.

In the wake of Randal's fury Chuck didn't look big anymore. Randal towered over him.

"Ha? What did I tell ya?" he demanded. Chuck was lost and couldn't speak.

Simon remained anchored in surrealism.

"He's-off-limits," Chuck stammered.

"Yeah! That's right!" said Randal nodding and scowling. Then he let go and Chuck fell to the ground. "Get out of his yard," said Randal and gestured toward his house.

Chuck glanced at Simon resentfully. Then he stood up and slowly crossed the street to the Wells' yard.

Randal turned around and looked at Simon. It was like he was surveying him, seeing him for the first time.

"Thank you," Simon managed to say.

Randal recovered his composer, gave a slight nod, and turned and walked away.

After exchanging a few quiet words the two boys walked down toward the park, tossing the football back and forth.

Quite some time had passed before Simon saw Chuck again, playing catch with Randal. He acknowledged Simon with a slight waive of his hand and a nod as if to say, "I'm sorry."

From that day forward no one, especially Randal's friends, picked on Simon. To Simon's dismay Chuck and his lackeys still picked on other kids from time to time, when Randal wasn't around.

✳ ✳ ✳

Randal was sitting on the cabin's porch, carving twigs with a blade. It was the same blade he'd been carrying around with him ever since his fifteenth birthday. It didn't seem like a gift Jessica or his parents would have given him, but no one in their family gave it a second thought.

For the past two years the blade, which was a large dagger, could easily pass as Randal's best friend. In that time Randal had spent countless hours sharpening, cleaning, and throwing the blade, with alarming accuracy. Concealed well, he took it with him everywhere. Randal had become quite the expert with the dagger. Even now, as Simon watched him carve the twigs, Randal handled the dagger with such ease it was like an extension of his own hand.

Every few moments Randal would glance at the van. Simon didn't think he could see him through the van's tinted windows, but Randal watched anyway.

Simon was still tired so he remained in the back seat, his head propped up against a headrest. He thought if he closed his eyes, he could sleep through the whole day and night too.

Why am I so tired? he wondered.

Then Jessica stepped out of the cabin. Her eyes wandered over to the van. Standing on the porch she looked more like a young woman than a fourteen-year-old girl. Her expression was serious and perplexed. She was contemplating something. She looked down and said something to Randal, who was still sitting on the edge of the porch letting his legs dangle. He just shrugged his shoulders.

Jessica glanced at the van and then at the porch's steps. She took a couple steps down and then stopped. Her expression changed from confused to concern; she pivoted on her heel and went back inside the cabin.

Simon decided he had better get up, regardless of how tired he was. Jessica must be upset at him for sleeping so long, although that didn't seem like her. But then he remembered something.

✳ ✳ ✳

As Simon waited in the van with Jessica and Randal while their parents grabbed a few last minute items before hitting the road, Jessica handed him and Randal each a water bottle filled with a dark beverage.

"Here," she said, "I mixed up some of my homemade tea for us."

Jessica had been on a weird kick making beverages and dipping sauces from scratch. She made punch with real fruit that she crushed, tea from actual tea leaves, and other drinks Simon couldn't identify. One of her fruit punches, with fresh blackberries and raspberries, helped clear up one of Simon's headaches a few months ago. But it didn't taste good. He remembered it had an earthy aftertaste. He was happy she hadn't asked him to taste her dipping sauces.

Simon took the water bottle Jessica offered him. Randle declined, "No thanks," he grunted. Jessica silently insisted he take the bottle by tapping him with it. "Okay, fine," he retorted and snatched the bottle.

Jessica took a gulp from her bottle, made a sound like she was refreshed, and smacked her lips together.

"I think this is my best one yet. What do you think?" she asked Simon.

Simon was reluctant to taste it because her concoctions had either been not so good or were down-right gross. He sniffed the top of the bottle.

"Come on. It's not going to kill you," said Jessica playfully.

He couldn't smell anything, so how bad could it be? He took a sip. Not tasting much, he took another. He was pleasantly surprised it wasn't horrible. It was way too sweet, but too sweet was better than earthy, pungent, and sour. He took a couple of gulps to please her and then made the same refreshed sound she had.

"Refreshing," said Simon.

Jessica was rattling through the ingredients of her new tea when her parents got into the van.

"Do you kids have everything?" asked Mrs. Wells politely looking back at the three of them.

"We're good to go, Mom," Jessica quietly answered, and continued explaining to Simon the mundane process of making the tea.

Simon took another gulp. It was cool when it touched his lips, but it felt warm going down his throat.

The last thing Simon remembered was Jessica explaining the best way to take a leaf off of a plant was to pinch it at the base of its stem so you don't rip and damage its integrity.

✳ ✳ ✳

That's it. That's all Simon could remember. No stops at a gas station, no conversation; he couldn't recall a thing.

Before getting out of the van, Simon decided to rest his eyes just a few more minutes. His eyelids were heavy as lead. He closed his eyes and recalled the other incident that had redefined his relationship with Randal.

✳ ✳ ✳

It happened about two years ago; Simon was twelve. Although there had been other circumstances in which Randal had displayed an uncharacteristic concern for Simon's wellbeing, this particular situation stood out because of its intensity involving a social castaway, a boy named Mitch Torkelson.

Mitch Torkelson wasn't a jock, he didn't join any school clubs, and he let it be known he hated school concerts, plays, or gatherings of any kind. He played the role of lone wolf. Although he tried to pride himself of being a loner, it was evident to everyone, except Mitch, he was desperate for attention.

In school Mitch made his way from clique to clique displaying an I-don't-need-you mentality every chance he got. This usually consisted of crass comments, witty snubs, and crude innuendos that inevitably resulted in being rejected, shunned from the group, and every once in a while a spat, from which Mitch would quickly depart. Mitch was not blessed with physical strength so he had to choose his battles wisely.

One of Mitch's signature phrases was, "What a suck-up!" This he said upon witnessing any act of kindness and generosity. He believed the only reason people acted out of kindness was for personal gain. If Mitch Torkelson was around, one was sure to hear, "What a suck-up!"

Mitch Torkelson did not have any friends, but he had a younger sister, Allahna, whom he watched over with a protective eye. Mitch once bit another boy's earlobe off because he laughed after Allahna had tripped.

Although he was scrawny and dexterity deficient, Mitch Torkelson was a ticking time bomb who could go berserk any second.

Allahna was a grade below Simon; Mitch was a grade ahead of Simon.

Allahna was built much like her brother; she was petite with fair skin. However, unlike Mitch, who had dark black hair that was in a constant state of disarray, Allahna had rich, golden-blond hair that fell to the middle of her back. She had far more poise than her brother. The two were an epitome of opposite, but the brother and sister got along nonetheless. Allahna was the one person Mitch was careful around; his manners were more controlled when his little sister was present.

The incident involving Simon and Mitch occurred on a bright and calm winter's day, not a cloud in the sky. The air was brisk. Simon stood at the top of a large hill waiting patiently for Scott and Jessica. Children sliding down the snow-covered hill laughed and screamed joyfully as they went faster and faster. Scott was trailing behind Jessica rolling a large, black inner tube up the hill. He looked like a locomotive chasing her with his rapid puffs of breath.

Jessica was still giggling from their last expedition down the mammoth hill. Simon smiled at the sight of her. She looked like a jubilant snowman. Snow was packed in the folds of her scarf, the tops of her boots, and in the brim of her hat. Even her wool mittens had snow still sticking to them. On their last trip down they hit a mound of packed snow that sent the three of them air-born; Simon and Scott managed to hang on to the tube, but Jessica flew two feet above them, landed on Scott and then bounced off of the tube into a snow bank. She hadn't stopped laughing since she dug herself out of it.

They decided to go down one more time before grabbing some hot cocoa in the Snack Shack at the bottom of the hill.

"Let's aim for the same jump," said Jessica catching her breath from the climb.

"Are you crazy?" Scott panted. "You almost got your-self killed down there." Steam rose from Scott's head. "I think we better stay away from there."

"Come on," Jessica pouted. "Are you chicken?"

"No!" he said.

"Okay, let's vote on it. Majority rules," she said. "Everyone in favor of having a blast raise your hand," she said raising her hand and looking at Simon with her lower lip puffed out in one of her best pouting sessions yet. Simon slowly put his hand in the air too. Scott grunted in protest.

"Fine!" Scott said putting up his hand too. "But if I land on either of you, you're not getting any sympathy from me." And he dropped the large tube in front of them.

Jessica jumped on first and then Simon and Scott got on either side of her to even out the weight.

"Squish me in good and tight boys," she said. Simon and Scott drew in tighter.

"Hang on," said Simon. "Better yet, loop your arms through ours so if you do let go we can hold onto you."

"Good think'n capt'm," Jessica saluted and did as he suggested. "Okay. On the count of three! One-two-threeee!" she yelled and they pushed off with their legs and leaned forward.

Two seconds later they were gaining momentum like a plane on a runway, throwing loose snow on either side of the tube. The air was bitter cold as they picked up speed. Each little bump caused the large tube to bounce, kicking snow into their faces. Jessica was giggling uncon-trollably and Scott was hooting between waves of snow hitting his face.

Simon felt so free sailing down the hillside. He tried keeping an eye out for the jump, but it was difficult with snow flinging into his face and the sun lighting up the snow-covered ground. But then he saw the mound like a large, white thumb sticking out of the ground. The jump was to their left.

"Hard left!" Simon yelled tightening his hold on Jessica.

Together the three leaned left and Simon pulled up his side. Like a large cruise liner on the open ocean, the mammoth tube slowly started to turn and angle left. All three of them screamed in anticipation. They were going too fast and angling too slow. They were going to miss the jump. But the tube hit a patch of hard-packed snow causing them to angle over even more.

The three amateur tubers were launched in the air again, spinning like a large Frisbee. Simon almost bounced off when they hit the ground, but Jessica held on to him. Simon's legs whipped around the side of the tube and hit something hard. After bumping heads, and getting smacked numerous times by the bouncing tube, they came to a stop. No one had fallen off.

Scott rolled off the tube and onto his back, puffing like a speedy locomotive up into the cool air. Jessica and Simon remained on the tube. The ground was tilting back and forth. Simon looked up the hill to see what his legs hit. A group of tubers were getting up from the ground.

"Oh no," Simon said trying to catch his breath, "I think...we hit...another group of tubers."

Jessica flopped over on the tube and looked back. Scott lifted his head up to take a peek. They recognized some of the kids from school; Allahna Torkelson was among them. She was sitting on the hillside looking up and holding her mittens to her face. She was bleeding.

Simon felt terrible. "Come on guys," he said trying to catch his breath, "let's check on them." Overcome with guilt he forced himself to stand up. His head was spinning and his leg was throbbing, but Simon began making his way to Allahna.

Scott dropped back to the ground. "Okay. Just give me a minute," he said.

Jessica started yelling. It sounded like she was yelling "come out," but when Simon saw her pointing at something in front of him it was clear she was yelling, "Watch out!"

He barely had time to register in his mind what was about to happen. His brain tried to send the image of the oncoming sled with a snap instruction to his legs to jump out of the way; however, Simon only had time to see the sled plow into him at full ramming speed. He was knocked completely off the ground.

As he went air-born time seemed to slow down. It was like he was in a slow-motion video. The sled and its passenger slid underneath him. The ground connected to the side of Simon's face followed by a muffled thump. His feet snagged the backside of the sled. He was dragged behind the sled for about twenty feet. Someone grabbed the back of his coat and turned him around.

The left side of Simon's face was burning. Someone was leaning over him, but snow and sweat blurred his vision so he couldn't see who it was. The person seemed to be putting his arm down to help Simon up, so Simon reciprocated by extending one of his arms. But instead of receiving a helping hand Simon received a blow to the left side of his face.

Instinctively Simon put both hands in front of his face.

"What are you doing?" Simon yelled, out of pain and frustration.

He immediately received another blow to his head followed by a knee into his stomach. Simon kept his hands up to protect his face and curled into a fetal position.

"Who do you think you are?" the boy yelled along with profanities.

The voice sounded familiar. Simon caught a glimpse of a straggly kid before he received a blow to his right ear. Simon's ear began to ring. In a panic, Simon twisted to the left and with his right leg kicked the boy off of him.

Simon began to get up, but his persistent offender tackled him from behind sending Simon's face once again into the hard, packed snow. The straggly kid wrapped an arm around Simon's neck.

Simon's face was throbbing and his throat began to burn. He attempted to move back and forth, but the berserker was sitting on his back.

"You think you're so special don't you? Mr. Goody Two-Shoes!" the boy spat.

Simon heard other voices yelling. He couldn't tell if the crowd was jeering or cheering, but as hard as he tried he couldn't get enough air to call for help.

Why was this boy attacking him? Why wasn't anyone helping him? What did he do to provoke the attack?

Couldn't anyone see he was being choked? Was he going to die in front of a circle of witnesses?

These were the thoughts running through Simon's head as his vision blurred and his head burned from the lack of oxygen.

And then in two very long moments it all came together.

First, the manic boy yelled, "That was my little sister up there you dumb suck-up!" Simon instantly knew. It was Mitch Torkelson! With crazy Torkelson as his attacker, Simon knew why no one was helping him. Most kids feared being where Simon is now, at the blunt end of Mitch's crazy rage.

Then, Simon felt the weight of Mitch Torkelson lift off him, quickly followed by a grunt as an unknown confederate tackled his assailant. Mitch's fingernails scratched Simon's face as he was torn away.

Simon rolled over onto his back gulping the cold, winter air, which stung his throat. Rolling his head to the side he saw Randal Wells wailing on Mitch Torkelson.

Although Simon would later feel sorry for Mitch Torkelson for getting his nose broken trying to stand up for his sister in a misguided sort of way, at that moment a burn inside Simon justified Mitch's end result.

Jessica had started running after Simon as soon as she realized Mitch was heading straight toward him. By the time she arrived it was already over. She knelt down beside him.

"Are you okay?" she asked.

"I will be," croaked Simon as he held a hand around his neck.

He glanced at Jessica. She was watching her older brother giving Mitch a run for his money. It was difficult to tell because it was against her nature, but she seemed pleased at what she saw.

"Where did everyone go?" asked Simon.

"Everyone? No one else dared to get any closer," said Jessica with disgust toward the distant bystanders.

"I thought I heard cheering, or yelling," said Simon.

"Oh," said Jessica, "that was me and Allahna yelling at Mitch to get off of you on our way over here."

"Allahna?" asked Simon. Then it dawned on him why this happened in the first place. "Allahna! Is she alright?"

"You tell me," said Jessica and gestured with her head toward the dying fray.

Simon saw Allahna holding a bloody mitten to her nose and standing timidly about ten feet away from Randal, who was still having words with Mitch. She was holding out her other hand and pleading with Randal.

"Please stop," she said timidly multiple times.

Jessica patted Simon on his shoulder and said with determination, "Just keep lying down for a moment."

She stood and walked over to her brother as casually as if Randal were sitting down watching television instead of sitting on top of another bully, punching and yelling at him. She put her hand on Randal's shoulder and said something to her brother. The only word Simon could make out was 'enough.'

Randal looked up at his little sister for a moment, gave her words a thought, and then shoved Mitch back to the ground. Mitch didn't bother getting up once Randal was off of him.

Allahna approached Simon, who was still lying on his back. She took the red-splattered mitten away from her face, and satisfied there wasn't any more blood said quietly, "I'm sorry about this. Are you okay?"

Simon suddenly felt bad for Mitch. Not only had the tide turned against Mitch, but Allahna was more concerned for Simon than her brother. Allahna was genuinely sorry and embarrassed for what Mitch did.

"Yes, I'll be fine," said Simon, slowly sitting up. "But I should be apologizing to you," he said. "I feel terrible crashing into you. I'm really sorry! Are *you* alright?"

"Oh, don't worry. That's part of the hazard of the hill, right?" she said, then chuckled and smiled.

Simon also smiled. "Is your nose going to be okay?"

Allahna's spirits lightened up. "Yeah, I've been hit harder than this by Mitch," she said matter-of-factly. "At least *you* didn't try hitting me. He usually hits me dead on," she said gesturing over to Mitch who was still lying on the ground in defeat. He appeared to be cussing the sky.

"He's got good aim, that's for sure," Simon said, and they both chuckled.

"Well, I better go check on him." Allahna smiled meekly at Simon for a moment and then turned and walked over to her brother.

Jessica rejoined Simon. Randal started walking away.

"Hey! Thanks!" Simon yelled out to Randal, his voice still hoarse.

Randal held up his hand and said, "Yeah," and without looking back continued walking away.

Simon and Jessica went over to Scott. He was still lying down next to their tube, panting, and oblivious to the recent event.

"Did you check on those other tubers yet?" Scott asked lazily.

"Come on, let's get inside and warm up," said Jessica.

"What'd you do to your face?" asked Scott as he leaned in closer to look at Simon.

Jessica grabbed Simon's arm.

"Scott! Get the tube!" she said impatiently leading Simon to the Snack Shack.

✳ ✳ ✳

Simon awoke to the fresh scent of a tropical paradise. Oranges, lemons, coconuts, and other exotic scents and spices tickled his nose and snapped his eyes open with a rush of energy. Jessica was sitting next to him in the back seat holding a small, steaming cup of tea. It smelled so delectable Simon's initial thought was to take it and gulp it down.

Jessica sensed his intentions; she handed the tiny cup to him gently.

"Sip it," she said softly. "It'll revitalize you."

Simon raised the cup to his lips. The aroma engulfed him like plunging into cool, clear water on a hot summer day. When he sipped the invigorating nectar, a spike of energy shot around in his body and mind, like an electric pulse. He felt great! Jessica smiled at him.

"How long have I been out?" asked Simon.

"About six hours," Jessica said. "It's the afternoon."

"I don't know what got into me. I hope I haven't dampened your trip," Simon said taking another pleasing sip from the cup.

Jessica's smile dissipated and a shadow of regret flickered across her face.

"No, not at all," she said, "I just..." she was lost for words.

"What is it?" asked Simon. "Is something wrong?"

Jessica looked out at Randal and Dr. Wells sitting on the porch with beverages. Jessica leaned in closer, but didn't speak right away.

"There's something I should..." she started to say and then stopped. They watched as Dr. Wells approached the van.

"Hi Daddy."

"Hi Pumpkin," said Dr. Wells. "How's our sleepy guest doing?" he said in slight jest.

"He seems better now," said Jessica.

"How are you feeling Simon?" Dr. Wells asked looking Simon over like he was one of his patients at the hospital.

"I'm better now, sir," said Simon, "I just don't know what happened. I wasn't tired at all when we left Riverside, but up until a few minutes ago I felt I could've slept for days."

Dr. Wells smiled reassuringly. "You just had a slight reaction to the tea Jessica made. She added chamomile, and apparently too much," he said rolling his eyes over to Jessica who was looking sheepish. "Well," he said turning his attention back to the cabin, "I better help your mother with lunch," and then left.

Randal stood as his father went up the porch and into the cabin. Then he turned and looked at the van. Randal's eyes narrowed like he was looking into the sun, only he was in shade. He held his gaze for a long while before turning and following his father into the cabin.

As soon as the cabin door closed Jessica turned to Simon. "We need to talk," she said urgently.

"What about?" asked Simon savoring the last sip from the small cup.

"Not now, and not here," she said. "After lunch I'll tell them we're going for a hike." She seemed to have thought this out already. "We'll have to sneak some extra food along without my family noticing anything peculiar," she said. "And I have everything else we'll need."

"What are you talking about?" asked Simon, "What other things do we need, and why do we have to sneak around?"

"Jessica!" Randal yelled from the doorway. Simon and Jessica both jumped in their seats. "It's time to eat! Get in here!" Randal yelled impatiently.

"Don't ask questions and don't act suspicious," said Jessica. "We'll leave as soon as we can. Just have a nice time," she said under her breath as she stepped out of the van.

"I thought that's why we came here in the first place," Simon muttered.

She turned around, stopping Simon in his tracks. She looked him in the eyes and said, "You're in for a big surprise…"

"Come on!" barked Randal.

Jessica turned back toward the house. "Okay!" she yelled.

As they passed Randal going into the cabin she said matter-of-factly, "You still need to learn patience big brother."

"And you still need to learn to listen little sister," Randal hissed closing the door behind them.

7

RAINBOW ROCKS AND COMPASSES

The meal was bountiful and exquisite, not at all what Simon was expecting. Sandwiches and potato chips are the norm on a camping trip. But Mrs. Wells had been cooking up a storm while he slept. By the end of their meal she had served seven courses.

The place settings on the large, wooden table were casual and homey. The table and kitchen were adorned with flowers of all kinds, but primarily chrysanthemums and an assortment of red, white, yellow, and blue roses, the most vibrant and prettiest roses Simon had ever seen. The cabin smelled like a perfume boutique, and the scents tickled his nose. He, along with the entire Wells family, sneezed quite steadily throughout the meal. And although it was light outside, there were at least a dozen candles set in various places on the table and around the kitchen. Simon thought the whole setting pleasant, yet odd.

Mrs. Wells put forth her best effort in preparing and serving the meal. The first course was filled with tasty hors d'oeuvres of all kinds. Simon's favorite was hot crab puffs. Mrs. Wells said the secret was in the cheese and the amount of garlic she uses. Then came a light Caesar salad with just the right amount of seasoning and topped with Parmesan cheese and homemade crispy croutons. Next was homemade cream of lemon soup with bits of tender chicken, which was capped off with lemon and lime sorbet.

Simon was already full when Mrs. Wells announced the main course, smoked salmon. The second main course was the most tender, tastiest, and juiciest meat Simon could remember eating; it was lamb, and Mrs. Wells went into great detail on how to prepare the dish. Mrs. Wells enjoyed explaining her dishes to her captive audience. Dr. Wells, Jessica, and even Randal responded with genuine interest. Simon even found himself interested. Mrs. Wells had a way of taking the simplest tasks and spinning them into a unique tale with a delicious ending. Her descriptions were so vivid that each tale made Simon hunger for the next one.

During the first course Simon was nervous; he didn't think he could eat. He kept hearing Jessica's urgent voice in his head, "We need to talk! Not now and not here!" What was so important? And why didn't she want her family to know?

By the time Simon finished his salad he was no longer nervous, just suspicious. He tried convincing himself Jessica was playing him like she had done in the past. She had a great imagination and a knack for coming up with some of the most exciting adventures.

Once, when they were nine, she had him convinced there were secret portals leading to other realms with great creatures and even greater treasures, and for almost two months they looked around. They never found one. It wasn't the story she told that convinced him, but the fact she believed it.

The Wells family was known for lengthy meals. Mealtime was a social time. They didn't eat just for the sake of eating; they ate to visit and learn more about each other's day, feelings, and even aspirations. By the time dinner was over it was late in the afternoon. Simon couldn't believe it. They had dined for over two hours, which was lengthy even for the Wells family.

Still...there was something peculiar about this dinner.

First, Dr. and Mrs. Wells seemed unusually interested in *Simon's* aspirations. Every other question was directed to him, and most of them pertaining to Simon's future such as where he would like to live, what professional fields he's most interested, had he considered law enforcement, does he like science, and other such probing questions. Nearly every topic was either about Simon, or led back to him. And when Simon tried bringing up a different topic in an attempt to take the attention off of him, the discussion was completely dropped and either Dr. Wells or Mrs. Wells focused on Simon again. So many times he was the center of attention, Simon felt uncomfortable; he never did like being the center of attention.

Even more disturbing was that Jessica made no attempt to change the subject and take the attention off of Simon. Despite several attempts to change the topic, Jessica remained content, listening to her parents' questions and Simon's answers. Even Randal was interested. This was most unsettling.

The dinner's second peculiarity was that Dr. Wells and Randal intermittently excused themselves from the dinner table to step outside onto the porch. The Wells family considered it impolite to leave the dinner table unless it was important. However, both of them left the table at least four times throughout the near two-and-a-half-hour meal. Neither Mrs. Wells nor Jessica gave any notice to their coming and goings. If it were any other family, Simon wouldn't have thought twice about it. But the Wells family was not any other family. Every meal together, regardless how small or large, was a formal meal. Their time together as a family was a high priority and one not taken lightly.

It didn't add up. A sudden trip, an extravagant meal in a small cabin, an excessive amount of attention on Simon, the aimless pacing on the porch by Dr. Wells and Randal, and Jessica's instructions, which were more like warnings, right before the meal.

Simon was trying to follow Jessica's advice to have a good time and not act suspicious. He was annoyed at the fact that if she hadn't said anything in the first place he *would be* having a good time and he definitely wouldn't have to worry about acting suspicious.

Whether it was the large meal, or making it through the one-hundred-and-one questions thrown at him, Simon was exhausted. Jessica and her mom were in the kitchen cleaning up, and Randal and Dr. Wells were both outside on the porch again.

Mrs. Wells had instructed Simon to rest on the sofa until she and Jessica were finished with the dishes. Each time he looked over his shoulder Jessica was watching him. He finally decided he may as well take a small nap while he was waiting. Besides, it was nice not having to answer a barrage of questions.

As soon as he closed his eyes he started drifting off to sleep. He smiled at the thought that he had only been awake for about four hours and was already tired. Before slipping into dreamland he heard Jessica ask, "Simon! Would you like a cup of cocoa?" She sounded faraway and desperate.

"Let him sleep Jessica," said Mrs. Wells. "It will make things easier for him."

Make things easier for me? What does she mean?

The cup of orange mango juice Mrs. Wells made Simon after dinner slipped from his fingers and fell to the wooden floor with a thump. Simon slumped over on the sofa and fell fast asleep once again.

A rush of energy jolted Simon awake. Startled, he sat up, choking on a familiar tropical sweetness. Jessica was sitting beside him on the edge of the sofa holding the same little cup she had earlier. Steam rose from the cup and the aroma enticing Simon to grab and gulp it down.

Jessica handed him the cup, "Here, drink the rest of it," she said. "You'll need it."

The room had darkened since their meal; it was already dusk. He had been sleeping for hours. He looked down at the little cup in his hands; the aroma infused his thoughts, and his mouth watered. But he fought the urge to drink the little cup's content. He wanted some answers and he wanted them now! He looked around the cabin and no one else was around.

"Jessica, I want to know what's going on! This doesn't feel like a camping trip, it feels like some kind of a game and I'm at the center of it!"

Jessica's dark brown eyes were vibrant; without a flinch or a blink she said, "This is not a game." And her eyes confirmed it. She was telling the truth, whatever the truth was.

"Then what's going on?" Simon asked. He suddenly felt a shift from energetic to tiredness and back again. Shaking his head he said, "Whoa! I'm feeling a little dizzy."

"You better drink the rest of that or you'll fall asleep again," Jessica said with urgency. "And once everyone is back I may not have this opportunity again."

"What oppertooonicty?" Simon slurred and could feel sleep quickly overcoming him.

"Just trust me for now and drink the rest of the potion! I'll explain later! I promise!" Jessica exclaimed.

"Possshhion...okay? I trusht yoou." Simon lifted the cup, but he couldn't hold it; he just wanted to sleep. He leaned forward in an attempt to meet his hand halfway to his mouth, but fell forward. Jessica grabbed his shoulders and pulled him back, spilling the potion on his shirt in the process. Simon slowly turned to Jessica, who looked like she had just witnessed a murder.

"Oh, God!" She said. "I can't believe this just happened!"

"What'sss the big deeal," asked Simon, "just give me another cup," and he lay his head against her shoulder.

Jessica held Simon's head between both of her hands; his cheeks squished together from her grip making him look like he was pretending to be a fish.

"You don't get it!" she said intensely, "I only made the one cup and I don't have time to make another before everyone is back." She lifted Simon's wet T-shirt to his nose. "Take a deep breath," she said.

Simon did what she said; he took a deep breath. The tropical coconuts, fresh herbs, and citrus aromas tickled his nose giving him newfound energy.

"Good," said Jessica with relief, "that'll do for now. Take off your shirt!"

"What? What for?"

"You'll need to breathe in the aroma for as long as it lasts," she said grabbing a shirt out of her father's bag and handing it to him. "Just put this one on and get your jacket; we have to go. Now!"

"Where is everyone?" asked Simon as he changed shirts.

"My mom and dad had to go somewhere and they left me and Randal in charge of watching you," she said. "Randal went to collect more firewood so he'll be back any minute."

Feeling tired he stuck his nose into the T-shirt, inhaling the revitalizing aroma.

"Watch over me? Why would you watch over me?" he asked, his voice muffled in the shirt.

Jessica zipped up her jacket and handed Simon his. She flew to the counter and grabbed a satchel. "Come on!" she said, throwing Simon his shoes. "I'll tell you on the way."

Simon didn't move. He was annoyed with the whole situation. Either this was a joke and she was pushing him to go along for the ride, or something was really wrong and she was trying to protect him from something. Either way, he wanted to know.

Jessica looked at him and took a deep breath. Sympathy quickly replaced her frustration.

"Simon. I know this is frustrating for you. Believe me. I truly understand. I didn't believe it either when I first found out about it." She walked up to him and placed a hand on his shoulder. "I promise I'll explain everything. We're best friends. This promise shouldn't be taken lightly. But right now we have to go or it'll be too late." Her eyes twinkled in the cabin's dim light.

Once again her eyes said it all.

"Alright," said Simon placing a hand on her shoulder. She smiled with delight, which melted into a scorn when she looked behind him.

"We have to go now!" she said, staring at something behind Simon.

Simon turned around. From the back door's window he saw a small light bouncing about the trees. Someone was coming up to the cabin. Dusk had turned to night. He bent to put on his shoes, but Jessica grabbed him. "We don't have time," she said. "Let's go!"

They ran out the front door and into the night, with Simon holding his shoes. His stockings were of little help against the sticks, shrubs, and the chilly autumn air nipping his feet. He sighed with relief when Jessica finally stopped and turned on her flashlight.

"You better hurry and put those on," she said. She kept the light low to the ground.

Simon was never more appreciative for his shoes. He was sure his feet were covered in cuts and scrapes, but they were so cold it was hard to tell. He didn't know the temperature outside, but their breaths were like puffs of smoke. It was cold enough.

"Why are we running from your family?" Simon asked, taking this moment to catch his breath. He put the crumpled shirt he was holding to his nose, smelling the revitalizing tropical aroma, which probably wasn't needed because the cold was doing the trick. Looking back all Simon could see were trees as far as the darkness would allow him.

"We're not running from my family," said Jessica, puffs of steam bellowing from her mouth.

"Really…" said Simon sarcastically. "Ironic coming from the girl catching her breath because she's running from her family, and not wanting to be seen I may add."

"We're not running from my family," said Jessica. "We're running from the cabin."

"Oh…that's smart," said Simon standing up. "Okay. I'll play that game," said Simon. "Then why are we running from the cabin…which is warm…and where your family will be?"

Jessica didn't answer. She was preoccupied, listening and looking around. She kept the flashlight on, but pointed straight down at their feet. Simon listened for a moment, but didn't hear anything other than the soft, rhythmic sighs from their breathing.

He was about to repeat his question when Jessica looked at him and said in a soft undertone, "Simon, you are in grave danger..." she paused for a moment looking for the right words, and then continued. "Some...one is looking for you, and if they find you they're going to kill you."

Simon waited for her to laugh or smirk. He was ready to laugh with her, but the look on her face matched her tone, grim and frightened.

"My parents brought you here to protect you, but I think they made a mistake," she said apologetically. "I know they don't agree with me, but I think it's best if you get out of here as quickly as possible!"

She waited for a response, but he just looked into the darkness. "I know this sounds ludicrous, but you have to believe me!" She stepped in front of him. "I have a plan," she said touching his arm. She opened her mouth to speak, but a twig snapped, cracking the silent night.

Simon and Jessica looked at each other.

"Run!" she muttered, squeezing his arm.

Simon found himself jumping over logs and ducking under branches with nothing but the silver glow of the moon and the bouncing spot from Jessica's flashlight to lead them. They were going down a slope, farther away from the cabin.

Simon struggled to keep up with Jessica. She was swift and moved with confidence, as if on a routine run. She only lightened her pace to either give Simon time to catch up, or find whatever marker she had been looking for, a particular tree or rock. She never looked back.

Simon's fear urged him to look back, to see his faceless pursuer before reaching Simon and pulling him down. Against his better judgment, Simon did. He looked back, but there was only darkness. Looking ahead he underestimated the height of a log Jessica leapt over. His first leg made it over, but his other ankle hit the log hard sending him crashing to the cold, hard ground.

"Are you alright?" Jessica whispered, pulling him up.

"Yeah, I'm fine," he said.

Then they heard the unmistakable sound of rapid footsteps crackling somewhere in the dark behind them.

Jessica tugged his arm, "Come on! We're not alone!"

Simon took off after Jessica ignoring his throbbing ankle and burning lungs.

They eventually came upon a paved road pointing in three directions. To the left and to the right the road continued through the trees, but the third direction lead straight into a large field. A wooden sign hung awkwardly to two posts. As they ran past it toward the open field Simon saw MISSISSIPPI...in orange lettering, but couldn't see the rest of the sign other than an orange arrow pointing in the direction they were running.

"Come on!" Jessica pressed Simon along.

He needed to stop and rest, but he gave it all he had. When they ran into the opening Simon's feet didn't find grass because it wasn't a field...it was a parking lot. Jessica was making a beeline to a single-story building tucked among trees on the other end of the lot.

Simon dared to look back. He saw no one.

They ran up the wide walkway leading up to the building. At its mouth, two stone columns supported a large archway made of thick timber stretching overhead. On the right side stood a seven-foot tall, metal globe encircled with short poles holding up a limp chain. On the left side was a long, low, wood sign, which read:

Mary Gibbs

Mississippi Headwaters Center

Jessica turned off the flashlight as they ran under a large portico. Moonlight streamed in from large windows above. They hunkered down in the darkest corner next to a set of doors. Above the doors it read:

GIFT SHOP

There was another set of identical doors at the opposite end of the building. The sign above read:

RESTAURANT

Panting as quietly as possible they listened for any sound. They waited anxiously. A few moments passed. Then a minute. Nothing. The silence became deafening.

Jessica scurried to a nearby pillar, peeked down the walkway, and scurried back.

"No sign of anyone," Jessica whispered, perplexed.

Perhaps it was their imagination, or an animal.

"What next?" Simon quietly asked.

"We wait for another minute to see if we can spot whoever was running after us," Jessica whispered. Then she reached in her back pocket and pulled out a sealed envelope and handed it to Simon. "Then we open this and read the directions."

Simon and Jessica snuck back to the dark corner beside the gift shop. Jessica kept watching the other doors under the portico leading into the building. She was restless, which wasn't at all her nature.

"Jessica, if this is some kind of a joke I want to know right now!" Simon whispered demandingly. "And if this is one of Randal's pranks I'm not going to be happy...at all."

"Shhh."

He saw fear in the whites of her eyes. Her voice trembled. "Please. Just wait until we're safe...then I'll explain."

Simon just nodded. Her cold, smooth hand touched his.

They sat still without saying another word. There was no way of knowing exactly how long they waited.

Fear has a funny way of distorting thoughts, emotions, and a person's internal clock. Every bird taking flight from a nearby branch was someone taking a step closer. Every second was a minute, waiting for a faceless man to jump out of a nearby shadow.

Simon's thoughts were soon cluttered with who's, what's, and why's.

He wondered if Randal finally snapped and Jessica knew it. It would explain why she wanted to leave the cabin before Randal returned. He couldn't think of anyone who had ever had a personal vendetta against him... other than Randal and his hooligan buddies. But Randal didn't seem to hate him. At least not enough to *kill* him.

Someone tapping his leg broke his thoughts. Jessica was trying to get his attention.

"I'm going to turn the flashlight on," she whispered close to his ear, "but I'm going to cover it with my hand so there's only enough light to see the envelope. You need to open it and read the message."

"What if someone sees the light?"

"I'll keep watch as you read. If I see anyone, we run! No matter what happens, don't lose whatever is in that envelope!" She squeezed his hand.

Her tone and demeanor erased any doubt he had that this was real and wasn't merely a joke. She was speaking from her heart and soul.

This has got to be a dream! Simon thought.

He heard a click. Then Jessica looked around before allowing a thin beam of light to escape her palm.

Simon suddenly felt vulnerable. Such a tiny amount of light was a beacon in the night to anyone looking for them; she may as well have turned on a strobe.

He took a deep breath and then shook the thought from his mind. His fear amplified his emotions.

The envelope was peculiar. In fact, once his eyes adjusted to the light, he saw it was parchment that had been folded and sealed with the capital letter "G" pressed into red wax. It looked like a formal invitation from a grand duchess. Simon was going to ask Jessica who gave this to her, but she was keenly looking around and listening. He decided now was not the time, so he broke the seal.

The wind growled and a gust of hot air swept through the portico. Simon and Jessica looked at each other.

Simon unfolded the parchment and read the elegant handwriting:

In the shop you will find
Rainbow rocks of every kind

North, South, East, and West
Choose the colors that fit them best

Use the largest compass you see
Beneath your feet it ought to be

Place each rock on its cardinal point
And every course will become conjoint

Read the message; don't be meek
And follow the path that you seek.

-G

"I don't get it," said Simon.

"It's a riddle," said Jessica. "We have to follow its directions to find our way."

"Our way where?" Simon was confused.

"It'll be easier if I show you," she said already deep in her thoughts. "Did it say 'in the shop'?" Jessica allowed a little more light to shine on the parchment.

They both looked into the moonlit night. There were so many shadows and dark hiding places out there.

"Yes," said Simon, looking down at the parchment. "It's where we'll find rainbow rocks...whatever those are."

"Good," said Jessica optimistically. "We must be in the right place. My father said if it came down to this we were to go to the shop near the headwaters."

Simon had wanted to see the headwaters to the mighty Mississippi River since the third grade. The great river flows down from the northern tip of the United States all the way down to its southern border where its waters empty into the Gulf of Mexico. The fascinating part is the great river's headwaters, which originate from Lake Itasca, start out a fresh-water spring so small a person can walk over it. He had always wanted to walk over the headwaters so he could say he walked over the mighty Mississippi River, one of the greatest river systems in North America.

Jessica was shining the flashlight in the store.

"We have to get in there somehow," she said more to herself than to Simon.

"Maybe you should check to see if it's even locked," said Simon.

Jessica gave him the how-stupid-do-you-think-I-am look and shook the handle hard. "I already tried that genius."

She looked at the flashlight, and without a second thought thrust the butt of it into a lower windowpane. Shards of glass shattered on the concrete floor. They cringed at the intense sound. With the flashlight, Jessica quickly cleared away the extra pieces of glass in the pane, reached through it, and unlocked the door. If the flashlight didn't give them away, the shattering glass did.

"Come on," she said stepping into the shop. She closed the door and locked it behind Simon. "It'll buy us a little time if someone comes."

The moonlight came into the gift shop through the paned windows lining two of the three outside walls.

"So, what are rainbow rocks?" asked Simon.

Jessica pointed the flashlight to something behind him. "I think I have an idea," she said. Simon turned around and the light illuminated a small, handwritten sign that read 'Rainbow Rocks – 35¢ Each' taped to a sign post with an old style oil lamp hanging from the arm of the sign. Atop the arm a decorative sign read 'ITASCA STATE PARK.' At the base of the signpost was a container made to look like a large stone well filled to its brim with multi-colored rocks sparkling like water in the light.

"Read the second part again," Jessica said peering down at the colorful rocks.

"North, South, East, and West. Choose the color that fits them best," Simon read from the parchment.

She was deep in thought again. Simon admired how quick Jessica could think through problems and dilemmas.

"'Fits them best,'" she repeated allowed. "He must mean 'represents best' in this context because how can a rock or color 'fit' a direction," she said. "I can't think of what else would work," she said with growing excitement. "What do you think?"

Simon just gaped at her. "Uh...yeah. Sounds good."

"Simon, I really need your input," she said, keeping the flashlight on the display of colorful rocks.

"I mean it," he said sincerely, "that sounds good! So what color represents each direction best?'"

They both gazed at the rock-filled well.

Simon reached in and cupped a handful of rocks. A few fell out of his hand and back into the pile; they sounded like marbles. "There are so many different colors. I don't even know what some of these colors are called."

Jessica started naming different colors that may best represent each direction. White could represent north for all the snow it gets, but so could a particular greenish-blue rock she saw because of the northern lights. South could be represented by a sand-colored rock for deserts, or perhaps red or orange for being hot. Simon pointed out yellow could also be for south because of all the sun. Jessica didn't think yellow would work, because the sun was more popular for the west, as in the sun setting in the west, or sunny California.

For east Jessica picked out a light purple with a tad of pink in it.

"You know, the colors of the sun rising," said Jessica caustically when Simon looked at her funny. Simon picked out blue for the Atlantic Ocean, but then decided that blue could just as easily work for the Pacific Ocean.

Frustrated, Simon tossed the rocks he was holding back into the well. There were just too many options. Then he froze. Out of the corner of his eye he saw the silhouette of a person standing in the parking lot.

"Get down!" he croaked, pulling Jessica down with him and sending all the rainbow rocks she was holding flying in the air.

"What is it?"

"There's someone out there," he whispered.

Jessica looked around the room, and then pointed with the flashlight. "Grab one of those and stand by the door," she said.

"A stuffed animal?"

"NO," she hissed and moved the light over a few inches. A small display of walking sticks and hiking staffs were next to the rack of stuffed animals.

"OH...I see!" He felt sheepish. "Hold it! You want me to go out there and attack him?"

"NO. Just stand by the door and if he reaches his hand in to unlock the door deck him...hard!" Jessica started gathering some of the rocks she dropped.

"What are you doing?" He was feeling rather unsure of himself.

"One of us has to figure out the riddle as the other one stands guard," she said.

"So, why do *you* get to figure out the riddle?" asked Simon.

Jessica rolled her eyes. "Because I've been coming up with better ideas."

"Yeah...alright," said Simon. She had a good point.

They both peeked over the nearest windowsill; the parking lot was deserted. No lights, no movement, no sign of anyone.

"Hurry Simon! He could be heading for the door right now!"

Simon swung around, and as he ran to the door he grabbed the first hiking staff he saw. Looking out the broken window he saw no one. He backed up against the wall clutching the wooden staff. His hands were sweaty and he could feel his heart beating in his throat.

Jessica was dashing around the small isles in the gift shop.

"What are you looking for?" Simon whispered as loud as he could.

"I can only find one size compass," Jessica whispered while frantically searching the shelves.

"Don't we need just one?" asked Simon glancing back and forth from the door's handles to Jessica's fiasco.

"'Use the largest compass you see. Beneath your feet it ought to be,'" she read from the parchment. "To be the largest, it would have to measure up against others to gain that title."

"Maybe it's the biggest one we can find because we will have to stand on it," said Simon earnestly.

Jessica thought about it for a moment. "You have a point. Besides, we just have to place it at our feet, right?"

"It's the best shot we got at the moment," said Simon shrugging his shoulders. "What is it?" asked Simon, as Jessica studied something outside the building.

"I saw something move out there," said Jessica as she ripped open the packaging to one of the compasses. "Are you watching the door?" she asked, placing the compasses at her feet.

"Of course," said Simon looking back at the doors.

"I did it," said Jessica looking baffled at the compass with four rainbow rocks around it at her feet.

"So...what happened?" asked Simon enthusiastically.

"Nothing!" she said disappointingly to the display at her feet. "I don't get it!"

"What's supposed to happen?" he asked.

"'And every course will become conjoint,'" she read from the parchment. "Whatever that means," said Jessica shaking her head in disgust.

Determined, she started trying different colored rocks at each cardinal point. With every switch she would stand up, look down, and wait a few moments. When nothing happened she tried a different rock at a different cardinal point.

"Hey, I got it!" said Simon with a sudden realization. "Maybe 'beneath your feet' is literal. Try standing on it!"

"Are you crazy? I'd break the compass."

"What about standing on a stool or chair and placing it under that?" asked Simon.

Jessica looked at him and nodded her head. "I'm impressed! That's a great idea!"

Jessica was taking the stool from behind the checkout counter to place above the compass and rainbow rocks when a light shone in from a side window into the shop. They both ducked. Simon got down next to the door and Jessica jumped in one of the display aisles. Whoever was outside was shining their flashlight at the spot where Jessica had ducked. After a few moments the light started darting around the room.

"I think they saw me," said Jessica as quietly as she could in a panic. "Simon, we have to see if this works!

It could be our last chance! On the count of three I'm going to jump up on the stool!"

"I have you covered!" Simon stood and gripped the wooden staff like a baseball bat.

"One...two..." but before she said three, a hand thrust through the broken pain to unlock the door. "Three!" yelled Jessica jumping up from behind a display of nick-knacks. At the same time Simon whacked the intruder's hand as hard as he could with the staff.

The intruder yelled some obscenities and kicked the door. "Simon! If that was you I'm going to slap you up!" yelled a familiar voice.

"Randal?" asked Simon hoping it was in fact him despite his last threat.

The door burst open. Randal stepped in the shop and pointed his flashlight at Simon's face.

"What do you think you're doing?" barked Randal shaking the pain from his hand. Simon looked like a deer in headlights holding onto a staff in the bright light.

Randal turned and shined the light on Jessica. She was balancing on top of the three-legged stool looking both surprised and disappointed above four rainbow rocks and a compass.

"Sis! What are you doing?" asked Randal looking per-plexed and amused.

"It's not working," she whimpered, holding back tears.

Simon knew why she was upset. She was relieved it was just her brother outside, but devastated she couldn't figure out the riddle. She failed because she hadn't figured it out before someone arrived. Whatever 'it' was all for.

"I take it you opened it," remarked Randal, changing his tone after seeing Jessica's watery eyes. He was looking up at his sister, still balancing on the stool.

"Yes," she said with great disappointment.

Simon closed and locked the door again; he felt better with the door secured instead of wide open. He still had a feeling they were being watched.

Randal extended a hand and helped Jessica down from the stool.

"Let me have a look," he said modestly.

Jessica reached in her back pocket and handed the parchment to her brother.

"Why did you open it anyway?" asked Randal sympathetically before opening the parchment.

Jessica glanced at Simon; she seemed apprehensive. Randal just stood and waited for her to say something.

"I didn't want the seers to catch up with him," Jessica meekly answered her brother with tears swelling in her eyes. She looked ashamed.

Simon felt terrible seeing Jessica so defeated, almost heartbroken. After all, she was just trying to help.

Simon was having a difficult time believing it, or perhaps grasping the entirety of it...someone wanting to kill him. Although it made no sense, there was no denying the reality of seeing Jessica, his best friend, so afraid and so determined. He was even seeing a different side of Randal.

Randal opened the parchment and read it. Simon was expecting him to laugh or crack a witty remark at his and Jessica's expense. But he didn't. He didn't laugh. He was doing something Simon wasn't used to seeing Randal do – thinking. As he read through it a second time he studied the rocks they had chosen and the compass.

"How did you come up with the colors to represent each point?" asked Randal. Jessica explained their random ideas in what the different colors represented and why.

"Sounds complicated Sis," he commented. "Couldn't you come up with something a little simpler?"

"Like what?" she asked.

"I don't know, just simpler, like colors that rhyme with each point, or have the same amount of letters, or…"

"Or *begin* with the same letter!" Simon bellowed as soon as the idea came to him.

"Yeah, that too," said Randal shrugging off Simon's idea.

"No! That's it!" said Simon with animated excitement. It made perfect sense. "It *is* simple!" Simon sprang over to Randal and Jessica. "Something hasn't been sitting right with me about part of the riddle. Look at how the cardinal points are listed," he said. "See how large the letters are?"

"So what!" Randal jeered. "Capital letters are supposed to be bigger, duffus."

Acclimated to Randal's insults, Simon continued, "But these capital letters are bigger than the other capital letters in the riddle, *and* when referring to directions the letters are not supposed to be capitalized." Simon was beaming.

"How do you know that?" asked Randal challenging his reasoning.

"He's right!" said Jessica with renewed enthusiasm. "North, south, east, and west are common nouns so they are not capitalized, unless they are used as a specific place. You can go north, lower case, or go to the North, upper case!" Jessica put her hand up to Simon, and he gave her a high five.

Randal sighed and rolled his eyes. "You two are both nerds, you know that?"

"See? It pays to study, big brother!" Jessica teased.

Happy to see Jessica's confidence restored, Simon turned around and quickly found a pad and pencil at the checkout counter. The three of them called out all the colors they could think of that started with the letters n, s, e, and w.

As Simon wrote down the colors they named, Jessica and Randal sorted out a rock for each corresponding color. They found the most rocks with colors starting with the letter *s*; they had five - sand, sea green, sapphire, silver, and sky blue. Much to Randal's dismay, they couldn't find one that looked like school bus yellow. Jessica said she didn't think a school bus was in mind when the riddle was written, but helped look anyway.

The other three were harder. They couldn't think of many colors starting with *n, e,* and *w.* Many of the rocks had multiple colors making it even harder to identify what color some rocks may be considered. Eggshell, eggplant, and emerald were the only names for *e.* They ruled out eggshell because they felt white was a better candidate for *w*, so they set that rock to the side. Between the three of them they couldn't agree what eggplant looks like, but Jessica put a purple colored rock to the side just in case. So emerald was their only hopeful option for the *e*'s.

For the *w*'s they had even less luck. White and wheat were the only two colors they could think of and find rocks with such colors. Jessica tried arguing the point that white wasn't really a color, but more the absence of color.

"That's black," demanded Randal. After a few minutes of bickering back and forth, Simon kindly pointed out it was irrelevant at the moment, and white was their best option for west. Jessica quickly agreed with Simon and dropped the subject.

Navy blue and neon were the only two on their *n* list. Neon was eliminated because, as Jessica pointed out, neon was only a type of color and not a color in and of itself, and there were no neon rocks of any kind in the display.

"Plus, I don't think Ganlock even knows what neon is," Jessica pointed out.

"Well then, he's not going to know what navy blue is either," Randal said matter-of-factly.

"Who's Ganlock?" Simon enquired, feeling he was forgotten in left field.

"You'll know soon enough! Just hold your horses... oh, favored one," said Randal sarcastically.

"What do you mean by that?" Simon snapped, tired of all the mystery.

"Nothing! Now let it be," Jessica intervened by stepping between them, "both of you! It's been a long night!" She glared at her brother and kept her palm on Simon's chest until they both backed down.

"Then we don't have a color for north," said Simon, after a thickening silence.

"That's not our only problem," said Jessica with increasing concern. "The compasses they have in this shop are too small to place a rainbow rock on the cardinal points." She went over and looked at the parchment they had laid out on the counter. "And I do not see how these stupid, little things are supposed to be 'beneath our feet,'" she said, holding one of the small gift shop's compasses up.

"For someone so smart, you can be awfully dumb at times," said Randal caustically, and took the small compass from Jessica's hand.

"What's that supposed to mean?" she asked impatiently.

Looking up from reading the parchment, Randal asked, "Where does it say the compass is in the shop… hmm?" Simon and Jessica both leaned over and read the riddle.

"It doesn't," said Simon still looking at the parchment in hopes of finding a different answer.

"That's right," boasted Randal throwing the compass over his shoulder after a dramatic pause. "If it *should* be beneath our feet, then we *should* be able to walk over it," he said smirking at his sister, "which, you already did," and pointed out the door.

"*Ought* to be," Simon interjected.

"What?" asked Randal.

"'Beneath your feet it *ought* to be,' not *should*," said Simon earnestly.

"Shut up, hero," said Randal.

"I can't believe I didn't think of that," said Jessica disappointedly.

"It's just outside the door?" Simon asked.

"Pretty much," said Randal.

"Great! Let's go!" Simon exclaimed gathering up the rainbow rocks they chose for the cardinal points.

Randal rolled up the parchment and Jessica grabbed the flashlight and started for the door. Then Simon remembered his speculation about Randal.

"Randal," said Simon, stopping before the door.

"What?"

"How long did it take you to discover we had left the cabin?" Simon heard his own suspicion.

"I don't know...not long," Randal answered curiously. "Why?"

"I told Simon...that someone is trying to kill him," said Jessica hesitantly.

"So, when you were chasing after us, why didn't you just call out instead of sneaking around?" Simon asked with growing concern.

"How much more did you tell him?" Randal asked frustratingly.

"Nothing...that's all I told him," she said. Simon detected fear in her voice.

"Randal, it doesn't make sense," Simon continued. "Why chase us with your flashlight off? Why not announce yourself when you arrived here?" Simon took a few steps toward the staff he left leaning against the wall as he spoke. "And why wait until we were inside the gift shop to finally come out of the shadows from hiding?"

Jessica looked at Simon, stunned from his apparent accusation, "Simon, you have it all wrong," she said, but then turned her attention toward Randal for his explanation.

Randal was more than upset; he was peeved.

"You're right," said Randal, gritting his teeth, "it doesn't make sense." He turned to Simon. "I *did* call out after you two!" he said raising his voice and slowly moving toward Simon. "I *didn't* have my flashlight off because there's no way I would have made it down the hill without it on!"

Simon felt around for the staff beside him.

"And I sure as hell wasn't sneaking around and watching you!" said Randal through clenched teeth. Fury was in his eyes, and he kept advancing slowly.

Finding the staff, Simon quickly swung it at Randal. With little effort Randal reflexively blocked the oncoming staff and disarmed Simon in the same defensive motion. The rainbow rocks scattered across the floor. Simon was pinned against the wall with Randal's arm pushed against his neck. Randal glared at him.

"Randal! Don't!" Jessica cried.

"How can you be so stupid?" Randal hissed, spittle flying from his trembling lips. "After all these years of protecting you, doing my job, you think I would want to kill you?" Randal's eyes glistened with tears and he pushed harder against Simon's neck.

Jessica grabbed Randal's heaving shoulder, but her effort was futile. "Randal! Please," she pleaded.

"If you weren't so important, I would kick the snot out of you right now," Randal threatened.

Simon felt faint and hot. Sucking in what little air he could, he managed to squeak out, "If not you...who then...?" His atom's apple burned.

Randal looked confused for a moment.

"Randal! Let him go! It must have been someone else following us!" Jessica cried.

Randal looked back over his shoulder to Jessica.

"Someone was following you down the hill?" asked Randal.

"Yes," she said, "Simon thought it was you!"

Randal cleared his thoughts, and then released Simon.

Simon sank to the floor choking and gulping for air.

"I didn't know," said Randal regretfully. "Did you see anyone?" He asked Jessica.

"Simon saw someone standing in the parking lot shortly before you arrived," Jessica explained. "And I heard more than one person running after us in the forest."

"Then it wasn't me because I didn't stop. I sprinted across the parking lot," said Randal. He looked down at Simon. "Are you gonna be alright?" he asked.

Simon nodded as he rubbed his throat. Randal bent down and helped Simon up.

"Someday...you won't have any trouble defending yourself...or kicking the snot out of me," said Randal with unusual sincerity, and then patted Simon on the shoulders.

Simon was lost for words.

"But for now you're a wimp, and it sounds like we have company," Randal deducted. "Why they haven't attacked yet, I don't know."

"Maybe they're waiting for us to open the portal," suggested Jessica.

"Portal? What are you talking…"

"Shut it. You'll find out soon enough," Randal interrupted. "For now gather up those rainbow rocks and the staff…and stay behind me."

Randal reached under his jacket behind his back and pulled out two identical blades, reflecting the moonlight like long, narrow mirrors. Randal cracked a smile. "Someone out there is going to get their butts kicked."

Simon looked at Jessica, expecting her to be as surprised as he was that Randal just whipped out two very large and lethal weapons. But her reaction, or lack thereof, was just as disturbing as Randal's two stainless steel buddies. Jessica reached into her coat pocket and produced a sling, along with some smooth rocks. She loaded the sling as routinely as tying her shoes.

This was surreal, like moving around in a dream. Simon was half expecting Randal and Jessica to start laughing hysterically as Dr. and Mrs. Wells, along with a crew of friendly pranksters, walked in the shop with camcorders and cameras saying, "*We got you good, Simon!*" His father would hug him and say, "*Son, this was for all the April Fool's jokes you played on us over the years.*"

"Simon! Are you ready?" asked Randal.

Neither Jessica nor Randal looked like they were anywhere near laughing.

"Yeah," Simon sighed, holding the rainbow rocks in one hand and the staff in the other, "as ready as I'll ever be."

8

HERE TODAY GONE TOMORROW

Roy compared his options before picking out a glass from the bar. "Jak, you let your mother down. You never got along with your father. You disobey authority. You are ungrateful, a rebel without a cause, and…." Roy Jakobsin waved off the thought with the tongs in his hand. More interested in his drink than talking with Jak, he took his time looking for the perfect ice cube from the bar. "As for me…I think you're just another inconsiderate teenager trying to find his place in this world. Unfortunately, your bad attitude and egocentric behavior make you intolerable. You are a stain on our family's name. Your place is certainly not here."

Roy carefully plucked an ice cube from the ice chest, which was made to look like a real treasure chest; its gold trim glimmered under the dim light in the study.

Standing in front of his late father's desk, Jak glanced back at the two men standing near the door, his uncle's bodyguards. His uncle told Jak's mother and the rest of the family he didn't feel safe around Jak.

Roy openly accused Jak of killing his brother, Jak's father, but there was no proof. However, Jak was held in juvenile detention during an investigation based on his uncle's accusation. Eventually, the judge released Jak and he was brought back from juvenile detention to live with his mother and sister in their mansion in New York. While Jak was away his uncle had moved in to take care of his mother and take over the family business. In addition to personal belongings, his uncle brought his accusations.

Rumors are like weeds. They grow and spread fast, choking life around them. The damage was done before the investigation started. Although Jak was never proven guilty, he never regained his innocence. His uncle's finger pointing condemned Jak. His family and so called friends looked at him differently, and judgmentally. It was as if they had been there that night and watched him take his father's life. It didn't matter that his father's body was never found at the bottom of Jakobsin's Pond, or that it was never found at all. It didn't matter that Jak was the one who called for help. His uncle was right. Jak and his father never got along. It was no secret. Everyone knew it.

Jak's tendency was to do the opposite of what his father told him to do, or what he suspected his father would want him to do. The more strain it put upon his parents, the more Jak would act out.

Jak believed he had good reason for his rebellion. He resented his father for never giving Jak any of his time. He never stopped in the middle of his busy schedule to spend time, even a little, with Jak. His accuser and judgers were quick to point out all the money his father spent on him, all the stuff he gave Jak and the rest of the family. But no one cared an iota he spent no time with his son. His father never knew Jak.

Roy smiled at the cube and dropped it in his glass with a clink. Then he looked for another perfect ice cube.

"Just because they released you from juvenile detention does not mean we have forgotten what you have done. However, since we have to take you back by law, and your poor mother has it in her heart to keep you under our roof, a dramatic change is in order." He finally found another cube. After admiring it, he dropped it in the glass with the other cube and listened to them clink. "We are leaving all of these wretched memories behind," said Roy gesturing around the room with the tongs and glass, "and moving to Tuttle Point, a quiet place just outside of Riverside, Minnesota."

Roy set down the tongs, poured his drink, and casually brushed unseen lint from his suit before looking at Jak for the first time since he arrived back home. "Do you have any problems with that...Jak?"

Jak loathed him. He hated the smirk on his face. Hated his pompous attitude. He hated everything about his conniving uncle. But Jak didn't care anymore. He didn't care about anything, or anyone.

"I want to see my mother," said Jak.

"Oh...I'm so sorry, but she doesn't want to see you." His uncle's smirk grew.

"I want to hear her say it," said Jak, but he wasn't so sure if he wanted to. After all, his mother let them take Jak to juvie and did nothing to defend him. She shut herself away from Jak, and from the world.

"That is not going to happen," his uncle sneered. "Anything else?"

Jak stared at him from across the desk.

"No? I didn't think so."

Roy glanced at the two men. They escorted Jak out of his father's personal study, a shadow of his father's existence.

✳ ✳ ✳

Jak woke up with a throbbing headache, but he preferred the physical pain over dreaming of his past. Jak rubbed the back of his head. He had been out for quite some time, and was groggy. While unconscious, night had departed and day had arrived. What time of the day, Jak had no idea.

His muscles were stiff and aching so he crawled to the nearest tree and leaned against it. There were trees in every direction. Oh, how he hated the outdoors. What people found so great about camping was beyond him.

His attention fell upon the area strewn with ashes. Whatever hit this area disintegrated all the trees in their entirety leaving a perfect circle in the middle of the forest roughly thirty feet in diameter.

Jak tried recalling events from last night, assuming it was last night and not a few nights ago. The last place his uncle would think of looking for Jak is in the wild.

Then he remembered he wasn't alone…there was a strange man talking to the trees.

And he attacked me!

Jak tried standing up, but the ground swayed back and forth like a boat bobbing at sea. He quickly sat back down. He looked around for the man, but there was no sign of him.

I hit the bum pretty hard.

And then it all came back to him. He missed on the first swing. And before he could try again, someone hit *him* on the back of the head and he fell unconscious.

After I find the bum, I'll find the guy who attacked me from behind. Then I can take care of business.

He flinched from a sharp pain on the back of his head that shot straight into his skull.

"Ouch!" he yelled.

"What do we have here?" The guttural and sinister voice was behind him.

Jak spun around.

Two hooded beings in dark, tattered robes approached him. Their faces were obscured by dark, long hoods revealing nothing more than a pair of solid silver eyes. Their robes bore rips and tears, and hung on their bodies like loose flesh. Their flesh resembled their cloaks in both texture and color.

Jak froze as they moved closer. One lifted a bony finger and pointed down at Jak, stopping just a few feet away. The blackened flesh was rotting, shedding dead skin.

The other one stopped ten feet away. Nausea overcame Jak when he caught scent of their flesh and got a better look at them. There was no telling where their dark robes ended and their skin began; the decayed material and decaying flesh were fused together.

"He wasn't dead," said the one pointing at Jak. Jak scuffled backward. A guttural chuckle escaped the creature. Then it bent over, looking Jak up and down from head to toe.

Jak placed both hands on the ground. He was waiting for a window of opportunity to get up and run, but he was still groggy from his head injury and now nauseated from the likes of these two. As frail as they looked Jak was confident under regular circumstances he could outrun them, but right now he probably couldn't even stand.

Still looking him up and down, the one said, "Do you see it? Do you?" He sounded excited, or perhaps angry.

"Yes! Yes I do," said the other more calmly, his lifeless eyes boring into Jak's mind. His head cocked to the left as he stood, with a slight sway, staring into, or through, Jak's eyes. The two silver orbs didn't blink.

Jak's mind was screaming, "*Get up and run,*" but his body was heavy and anchored to the ground.

"Is this the one?" hissed the creature nearest to Jak. "It is a boy! He said it would be a boy…."

Jak could hear the ill-tempered hissing uncomfortably close to him, but he couldn't turn his head. He couldn't look away from the frosty eyes ten feet from his, peering into his head.

The creature's eyes widened and a heavy force fell upon Jak and held him to the ground. A strange sensation overcame him, like darkness itself was seeping down into his pores and violating the inside of his body. He tried pulling away from the creature's glare, but only managed a few jerks and tugs under the massive, invisible grip.

Something stirred inside Jak, a part of him wanting desperately to lash out. Anger, resentment, hatred, and sorrow became so overwhelming tears streamed down his cheeks and sweat ran down his face. Each breath was more difficult than the last. Still aware of his surroundings, Jak fell into a dream-like vision.

✳ ✳ ✳

"Jak, what are you doing here?" asked his father. He sounded concerned, but Jak knew he wasn't. He must be annoyed.

"Nothing...just wondering what you're doing out here," said Jak, trying hard to sound interested.

"Never mind," said his father glancing down at the small rowboat at the edge of Jakobsin Pond. In the boat lay a fishing rod, an extremely large tackle box, and a duffle bag. Suddenly taking notice of the boat and its contents, his father quickly pointed out the obvious. "As you can see I'm going fishing."

Jakobsin Pond was more like a small lake. It was man-made and used mainly for swimming and recreational boating. Because of laws about owning lakes, Jak's grandfather had it made just below the legal size of a lake and dubbed it Jakobsin Pond. Fish were never added to it.

"It's getting dark," Jak pointed out.

"It's dusk not dark…besides it makes no difference," said his father, preoccupied with a notebook in his hand.

"Reading up on how to fish?" Jak hated how engrossed his father was with his work. He could be standing next to his father, but may as well be worlds apart from how little his father noticed him. He hated it even more when his father talked down to him, or worse, lied. Jak knew his father wasn't fishing. His father just didn't want to tell Jak what he was doing. This made Jak mad.

"Since when do you fish?" He didn't mean to sound as accusatory as it came across.

His father sighed. "Jak, there are many things you don't know about me…"

"I wonder why that is?" said Jak, thick in sarcasm.

His father hesitated before he spoke. "Because I prefer it that way."

Jak didn't see it coming. The words hit him hard and he flinched. Not knowing how to answer, Jak stared at the little rowboat as his father continued to busy himself within the confines of his notebook.

He prefers it that way?

Jak was expecting his father to make up some stupid excuse: "Sorry, I'm just too busy," "I'm doing all this for you, your mom, and your sister," "Someday you'll understand," or "I've been meaning to spend time with you…."

But not this.

All my life he's been intentionally ignoring me…. I've been just another obstacle in his life!

"Why do you hate me?" Jak prided himself on suppressing his emotions, but right now he was struggling to fight back his tears.

His father sighed again and became solemn.

"I don't *hate* you...I just..." His father looked skyward. Faint twinkling of stars shown in the darkening heavens. "Power is everything," he muttered to the stars. "A man who has it can have anything he desires. Power separates a great man from a commoner." His father looked old in the dull light, his eyes somber and lost. "It divides kings from cowards."

"What are you rambling about?"

His father shook his head. "Not now Jak! I don't have time for this!" He huffed impatiently, his solemnity becoming anger quickly.

"You don't EVER have time!" Jak yelled, his face burning. "You're the worst father ever! You're a loser! I don't care if you hate me or not! I HATE YOU!"

✳ ✳ ✳

"Is it?" asked the impatient, hooded fiend next to Jak, "is this the one?"

Jak felt like throwing up and passing out, when suddenly he was pulled out of his vision. The agony stopped. But before the heaviness lifted and he could breathe once more, his mother's screams and sobs came back from the not-so-distant past. Jak took in a deep breath, choked on it, and then, turning on his side, threw up.

"NO..." hissed the other in reply. "This is not the boy."

"Then *I* get to eat him. You ate the last two!" scowled the other, stomping his foul claw near Jak's face.

"Stop!" the other growled in protest. "We can still use him."

"What! Why?" asked the other. "You said he was not the one."

"He's not!" He stepped a few feet closer, wrapping one of his long, bony claws around a fallen branch. "But he may be of use. If we go back with nothing you know what will happen."

They both looked down at Jak. He couldn't see their expressions under their hoods, but could sense their grins.

This was it. Jak had to do something or he was never getting away from these two. His flashlight was within reach. So he took several deep breaths, and grabbed it as fast as he could. A blood-stained claw came down on his wrist. Jak screamed in pain and frustration. The creature bent down, contorting its body in an inhuman way and placed its hidden face in front of Jak's.

"You live for now, boy," said the creature in a gurgle. Lifting its claw off of Jak's wrist the creature stepped on the lens of the flashlight, crushing it into the ground.

"It's time to go," demanded the other.

Reaching into its cloak the foreboding creature next to Jak took out an amulet. A faint blue glow emulated from it. Its companion reached into its cloak and took out two more similar amulets, and then approached Jak. It bent down, its body contorting in awkward, jerky movements, and placed one of the amulets around Jak's neck.

Jak didn't touch it. He remained on the ground, exhausted and defeated.

Both creatures placed their amulets around their necks. Standing on either side of Jak they each looked around. Satisfied, one of the dark figures once again reached in its robe and produced a glass orb about five inches in diameter. It stretched out its arm and spoke to the orb in a language Jak didn't understand. The orb filled with a bluish-white mist, which began whirling, and generating a sound like a strong breeze passing through a ravine. The contents in the globe looked like swirling clouds in a small sky.

Then the mist shot out in a straight line to the center of the thirty-foot clearing. Once the orb had depleted all of its content, it hovered in the exact center of the clearing for a split second and then exploded into a geometrical perfect oval, followed by a thunderclap. The small explosion blew the ashes into the air. The oval was highlighted with the same blue glow as the amulets, which Jak noticed were glowing more prevalently as if they were responding to the portal in front of them.

That is what hovered just inches above the forest's floor, a portal. It looked like someone hung a picture in the air of a different landscape. Only Jak didn't like what he saw. The trees were much larger and darker, almost black, with gnarled trunks and twisted branches as if they were reaching for him. A small clearing revealed dark and gloomy mountains in the distance.

"Let's leave this wretched land. I'm hungry and need to feed!" said one of the dark strangers. And with little effort he grabbed Jak by his collar and dragged him to the portal. Jak screamed for help and tried to pry the bony hand from his shirt. When he gripped the rotting hand he got a fistful of dead skin and tendons. The two dark beings chuckled sinisterly while pulling Jak through the portal.

Surrounded by gnarly trees with thorny branches, Jak now saw a picture of a more familiar landscape hanging in the air. It was the forest in Riverside he was in just moments ago. The tall pines stood proud. And although he couldn't see it, he knew, with a saddened heart, Tuttle Point was beyond those trees.

On a cold, autumn day, in a clearing strewn with ashes in the forest between Tuttle Point and Riverside, a portal to another world slowly closed and vanished, cutting off the horrified screams of Jak Jakobsin, and leaving behind the sole sound of a wispy, autumn breeze playing among the trees.

9

A SUNRISE ON THE RIVER BOTTOM

Crouched down, Randal quietly opened the door. "Wait here by the door until we give you the signal," Jessica whispered. She paused after looking at Simon. She looked sad and worried. "I'm really sorry you have to find out this way. I wanted to tell you everything myself over a pizza after one of our movie nights, but it was forbidden." Her dark eyes filled with tears. She brushed her long blonde hair from her face, leaned in, and kissed his cheek. "Just know, that whatever happens tonight, you're the best friend I have ever had." Then she ducked out the door and into the shadows with Randal following her.

Simon held his breath as he watched her leave. He leaned against the open door. A million thoughts went through his mind.

Randal moved quickly and quietly to the outside edge of the portico from column to column. Every few moments Simon glimpsed the moonlight reflecting off of Randal's blades like two fireflies dancing in the night.

Simon reacted to a sudden movement about fifteen feet from him. Jessica had darted out of a shadow to the center of the portico. Once there, she turned on her flashlight and began searching the ground. Finding what she was searching for, she walked around it, studying it under her light in quick scanning motions. Then her light went out.

Too much time elapsed. Simon began questioning their plan. Maybe something happened to her…. Then it finally came, three quick flashes from her light.

As Simon made his way to Jessica, the staff in his hand knocked against the concrete several times. In the silent night, each knock may as well have been a gunshot. Jessica lightly shushed him, and he was sure he heard muffled grumbling from Randal. Simon was embarrassed; he wasn't used to sneaking around.

When he reached Jessica, she took his hand in the dark and guided him to a spot next to her. "We're standing on a compass etched in stone," she said quietly. "When I turn on the flashlight we need to place the colored stones we agreed upon on each of the cardinal points. And act fast. I saw something moving in the trees."

Something? Doesn't she mean someone?

"Are you sure we should do this now?" Simon asked, rethinking his options. "Maybe we should get your parents to help…"

"Randal will keep watch," she whispered confidently. "He has our backs."

Simon couldn't believe how well Jessica held her cool. He wanted to jump out of his skin.

"Ready?" she asked.

"I guess so," His stomach kept flipping about.

"Okay…go," Jessica turned on the flashlight.

The light revealed a magnificent compass etched into dark gray granite. In the outer circle of the compass were the four cardinal points, four extravagant arrows sharply pointing to the letters: N – S – E – W. A smaller circle housed sixteen more arrows, which were longer and pointier, representing the sixteen intermediate directions of a compass. The very center of the compass resembled a sunflower, in which a solid, dark circle contained sixteen sections, like pedals, stemming from it.

Simon couldn't read what they said because it was too dark, but there were quotes etched on the outside of the compass by each cardinal direction. The only thing he could make out was a date, 1836, in one of them.

He knelt down in the center of the compass. Jessica remained standing and lifted the flashlight as high as she could so he could see everything.

Place each rock on its cardinal point, he read from the parchment. Opening his fist full of rocks he plucked out the white rock and placed it in the arrow pointing to the W. As the white rainbow rock touched the compass it lit up and melted into the arrow, leaving the arrow glowing bright white.

"How is it doing that?" asked Simon staring dumbfounded at the glowing arrow pointing west.

"It's magic," she said, almost laughing with joy. "Quick! The next one!" said Jessica excitedly. She was as fascinated as Simon.

Simon placed the emerald green rainbow rock in the arrow pointing to the E. Once again the rock lit up and melted into the cardinal arrow. The glow, like a pulse, was emerald green.

"That is SO awesome!" Randal whispered loudly from one of the shadows. Simon looked at Jessica, her face radiating with excitement.

He turned to the south cardinal point and took out the sand colored rock and placed it in the arrow. Nothing happened. He brushed that one off and placed the silver rock in the arrow. Nothing happened. He looked up at Jessica.

"Try the next one," she said encouragingly.

Simon placed the sea green rock on the arrow. Again, nothing happened.

He only had the sapphire and sky blue colors left for south. Since the sky blue rainbow rock had some white in it, he laid the sapphire colored rock in the arrow. Simon sighed with relief when the rock lit up and melted into the arrow, which illuminated majestic sapphire blue.

"What next?" asked Simon.

"What do you mean?" said Jessica. "Place the rock for north down."

Simon looked at the rocks he had remaining.

"We didn't come up with a color that fit north... remember?"

Jessica looked out into the darkness. "Just try them all!"

Simon tried the rest of the rocks he had, but none of them produced a result. The other three cardinal points continued glowing in a rhythmic motion as if they were waiting patiently for their fourth comrade.

"That's it! I tried them all!" Simon was frustrated. "Are we set up to fail? Is this all a trap?" No colors he could think of started with n.

"Hey guys!" Randal half whispered from his post. "Whoever, or whatever, is out there just moved in closer! Finish it up, now!"

"We can't," said Jessica, scanning the distant trees while holding the light steady for Simon. "We have no color for n."

"Nothing?" grunted Randal.

"Can *you* think of something?" Jessica asked, agitated.

There was a small pause. Simon was hoping Randal was going to point out an obvious color they hadn't considered.

"No, not really," he finally said.

"Okay then, we have nothing!" Jessica retorted.

Having the epiphany almost simultaneously, Simon and Jessica looked at each other and exclaimed, "That's it!"

"Here!" said Jessica, handing the flashlight to Simon. He grabbed it and ran back into the shop and to the rainbow rock well. He dug around in the display of shiny rocks. He had seen a couple of them earlier, but it was like they knew he was looking for them and were avoiding him.

"Come on!" said Simon aloud, "I know you're…"

And there it was. A clear rock. He slowly picked it up like he was afraid he would scare it off if he moved too fast. Holding it up to the light he looked at it closely. "Nothing," he said to the rock. "No color at all. You're my n."

"Simon!" Jessica yelled from outside.

He turned and ran as fast as he could. Jessica was standing in the white, emerald green, and sapphire blue glow emanating from the compass below her, slowly swinging her sling.

"There was definitely movement out there!" she informed him.

Simon slammed the clear rainbow rock in cardinal north. Instantly the rock lit up and melted into the arrow. The arrow glistened in the likeness of the skin of a bubble; it was clear, with a thin spectrum of colors. Then, beneath their feet, each of the sixteen points lit up, one after the other, until all sixteen were conjoined. Simon and Jessica jumped off of the compass. Four points were white, four were emerald green, four were sapphire blue, and four resembled the color of a bubble's skin.

The compass became brighter and brighter until the entire portico and beyond was lit up. In those few short moments Simon saw Randal hiding behind one of the large columns, and beyond him were two strangers standing among distant trees, watching.

Simon pointed to them, "Look!"

"I know!" Randal growled.

The light dimmed quickly as the four different colored lights from the compass all came together at the center circle and compressed into a small orb of light just inches off the ground. Then the orb exploded with a flash of dazzling colors.

And then it went dark.

Simon didn't notice it at first because it took a few moments for his eyes to adjust, but then he saw one of the sixteen points glowing red, the point for southeast. It was the only point left that was glowing at all. There were only two paths that lead into the forest, one went east and the other went south. There wasn't a path going southeast.

"The three guys I've seen are choosing to sit back and watch," said Randal joining Jessica and Simon at the compass. "I don't know what they're waiting for. And I really don't like that I haven't seen any sign of the soul seers."

Simon wanted to ask what soul seers were, but could already hear Randal's remark in his head, *Can it!*

"At least we know we need to go that way," said Simon pointing southeast into the trees.

"But that will take us off both paths and lead us directly into trees. That will slow us down and make it easier for the three weirdoes to catch us," said Randal, looking into the darkness.

"There's still one more piece of the riddle," said Jessica taking the flashlight from Simon and looking at the parchment. She read aloud, "'*Read the message; don't be meek. And follow the path that you seek.*'"

When she finished reading, some of the words in the quote carved on the north side of the compass began to glow the color of a bubble, as if someone were highlighting the letters by hand. Simon and Jessica walked over to it.

"You guys take care of this," Randal said gripping his blades, and then disappeared into the shadows again.

"*There is one remarkable course and its waters...*" Jessica read as random words in the quote lit up one after the other. "That's all," she said disappointingly.

"Over here," said Simon standing on the east side of the compass as more words in the quote etched in the stone began glowing emerald green. "*Guide the way what had been long sought, at last burst upon view...* "

"*To the watershed,*" Jessica read from the glowing sapphire words from the quote on the south side.

"*The country you are going to see will guide you onward step forward to them,*" Simon read from the words glowing white by the w. "It doesn't make sense," he said.

"We need to read it in the same order, but pause where a new sentence should start," she said, and finished writing it all down.

Looking around there was no sign of the strangers, or Randal.

It didn't take them long to figure out the message. It was clear where each sentence should start and stop once they had it all written down.

> *There is one remarkable course, and its waters guide the way.*
> *What had been long sought, at last burst upon view.*
> *To the watershed.*
> *The country you are going to see will guide you onward.*
> *Step forward to them.*

"So which path do we take?" Simon asked eagerly.

"I don't know," said Jessica looking at the message indecisively. "But I don't think it matters," she said looking at the spot where both paths begin.

"Of course it matters," said Simon. "We'll end up in two completely different places."

"That's just it," said Jessica shining the light down each trail, "they both lead to the same place...the headwaters of the Mississippi."

Simon was even more confused. "Why would we be given two different paths to follow if they lead to the same place?" asked Simon.

"We weren't," said Jessica more to herself as she remained in deep thought. "These paths were here before the portal was even put into place."

"Then let's choose one," said Simon with some authority. "We don't know how much time we have, or how many more people are on their way here after that light display!"

"We can't just rush into things," Jessica countered with equal authority. "This is important Simon! We're so close; we can't make a mistake now!"

"What's the worst that can happen if we make the wrong choice?" asked Simon in a heartfelt tone. Before Jessica could answer he asked, "What's the worst that can happen if we wait too long to make a choice?"

Jessica looked down at the southeast point on the etched compass near their feet. The red glow was slowly fading.

"I don't know the worst that can happen if we make the wrong choice," said Jessica with sudden realization, "but if we wait too long the portal will eventually close, if it's already open down there."

"Well, isn't this *portal* why we came here?" Simon asked feeling weird saying 'portal' like it was just another landmark to see.

"Well...yes," she said.

"Then I say we head down a path and figure the rest out when we reach the next destination," said Simon encouragingly.

"Look! Whatever you're going to do, do it!" said Randal from out of nowhere. "Our visitors are tired of watching! They're closing in!"

"Simon! You choose!" Jessica blurted out.

"This way!" Simon started down the path going east.

Jessica and Randal weren't far behind him. Randal sheathed one of his blades and took out his flashlight. Their flashlights illuminated the path enough to keep up a sturdy jog.

The path took them under an archway made of stones and wood. Then it snaked its way into the forest. Not far down from them it looked like someone crouching near the path, but it was a strange bronze-colored statue of a girl playing with baby turtles and smiling at her passersby. On the other side of the trail from the happy bronze girl was a brown sign with yellow letters that read MISSISSIPPI HEADWATERS 600 FT. and an arrow pointing down the trail they were on. This made Simon run even faster.

They quickly came upon a bridge made much like the archway they had passed under, rocks and solid wood. Simon was about to cross the bridge when Jessica stopped him.

"Over here!" she said huffing and puffing. Her flashlight revealed steps made from wood and rocks leading down to the Mississippi River, which couldn't have been more than two feet deep and ten feet wide.

"There are more steps on the other side," Randal pointed out.

"Maybe this is the place," said Simon hopefully.

"But in the message it clearly states 'To the watershed,'" said Jessica, quickly thinking it through, "and this isn't the watershed."

"Then why the steps?" Simon asked in anticipation.

"Why all the stupid questions?" Randal barked. "They're hot on our trail!"

Simon grunted and ran back up the set of steps he started down and crossed the bridge with Jessica and Randal. Jessica took the lead and Randal stayed behind Simon.

They passed another brown sign with yellow lettering that read HEADWATERS 450 FEET with an arrow pointing to the right; the trail had broken to the left and to the right. An isolated, wooden bench sat near the tree line.

The trail, lined with small rocks, twisted and turned among the red and white pines. Moonlight made its way to the foot of the trees until they reached a thick canopy of low pine boughs. Large Norway pines hung their branches low, not allowing the moonlight to pass through. The branches were so low and thick, it looked like a tunnel. On the other side of the tunnel, a pool of moonlight revealed an opening in the trees. There also came the clear and distinct sound of running water. The headwaters!

They stopped just outside the foreboding canopy tunnel. No wind or sound made its way out.

"The watershed is just on the other side of this tunnel and to the right," said Jessica with determination. "Let's keep going before they reach us!"

"Hurry!" Randal warned, "They're coming down the path."

Simon glanced back. A flickering light came from around the last bend in the path.

"Come on!" Simon demanded.

They started running through the tunnel of tree branches. Midway through the tunnel the sound of high-pitched chirps, followed by a methodical humming, enveloped them. Tiny shadows darted in and out of their lights like giant mosquitoes.

Instinctively all three of them started swatting blindly at anything fluttering near their ears. Jessica and Randal were swinging their flashlights about so fast, Simon couldn't get a close enough look at whatever these things were that were quickly growing in number.

Near the other end of the canopy tunnel Jessica let out a cry, stopping Simon and Randal dead in their tracks. A wall had materialized in front of her. Moonlight peeked through small holes in the wall.

Jessica walked backward toward Simon and Randal as the wall closed in on her. From the hovering wall came loud humming, buzzing, chirping, and fluttering. It moved in a fluid motion, like a flag waving in a slight breeze, getting ever so closer.

"What are they?" Jessica yelled. "They look like giant bugs!"

And indeed they did, like giant mosquitoes. They were large enough that four or five sucking blood out of a human could cause serious damage. There were hundreds of them flying abreast to form the wall.

"Randal! Do something!" Jessica cried.

Randal stepped in front of Simon and Jessica.

"We're going through these blood suckers," said Randal as he drew his other blade. "Simon! Catch!" Randal turned and tossed his flashlight in the air.

What happened next shocked Simon.

As if the swarm knew his intentions, in a single, fluid motion they rolled up like an ocean wave, and like a wave came crashing down on the three of them. Randal started to swing back around to face the oncoming wall, but in seconds his motions were so slow it looked like he was under water.

Even more bizarre was the flashlight Randal had tossed. It was still in the air floating sluggishly toward Simon. He tried reaching out toward the flashlight and then realized he too was moving in slow motion.

Out of the corner of his eye, to the left, he saw Jessica...slowly...slowly turning around to run. The swarm came down upon them like water pouring from a giant glass, but the flying creatures didn't attack them. They didn't even touch them. Darting around at blinding speeds, they formed a dome-shaped perimeter around and above Simon, Jessica, and Randal.

The humming and chirping became rhythmic and hypnotic. Intermittently the fluttering creatures weaved in and out of the perimeter, three and four at a time. The rest appeared to be watching the scene before them as they hovered.

It must have been an amusing scene. Simon was still reaching for the flashlight that was slowly getting closer.

Jessica's long hair remained fanned out as she slowly turned around. Randal looked like he was performing an odd dance, or perhaps trying to fly, with his arms splayed about, holding his two blades.

One of the curious creatures fluttered passed the floating flashlight down to Simon's outstretched arms. While in the perimeter, it too moved slower. But its slow motion was still fast in comparison to Simon and the airborne flashlight. As it neared Simon's hands it stopped and hovered an inch above one of his palms. Its tiny, pointy wings flapped gracefully. Its small bill appeared to don a smile, and its miniscule black eyes were curious and kind. It wasn't a giant mosquito; it was a hummingbird.

The little bird showed no concern for being in the path of the floating flashlight. It seemed intrigued with Simon, cocking its little head to one side. With a delicate poise it puffed up its shiny, green chest and flew within a few feet of Simon's face. It appeared the miniature bird wanted to say something to Simon. Instead it bowed its bright ruby head and returned to the perimeter with the rest of the hummingbirds.

Then six figures in hooded cloaks, one holding a torch, walked past the swarm that encased Simon, Jessica, and Randal, and stopped near the headwaters. Simon suddenly realized it was only the three of them that were affected by this time manipulation. Everything outside the hummingbirds' perimeter was unaffected and moved about normally.

The six figures formed a single row and faced Simon, Jessica, and Randal who were still floating within the swarm of hummingbirds.

One of the figures lifted a hand, palm up. Then two of the hummingbirds zipped over and landed on the palm. They were looking at the concealed face as if listening. The two tiny birds zipped back to the perimeter chirping excitedly and all the hummingbirds scattered up into the trees.

As the miniature birds departed and the perimeter broke apart, time once again resumed its normal pace. Simon caught the flashlight, Jessica finished turning around, and Randal swatted the air and yelled in a fit of rage, until he realized circumstances had changed.

Simon looked down at the flashlight in his hand and then up to the branches above him. He wasn't sure what he was looking for, but he expected to see strings or cables or...something to explain what had just happened.

"Hello Simon." The soft and amiable voice was from one of the six hooded figures, who all stood still between Simon and the headwaters.

Hearing his name come from the stranger's lips surprised Simon. He and Jessica shone their flashlights on the cloaked figures, and then moved over to Randal.

"Who are you?" ordered Randal adjusting his stance for fighting.

"Please," the soft, feminine voice responded, "lower your lights so as not to shine in our faces, and I promise I will tell you."

"We're calling the shots here lady!" said Randal as authoritarian as he could. Simon found this somewhat amusing considering *they* were in no position to be calling anything. Not only were they outnumbered two to one, but the hummingbirds hovered just ten feet above them.

"How do you know my name?" asked Simon out of both curiosity and concern.

"Because you are the reason I am here," spoke the stranger with a hummingbird companion on each shoulder. "You can trust me Simon. I mean you no harm." She sounded sincere.

"It's a trick Simon!" Randal shouted without taking his eyes off of the six strangers.

Simon pointed his flashlight down, shining it on the ground between the two groups facing off. "Jessica," said Simon subtly. She responded by lowering her light as well. Randal grunted disapprovingly.

The two distinguished hummingbirds hovered off of her shoulders while the stranger let down her hood, and then they perched upon them again when she lowered her arms. Her beauty was naturally superlative. She had long auburn hair and fair skin. Her eyes held much compassion and wisdom, eyes easy to trust. A thin, silver circlet rested upon her head.

"As promised, I will introduce myself," she said politely. "My name is Sonica Wintergreen. I am from Magnanthia." Gesturing to the five standing by her she said, "These are friends. They come from the Cordon Society to assist me."

The others took their hoods off and opened their cloaks. Beneath their cloaks the five males wore leather armor, and donned swords and daggers. Two of them couldn't have been older than twelve, and one must have been around Randal's age, sixteen or seventeen. The other two were adults.

Simon took a step back upon seeing their heavy gear. His first thought was to run. But he was also intrigued and wanted to know what was going on.

"Tanner!" Randal yelped addressing the young man his own age. They met each other halfway and embraced. Simon had never seen Randal so happy, didn't think he was even capable of the emotion.

"Randal! You look mighty fine mate," said Tanner as they patted each other's backs. He had a thick accent.

"Why didn't you guys say who you were to begin with?" asked Randal, still elated by the turn of events.

"We had to be sure the soul seers had indeed passed through the other portal as we suspected," explained Sonica, "and the only way to be sure of that was to watch from afar, in case we needed to get the jump on them." She looked at Simon. "More importantly, I had to be sure this was *the* Simon Whittaker," she said, satisfied.

"And just how did you confirm that?" asked Jessica bluntly.

"Because you were with him," said Sonica, her lips spreading into a casual smile. Jessica looked a little uneasy. "And Simon, *the* Simon Whittaker, was the unmentioned element in the spell to open the portal. It wouldn't have opened without him."

"How...I mean, really?" said Jessica.

"Ganlock has his ways," said Sonica, leaving it at that. "Simon, we must leave soon," said Sonica.

"Us?" asked Simon gesturing at Jessica, Randal, and himself. "Where?"

"No," said Sonica softly, "you and I...to Magnanthia."

Simon looked at Jessica. Her eyes were already filling with tears. Randal shook his head and looked down at his feet like a boy just caught with his hand in the cookie jar.

"I don't understand," said Simon.

"Come. Look," said Sonica leading him to the headwaters.

Water flowed over a row of large rocks separating Lake Itasca from the headwaters, the birthplace of the mighty Mississippi River. Here, the Mississippi was merely a stream, no more than two feet deep and twelve feet wide. A magnificent sight nonetheless.

Sonica pointed at the headwaters. "Look into the water, Simon."

"I just see the moonlight," said Simon.

Sonica held her hand out. "Come closer."

Simon walked up to her and she took his hand. She led him a few steps into the icy waters.

"Now, look *into* the water, beyond its surface."

Simon leaned forward, still holding her hand.

All he saw was the reflection of the moon dancing on the surface of the clear water. Disappointed he started shaking his head...but then something caught his eye. There was a faint light *below* the surface. He looked closer and discovered it was at the river bottom. It was the size of a doorway, only oval in shape. The colors at the bottom were sheer, like he was looking through thick glass. They were colors in a sunrise, orange, yellow, pink, and red. The sunrise on the river's bottom danced to a different rhythm than the moon's reflection on top of the river.

"I see it now," said Simon still gazing into the fresh spring water. "It's beautiful."

"It's Magnanthia," said Sonica placing her hand on his shoulder. "It's where I must take you."

Simon looked at her. Her eyes were already fixed on him. "That is *our* portal," she said gently, her eyes full of strength.

Simon kept looking at her. A small part of him wanted to jump in. But none of it made any sense.

"I can't go with you," said Simon aware of the disappointment in his voice. "I have my dad here, school work due next week...the choir concert!" he rambled. "My whole life is here!" he said stepping out of the water and leaving Sonica standing alone in the river.

"Simon," said Jessica, trying to hold back her tears, "*This, this* is your life," she said softly gesturing to Sonica and the portal.

"Jessica...what are you saying?" said Simon. His mind was foggy, as if in a dream.

"You have a greater calling," said Jessica stepping closer to him. "I know because our family has had the honor of watching over you and your father, to make sure no harm came your way."

She went on to explain that for years she had known how important he was. The day she found out was the day she brought him an ice cream treat. Her parents had sat Randal and Jessica down that day and explained what their family was doing. They were watching over the

Whittakers because the people of Magnanthia would one day need him.

Upon Simon's sixteenth birthday he was to be introduced to the Cordon Society. This society consists of Magnanthians who live on Earth and monitor any and all spell casting or magical phenomenon, especially portals. Simon would live there for two years to learn who he was and begin his training to prepare him for Magnanthia and his important role. There was going to be a great celebration the day he crossed into the land of Magnanthia.

"However, something went wrong," Sonica added to Jessica's explanation. "A portal had been opened near Riverside, and it was difficult to find. No one in Magnanthia knew who opened it.

"There are those in Magnanthia, like the Cordon Society, who possess the ability to detect when a portal is opened, because it takes powerful magic to open a portal. The more powerful the spell, the easier it is to detect. Opening a portal takes so much power that the right magic-user can often identify when it was opened, where it was opened, and what kind of magic was used to open it. However, this portal either opened on its own, which seldom happens, or a different kind of magic opened it, one very difficult to track."

"When we arrived at the portal's location, much damage had been done to the surrounding trees," said one of the Cordon Society men, "and a local youth was attacking a man who must have come through the portal, a ranger from Magnanthia. We knocked out the local boy and took the Magnanthian with us. Unfortunately, the ranger didn't make it."

The Cordon Society had to act quickly so they ordered Simon be taken to a secret portal designed by grandmaster wizard Ganlock Gammelgard and located at Itasca State Park.

After the Wells family and Simon left Riverside, the Cordon Society believed the portal was reopened. When the same team of rangers investigated they found the unmistakable tracks of two demented soul seers dragging someone back with them through the portal. The tracks indicated it was the same local youth the Cordon Society rangers had knocked unconscious.

Jessica admitted she gave Simon a sleeping potion before their journey to Itasca.

"I'm really sorry, but I had to," said Jessica.

It was the only way to move Simon safely because they suspected soul seers were looking for him. Putting him to sleep would make it more difficult for the soul seers to see or smell him.

Mrs. Wells had felt bad that Simon wasn't going to get a big celebration, so that's why she made him the extravagant meal in the cabin. The flowers and candles were meant to cover up Simon's scent, making it harder for the soul seers to track him. Simon figured it must have worked because the cabin smelled like a potpourri factory.

"We were supposed to wait for Mom and Dad to get back from the Cordon Society, but this one here," said Randal pointing to Jessica, "got a little hot under the collar and decided to take things into her own hands."

"I overheard my parents talking. The Cordon Society had informed them that there might be soul seers on our trail. They were communicating with the Cordon Society by means of a paper passage," said Jessica, a little defensive. She explained to Simon a paper passage is a small and simple passageway used for transporting letters and documents. They're not big enough for people to pass through. They're a book, a shoebox, a jewelry box, pretty much anything able to hold paper. "I know Mom and Dad had other magical items at their disposal in case it came to a fight," said Jessica. "My final decision came when they left to consult with the Cordon Society."

"You didn't have to steal the parchment and take Simon on your own!" Randal grumbled. "Why did you anyway?"

"Because soul seers instinctively detect and smell magic," said Sonica understanding Jessica's intentions. "If your parents were using a paper passage, and keeping among them magical items, there would have been a good chance a soul seer would pick up on it, especially in this world where magic is not abundant."

Jessica grinned at Randal, pleased with herself.

Simon was dumbfounded trying to sort out all of this new information. And Jessica, his best friend, seemed like a complete stranger to him.

"So all these years you were lying to me," said Simon somberly. He couldn't look at her.

"I had to," she pleaded, "there was too much at risk if you knew."

Simon felt confused, betrayed, angry, and didn't know who, or what, to believe. "So all these years, all the things we did together, we did because you had to be with me?"

"No..." she sighed. Tears slid down her cheeks. "We became friends because we had so much in common! I love being with you!"

"Why me?" Simon was skeptical. "What makes me so special?"

"Because you were chosen. You were given a rare gift," said Sonica quietly.

"What gift?" asked Simon.

"That is not for me to know. It is for you to uncover," said Sonica. "Simon," her soft tone was calming, "Jessica did the right thing. And she did it because she cares for you." She walked out of the stream and placed her hand on his shoulder. "All of us here care for you. You bring us hope we have not had in many years."

Simon walked up to Jessica and she flung her arms around him just before he reached out to hug her.

"I'm sorry," said Simon hugging her tightly. "I don't know what to think about all this. But you're my best friend."

"And you're mine," she said. "Don't worry. We will see each other again."

"Promise?" he said wiping his tears away.

"Promise," she said.

"This just doesn't seem real, like this is all a joke on me," said Simon looking at Jessica, Randal, the five armed guys, Sonica, with the two hummingbirds staying close to her, and the mass of hummingbirds jetting around the trees behind them.

"Well, if you step over the portal and nothing happens...then the joke *is* on you and we can all go home," said Randal in his usual mocking tone. "But if this is real…."

"If this is real," Jessica interjected, "than you have a big responsibility. Your life will be forever changed."

"What about my dad…and school…?" asked Simon suddenly realizing the obvious.

"We got your father covered," said Randal. "That's our job."

"The Wells family, along with the help of the Cordon Society, will take good care of your father," said Sonica. "In this you will have to trust the Wells family."

"What about school?" asked Simon.

"Let us worry about the details, hero," said Randal caustically. "You're already forgetting, genius…trust!"

Simon turned around and studied the portal at the bottom of the Mississippi River; then he looked at Sonica. "How come you're not worried about this portal being detected?"

"You're very inquisitive," said Sonica with a smile. "Ganlock designed this portal to appear under water, one of the few places portals cannot be detected…by most."

"How is it the water doesn't drain into the portal?" asked Jessica, gazing into the portal.

"Because the portal leads into another body of water in Magnanthia," said Sonica.

"That's ingenious!" exclaimed Jessica. Simon was glad to see her smiling.

"Yes," said Sonica, "but if not done correctly one body of water could pour into the other, causing a catastrophe. That's why no one has attempted it and lived to tell about it."

"Whoa! What?" Simon didn't like how that sounded.

"Don't worry. If any wizard knows how to do it best, it is Ganlock," Sonica reassured him, "but it's all the more reason, aside from being seen, we need to go, Simon."

She reached in her cloak and pulled out a ring that was hanging from her neck. She untied the necklace that was threaded through the ring. The others gathered around Simon and Sonica to watch, intrigued by what was happening.

"I'm sorry there is no ceremony and celebration to accompany this iconic moment," said Sonica as she handed it to Simon, "but this is yours, and you will need this to pass through the portal safely." Leaving it in his palm, she closed his fingers around it and held his fist in her hands. "This is a Ring of Affinity. Forged for only one to bear," said Sonica looking Simon in the eyes. The ring was warm and felt alive in his hand. "Once you don the ring it will be yours and yours only; it will become a part of you. In time it will enhance your strengths and help you overcome your weaknesses. And most importantly," said Sonica tightening her hold around his fist, "when the time is right, the ring will reveal gifts others sacrificed so you may have them."

She cupped his fist in her hands for a few moments; no one spoke. The sole sound was the passive gurgling of the headwaters. Sonica slowly let go of his hand and took two paces back leaving Simon in the middle of everyone.

He slowly opened his fist. An orange and red glow emanated from the ring's jewel. The polished silver, with tiny scales, glittered in the moonlight.

Simon hesitated for a moment and then picked it up. He had never seen anything so beautiful. The fire-ray cut revealed what looked like faint, small flames dancing in the heart of the gem.

Simon looked at Jessica and then to Sonica, not knowing what to do with it.

"Since you are right-handed," said Sonica gently, "place it on the ring finger of your left hand."

Jessica, Randal, and the others were awestruck, watching in anticipation. Sonica's expression was difficult to read; she appeared excited and concerned at the same time.

Simon stretched out his left hand, and holding his hands outward for all to see, slowly slid the ring on his finger. The ring moved of its own accord, tightening its grip on Simon's finger, until it fit perfectly. The gem lit up like stoked flames, illuminating the area with orange and red, flickering like a roaring fire.

A strong and sudden wind blew over Lake Itasca and down to the headwaters. The enormous gust of hot air spewed fog instantly in its wake. The wind encircled Simon, leaving him untouched, but blew amongst the others, throwing their hair and cloaks back, snuffing out the torch and the two flashlights.

A low growl-like rumble followed the hot wind into the forest. The heavy fog rolled in, trailing the enigmatic, passing wind. And then all was cool and calm. The fog quickly sank and crawled cryptically on the ground.

The orange and red glow returned to the heart of the gem leaving the group under the moonlight.

"It has begun," said Sonica in an intense delight. "And now we must go, Simon," she said kindly joining him at his side.

Jessica took Simon's flashlight from him. The sunrise at the bottom of the Mississippi was shining even brighter through the portal. Jessica hugged Simon and kissed him on the cheek. She held up the flashlights, "You can't take these with you," she said, forcing a smile.

"Good luck, Simon," said Randal. "Be seeing you soon."

Tanner and the others quickly expressed their thanks and gratitude as Sonica gestured to Simon it was time to go. Speechless, Simon smiled at Jessica and nodded to the others. He wanted to cry, laugh, and shout...for this was no dream.

Together, Simon and Sonica walked into the cold headwaters to the edge of the portal. The two humming-birds hovered in front of them.

"Thank you my friends," said Sonica to the little birds, "go in peace."

Simon heard two small voices say, "Go in peace," before the two birds vanished into the dense fog.

Sonica offered Simon her hand, which he gratefully accepted. Together they stepped into the portal with the sunrise at their feet and stars above their heads, into the land of Magnanthia.

10

LOUD ENOUGH TO WAKE
THE DEAD

Jak lingered in a state of consciousness between dreaming and fully awake. His body demanded rest, but his mind struggled to awaken, to sort out what was reality and what was fantasy. Recent events were both unbelievable and undeniable.

He could hear someone talking, but was unable to focus on the words due to his blurred thoughts. Was he dreaming that someone was talking? It seemed just moments ago he was flying through a forest, a cold and dark forest. And before that…he was reading in the library in their newest mansion…on Tuttle Point.

I must have fallen asleep while reading.

He definitely wasn't in the forest because he wasn't cold...but then again, he wasn't warm.

Maybe it's Mickey talking. For some reason it was comforting to think that the dumb buffoon was, in fact, the one in the room with him. Jak tried calling for Mickey, but his lips wouldn't move. They were heavy, or stuck together. He tried several times, but no matter how hard he tried or how much he concentrated on his lips, he couldn't open his mouth.

Slipping in and out of reality he tried to sort out what had happened. His mind went from the mansion on Tuttle Point, to the streets of New York; from the limo rolling down Riverside, to a strange door leading to a distant land. He wasn't sure where he would be when he awoke.

Then he was aware he was lying on a bed...it was itchy. Wool maybe? He was relieved to find he could open his mouth. He took a deep breath, drawing cool air into his lungs.

"Mickey?" His voice crackled in his throat.

There was no answer.

Jak didn't open his eyes. He was hanging onto the thought, or perhaps a hope, he was in his bedroom on Tuttle Point, even though it didn't feel like it. The sound of a bird fluttering its wings nearby convinced him to open his eyes.

The worst scenario was realized. The recent events were no dream. He was lying on a small wooden cot with a large sackcloth bag stuffed with straw, by the smell of it, as a mattress. A shoddy wool blanket covered his legs. A candle burned on a tiny nightstand, and a mug held what he hoped was water, because he was parched.

The room was round, made from stone, and about thirty feet in diameter. A single window, about two feet wide and four feet high, its shutters wide open, revealed it was nighttime. The moonlight made a trapezoid shape on the floor of the small room. A black raven shuffled anxiously back and forth on the windowsill. A door stood on the other side of the room.

Jak sat up. His head hurt, his body ached, and he was already feeling moody from hunger pains. He grabbed the mug next to the candle, sniffed it and looked inside. Then he took a taste. Sure enough, it was water. It was stale, but it was water nonetheless. He gulped it down greedily. Wiping the water from his chin, he looked at the raven.

"What are you looking at?" he asked rhetorically.

"I don't know," said the raven in a worried and quiet voice, "I hope not a dead man."

Jak jumped up and away from the window.

Stunned, he stared at the creature.

"No way! That thing just spoke," mumbled Jak. The bird shuffled back and forth, its claws tapping and clicking on the stone windowsill.

"I'm a raven, not a thing," it said. "I thought you would know that."

It was amazing! The raven's beak even moved when it spoke, like a puppet.

"I know...you're a bird," said Jak feeling silly and awkward talking to a raven.

"Then what's the problem?" asked the raven quietly. He started pacing back and forth even faster.

Jak thought the problem was obvious. "You're talking."

"Oh...that," said the raven as if it were a minor oversight. "Sorry, but I can't take on a human form. Plus, I had to be able to fly to get all the way up here."

"Wait! You think..."

"Shhh," interrupted the raven, reaching a wing around to his beak, like a finger to lips. "You must be quiet or you'll wake him up," he whispered.

Jak looked back at the empty cot. "Wake who up?" he said, bringing his voice down.

The raven extended his shiny, black wing and pointed to the foot of the makeshift cot. In the heavy shadows someone was hunched over.

Jak cautiously walked over to the nightstand. The candle was melting over the edge, but Jak eventually snapped the candlestick off. Hot wax spilled onto his hand, and instead of yelling he replaced his unspoken curses with cringes and gritting teeth.

Turning his attention back to the hunched sleeper, Jak leaned in for a closer look. He gasped and stepped away. It couldn't be real!

"Is that..." Jak started to ask, but he realized the irony of asking a talking bird if what he was looking at was indeed a skeleton. It sat motionless, no breathing, no twinges, nothing. Its wooden helmet covered its eyes. Tattered leather armor covered parts of its body. And its left hand rested on a sheathed short sword strapped to the skeleton's waist. It looked dead.

Of course it's dead; it's a skeleton.

"What's going on here?" asked Jak, raising his voice enough to show he wanted answers from the beaked one, but not enough to wake the dead.

"Return the candle to the nightstand," said the raven. "The undead are easily startled by light and fire. Keep him in the shadows where he belongs and I shall tell you."

Jak thought of his options, which were limited, so he returned the candle to the nightstand and approached the open window. The raven scuttled over to make room as Jak leaned over and looked down.

He shook his head in disbelief. Far below him narrow, cobblestone streets, with a few lanterns and torches, ran disorderly into and through one another, a cobweb of roads sprawling out for miles on and alongside a mountain range. Horrid noises echoed in the distance, screaming, crashing, pitiful laughter...the din of fighting and combat.

Jak was imprisoned in a tower of an enormous castle. The dark, loathsome castle loomed over the abandoned streets, which were lined with ruined cottages and forgotten establishments.

There was more. What first appeared as a single colossal structure, which dwarfed the castle, was instead a hoard of coalesced towers, castles, fortresses, battlements, bridges...all spewing and jutting out from the mountain. Some of the structures were new and still stood strong, like the one Jak was in. But most of them were old and broken down. So many had fallen into one another it was difficult to tell where some started and others ended, like long forgotten dreams.

What is this place...condemnation?

Jak's heartbeat quickened and the need to get out overcame him. He hurried to the door, but to his dismay there was no handle, just a keyhole. He pushed, but it didn't budge. He started pacing, trying to think. His face was warm despite the cool air coming from the open window.

He decided he would break the door open; the keyhole should be its weakest point. He was scrawny, but if he put all his weight behind it he figured two or three runs at it might be enough.

"Uh, uh," warned the small, singsong voice from the windowsill. "If you wake lazy bones over there and he thinks you're trying to escape, he will subdue you in any way he can, without killing you of course. That includes taking off one of your legs so you can't run, if need be."

Jak thought twice about his plan. The talkative raven was probably right.

Slouching, he dragged his feet back to the window.

"How do you know this?" asked Jak.

"I heard the overlord give the order," said the raven ruffling his feathers. "Besides, that door is six inches thick and is barred on the other side. The only way that door is opening is if one of the guards out in the hall open it."

Jak sank beneath the windowsill.

"Are you ready to listen?" asked the raven.

"Yeah," said Jak, hopelessly. What choice did he have?

"Tell me your name," the raven kindly inquired.

Jak hesitated, but then figured it didn't make any difference. "Jak."

"Don't look so forlorn, Jak," the raven whispered, leaning down to Jak's ear. "You were brought here for a very important reason. I know because I listen. Besides, you would not have been locked in a tower so close to the overlord's section of the castle if you weren't so valuable. You would be sitting down in the dungeons with the rest of the unfortunate souls awaiting the...trial."

"Trial?" He didn't like the sound of that. His stomach turned over. "Why am I being put on trial? I didn't do anything to anyone..." but his thoughts trailed off and he remembered the weird man in the forest he attacked.

But he attacked me first! It was self-defense.

"You're not being put *on* trial, you're *going out on* a trial," said the raven. Noticing Jak's bewildered look, the raven reiterated, "You're going to be tested."

As Jak was processing this piece of information, the raven jumped down on his knee. Jak's first instinct was to bat him off. He didn't like animals much and even less when they crowded him. But he thought better of it since this feathery informant was his only source of information and hope of getting out of this mess.

The raven must have sensed Jak's initial reaction because he spread his wings in flight-ready position, and Jak saw fear in his little black eyes for a moment.

Once Jak relaxed, so did the raven. He stood on Jak's knee and continued.

"You're confused right now and desperately want to know why you are here. But let me tell you *how* you got here, and the why and where will fall into place." The raven tilted its little black head, awaiting a response.

"Okay," said Jak. "Let me have it."

"The other night a portal cracked opened into our world…"

"Which is…" interrupted Jak.

"A magic door, much like a passage, but between two worlds," said the raven.

"I figured that out on my own," said Jak. "I meant the name of this world."

"Oh, yes of course," the raven interjected, "Magnanthia, you're in Magnanthia. What's the name of your world?"

"Earth," said Jak.

The raven contemplated. "Hmm…Earth. How simple. It doesn't reflect the nature of a world, only its contents."

Jak didn't have a rebuttal because the feathery freak had a good point.

"Continue."

"The news of this cracked portal traveled quickly. Nothing like this has ever happened. The greatest wizards and warlocks weren't sure of its ramifications and both sides thought the other cracked it open."

Wizards and warlocks?

If he weren't hearing this from a talking bird, Jak wouldn't have believed any of it. But considering the source he kept his mouth shut.

"To understand the importance of this incident you must understand the laws and principles of magic. There are many, but one of the most basic laws, and probably the most important, is when casting a spell, the spell-caster must have complete control over it so he can contain and maximize its power. He must master it. If the spell-caster conjures a spell he has not mastered, he runs the risk of losing control over it, or worse, a sever-decimation, which can obliterate not only the caster, but all living things around him."

"A sever…what?" asked Jak.

"A sever-decimation," the raven slowly explained. "It's when a spell completely severs itself from the caster and with its remaining energy decimates itself and all that's around it. It's referred often as The Maker's Wrath."

Jak was intrigued. The mere idea of such power thrilled him; the bird had his attention now.

"How far 'around' gets incinerated?" asked Jak with growing interest.

"That all depends on the size of the spell," said the raven. "A small spell may incinerate only parts of a caster. I've seen a magic-user blow up his hands trying to cast a holding spell. I have also heard stories of casters inciner-ating themselves along with small villages or constructs. Of course, few casters have ever survived to tell which spell it was they were casting when the sever-decimation occurred. I only know of one."

The raven looked over at the skeleton by the foot of the cot; he was still slumped over. Speaking even quieter than he had been, he said, "You will be meeting him soon. Because of his foolish mistake, for only a fool would cause a sever-decimation, he was stripped of his former name and was given the name, Severn. He's cruel, bitter, and a powerful warlock."

"Powerful?" Jak said mockingly. "You said yourself he would have to be an idiot to do such a thing."

"There's no mistaking it," said the raven somberly. "To survive such a blast, one would need to be powerful."

"How big was it?" asked Jak. He wanted to know more about spells.

The raven looked saddened as he considered it.

"A castle was decimated. Only a few walls remained standing. Somehow, he alone survived," said the raven. "So do you understand the power behind magic?"

"I do," said Jak in wonderment. And he wanted to understand much more.

"So a crack in the portal meant someone didn't know what they were doing when they tried to open it; they just cracked it."

"So what? What's the big deal? And what does this have to do with me?" asked Jak in a suppressed whisper.

"This crack is like a crack in a window. You can close the window, but the window's integrity is compromised. It's easier to break. Wind can freely pass through a broken window, only it's not the wind that is of any concern if a portal breaks open." The raven hopped over to Jak's other knee. "And to answer the second part of your question…everything," answered the raven, looking over at the motionless skeleton. "You have everything to do with the crack. Severn believes you may be the one who cracked it."

"But I don't know magic," said Jak, "So I couldn't have."

"But you were found on the other side of it," the raven said suspiciously. "What were you doing there?"

"I...I don't know," said Jak trying to recall what had happened. He didn't recall seeing a crack; what he saw was a whole 'window.' "Someone hit me on the back of my head. And when I woke up there were two freaky look'n things that attacked me and dragged me through the window, or door...whatever it was. And it wasn't a crack, it was a whole door!" Jak uttered angrily.

The skeleton stirred and grunted. They both looked at him and waited, but he didn't move again.

The raven put one of his wings up to his beak. "Shhh. You must learn to hold your tongue, or it could end up on the floor."

Jak leaned back against the wall below the windowsill. Cool air touched the back of his head and neck, rolled over his shoulders and down his arms. The air carried with it the scent of burning wood, meat cooking over an open flame, and a pungent smell he couldn't identify; something told him it was best if he didn't know. Whatever the stench, it didn't sit well with him. He quickly sat up and scooted a few feet away from the window. The raven hopped off of Jak's lap and onto his arm and then scuttled up on to his shoulder.

Jak felt uncomfortable with the large bird standing so close to his face. His sharp claws clutching his shoulders weren't comfortable either.

"What are you doing?" whispered Jak cautiously, watching the skeleton for any sudden movement.

In an ever so slight whisper, the raven said, "This way I can speak into your ear and we both can be a little quieter. We'll lessen our odds of waking skinny over there. Listen to me," said the raven, his voice so small it could pass as Jak's conscience. "The soul seers would not have brought you here if they hadn't seen something about you they believed the overlord would like."

"Soul seers?"

"They're the 'freaky look'n things' who brought you here."

"I don't even remember arriving."

"What *is* the last thing you remember?" the raven enquired.

"Being dragged like an old coat through a weird forest. The trees were grabbing me; it was as if they were alive. I could feel branches scraping my legs and ankles…and that's it. I don't remember anything else." Jak examined his legs. Sure enough, his pants were torn and ripped at the bottom and his ankles were covered with scratches, as if a cat had mistaken them for scratch posts.

"Severn opened another portal over the cracked one and sent the two scouts, soul seers, through it to investigate. He told the two scouts that if they found 'him' to bring 'him' back…then they brought *you* back. However, apparently you are not the 'him' Severn was looking for because he almost killed the scouts for failing their task. In an attempt to save their hides the scouts quickly explained that what they saw they believed would be of great interest to the overlord. This made Bedlam's Keeper interested as well."

"What? What did they see?" asked Jak, "And what is a bedlam, and who is the keeper?" He didn't like the thought of someone checking him out, especially weird freaks resembling something out of a Wes Craven flick. And he was becoming increasingly annoyed not knowing half of what the raven was talking about, despite the fact he still couldn't believe the bird was even talking.

"Bedlam is where you are," said the raven as he spread his wings and motioned to the space all around them. "It is the home of the overlord and his army of undead. It's mammoth and majestic. It's a maze of grand halls, haunted chambers, and dark corridors. Bedlam is so grand, creatures of all kind dwell within its walls and can go unseen for years, creatures you want nothing to do with." The raven gestured to the armored skeleton. "Even the undead minions move about in packs in fear of the unknowns lurking around dark corners and abandoned corridors searching for food and prey.

"For centuries warlocks, necromancers, and other powerful beings have made their home here, attributing to the size and greatness of Bedlam. Every one of them wanted to leave behind their own mark. What started as one castle has become a colossal labyrinth of castles, dungeons, and towers. The tower you are in is one of hundreds. No one knows Bedlam's entirety, not even the overlord and his great warlocks. No one has ever been able to map out Bedlam in its entirety. They either give up, or are never seen again."

Jak was hoping he would wake up from this nightmare.

"Sounds like it's best our door is locked," Jak mumbled.

"Indeed," agreed the raven. "Come to think about it…they probably did lock the door to keep things out. After all, you wouldn't last long if you were to escape. And they know it."

There was an awkward pause. From the corner of his eye Jak could see the raven studying him in a wild fascination.

"You must be very important for the overlord to secure you away from the others...but why?" said the raven to himself and studied Jak a little longer. "Someone must covet something you have." His black, beady eyes stayed on Jak. "This brings me to the third part of your question.

"Bedlam's Keeper is a warlock, whom the overlord places in charge of the undead army. Bedlam's Keeper carries out the overlord's biddings, and in return the overlord gives Bedlam's Keeper the Scepter of Zalaruz as a gift to help keep things in order, if it's possible for chaos to have order," said the raven followed with a hasty chuckle. "The most recent warlock to be given the title of Bedlam's Keeper is the one and only, Severn."

"Who's the overlord?" asked Jak, stuck in a state of surrealism.

"Ahh...the ultimate unanswered question," said the raven. "Who...or what, is the overlord? Allow me to summarize. Few have ever seen him, but many have witnessed his destructive powers! If you are ever in the presence of the overlord, Jak, then you will have either reached the pinnacle of your success, or have fallen to the deepest depths of hell. The latter of the two being more probable. Either way, if you do find out, please share. Then we'll both know."

Jak was at a loss for words. He wanted to kick back a witty remark to the cocky crow...but perhaps he was telling Jak in a nice way to keep away from the overlord. Jak held his tongue.

"I've yet to answer the first of your three questions, and the most important one," the raven continued.

"What the scouts saw."

"Precisely," said the raven, his voice low and enigmatic.

"Well, don't take your time with it. What did they see that was so important? Why did they bring me to this God-forsaken place?"

The raven leaned closer to Jak's ear and whispered, "Your soul."

A chill swept through Jak, covering his skin with goose bumps.

"My soul?" Jak shuddered. "What do they want with my...do they plan on killing me?"

"Much depends on the path you choose," said the raven. "Severn took care of the cracked portal, so no permanent damage was done. By opening a new portal over the crack, the portal sealed the crack shut...." The raven thought about it for a moment. "Quite brilliant, really," said the raven with admiration. "Most magic-users would have been too afraid to attempt what he did."

"Why?"

"Sever-decimation of course.... Hmm...brilliant, just brilliant," commented the raven.

"Focus!" said Jak in a gruffly tone. "What paths do I have a choice of? I don't seem to have any choice at the moment, except perhaps jumping out the window to a quick, and grotesque, end...no thank you."

The raven leaped up to the windowsill and looked down to the glowing torches far below. "It certainly is a choice," said the raven gawking in the direction of someone, or something, hollering in the distance. "I guess we always have choices. Perhaps unseen choices…much like the paths soon to be revealed to you."

Jak grew suspicious as he watched the raven.

Why is he here? Why is he telling me all this?

Jak broached the subject the best way he knew how.

"Why are you here? Why are you telling me all this?" Jak asked pressing the issue. "What's in it for you?"

The raven looked at Jak; his beak was contorted in such a way it didn't look real. He was smirking.

"What makes you think I'm here for my own personal gain?" asked the raven in jest.

"Why would you be here with a guy locked in a tower with nothing more than a bleak immediate future?" asked Jak accusatorily, standing up to look down on the raven on the sill. "You're either a very sick and twisted fiend who enjoys watching others suffer, or you have a motive."

The raven admired Jak for a moment. "Perhaps I made the right choice after all," said the raven to no one in particular.

"I'm happy for you!" said Jak sarcastically. He was becoming annoyed knowing this oversized, black chicken has been holding out on him. *He knows something.* "And just what choice are you so proud of making?"

"I said 'perhaps,'" said the raven, his tone dry and direct. "But we'll need to see how circumstances develop from here on."

"What do you mean?"

"You'll see soon enough," said the raven. "For now, it's time to give circumstances a little shove."

"What are you talking about?"

A dark, red glow ignited in the raven's eyes. Spreading his wings, his feathery chest puffed up as he took a deep breath...and then cried out. In the silent, tiny tower, the raven's caws were deafening, shattering the stillness like an alarm, a call to arms.

To Jak's horror, the undead skeleton awoke from its slumber and jumped to its feet.

11

MOONLIGHT STARLIGHT

The sensation was like no other. Simon was expecting to sink into the water, but upon stepping into the portal he and Sonica moved through the water at a tremendous speed. The water was cold in the Mississippi, but as they were propelled through the portal, the water was warmer. For a short time Simon lost his bearing and didn't know if he was falling into one river or rising out of the other. He held Sonica's hand tight.

Breaking the surface of the water, the warm air touched their faces.

Sonica laughed jubilantly, splashing about like she was on a water park ride. Caught up in the excitement, Simon joined in the splashing, being sure, however, to keep a good hold of her hand.

The landscape was a wonder. The river carried them around bends with bright-colored trees on either bank. The trees were almost celestial, radiating in the sunshine. The bark on the trees was sandy blond. Their leaves were massive and thick with a variety of colors, each tree having its own special color. There were green trees, red trees, orange, yellow, blue, ruby, violet, silver, and many others. The leaves and bark on the trees shown more brilliantly as the sun slowly made its way into the sky.

"We are the first to ever do that!" exclaimed Sonica still excited from their experience.

"To do what?" asked Simon as the soft current guided them around another small bend in the river.

"Pass through a portal underwater," Sonica explained enthusiastically. "There's no record of a portal ever having been opened underwater before, until now," she said with a smile stretching ear to ear. "Ganlock is going to be well pleased."

Simon could see the river's sandy bottom twenty feet below.

"Sonica, is this still the Mississippi River?"

Sonica giggled, her red, wet hair shining in the morning sun. "No," she said still giddy from their feat. They both watched as a school of large, bright yellow fish with a bright blue stripe running the length of their bodies swam carefree underneath them. Still watching the four to five foot-long fish she added, "This is the Tyberus River, which means spirited little one." Her tone carried a hint of sadness. "It was named hundreds of years ago after a toddler who drowned in the river. He went over one of the waterfalls and was never seen again."

"Waterfalls?" Simon kept his eyes downriver.

"Yes, waterfalls," said Sonica as if she were looking forward to one. "You have not noticed the river carrying us faster and faster?"

He hadn't really been paying attention. The many colored trees and blazing sunrise almost hypnotized him; it was dreamy. But now, since she brought it up… "You're right, it's carrying us along quite quickly now. We better get to the shore!"

Sonica didn't let go of his hand.

"Come on!" Simon prompted her with a few tugs.

"There is no need, Simon," said Sonica calmly. "The Tyberus is taking us to our destination. No worries. Just enjoy the ride. It's such a beautiful morning after all… oh, and the trees are happy you have arrived."

Simon tried to enjoy the scenery, but he soon heard it. There was no mistaking a waterfall was downriver and they were rapidly coming upon it.

"Um…I hate to rain on your parade," said Simon, "but I hope our destination is coming soon. I hear a waterfall."

"I know," said Sonica, "that is our destination." Her eyes lit up and she smiled at Simon; she was just on a water park ride.

She must have read Simon's expression because she pulled him closer to her and said reassuringly, "Although it's tragic and unfortunate the river took young Tyberus's life, no one has been killed, or even harmed, going down the river's waterfalls since. Tyberus, the toddler, sees to it. His spirit guards these riverbanks."

The waterfall's distant grumbling was soon a roar as they came closer.

Simon looked around frantically for a way out, a rock to grab onto, an extended branch...anything! This was insane! How shallow was it at the bottom of the waterfall? Or what about branches sticking out of the water, or the undercurrent.... Sonica gripped Simon's shoulders and looked at him, her emerald green eyes full of life and confidence.

"I promise you, Simon," said Sonica in a lullaby tone, "no harm will come to you. Trust me...the waterfall will bring us no harm."

Her eyes seemed so sincere.

Sonica and Simon started slowly swirling around in the current. A warm mist engulfed them before the waters washed them over the edge toward the frothy bottom below.

Simon couldn't hold onto Sonica's hand and she vanished in a whirlwind of air and heavy waters. What if she were wrong about Tyberus, or this was the wrong river?

Simon screamed out for her. He was sure they were both going to die.

A jolt from Simon's heart caused a pulse to travel down his left arm and to his hand where the energy accumulated to his ring finger and into the Ring of Affinity. A bright white light pulsed from the ring and all went silent. Hitting the bottom of the waterfall Simon could feel the cool liquid, but there wasn't a single sound. No splash. No roaring waters. And no current.

Instead of falling into flowing waters of the river, he fell into the still waters of a lake. There was no resistance.

It took a few moments of obscurity before Simon had an idea of what had happened. First he thought he had lost his hearing, but then realized it wasn't his hearing that was lost, but the sounds around him. He was unaffected by the anomaly; he was moving at regular speed. But everything else had frozen to a complete halt. The water he fell into didn't make any sounds and it didn't move, not one splash. The water Simon touched changed shape, but didn't continue moving. It was like falling into a lake of Jell-O. Bubbles formed underwater, but didn't rise.

Swimming to the surface, Simon rose out of the water, catching his breath. The water rose up with him, but upon leaving his body the droplets froze in mid-air.

The water above him was frozen like strands of diamonds, refracting the brilliant sunlight. Sonica, suspended about eight feet above the river, was motionless, like everything else immediately around him.

What happened? Did I do this? he thought.

He began to fear he might be responsible for Sonica's death.

He swam toward her in water that wouldn't splash, wouldn't ripple, and wouldn't make a sound. The silence was unnerving.

As he got closer to Sonica something caught Simon's attention. Midway up the waterfall, the water was still falling at its regular speed, but as the water met the invisible barrier separating normal time from the frozen anomaly, the water gathered in the air as if against a glass dam. Like snow or ice it stopped and piled higher and higher.

Downriver the last of the flowing water disappeared around a bend, leaving behind an abstract path of sand, mud, and fish frantically flopping about in an attempt to find the river.

Simon was close to Sonica when swimming suddenly became tedious. His arms and legs were heavy and each breath was harder to take. He progressively weakened.

Drops of water falling upon his head made him look up. Water slowly began to come through the invisible barrier like water on a leaky roof. Then it came down like rain. And Sonica started falling again.

Everything picked up speed. Water trickling downriver amongst the flopping fish started running again. All around Simon the splashing waters grew louder. He fought to get to Sonica, but a heavy slumber fell upon him. The water rippled and splashed from his strokes as he fought to stay awake.

Before Simon passed out, the invisible barrier six stories above him suddenly shattered. The Tyberus came down with vengeance in a thunderous crash continuing its natural journey and taking Simon and Sonica with it.

Water gushed into Simon's lungs.

"You're lucky you survived," said a young man, raising his voice, "and we're all lucky *he* survived! He has no right casting spells! Wheelock will not be pleased when he hears about this."

"I disagree," said Sonica matter-of-fact like. "I think Wheelock will be quite intrigued with the recent event."

"How did he do it? I thought he wasn't able to cast spells, or use any of the ring's possessions, until after he was trained," said the young man ill at ease.

"I don't know," said Sonica curiously, "but I've never seen anything like it. He didn't have the ring on for more than five minutes and was able to call on it."

"But he was unable to *control* it," said a woman. She spoke with caring authority. "Discovering his abilities will be easy for him if he listens and learns. Teaching him control over these abilities is our most important responsibility."

"Thianna?" asked the young man.

"Yes," replied the woman.

"What he did...the fact he was able to do it..." the young man reluctantly stopped.

"Speak whatever is on your mind Heaton," Thianna said encouragingly, "after all, we'll be spending a lot more time together from this moment on."

Heaton cleared his throat. "Is it a good sign, or a bad omen, he was able to use the ring so soon...and with such power?"

"That's an intriguing question, but one I cannot answer. Time will be our most accurate indicator, but I have a feeling Wheelock will have a few of his own hypotheses," said Thianna. "Which reminds me...Sonica, could you check on our newfound friend? He should be waking soon and we will go as soon as he's able to walk. Wheelock has been anticipating his new protégé's arrival for some time."

Simon heard footsteps. Sonica's hand was soft and cool against his forehead. "He is greatly improved," said Sonica.

"Then I haven't lost my touch," said Thianna with a light laugh.

Simon didn't see the humor. His body ached and his head throbbed. He was especially tired and very willing to stay in this semi-conscious state.

"Simon," said Sonica lightly touching his chest, "Simon…can you hear me?"

Simon's eyelids were heavy, but he managed to open them. The bright light stung momentarily. Sonica leaned in, blocking the sun from his eyes.

"It's time for us to go, sleepy head," said Sonica and smiled.

"How long have I been out?" asked Simon. The sun was much higher in the sky.

"Out of what?"

"I mean, how long have I been sleeping?" asked Simon.

"About six hours," said the woman as she knelt down on the other side of Simon. "I'm Thianna Furrow," she said reassuringly. "We're here to help you."

"I'm Simon…Whittaker," he said, reciprocating the courtesy of sharing her last name with him.

"We are well aware who you are, Simon Whittaker," said Thianna. "We have been expecting your arrival to Magnanthia for some time."

"Who's we?" asked Simon attempting to sit up, but his head was heavy and he started feeling nauseous.

"Wait," said Thianna placing her palm on his abdomen. He was going to lie back down, but a faint, white glow under Thianna's palm caught his attention. His stomach became warm and then his nausea instantly went away. The warm sensation traveled quickly up into his lungs, chest, neck, and in his head. His aches and pains dissolved. He was reenergized before she removed her hand. Thianna cupped her hand and the glow vanished inside her fist.

"Better?" asked Thianna, but she already knew the answer.

"Yes…thank you very much," said Simon.

"Then it is best we set pace since we have far to go and dusk will be upon us soon," said Thianna. Sonica assisted her in helping Simon up. "But before we go, let us answer your question, who we are," Thianna exchanged looks with Sonica and a young, fit man.

"We haven't properly introduced ourselves. I am Thianna Furrow, handler and high cleric to the guardian," she said looking to Sonica for her introduction.

Sonica searched for the words. "I'm Sonica Wintergreen, handler and journeyman ranger to the guardian," she said awkwardly like they were new words on her tongue. Sonica looked to the young man clad in leather and chain mail armor.

Looking down at the ground he resembled a little boy on the playground of a new school, stepping from side to side in place with his hands behind his back. He looked nervous for a man with so many weapons. A medium shield hung on his back, various daggers were tucked in close, and a broad-handled sword was sheathed at his side.

He looked up and glanced at Sonica and Thianna, who were both looking at him. Simon saw Sonica give the hesitant young man a nod of approval. He took a deep breath.

"I am Zacharia Heaton, handler and soon-to-be master swordsman...to the guardian." He spoke as if it were against his will, but with poise nonetheless. "Just call me Heaton...if you will," he said.

As the three of them picked up their gear and prepared themselves, Simon saw how their appearances defined who they were.

Heaton and his many weapons, apparent strength, and the ease in the way he handled and carried his gear, was certainly built for fighting.

Thianna wore some armor, a light chest plate, high leather boots, and a small shield strapped to her left arm. Dangling from her right hip was a small mace hooked to a wide, leather belt inlaid with various pouches and pockets. A hooded cape straddled her shoulders.

And then there was Sonica. Her hooded cloak was thinner and shorter than Thianna's, but it still concealed a couple of daggers and light leather armor, which was dark brown and black. She picked up her bow and a quiver full of arrows and placed them on her body like another garment.

Simon was starting to get the idea what a ranger was skilled in.

Simon felt underdressed in sneakers, jeans, T-shirt, and light spring jacket he had taken on their "camping" trip. Thinking about the trip the Wells family had taken him on, Simon shook his head and smiled. Funny how suddenly life can turn in a different direction, a completely different direction.

Earlier this week Simon's main concern was preparing for the choir concert. Now he's in Magnanthia, an entirely new world, following a ranger, a swordsman, and a cleric into a forest.

Thianna and Heaton took the lead. Sonica walked with Simon, dropping back and letting him go ahead of her any time the trail narrowed to a single path. Little was said. His three travel companions all seemed to have something either on their minds or they were busy paying close attention to their surroundings as they traveled deeper into the forest. This gave Simon the chance to see this other world, to see Magnanthia. It also gave Simon time to replay recent events in his mind, trying to grasp it all.

Thianna said they had been expecting me for some time. That means they were expecting me to go to Itasca and open the portal. Who set it all up? And what exactly is the Cordon Society, and how long had it been watching me? I don't understand why all the sneaking around and secrecy.

Who is Ganlock and what does he want with me?

Who is the guardian these three work for?

As Simon pondered everything and tried to make sense of it, which wasn't proving successful, he also admired the beauty around him. The colorful trees lining the Tyberus River along the falls were no longer in site. Instead, their party was amidst more common looking trees. These trees were larger and healthier than any Simon had ever seen.

"What kind of trees are the ones with the different colored leaves, which were along the river?" Simon asked Sonica.

"They are rare," she said, "found only on ground a spirit has walked upon."

"Tyberus, the young boy who drowned?" Simon deduced.

"Yes, his spirit left the gift of guidance, so no one would go over the falls and die ever again," said Sonica, appreciating Simon's curiosity. "They're spiritwood trees. They grow from the essence a spirit leaves behind. The color of their leaves and trunks reflect much of the spirit from whose essence they stem."

"That's amazing," said Simon. "What else can you tell me about them?"

Sonica chuckled softly. "We'll have plenty of time for that when you start training," said Sonica, "but I'll leave you with this." Her tone suddenly sobered. "Spiritwood is sacred. There are consequences for taking and using the wood from a spiritwood tree...always," she warned. "Some of them dislike, and even hate, to be disturbed. Some...long for it."

As the day waned, so did Simon's energy. His legs were sore. He had never walked so much in his life. The few breaks they took were for Simon. Sonica, Heaton, and Thianna all seemed unaffected by the day's journey. He wondered how many miles they had put behind them.

The forest had grown dense and the trees were large. The trees were about twelve stories high, and stood as marble pillars. They weren't so common anymore. They were wooden giants stretching their arms and large green hands toward the sky. The bases of some of the trees were as big as a small house and some of their branches were over ten feet in diameter. The farther along the party walked, the larger the trees were.

"I see you like the shiftwood trees," Sonica commented to Simon who was gazing up and down the indigenous plant life.

"They're breathtaking! They're mammoth, and yet they seem so strong and healthy," said Simon admiring a large shiftwood next to him. He walked up and touched the tree. Its bark was rock solid...and warm. The shiftwood was warmer than the air despite the few sunrays coming through the heavy canopy of leaves above them.

"Why are they so warm?" asked Simon; his hand still pushed up against the shiftwood's bark.

Sonica smiled. "Why are you so warm?"

Simon was puzzled. The answer was obvious, but didn't make sense. "Clothes?" he said unsurely.

"Clothes *keep* you warm; they don't make you warm," said Sonica congenially.

"But the more clothes I put on the warmer I become," said Simon. "I may even become hot if I put on too much clothes."

"Is it the clothes you wear that make you warm, or is it what's underneath that becomes warmer, and eventually hot?" Sonica prompted. "You can wrap a boulder in many blankets, but if there is no heat coming *from* the boulder, it will not become warm."

"Are you telling me this tree has body heat?" asked Simon pointing to the tree.

"*You* figured it out; I just guided you." She gave it a moment to sink in.

Simon looked at the tree with a whole different perspective.

"Shiftwood trees are personified by their environ-ment," said Sonica walking up to the shiftwood Simon was pointing to and gently laid her hand against it. "They cannot help but conform to the forces and energy around them from other living beings. The greater the force, the greater the impact it has on their lovely lives. We strive to keep ourselves healthy, strong, and faithful as long as we dwell in Shiftwood Forrest so the trees have positive energy to help them grow strong and healthy, as you can see. In return we can learn much from their knowledge."

Sonica closed her eyes and kept her hand on the tree. Her breathing became long and rhythmic. Slowly open-ing her eyes, she gazed upon the tree as if it were a long-lost friend.

"Thank you loved one," said Sonica to the tree.

Simon thought the moment with the tree was odd, but didn't say anything.

"The overlord sent two soul seers through the cracked portal," said Sonica, addressing the group. Thianna and Heaton, who were discussing other matters, came in closer to listen. "This confirms what the Cordon Society suspected. Apparently the soul seers took a boy from Simon's homeland through the portal to Bedlam. There has been no sign of him since."

"Perhaps they mistook the unfortunate soul for Simon," said Heaton.

"That is not likely," said Thianna, mulling it over. "They are soul seers. They wouldn't mistake Simon for someone else. Whoever they brought back, they brought back for a different reason."

"It must be an important reason," said Sonica grimly, "because bringing someone, or something for that matter, from another realm can have repercussions beyond even the greatest prophets' insights. The overlord should know this better than anyone else."

"Remember the fire giant they summoned from an undiscovered realm?" Heaton jeered. "It took two master wizards and three high clerics to contain the giant. They were unable to send it back to whatever realm it came from."

"There were many lives lost that day," said Thianna sorrowfully.

"What happened to it?" asked Simon.

"No one knows for sure," said Heaton, "but some believe the raging fire beast still roams somewhere in Bedlam. I hope he burns the whole damned place down; it would serve the overlord right. What do you think Thianna?"

"Yes...it would serve them right," Thianna answered with a faraway look on her face. "Alright," she said, regaining her focus, "we should set up camp. Dusk is upon us and night is near. Sonica! Let the trees know the significance of our present situation. Heaton, do a perimeter check, but don't go too far. I don't want us to be separated too long. Meanwhile, Simon and I will collect whatever wood the trees have shed."

Sonica looked reluctant. "Simon," she said with concern, "it's important you do not pick any wood off of the trees. Only take branches or foliage that are dead. If you're unsure, then don't take it."

"I'll be with him Sonica," Thianna reassured her. "I promise to show him the proper way."

Satisfied, Sonica turned and went to the tallest tree around, gently placed her hand on it, and closed her eyes.

"Come," said Thianna, "we have work to do before darkness is upon us." They left Sonica by the tree, and Heaton had already disappeared out of sight.

When Simon felt they were far enough away, he asked Thianna, "Why are these trees so important to Sonica? What makes them more special than other trees?"

"They are not *more* special than other trees," explained Thianna walking toward some fallen branches, "they are special like all trees, plants, and animals." A thought came to her and she smiled as if she were looking upon an adorable puppy or kitten. "Well, perhaps she holds a special place in her heart for the shiftwoods, but she loves all creatures with her whole heart."

"Why does she hold shiftwoods close to her heart?" asked Simon.

Thianna pondered his question for a moment. "That is not my story to tell," said Thianna with an air of serenity. "You will find, young Simon Whittaker, silent patience will bring you more answers to your heart, than spoken words to your ears."

Thianna went on explaining that shiftwood trees shed their bark and undesirable branches as they grow. The trees take no offense, and they even appreciate it, if this wood is used.

As they walked Thianna pointed out the dead bark and branches that were safe to take. If moss or other plant life was growing on, or even near, the dead wood, they left it alone. Along with wood they picked up dry foliage. Some of the leaves were the size of pizza boxes and as dense as cardboard. Other plant life was left untouched.

"What did you mean when you told Sonica to let the trees know the significance of our situation?" asked Simon, adding more foliage to their pile.

"Bringing you here, to Magnanthia, is a significant event," Thianna explained.

"I'm starting to realize that, although I don't know why," said Simon, feeling embarrassed and self-conscious from her remark.

He wasn't sure if he should ask the question dangling at the tip of his tongue. Perhaps it was too personal, or none of his business. Apparently his indecisiveness was not well hidden.

"Go ahead, Simon," said Thianna. "Say what is plainly on your mind."

They added more to the stack of wood in their camp and were going back for more.

"Why, and *how*, is she telling the trees we're here?" Saying it aloud sounded sillier than it did in his head.

Thianna chuckled softly. "You do have much to learn," she said. "There is no more need to tell the trees we are here as there is for the trees to tell us they are here. She is sharing with them the vital information they need to know in order to understand the importance of our situation. We do not want our allies taken by surprise, now would we?"

He wasn't sure if that was a rhetorical question, so he came up with his best response, "N-no, I guess not."

"As for *how* she speaks to them, I do not know. It is her gift."

"Seems like a really nice gift," said Simon, not knowing what else to say.

"Then I pray you grow to appreciate it as much as she does," said Thianna earnestly.

Nighttime soon gobbled up all the long shadows that dusk had cast.

Surveying the wood and foliage they gathered, Thianna said, "That should get us through the night... would you agree Heaton?"

"I do," said Heaton immersing next to Simon from the shadows. Startled, Simon jumped back. Until Thianna had acknowledged him, Heaton's whereabouts was unknown to Simon.

Heaton grinned at Simon like a schoolboy who had just played a prank.

"I didn't intend to startle you," said Heaton, but his caustic expression said otherwise.

"I...I wasn't startled," said Simon, his face burning from embarrassment, "I just wasn't expecting you...to be right behind me."

"Sounds like the makings of one being startled...if you ask me," said Heaton in an easy chuckle, and his grin grew wider. Simon glanced at Sonica. She was watching him through the corners of her eyes so he quickly broke eye contact. Simon didn't say anything else. He just watched as Heaton prepared their fire.

When the campfire was burning strong they sat around it. Simon's legs ached and began stiffening. Sonica, Heaton, and Thianna took out wrapped portions from their satchels and packs. Sonica unwrapped a handful of nuts, berries, and greeneries. Heaton had a chunk of cooked meat resembling makeshift beef jerky. Thianna laid out a small loaf of bread and a jar of honey. Then she took out another cloth and broke a piece from the loaf, drizzled some honey over it, and handed it to Heaton. Heaton added a portion of meat to it and handed it to Sonica. Sonica added some berries, a variety of nuts, and some green leaves to the mix and handed it to Simon.

"Thank you," said Simon quietly. He was ashamed he had nothing to add…and they had such little food. He felt like a burden.

The Wells family taught Simon much about dinner table etiquette over the years, or in this case a dinner campfire, so Simon waited for everyone to be served. He watched as the others exchanged food with one another so they all had a variety on their cloths.

When they all had a portion, Thianna folded her hands.

"Now we pray," she said.

Simon folded his hands and listened as Thianna gave thanks for their food, their day, and that Simon had been safely found. At the mention of his name offered in prayer, he was honored, but felt bad too. They were all out here because of him. And for what purpose he still didn't know.

They ate in silence around the fire.

When Simon finished his meal he studied the ring. The ring was in the form of a dragon resting contently around his finger. A flamed-colored gem rested on the dragon's chest. It was enchanting. What appeared to be tiny flames inside the gem sparkled and flickered. Watching the gem, wonderment grew within him, and spread from his mind to his heart, stirring warmth…and hope.

Then Simon looked down at the crumbs on the small cloth before him, and suddenly sadness overcame him. He thought of his father giving up so much to raise Simon all alone. He thought of his mother, whom he knew so little about, and how she would never come to know her son. He thought about Jessica, his best friend, his *only* true friend, and how she was always supportive and was there for him.

A cold thought crept into his mind. Was Jessica's friendship genuine or manifested for the sake of this ring and its purpose? He quickly let go of the idea.

And then he thought about Sonica, who seemed to have so much hope in him.

Why? What's so special about me?

Simon was the most plain and ordinary guy he could think of. There are so many stronger, smarter, more creative, and more popular teenagers than he. Up until he stepped into the headwaters, up until the moment he stepped into the portal, he was expecting everyone to yell, "Surprise!" and laugh about the silliness of it all and how scared he looked and how everyone was so convincing.

And yet there was a part of him that wanted the portal to be real and be a life-altering step. And it was.

Suddenly Simon felt compelled to go home. He was afraid. He pulled on the ring, but it didn't move. He tried several more times, but it wouldn't budge. He couldn't even turn it around his finger, as if the dragon's tiny, jeweled eyes insisted on looking forward.

Simon stood up and with all his might pulled the ring.

"Guys! I can't get this thing off!" he said irritably.

Sonica jumped up and grabbed hold of his hands.

"It's alright," she said, "it's meant to stay on."

He yanked his hands away, "But I don't want it to!" he said, growing more irritated. "You've all made a terrible mistake! I'm not the one you are looking for! There's nothing special about me!" The more he pulled the ring the angrier he became.

"You can't stop your destiny any more than you can change the stars in the heavens," said Thianna calmly.

Simon felt tears swelling in his eyes as he continued to tug at the ring. This wasn't part of the deal. In fact, there never was a deal. Everyone just expected him to go along with this, to do the right thing. No one asked how he felt about it! No one even offered to explain what was going on!

"I certainly hope you're not going soft on us now," said Heaton and rolled his eyes.

Simon glared at Heaton. He had it with Heaton's I'm-way-better-than-you attitude.

Heaton mumbled another one of his trademark bantering comments and started around the campfire toward Simon when something happened.

"Don't come near me!" Simon yelled as tears of frustration rolled down his face. Then he thrust his hands out gesturing to Heaton to back away, but as he thrust his hands forward he glimpsed a flicker of light, like a spark, from the ring. The campfire exploded sending flames and hot coals in almost every direction.

Thianna shielded her face with her arms as the explosion lifted her off the ground and into a backward somersault. Sonica was thrown to the ground near Simon's feet with speckles of flames and coals landing about her. And to Simon's horror a large flame leaped from the explosion and lashed out at Heaton...but Heaton reacted quickly.

The flames barely licked his face as he turned and dived for his shield in a forward somersault, taking refuge behind it. The raging flames crashed onto his shield, and then disappeared.

And as quickly as it happened, it was over.

"What was THAT?" Heaton bellowed, breaking the intense silence, smoke rising from his shield.

Simon's heart beat fearfully. He didn't dare move. He just looked at the others.

Thianna was dusting herself off. Heaton was crouching behind his shield. Sonica was yelping as she brushed frantically at the remaining tiny, red-hot particles.

The fire was gone. It wasn't just put out; it was gone. A hole in the earth about a foot and a half deep and four feet in diameter occupied the area where the fire was crackling just moments ago. The forest's ground was speckled with glowing lumps of firewood, which for a few minutes kept the area illuminated with an eerie glow.

The only areas not affected were where Simon stood and directly behind him. The area taking the brunt of the blow was on either side of Simon. Red-hot coals formed a perfectly symmetrical V just inches from Simon's feet and then panned out behind him.

Simon was unscathed.

Thianna lit a torch.

Simon and Heaton didn't move.

Then Thianna ran over to Sonica, standing a few feet from Simon, and started attending to her. Simon's heart dropped to his stomach. The right side of Sonica's face was pitted with burn marks. Her hands burned and bled after wiping the hot coals from her body. If it were not for the cloak she donned for evening warmth, she would have been injured more severely. Her cloak was riddled with holes and burn marks.

"Hold this," said Thianna sternly handing the torch to Simon.

Holding Sonica's hands gently in hers, Thianna closed her eyes and spoke so softly Simon couldn't make out her words. After a few moments a white light passed from Thianna's hands to Sonica's. The wounds on Sonica's hands slowly closed, leaving pink blemishes upon her pale hands.

Simon finally managed to speak.

"I am so sorry Sonica…to all of you," said Simon. "I don't know what's going on, or even how that happened, but I meant no one any harm."

"We know you meant no harm," said Thianna laying her hands on Sonica's face as the same light passed from her hands to Sonica's burn wounds. Although Thianna seemed sincere, Simon heard fear or anger laced in her tone.

Heaton leapt over the pit where the campfire once was and pushed Simon with his shield; Simon landed with a crash and thud. Then Heaton jumped on Simon and pinned him down.

"That's no excuse!" Heaton bellowed. "He almost killed Sonica at the waterfall! And now this stunt! He's too dangerous! He is certain to get someone, if not all of us, killed!"

"Heaton," her voice was soft, "calm yourself. He is not our enemy."

Heaton's shoulders were heaving. "But…"

"It is not his fault. We are to blame," said Sonica tenderly as she walked over and laid a hand on Heaton's shoulder. The healing pink blemishes on her face extinguished any anger Simon had toward Heaton for pinning him down.

"We owe him an explanation," she said.

"Yes, we do," said Thianna, "but we told Wheelock we would wait until we were all together to do so."

Sonica looked at Thianna and then gestured to the boys, pointing out the situation at hand. Heaton was sitting on Simon and holding him down with his shield.

"Perhaps we could go over some of the basics, for all our sakes," said Thianna. "Let us start by preparing another fire in the pit Simon has so kindly provided us."

Sitting around their new campfire, Thianna spoke first.

"Simon, you have been chosen. The Ring of Affinity has been bestowed to you. This is a high honor. Someday you will understand and, I hope, fully appreciate it. The ring's abilities and powers are unparalleled; however, many covet such power and even more fear it."

"What is this *honor*?" asked Simon, but he wasn't sure he wanted to know. "Heaton's right! I might kill someone, including myself."

"That's for sure," Heaton added, but threw his hands up in the air and remained silent after Thianna and Sonica gave him sharp looks.

"The answer to that question will have to wait until we reach Wheelock, who is awaiting our arrival at Domic's Haven," explained Thianna. "Once there, as a group, we will go into greater detail. For now it is probably best if you know some basics so we can avoid any more... incidents.

"The ring is acclimating itself to you, your emotions, your thoughts, your movements...everything about you. You will need to acclimate yourself to the ring, something you do not know how to do yet. This is crucial.

"You need not worry about killing yourself," said Thianna assuredly. "The ring will protect you at all costs, even if it means destroying those around you, friend or foe. When you froze time at the waterfall, the ring kept you in the safest place, which, incidentally, was precisely where you were falling. Your inexperience and lack of trust is why you almost drowned...and burned Sonica."

"What?" Simon was on the defensive. "Inexperience, yes...but lack of trust?"

"Identifying the alignment of spiritwood trees may not be common knowledge, and neither is the story behind Tyberus Falls," said Sonica delicately, "but I explained to you the spiritwood trees would see to it no harm would come to us going over Tyberus Falls."

"How was I supposed to know it would work?"

"Because I told you," said Sonica.

"Yes, but..." Simon sighed. How does he justify himself? Trusting a complete stranger is hard enough. Trusting no harm will come from going over a waterfall is a pretty big order to fill.

"You have much to learn about the ring and its ways," said Thianna.

"But I didn't ask for this," Simon retorted. "This is all happening so fast! I don't think I can do this. You made a mistake choosing me! I think it's best if I go home!" Simon hung his head. He felt shame, selfish, and alone.

Everyone was silent.

"We are not the ones who chose you," said Thianna earnestly. "Like you, we are mere servants to destiny." Thianna took a deep breath; a sigh escaped her. "We understand how you feel Simon. None of us asked for *this*, and yes, this is all happening very fast. We too are struggling to understand the ring and the recent events. We too would rather be home spending time with loved ones, sleeping in our own beds, and having hot meals around the dinner table.

"Life presents moments, and even long spans of time, that in our hearts we desire to ignore. The heart thinks only of itself and wishes to do what is easier, safer, and even more profitable for oneself. But deep in our soul we know what is right."

"We had to give you the Ring of Affinity so you could cross over," said Sonica. "This is not how you were supposed to come to know Magnanthia. The Cordon Society was to enlighten you upon your sixteenth birthday. You were not meant to cross over into Magnanthia until you turned eighteen, so you had time to learn and train. But the discovery of the cracked portal altered everything. You have arrived over three years early and have no training. Heaton and I were also unable to complete our training, to master our craft within our guilds."

"Speak for yourself," Heaton grumbled.

Sonica ignored him. "You had to wear the ring to pass through the portal, or you would die. Ganlock believed it would assure your safety once you arrived in Magnanthia. Please understand we had no other choice than to give you the ring before you were properly trained." Sonica was nervous and looked to Heaton and Thianna for guidance or assurance.

Heaton offered her no assistance.

"We did not expect the ring would respond to you so quickly...if at all." Thianna patted Sonica's knee reassuringly. "We were told the ring would need time to acclimate. Weeks, perhaps months. For this reason alone you should be assured the ring did not choose you in error."

Simon had to clear his throat. It was obvious everyone was uncomfortable discussing this at the moment. When he first spoke it came out a whisper. "So...why did I need the ring to cross over?" He genuinely wanted to know.

"Starlight is needed to cross through a portal unharmed," said Sonica. "The Ring of Affinity has something even better, stardust. Starlight is used and then gone, whereas stardust continues to generate starlight, so the bearer can cross through portals as often as he or she desires."

Simon looked at the ring. Among the colors within the stone was a bright bluish-white twinkle.

"Does this mean I can go back home whenever I want?" asked Simon.

"It does mean you will be able to go back home..." Thianna answered apprehensively, "but you cannot go back whenever you want. It's not that simple."

Simon sighed.

"In time, Simon...in time," said Thianna kindly.

Simon forced a smile.

Quickly changing the subject, Thianna said, "Moonlight is the element needed to stop time. Your ring contains moondust. So once you are trained and skilled at it, you will be able to manipulate time in your favor."

"Why did he almost drown if he was controlling time?" Heaton wasn't impressed.

"Having an element, as rare as some are, does not assure a spell will work," said Thianna ignoring his tone. "It also takes knowledge of a spell and inner strength. Having no knowledge of the spell, of any spell, and able to cast like you did is an anomaly. However, you passed out from trying to sustain the spell. The ring needs to tap into your innermost energy, which it must, and you, with no knowledge of how to store and control it, quickly lost your strength.

"Use this experience to remember how dangerous magic can be if a caster does not know how to cast, control, and sustain a spell. The ring cannot protect you once your inner energy is depleted. You would have drowned if Heaton and I had not been there to pull you out of the water.

"As for blowing up our campfire," said Thianna reading the looks on Simon and Heaton's faces, "I am at a loss. This magic is arcane, the kind only wizards yield, and will be best answered by Wheelock," she explained. "Who, by the way, is expecting us tomorrow. We need to get some rest. It has been a long day for us all.

"The best advice I can give you for now Simon, is be mindful of your emotions; do not let them control you. Emotions are linked to our inner energy, and they can be the quickest, but not safest, route to access that energy."

"I can take the first shift," said Heaton reaching for his sword.

"That won't be necessary, although kind of you," said Sonica. "These shiftwood trees have been our sentinels all night. We are close to Domic's Haven. I trust they will guard us well."

"How will they do that?" asked Simon.

"They will alert me if anyone comes," she said.

"Or they'll drop a branch on our heads," said Heaton looking at Simon over the fire.

Simon looked at Sonica for a response to Heaton's remark.

"He's teasing you. They would not drop a branch on our heads. That would surely kill us," said Sonica.

"Sonica," said Simon lying down near the fire, "what's Domic's Haven?"

"Our destination," said Sonica, her smile renewed, "and a wonderful treat! You are going to love him! He's been waiting for quite a while to meet you." She giggled at a thought and then closed her eyes.

Left to his thoughts, Simon realized how selfish he had been. He didn't think they would be missing loved ones, or were afraid. He assumed they were all in this together and this was their life. Thianna was right. He did have a lot to learn about Magnanthia, but he also had a lot to learn about his companions.

Simon closed his eyes and wondered what tomorrow would bring. Exhausted, he fell fast asleep.

12

BLUE QUAGMIRE

The next morning Simon woke abruptly to someone huffing and yelling. He scrambled to his feet. Dumbfounded, he looked at the towering trees. The Ring of Affinity shimmered on his left hand. Yep, no doubt yesterday happened.

Simon spun around when he heard grunting behind him. Heaton was practicing with his sword, huffing and yelling with each swing, parry, and thrust. He was determined to beat an invisible foe. After a couple of sets Heaton spun around, taking on a new invisible foe creeping up behind him. Heaton's eyes met Simon's. He continued attacking his unseen opponents.

"Didn't think...you were ever going...to wake up," said Heaton in the middle of his sword fight.

"Never mind him," said Thianna, rearranging her supplies, "we're just finishing up our morning routine. Sonica has breakfast laid out for you over there." She gestured to Sonica, sitting down on a blanket.

Portions of fresh berries, leftover bread with honey, and dried meat were neatly placed on one of the corners of the blanket. Simon's stomach growled as he sat down, but there was no way the amount portioned would fill him up. His stomach must have been protesting. He ate his meal, savoring every bite knowing he had to make it last. He wanted to ask for more, but didn't want to be impolite, or ungrateful. He wasn't sure if these were normal portions. And, after all, they were kind enough to share.

"How was breakfast?" asked Sonica.

A blue and black butterfly, the largest Simon had ever seen, flew off her knee and made its way high up in the branches.

"It was nice, thank you," said Simon watching the butterfly rising toward the glimmering sunshine coming through the canopy of leaves dancing in the morning breeze. A faint wisp is all that was left of any breeze by the time it made its way to the forest's floor.

"He said the weather will be fair today, so our travels should be easy," Sonica said as she bundled the blanket.

"Who's he?" asked Simon.

"The butterfly," she said. "He was kind enough to deliver a message from us to Wheelock and Domic, letting them know we should be there by dusk, if all goes well." Sonica looked at Simon, trying to read his expression. "He was heading in that direction anyway," Sonica justified this as if Simon's lost look was because he thought she was asking the poor butterfly to go out of its way.

They headed north with Heaton and Thianna taking the lead again. The plan was for Heaton and Thianna to keep a safe distance ahead of Sonica and Simon to make sure all was safe as they traveled. Sonica would stop from time to time to ask the trees if anyone was following them.

A black squirrel came down one of the lower branches of a tree, sat contently, looked Sonica in the eyes, and squeaked to her in intervals. The squirrel pointed up the tree with his tiny claws.

"Thank you my friend," she said and the squirrel turned and scuttled back up the tree.

"He'll hang around the lower branches for a while and keep an eye open," said Sonica. "He seems very kind."

Simon was amused how normal Sonica made it look talking to trees and wildlife.

"I don't get it," said Simon. "How do you speak to them without opening your mouth, or understand a tree that has no lips?"

"A small portion of communication comes in the form of words," said Sonica glancing ahead at Thianna and Heaton, who were about thirty yards ahead of them. "We needn't use our tongues in order for our souls to speak, and we needn't use our ears for our hearts to hear. Not all living things have a tongue and ears, but all living things communicate."

What she said made sense, but the passion behind what she said made him think. Sonica dropped a few feet behind him, leaving him to his thoughts.

Simon's thoughts drifted to yesterday's events. They were surreal…and miraculous. The rush of emotions and energy he felt, which were overwhelming and hopeful, when he put on the Ring of Affinity. Walking through the portal and into Magnanthia. Stopping the flow of the Tyberus River. And the campfire exploding.

Magnanthia… "Magnanthia," he said in a nearly inaudible hushed voice, to feel it on his lips and tongue. Saying it was almost as majestic as the land itself.

There was already much to say about Magnanthia: the strong, enormous shiftwood trees; the vibrant colors of the spiritwood trees; Sonica's interaction with the black squirrel; and how significant the people treat everything. Magnanthians, albeit he has only known the three, take time to see their environment, use resources sparingly, and leave nothing to waste. Even Heaton, who has little patience for Simon, has pointed out particular plants and their uses. Time is expansive in Magnanthia.

Hours had passed since anyone spoke. Everyone was entangled in their own thoughts, until Simon stopped.

"What is that?" asked Simon pointing to a bright light in the distance.

"It's an opening in the forest," Sonica answered, studying the distant glow, "a field or lake perhaps."

Simon looked up at the gigantic tree limbs extending out like wooden highways, crossing each another as if they were holding hands. It appeared to be a cloudy day from the lack of direct sunlight, but as they came near to the break in the forest Simon saw it was a clear, sunny day. Little sunlight passed through the treetops in this part of the forest because some of the shiftwood trees were over two hundred feet tall. Their arching branches with leaves reached out like green clouds giving the illusion of an overcast sky.

Thianna and Heaton waited for Simon and Sonica at the break in the forest. Simon had to shield his eyes with his hand, like a sailor overlooking the sea, when he stepped into the bright sunshine. A cool breeze brushed by. Simon breathed it in. He hadn't realized how warm and stuffy it had been in the forest until now. Back over his shoulder the forest seemed dark to his adjusting eyes. Sprawled out before them was a mass of glistening blue in a basin roughly three hundred yards long and half as wide.

"I've never seen a body of water move like that before," said Simon looking down the basin's embankment with the others. The water didn't have waves that beat against the embankment, nor did it make any sound. No splashing or lapping. The sparkling mass rippled back and forth in the breeze, swishing with the leaves in the nearby trees in sync with the wind. Yet, as he watched the water he could see small areas of it moving ever so subtly in their own direction.

"That is not water," said Sonica as she studied its girth, "it's sea silk."

The sea silk glistened like water and even moved like water in the wind. Sonica explained that sea silk usually grew in low-lying areas to hide its depth underneath its water-like surface.

"It's so peaceful, like the waves on a lake," said Simon admiring the plant's beautiful ability to mimic water.

"This is true," said Sonica, watching the anomaly, "but there are a couple of problems with this peaceful scenery."

Simon looked at Sonica. She wasn't admiring the wide, blue expansion. She was studying it, concerned with it.

"Like what?" asked Simon.

"Sea silk feeds on other living organisms," said Sonica, staring at it. "Because the plant resembles water in both color and motion, sea silk is often called blue quagmire. Its very thin, fine tentacles look and move like water to attract its prey, usually small to midsize creatures who believe they are coming upon water to fulfill their thirst. The sea silk latches on and drags the unfortunate prey out into the deep where it pulls the creature under. Sea silk feeds on both plants and animals.

"Although sea silk has some ability to strangle its prey it usually doesn't need to," Sonica continued, "because below its beautiful surface there is very little oxygen. The victim chokes on the silky tentacles and eventually suffocates as it falls deeper to the bottom. It is at the bottom where the prey is slowly digested for its nutritional value."

Sonica had not moved her eyes from the rippling, blue mass. "The other problem is," she continued, "this sea silk has only been here for two weeks and its size is of considerable concern."

"How do you know it's only been here two weeks?" asked Simon curiously.

She took a deep breath, and sighed. "The trees told me. They are in terrible fear for their lives, for they have had to watch their fallen comrades taken down, overrun, and forever lost in the depths of the blue quagmire."

"I have never known sea silk to take down large trees such as these shiftwoods, or spread so quickly," said Thianna

"I have never seen, or heard of, sea silk in this part of Shiftwood Forrest." Sonica studied the area, no doubt thinking of a plan. "The shiftwood trees have always overpowered the blue quagmire on their own accord by depriving it of sunlight. Sea silk can live longer without feeding than it can without sunlight. I have a feeling this was no natural event. A large opening in the forest would have been needed for it to start growing, and there is no way it had consumed enough animals to grow like this. This area was covered with shiftwood trees two weeks ago. Unfortunately, the trees cannot recall what happened." She scanned the area around the blue quagmire. "What did it consume to grow so fast?"

As if to answer her question there came a deep and loud moan reverberating nearby followed by intense snapping and cracking like a wooden building toppling over. Only it wasn't a building.

"NO!" yelled Sonica bounding along the blue quagmire's embankment.

"Sonica!" Heaton hollered, running after her.

Sonica ran toward a shiftwood tree being pulled over the embankment. Although small in comparison to its surrounding companions, the shiftwood was about eighty feet tall. Sea silk had latched onto the tree's trunk and lower branches, slowly pulling it down and ripping chunks of bark off.

The deep moans reverberated from the tree, as the blue quagmire's long, water-like tentacles made their way up to more branches. Some of the branches fell from the tree before the blue quagmire could get to them. The tree wasn't going without a fight.

"Come quickly," said Thianna to Simon, "stay afoot and close by me!" And they ran after Heaton and Sonica.

When she reached the tree Sonica placed her left hand upon its trunk and held out her right hand, palm out like a traffic cop, to the sea silk. She closed her eyes tight. Her lips trembled.

Heaton stopped when he reached her. His right hand rested upon the hilt of his sheathed sword.

Simon had never seen anything like it. The tree had fallen about a quarter of the way. Some of its roots were tearing loose, ripping the soil around it. The sea silk gave the illusion of water rising up and pouring over onto the tree. It looked so much like water, Simon could see himself cupping the refreshing drink in his hands and sipping.

The sea silk eased its grip on the tree and the watery tentacles stopped climbing. Some of the short sea silk closest to the embankment reached out in fluid motions toward Sonica, but they were much too short to reach her. Sonica rubbed the tree trunk with her left hand.

"You are going to be fine dear one," said Sonica compassionately.

She quickly averted her attention toward the sea silk that started moving in an odd fashion, like a pit of mad snakes. The sea silk flickered and flailed losing its fluid luster, revealing the bottom half of some of the larger tentacles. The bottom half of the sea silk looked nothing like its top half, its counterpart. Instead of fine silky threads, the bottom portion was thick and murky gray-green, covered with suction cups, and sharp thorns.

"No...no," Sonica uttered softly and then extended her palm out farther, emphasizing her gesture to the sea silk to stop. Her eyes remained closed, but she sensed something amiss. Heaton and Thianna remained steady, careful not to make any sudden moves. Simon, in awe, didn't move except to look back and forth from Sonica to the sea silk. It looked like a wave of water hugging the tree's torn trunk.

Simon sensed anger, resentment, and hostility rising out of the blue quagmire. And then the emotions collapsed upon all four of them like a massive, unseen shroud. The tentacles suddenly stopped flailing, and for a moment looked like ice. Sonica's eyes flashed wide open and she cried out, "Heaton!"

The sea silk quickly regained its grip over the tree's trunk with a heightened fury and found its way around more branches. The sound of the tree's deep moan in the midst of loud snaps and cracks was eerie. The embankment under the tree began to crumble and fall into the blue quagmire, bringing the groaning tree down with it.

Heaton drew his sword just in time, as a large tentacle near the shore reached for him. It splashed into particles like water as the sword's blade sliced it open. The injured tentacle slithered back into the confines of the field of sea silk.

Heaton pursued, slicing and slashing the clear sea silk as he made his way closer to the shiftwood tree. With each stroke of his sword, Heaton sent water-like pieces flying in the air.

And then Heaton connected with one of the larger tentacles wrapped around the shiftwood's trunk. He struck the lower, ugly portion of the tentacle. The sword bit into the thick, greenish skin, splitting one of its suckers. The sea silk's lower portion was stronger. The sword didn't slice through it, but sank into it. Heaton yanked the blade from the flailing weed. Thick, pea green ooze spat from the cut.

Thianna jumped in with Heaton and joined the fray. She fought to hold back the sea silk reaching for Heaton as he hacked away on the larger tentacles on the tree. Out of desperation, Sonica shot arrows randomly into the spastic field of blue quagmire, but it did little damage. Between shots she laid her hand upon the tree's trunk and gently rubbed, as if comforting a dying soldier. The harder they fought the faster the tree came down.

Simon felt helpless. Heaton and Thianna were wet and covered in green slime, swinging wildly about. Sonica fought back tears as she shot an arrow into the mass of sea silk, staying next to the tree as it slowly slipped from her.

There were series of horrible cracking and crashing noises as more large branches gave way to the blue quagmire, and were pulled away to the center of the field of glistening blue. Running out of a hole in one of the broken branches, Simon saw two brown, furry marmots scuttle down the mighty trunk being pulled apart from under their paws.

"Sonica!" Simon yelled pointing at the two critters trying to keep steady on the shiftwood's shaking trunk.

Sonica's eyes lit up and she waived them in. "Come on! You can do it!" she called to them encouragingly.

The smaller one looked scared as the other one looked around, as if weighing their options.

"Come on!" Sonica called over the splitting, and snapping wood, "you're running out of time! Jump and I'll catch you!" The larger one looked at Sonica and then to its smaller companion. The small one was frozen, its pearl black eyes looking frantically around the trunk splitting beneath its tiny paws. The larger one took a few steps, but when its companion didn't move it went back. This happened several times before the bigger of the two gave up.

Heaton and Thianna had to retreat to the shore from almost being overcome by the frantic tentacles. Simon knew they were going to lose this fight, even before he heard the woeful, broken moan reverberating from the depths of the shiftwood tree.

Suddenly, Simon sensed great sadness alongside the bitter anger around him.

"What?" Sonica asked the tree in disbelief.

Another moan, like that of a great whale, responded to her.

Sonica gripped her bow and reached into a small quiver of multi-colored arrows. She pulled out a dark red arrow and knocked it.

The tree's roots were all that were left on the embankment. The tree's trunk was slowly covered in the frenzy of blue and green tentacles as it was pulled out toward the deep.

Tears welled up in Sonica's eyes. "Take cover behind the trees, everyone!" She cried pulling the string back and taking aim at a large hole in the ripped body of the shiftwood.

Heaton looked at Sonica, and seeing what she was doing, grabbed Thianna and they both ran. Simon stayed.

"Get back, Simon!" Her voice quivered.

Simon reacted. He ran onto the thick roots of the disappearing tree.

"Simon!" he heard them shouting behind him.

He quickly climbed twenty feet of roots until he nearly reached the two marmots. The big one was tugging the little one and squealing, which sounded like pleading. The little one was clutching the tree trunk as if it were the only hope of survival.

Simon whistled. They both looked at him with their shiny black eyes.

"If you make it to me, I promise I won't let you go," said Simon, his voice sounded distant and foreign. He had never spoken to an animal like this before. "I promise with my whole heart, but you have to come... NOW!"

The sea silk was making its way onto the roots.

The marmots started running. Simon braced his feet firmly on the roots and held out his hands. The smaller one was gaining speed and passing the other. Seeing the blue quagmire behind the marmots, Simon coaxed them.

Ten feet from him a watery tentacle grabbed the small one's paw. It squeaked and fell down, tangled in the shiny grip. The other marmot attacked the sea silk, freeing the small one and they both ran as fast as their little legs would allow.

The little one was the first to jump, landing into Simon's arms like a football. He curled up tight into a ball, covering himself with his tail.

The other marmot had also jumped, but never made it to Simon's outstretched arms. Several tentacles grappled the marmot as it jumped, and dragged the critter over the edge of the roots. The squealing was soon lost in the flailing madness of the blue quagmire. Simon looked over the edge hoping to see the furry critter, but the marmot was gone.

Simon covered the little marmot with part of his shirt and started down the roots. Looking back, his heart sank. The roots had been pulled out of the ground and were twenty feet from the edge of the shore as they were slowly dragged out.

The area Heaton and Thianna had cleared away from the shore was only ten feet away. Simon couldn't tell how deep the sea silk was between them, but without hesitating he jumped in.

He didn't land hard. Like water it slowed his momentum as the tentacles immediately grappled and twisted about. Unlike water, he didn't get wet. He freed himself several times, ripping the watery tentacles as he fought to reach the shoreline, but within seconds he couldn't move; the silky plants twisted around his ankles and legs.

Sonica still had her bow fixed with determination on the dying shiftwood tree behind Simon.

"Hang on Simon!" Heaton yelled jumping in the blue quagmire with Thianna close behind. Sweat trailed down Heaton's face as he cut a path to Simon.

"Hurry!" Sonica yelled holding steady the red arrow.

The sparkling blue silk had covered much of Simon's waist by the time Heaton made it to him. Heaton continued to clear an area around Simon. Thianna stepped up to Simon and held out her arms like she was going to hug him, but instead she whispered a spell as she looked Simon in the eyes. Her hands were illuminated in a blood-red glow. Careful not to touch Simon, Thianna touched the sea silk that was wrapping itself around him. As her blood-red hands touched the plants their blue top halves burst like water balloons, and their green bottoms shriveled and fell to the ground. When Simon was freed, Heaton and Thianna lead him to the embankment.

A weak moan rumbled from the tree. Sonica released the arrow. It whistled over Simon's head as it cut through the air. Before hitting its intended target the arrow exploded into a raging fireball. The tree lit up like a Roman candle and blew up. The percussion lifted Simon, Heaton, and Thianna over the embankment. Water and pea-green slime covered the area.

The explosion killed over half of the massive sea of blue quagmire. The water in the upper portion of the plant eventually prevented the flames from spreading to the rest of the field, like built-in fire extinguishers, but much damage was done nonetheless. A smoldering trail of ashes and coals lead from Sonica to the massive bonfire.

Tears ran down Sonica's pale cheeks, but she stood tall and poised watching the remains of the fallen shift-wood burn.

Simon saw how sea silk could be so deadly even to large animals and these enormous trees. The burning remains revealed the landscape the blue quagmire occupied. It grew in a steep ravine, earlier hidden by the sea silk. Although the ravine dropped sixty feet or more at its center, the sea silk gave the appearance it was maybe five or six feet deep. Even now, knowing it was a plant, the sea silk looked like water high above dark green earth, near the burning tree. The tentacles, with brilliant blue tops and dull, greenish-gray bottoms, swayed back and forth as if nothing had happened.

No one spoke as Thianna healed their cuts. Sonica was relieved when Thianna checked the little marmot for wounds, and found he had none. The frightened little thing refused to leave Simon, so Thianna did her job as Simon held the marmot close.

Simon tried releasing the marmot into the forest and even onto several different trees, but he clutched Simon's T-shirt and cried with intermittent whistles from his two front teeth. Simon soon gave up and conceded to holding him.

Sonica closed her eyes until two sparrows landed on her shoulders.

"Look upon this dismal scene," she said facing the blue quagmire. "Inform Domic of what you see. Tell him the rest must be destroyed, but we have not the means. Go in peace my friends."

A few chirps and then the two sparrows flew away.

There was nothing more they could do, so the party left in somber silence. Heaton and Thianna lead the way with a safe distance between Simon, Sonica, and Simon's newly acquired friend.

After enough time had passed and some distance was between them and the fallen shiftwood tree, Simon broke the silence.

"What was the deep sound coming from the shiftwood tree?" he asked politely.

After a seemingly unending silence Sonica finally said, "He was crying out for help."

She didn't seem to be in the mood to talk, so he didn't ask anything more.

"I'm surprised you heard his cry," she said after a few minutes.

"It was awfully loud. Hard not to."

"I know…but you have had no training and yet you heard his cry for help. Most people do not take the time to learn or care enough to hear such things. Nature has much to say, but very few listen," she said somberly. "If you were to ask Heaton and Thianna what they heard, they would describe the sounds of the tree falling, but not crying out." She looked at Simon, her eyes pink and tender from crying. "I am proud of you Simon Whittaker. You have shown that you have a good heart. You care for those who seldom receive even a second thought from most people."

"If you don't mind me asking," said Simon reluctantly, "I heard the tree moan right before you took out your bow. What did the shiftwood tree say?"

Sonica was quiet for so long Simon thought she wasn't going to answer.

"He asked me to burn him if I had magic fire, to save his kin," her voice was hoarse from holding back more tears.

She swallowed a lump in her throat. "To understand the significance of his request, it's important to remember he's a tree. They fear fire over everything else. The shiftwoods on this side of the forest will shed dead bark or branches and allow us to burn it, because they trust us. There are parts of the forest where the trees hate those living amongst them and do whatever they can to protect themselves."

"I could tell it was difficult for you to do," said Simon.

"You have no idea," she said.

Simon hesitated before asking, "Why did the tree blow up? Was it the arrow?"

"No," she said, "I do not have an arrow powerful enough to produce damage of such magnitude on its own accord. The shiftwood caused the explosion." She marveled at the shiftwood's final act. "I'm sure you are already aware, trees produce oxygen for us to breathe. Shiftwood trees, being many times larger than the average tree, produce an enormous amount of oxygen. Shiftwoods can hold their oxygen, like you and me holding our breath, and release it to produce a breeze, or gust of wind. One or two trees may not cause much of a ruckus, but a large group of shiftwoods orchestrating their ability together can create damaging windstorms. I've heard shiftwood trees have blown horses, wagons, drivers, riders, and all their contents off of trails because they didn't like what they were doing, such as cutting down other trees who weren't ready to be cut down."

"I don't understand," Simon interjected. "How can a breeze make an explosion?"

"It wasn't the act of breathing, per se, which caused the explosion," Sonica explained. "It was the act of holding all the oxygen it could and releasing it all at once when struck with the fire arrow. The shiftwood shared this with me when he was sure the sea silk was overtaking him."

Sonica's mood grew more dismal, so Simon changed the topic. "How do you come by arrows like that?"

"Wheelock cast spells on some of my arrows for such occasions." Sonica looked distant. "Under most circumstances his magic arrows are fun and exciting to use."

They walked in silence, amid their own thoughts for a while. Then Sonica glanced at Simon.

"You have not asked me about the blue quagmire," said Sonica.

"What do you mean?" asked Simon.

"The blue quagmire is a living thing as well, is it not?" she said didactically.

"Yeah...of course," said Simon. It seemed an obvious answer.

"Then why have you not asked me the reason I favored the life of the shiftwood tree over the sea silk?" She stopped walking, so Simon turned and faced her. The marmot was wrapped contently in Simon's arms. Sonica walked up to Simon and stroked the marmot.

This must be a trick question.

"I assumed you don't like blue quagmire because it eats trees and it's dangerous." He felt satisfied with his answer, but somehow knew she was going to find holes in it.

"Yes, trees, especially shiftwoods, have a special place in my heart, and for good reason, but that is not the reason I interjected," said Sonica petting the relaxing marmot. "Simon, it is imperative you understand and learn that *all* life has meaning and purpose. None are more important than others." She looked down at the marmot. "Why this marmot survived and the other perished was a matter of a few seconds. His brother stopped to free him from the sea silk, but in return he lost the few seconds he needed to be here with us, sleeping contently in the arms of a protector." Sonica looked into Simon's eyes. Her dedicated stare made Simon a little uneasy. "Nature has its way of dealing with its own problems. There is a natural cycle of life we should not disturb, especially for our own benefit and selfish reasons. However, there was something unnatural about that blue quagmire. It was full of hate and anger. It was consuming to destroy, instead of survival. When I sensed the blue quagmire's hatred and heard the cry from the shiftwood tree, I had to do something."

"So, what you're telling me is you would not have intervened if the sea silk was feeding for natural reasons, eating to survive?" asked Simon studying her reaction.

"Yes...correct," said Sonica defending her answer. "We may not like certain aspects of the circle of life, but it is important we respect it nonetheless. If the sea silk plants were only feeding, I would be just as wrong in saving the shiftwood tree as I would be taking away your dinner tonight," she said smirking and patting the food pack in her satchel. "But I knew there was a different reason, and it had to be stopped. Sea silk usually does not attack other plants unless it is desperate for food. It prefers birds and small critters. And it's a passive plant that usually grows slow. It doesn't live to eat; it eats to live.

"I think the blue quagmire was placed there for a reason and was manipulated so it would destroy the shiftwood trees." Sonica was talking more to herself as she sorted her thoughts.

"Why would anyone want to destroy trees?" asked Simon curiously.

"Not just any trees, but shiftwood. The shiftwood trees have as many enemies as they do friends." Sonica regained her focus and continued walking. "Once we arrive at Domic's Haven you will gain a better understanding."

They picked up their pace to catch up with the other two.

"Is manipulating a plant even possible?" Simon asked.

"Anything that eats and breaths can be manipulated, even without magic," said Sonica impassively. "The more simple a creature or being, the easier it is to manipulate."

"I thought we were going to have to turn around and come searching for you two," said Heaton sarcastically as Simon and Sonica approached them.

"What is Domic's Haven?" Simon asked.

"We do not refer to Domic as a what, but instead who," said Heaton glancing at Thianna and Sonica staring at him. "What? I figured Domic would take offense if he was referred to as a thing."

"That will be enough Heaton," Thianna kindly cut in. "I believe the less said the better. It will be Sonica's choice what and how much Simon learns about our mighty companion." Thianna smiled at Sonica, who rolled her eyes and giggled.

"This will be a perfect time to strengthen your patience, Simon," said Sonica, taking the lead. "We shall be there by nightfall, and greeted with a warm meal and sweet drinks. Then, and only then, shall we speak in detail of Domic's Haven." There was a bounce in her step as she took them into the heart of Shiftwood Forrest.

13

BEDLAM'S KEEPER

The skeleton unsheathed his sword and held it high. "Who goes there?" he grumbled. The raven flew from the windowsill and disappeared into the night, his cawing echoing in the outer darkness.

"Cursed crows!" the skeleton droned, waiving his sword at the open window. Then he turned to Jak. The skeleton's eyes bulged from their sockets having no eyelids to cover them. His body was nothing more than bones, with some rags of hide hanging over his ribs and backside. He wore a wooden helmet held together with a rusty metal brim. His sword was chipped and notched.

"Finally you wake," said the skeleton moving toward Jak. Having no lips, it was difficult to tell if the skeleton was smiling or frowning.

Jak stumbled back until he was up against the door. The skeleton came closer, his bulging, bloodshot eyes staring at Jak's. He seemed to be waiting. Then he grunted and shoved Jak to the ground with one arm.

"Out of my way boy!" The skeleton was much stronger than he looked, having no muscles to speak of.

The skeleton pounded the door with the handle of his sword.

"Open up," he said, "the boy has awakened."

After a few moments, someone on the other side of the door asked, "Who is it?"

"Who do you think?" growled the skeleton.

"How do I know you're not the boy?"

"Open this door before I rip off one of the boy's arms and beat you with it!" the skeleton yelled into the old, wooden door.

"Okay, okay…I'll get the key."

The skeleton looked down at Jak, who was still on the ground.

Jak was too nervous to move. It was a skeleton, like some Halloween gimmick, walking and talking and making threats to rip off his arm.

"How long have you been awake?" asked the skeleton.

"Um…I think…" said Jak, but he couldn't stop staring at the skeleton. This couldn't be happening. A talking raven, an animated skeleton…what next?

"Come on! Spit it out boy!"

"Maybe…twenty minutes…or so," said Jak in disbelief.

"I guess I was dead tired…huh?" said the skeleton, chortling. It was the weirdest thing Jak had ever seen. The skeleton laughed like a living being. His jaw moved up and down and he grabbed the area where his stomach would have been as though his laughing was going to cause his side to ache.

Rattling and clinking came from the other side of the door. The latch made a dull thud, and the door creaked open.

"Come on," said the skeleton, "you've gotta admit, that was pretty funny." Jak just continued to stare. Instantly, the skeleton's mood changed. "Alright," barked the skeleton, "let's go!" Jak leaped up and stepped out of the tower and into the hallway.

Two more skeletons, donned in ragged leather, were waiting for him. The smallest, and seemingly the oldest skeleton, had a hunched back and a few, crooked teeth. He was holding a ring of keys in one bony hand and a torch in the other. Next to him was a large skeleton. His bones were thick with bands of muscle still attached to parts of his arms. The older skeleton was dwarfed next to the larger one, who stood a foot taller than Jak. He carried a two-handed war hammer stained from previous uses.

The skeleton with the sword shoved Jak, shoulder first, into the wall of the narrow hallway. Hitting the hard, cold stone sent a sharp pain through his shoulder blade and up his neck.

"I don't have all night," barked the skeleton with the sword, "so move it!"

The hallway was dark and quickly turned into a narrow stairwell leading down the tower. The only source of light came from the torch the aged skeleton carried, leading them down the winding stairwell.

Upon reaching the bottom of the tower they followed a cold and damp corridor, which lead to another, and then another, until eventually they turned down another corridor, and of course another one. Jak quit counting corridors after ten.

Along the way they passed doors of varying shapes and sizes. Jak wondered what was on the other side of them. Were there other towers? Were they cells? Then he remembered the raven's mention of haunted chambers. What else, other than talking ravens and skeletons could be behind the vast number of doors?

From time to time they came upon an intersection of two, three, and even four or more corridors splitting off into more directions. The aged skeleton would pause, look back and forth down the dark paths, and then pick one to continue down. If the raven was right about wandering monsters and other unknowns lurking about, Jak was hoping the decrepit, old skeleton knew where he was going.

Behind him, the large skeleton asked the other in a deep, drawled out voice, "Do you think they will let us rip him apart?"

"Doubt it," said the one with the sword, "but maybe they'll let us torture him," and then he hit Jak's sore shoulder. Jak yelped in pain and dropped to the floor clutching his shoulder.

"You bastard!" Jak yelled.

"BASTARD?" the skeleton retorted as he raised his sword.

"I wouldn't do that if I were you," said the aged skeleton, his voice weak, but stern. "We don't know why we're bringing him to Bedlam's Keeper. He may have plans for this one."

"Well I'm not you, you old fool," snapped the skeleton still holding the sword in a ready-to-strike posture.

"You're right, you're not me," cautioned the hunched skeleton, "but if something happens to this boy it's not just your skin, it's all of ours on the line," and he gave the large skeleton a nod. In a swift and effortless motion the large skeleton snatched the sword away.

Looking behind him at the large skeleton holding the war hammer in one hand and the sword in the other, the now weaponless skeleton conceded with grumbles and grunts.

"We don't know what may become of this one," he gestured toward Jak with the torch. "That's a chance you can take on your own, but I haven't lasted as long as I have by letting any skeleton with a thick skull do as he pleases. Now help him up!"

The skeleton under scrutiny didn't take long to heed the warning. He reached down, grabbed Jak's arm, and pulled him up. Then he turned and put his bony hand out to the large skeleton. The aged one nodded and the large skeleton handed the other his sword.

Holding the torch high above his head, the aged one turned and continued leading the way. Jak pondered the words of the raven and the aged skeleton. He had something the overlord wanted or he wouldn't have been dragged to this hideous labyrinth and then kept alive. Someone must like him…or hate him.

As they passed one of the doors Jak heard something on the other side of it. He gazed at the large door, reinforced with steel trim and large steel bolts over dark red wood. There was something ominous about it. He had a feeling there was something just on the other side of the door, listening to them. Jak slowly walked to the door, reaching his hand out. Behind him, one of the skeletons grunted, but all three watched him. They, too, must have heard the same noise.

Jak touched the door near the handle. The wood was warm, but the steel was cold. "Hello?" Jak managed in a raspy voice. "Is there someone in there?"

He couldn't be sure, but it sounded like someone, or something, was rubbing against the other side of the door. After a few moments Jak lost interest; whoever it was wasn't going to answer. He turned around to leave when a shaken voice on the other side cried out, "Let me out of here! Please let me out of here!" The person sounded desperate.

Jak turned back around. The door was lightly rattling; whoever was on the other side was testing to see if the door had been unlocked.

"Who are you?" Jak asked trying to sound less afraid then he was.

"Please…I promise not to do it anymore," the being on the other side said, almost whining. "You can trust me now…I PROMISE!" The whining voice twisted into a horrible shriek.

"We better keep moving fleshling," said the aged skeleton, looking at the rattling door.

"Fleshling?" the voice said curiously. The rattling stopped.

"We know not the many things that dwell in these rooms, hence we stay close to our quarters and keep moving in groups," explained the aged skeleton.

Jak looked back at the aged one. "You're not curious who's in there?" Jak asked. He was unnerved, yet thrilled.

"Yes fleshling," said the voice behind the door, "open the door and see for yourself my incredible wonder. I can offer you much in return." The voice was unnaturally calm and enticing. It made Jak uneasy.

"Doors in these halls that are locked are locked for a reason, fleshling," said the skeleton with the sword. "Under other circumstances I would invite you to open it so I could see you whimper and cry before being dragged into the darkness and eaten alive, but unfortunately we have orders."

"NO FLESHLING! Come here and see the wonders I can offer you," said the maddening voice. "I will free you from this wretched place! I promise! I won't do it again! You can trust me!" There was a hint of sadness mixed with its madness. "I PROMISE!" the voice screeched, and the door shook and convulsed as the unknown on the other side tried freeing itself.

Jak backed away from the door and the four hastened down the corridor. The violent screams followed them. "COME BACK FLESHLING! COME BACK! I PROMISED!" The door kept rattling. Jak hoped the lock on that door would hold.

Bedlam's dark halls were riddled with doors and rooms of various sizes, shapes, and structures. There was no logical order to the place. Some corridors had no doors in them at all, and others had too many clumped in an area.

One corridor was long, straight and seemingly endless, and not one door. Another corridor twisted around like a worm, and the doors were crooked and either too small for a human, or extremely wide. One door was so wide it was wider than the hallway; there was no way it could have opened all the way.

Two corridors came to dead ends.

One of them was well lit. Its floor was level, and the stone walls were smooth and adorned with ornate carvings of creatures and scenery. The dead end came abruptly as they turned a corner. There was nowhere else to go, but back. Designed by the hands of a prankster, it seemed.

The other dead end corridor was more like a cavern dug into the mountain. Choppy and uneven, jagged rock jutted out from its walls, the ceiling hung low, and many rooms were started, but ended up mere holes chiseled into the walls. It appeared whoever was working on this corridor lost interest and abandoned it long ago, like many of the corridors in Bedlam. The strangest thing was the corridor went on and on for a long way. A lot of effort was put into a path leading nowhere with uninhabited, useless holes in its walls.

Throughout Bedlam, Jak found that the rooms they could see into were even stranger than the corridors. Many of the rooms were blank; no sign of life ever setting foot inside. Other rooms had signs of life from some time ago, like moldy food, moth eaten clothes on the floor, pieces of furniture, or random stuff thrown in and scattered about.

Some rooms were carefully designed and well furnished, like bedrooms, parlors, kitchens, and storage rooms. Many of these rooms were either enveloped in thick dust, which had been undisturbed for a very long time, or ransacked and left in disarray.

The rooms Jak found the most disturbing were the ones with signs of life, or at least signs of being used. Several bedrooms had torches on the walls, beds unmade, recently eaten food on tables, and a few with hushed voices around dark corners.

One study had stacks upon stacks of books leaning to one side or the other on the floor, on tables, and on chairs. Candles burned, without a flicker, on sconces. The candles left thick trails of wax running down the walls, onto the books, and covering much of the floor. The thing that caught Jak's attention was a faint, rhythmic swishing sound.

Leaning into the room for a better look Jak couldn't believe what he saw. On the only table with no stacks of books and the only empty chair in the room pulled up to it, sat a mound of wax that draped over several of the table's edges and onto the floor. The wax mound towered over the table, and at its summit perched a candlestick with a single, unwavering flame.

A large opened book rested upon the table, its pages slowly turned in a rhythmic swish. No one was in the room. Jak took one step onto the wax-covered floor, and the pages stopped turning. The candle on the mound flickered. Jak quickly backed out and hurried along his escorts. Behind them came a faint, rhythmic swishing sound.

Halfway down one of the many dark and dingy corridors there came a sliver of light through a cracked open doorway. From the other side of the doorway came the faint sound of a child humming; it echoed up and down the corridor. The other rooms down this corridor were abandoned, their contents all broken and smashed.

The aged skeleton insisted they take this corridor to avoid the nest of giant spiders he claimed was down the corridor they recently avoided.

"She sounds pleasant," he said listening to the soft, melodic hum. No one else agreed. Then he snuffed out the torch. "Just in case, be quiet."

The stench of mold, mildew, and rotting meat became more pungent the closer they got to the door.

As they snuck passed the door, Jak could see part of the room. It was a bedroom decorated in rich wood, silver, and rubies. The room was pleasingly beautiful. The warm glow came from a hearth.

Then, the humming stopped.

"What is that?" A little girl's voice asked curiously.

"What are you referring to?" The deep, guttural voice gave Jak goose bumps.

"That smell...it's familiar," said Little Girl politely.

"Maybe our visitor has arrived," said Deep-Guttural.

"No...no...it's...I know," said Little Girl excitedly. "Fresh blood!" The last two words were in a restrained hush.

"Are you sure?" asked Deep-Guttural.

Little Girl snapped and went on a rage. "Are you QUESTIONING ME?" she shrieked, loud smashing and crashing followed. "GO CHECK!"

Before Jak and the three skeletons reached the end of the hall, for they started moving right after they heard Deep-Guttural speak the first time, Jak looked back. A large, horned creature with elongated claws darkened the doorway right before Jak turned the corner.

After a few more twists and turns the hunched skeleton stopped unexpectedly. The skeleton behind him walked into him, sending his sword through the old one's rib cage.

"Hey, watch it!" exclaimed the aged one, pushing the blade back through his dried bones.

"What is it?" asked the skeleton with the sword.

"Something is coming this way," the aged one explained holding the torch a little higher. "By the sound of it, it may be a ghoul."

"We can take it," said the sword holder.

"No, not now," said the aged one. "We can't take any chances with the human."

They seemed eager to fight, all three of them. The big, silent one stood slapping the large war hammer in his palm with an unsettling eagerness.

"Come on," drawled the large one. "Let us have us some fun."

Jak peered past the torchlight and down the shadowy corridor. Approaching in the distance was a creature with long, skinny arms stretching out the width of the corridor. It moved unevenly, unbalanced; its scrawny legs didn't seem capable of holding up the creature's weight for very long. It held itself up with the help of its two elongated arms, pushing its weight from wall to wall, moving forward slowly but steadily, toward them.

Other than creepy looking, the creature looked rather frail. "You guys are scared of that stringy thing?" Jak mocked. "What are you worried about?"

"You," replied the aged skeleton. "Despite their appearance, ghouls have remarkable strength. And they have a ceaseless craving for flesh. One whiff of your scent fleshling, and he will stop at noth'n to get to you and then eat you alive."

"It's not our hides we're worried about, greasy one," snapped the one with the sword.

"I'm the only one here with a hide, bone head," Jak snapped back. His face felt hot. He was suddenly more aware of having a scent now than he ever had.

"All the more reason to worry about it then, ain't it?" the skeleton retorted, jabbing the sword toward Jak.

"Tempting, but let's go," ordered the hunched one.

And with that they turned and went back the way they came until they reached another intersection. The aged one scratched his skull with a bony finger looking to the left and right. Choosing to go right for no apparent reason, the hunched skeleton quickened his pace and after a few more twists and turns down more dark corridors they finally came to one that was much wider than any they had been down. It was about thirty feet wide and well lit with torches on either side.

They passed several large ballrooms, long forgotten in time, dust and cobwebs covered their once well-kept and extravagant contents. They were adorned for a ball that never took place.

Jak and his undead escorts soon passed a dining room, fully lit. The dining room sparkled from all the silver plates, gold goblets, silverware, gold candlesticks, and more. There was no food on the table, but Jak could smell something cooking, something good.

The skeletons brought Jak to a set of doors on the other side and two doors down from the large dining room. The delicious scent of roasted turkey followed them down the hall. Jak's mouth watered and his stomach grumbled.

The aged skeleton knocked on the double doors adorned with beautiful carvings. A latch on the other side clicked and one of the doors creaked open. Standing in the doorway was a beautiful girl. Jak couldn't take his eyes off her. Her long, dark hair was shiny as silk and ran the length of her back. Her cheekbones came to a narrow point to her lips. Her skin was dark, a bluish-gray, and had a sheen from being well kept. But her most beautiful quality was her eyes. Jak had seen none like them before. They were silver with blue pupils, and they were looking back at him. Her poise was perfect. Her hand remained resting on the door; her delicate fingers lightly caressing the old wood.

"They've been expecting you," she said, still looking at Jak. Her voice equaled her beauty in tone and spirit. Jak found her intoxicating.

"We were ordered to bring the boy as soon as he awoke," the aged skeleton replied.

"Then our boy is either very sleepy, or his escorts almost got lost," she said politely, still gazing at Jak. "Either way I guess it doesn't matter," she said playfully. "The three of you are to remain here while I bring our boy in with me," she said as her lips curved into an enticing smile. Jak smiled back at her, dumbfounded. "Thank you gentlemen," she said looking their way for the first time. If skeletons could blush, all three of them would have rosy cheeks. They bumbled about for a few moments before settling alongside the wall near the double doors.

She offered Jak one of her hands and said, "My name is Lonique."

"I'm Jak," he said. Taking her hand he trembled. Excitement, fear, confusion, all were adequate reasons he trembled, but he told himself it was from her remarkably soft, smooth touch.

"I know," she said smiling. "Come with me Jak."

He loved hearing his name from her lips. She led him into the room and closed the door behind them.

Like the dining room, this room was lit with many candles and adorned with gold and silver. It was a study, no doubt, with its shelves full of books from floor to ceiling. A hearty fire crackled in the grand fireplace, its mantle made of dark mahogany trimmed with more silver and gold.

There was so much gold and silver in the large study that it was easier to pick out things not made from, or covered in gold and silver. The picture frames were made of gold, and the furniture was trimmed in gold and silver. The bookshelves contained various golden statuettes. Even the bookshelves, every one of them, had silver and gold embedded in the wood. These items gleamed and shone between dancing shadows from the flickering flames.

There were five males, three men and two boys, sitting in extravagant high-back chairs along the wall opposite the fireplace. They all wore black robes with no distinguishing features.

Standing still in a perfect line on the opposite end of the room, were three women and two girls. They had dark hair and skin, sharing the same breath-taking beauty as Lonique. However, unlike Lonique, each of the five females was armed with a large dagger strapped to her hip and wore a thin circlet made of silver and adorned with a green jewel upon her forehead. To their left was a set of large double doors made of mahogany and adorned with gold, silver, and rubies.

Quietly and gently Lonique escorted Jak to the middle of the room where a Victorian style sofa was facing the five males. The sofa cushions were embroidered in gold. Lonique didn't sit, but instead stood beside Jak as he looked around the room.

The five males were staring at him, studying him, but spoke not a word. Afraid to look into their judging eyes, Jak stole glances of them as he surveyed the room.

The two boys were perhaps around his age. They were looking at him suspiciously. It was difficult to gauge their ages, because although they possessed the distinct features one normally does as a youth, their faces were distorted. It seemed as though their faces had been broken and then pieced back together.

He didn't dare stare, but the younger of the two boys had two different eyes. One eye was blue and one was almost orange. The blue eye seemed to 'fit' his face, but the orange one was larger and seemed out of place. A large scar ran down one side of his nose and below the large, orange eye. He looked unsure of himself when Jak looked at him.

The other boy's face had more broken pieces fused together, but not all the pieces of his face were the same. Some parts looked older and other pieces of his face were different colors and tones. Although white was the dominant color of the boy's face, there were brown and gray patches of skin, and a patch that looked like it was decaying. This boy did not appreciate Jak looking at him. His glare made Jak quickly turn away.

The three men wore masks. The masks were strange; they must have been custom made because the only reason Jak knew they were masks was because the colors and texture of their masks were distinctly different than their necks. They didn't look like real flesh. They looked metallic. One of them, the man in the center of the five, only had three quarters of his face covered leaving his chin and the lower part of his cheek exposed. The masks fit well, moving with each contortion of their faces as they looked at Jak in discussed, curiosity, and even concern.

Not a word was spoken until Jak looked at the five female sentries. The largest male, sitting in the fifth chair, spoke.

"Sit down," he said sternly. His large voice fit his size well.

Jak recoiled and quickly sat on the sofa. Lonique walked around and stood behind Jak. They both faced the five males. The fireplace behind Jak cast Lonique's slinky shadow across the floor. The five males continued to glare at him.

Usually Jak didn't care if strangers watched him, in fact he often drew attention to himself because the attention was almost addicting. But Jak was uncomfortable being gazed at by these strangers. He diverted his eyes away from them, trying hard to conceal his emotions, concerned and afraid.

He had to fight the urge to jump up and run out the door. It would be a feeble attempt to run anyway, because he was outnumbered eleven to one. Then there were the three skeletons standing guard in the hall, and if he somehow made it passed them he wouldn't have the foggiest clue how to get out of this labyrinth-castle, this Bedlam. He was probably safer in the room with these weirdoes...at least he was hoping.

The minutes slowly passed. Jak had no idea what time it was because there was no clock in the room. After sitting idly on the sofa for what felt like the longest ten or fifteen minutes of his life, Jak decided to break the silence. The suspense was wreaking havoc on his stomach.

"Can anyone tell me why I'm here?" Jak asked as politely as he could.

Getting no reply from the five males, Jak turned around to ask Lonique. Before he could repeat his question, Large Voice spoke again, "Face forward," he demanded. The man's voice resonated. "Do not look at the sentries! And you will not speak unless spoken to."

Jak faced forward. Orange Eye looked as nervous as Jak felt.

"Do I make myself clear?" said Large Voice spitefully, his glare matching his tone.

Jak bit his tongue when his face got hot. It took all he had to fight the urge to whoop and holler at this primitive scumbag. Jak wanted to yell, "*Who do you think you are? Do you have any idea who I am? My family is rich and powerful! My father's gun club's lounge is fancier than this place. They are going to kick your butt for pulling this stunt, you freak of nature!*"

However, due to recent puzzling events, he decided it was best to sit tight.

"Yesss," Jak hissed, "perfectly."

Moments later a loud metal-on-metal clank from the other side of the enormous double doors echoed in the study and down the corridors. The doors slowly parted; they were at least eighteen inches thick. They were barely open when, on their own accord, they stopped, leaving just enough space for a person.

Jak was curious how they opened since there had been no sign of electricity in this place, anywhere. His curiosity was quickly extinguished when he saw the same two creatures, the ones the raven referred to as soul seers, accompany a prestigious, well-groomed man, decked in robes fit for royalty. Seeing the soul seers again made Jak nauseous.

In his right hand the prestigious man held a tall, thin scepter about eight feet tall. It tapped on the floor with every other step he took. Atop the scepter was a crystal orb the size of a man's fist, which rested in the jaws of a silver and gold dragon's head. White smoke whirled about in the orb. Something else was also moving within the orb, but Jak didn't take the time to study it. He kept his eyes on the soul seers who seemed pleased to see him again.

The doors gradually closed on their own, but before the doors rumbled shut, Jak caught a glimpse of the dimly lit room. Strange and unconventional equipment hung from the walls around tables equipped with leather straps. The room was forbidding.

As the three newcomers approached, Large Voice stood. "Severn! What are *they* doing here?" he barked impatiently, gesturing to the soul seers, "and why have you called us together only to leave us waiting for so long?"

Severn approached Jak and Lonique without saying a word, leaving Large Voice standing and waiting for an answer.

"Sit down," said Severn in a firm and collective tone.

Large Voice hesitated. It appeared he wanted to say more, but took his seat.

Maintaining his rigid composure, Severn turned and looked down at Jak.

"Is this the one?" he asked as if he were picking out new furniture. He was looking over Jak with little interest.

Severn looked nothing like the other males in the room. His facial features were distinguished. Large collars billowed up from his robes accenting his handsome face. His stance was stern and controlled. Every move was conducted and specific. While the other five seemed to be dressed to bring little attention their way, Severn went out of his way to accent his features with fine linen and dazzling jewelry as if to say, "Here I am!" Upon Severn's head was a diadem, much like the circlets the lady sentinels wore only wider and garnished with large emeralds. And according to the raven, the scepter Severn held was the Scepter of Zalaruz, a gift from the overlord to help keep order, whatever that meant.

One of the soul seers reluctantly stepped toward the man. The two dark and mysterious beings looked out of place with their ripped and tattered robes stained in what could only be blood.

"Yes, your greatness, he is the one," the soul seer replied, its voice sounded old and parched.

Severn didn't seem impressed.

"We promise you," assured the other soul seer, "what we saw we have not seen or witnessed for many years." After speaking he reached up and touched his throat. A piece of his decayed hand was missing, revealing the bones and dead ligaments moving as the soul seer massaged his throat. Jak remembered grabbing that hand and getting a chunk of rotten flesh.

"Do you see it now?" inquired Severn as he slowly walked around behind Jak, his movement fluid and precise. The Scepter of Zalaruz in his hand loomed above them all.

Both soul seers skulked closer to Jak and gazed upon him. Under their hoods their dull gray eyes became more silver the longer they stood in front of him.

"Yesss," one slowly answered.

"Yess, indeed," the other said in a festering excitement. He opened his mouth revealing jagged, sharp teeth. Heavy drool slid from the sides of his mouth and down his chin forming shiny strings stretched out like fangs. The soul seer's silver eyes burst into a bright glow, and he lunged at Jak.

Jak only had time to put his arm up and draw back into the sofa. He braced for an attack, which never came. Before Jak's arm was even high enough to protect his face he heard a crack and then a bolt of electricity struck the attacking soul seer, pushing him back near the sentries.

Jak glanced back. A current of electricity coming from the orb held down the soul seer. The creature's intense shrieks and screams were unnerving. The other soul seer backed up. His eyes quickly lost their silver glow and turned gray.

"Spare him...I beg you," pleaded the soul seer.

The electrical current suddenly disappeared, leaving the injured soul seer writhing in pain.

"Now you may go feed...the both of you," said Severn cordially as if nothing happened. He walked around from behind Jak and over to the writhing soul seer. "And if this ever happens again, it will be death by fire. Is this clear?" he asked in a cold, calm tone.

"Yes, your greatness," and they both quickly left the room through the same door Jak had come.

After the soul seers were gone, Severn focused his attention on Jak once again. He stood still, studying him. His expression changed from one moment to the next, like he was contemplating his next move with Jak. He was in a near meditative state for several minutes. In that time Jak stole several glances of the five males. They were watching Severn intensely.

When he finally broke out of his trance, Severn came closer to Jak.

"I am Severn Fowl, Bedlam's Keeper," he said sounding like a parent setting a defiant child straight. "These are the five warlocks who carry out my orders," he said gesturing to the five males who were still seated. "They answer to no one, but me."

Severn looked at Lonique and then to his left shoulder. Lonique walked over and stood on his left side. Lonique looked younger than the five women standing at attention.

"Do you like what you see?" Severn gestured all around. "Because there is so, so much more," he boasted.

Jak couldn't believe someone was actually trying to impress him, a Jakobsin, with wealth. All his life Jak had been served from a silver platter, literally. The Jakobsins were so rich and powerful there wasn't a political officer in the world who wouldn't cancel last-minute plans if a Jakobsin called. Three of the top ten wealthiest people in the world were Jakobsins.

"Look, this is nice and all," said Jak trying hard to cover up his fear, his voice scratchy from lack of drink, "but my father's gun club is fancier than this place."

"Gun club?" Severn repeated the foreign words to himself. "How unusual…. How interesting."

Severn focused on something far away, listening to a subtle noise, then asked, "What motivates you boy?"

"Getting back home," said Jak.

He was hoping Severn didn't detect his annoyance, but he was annoyed with this dialogue. Jak was used to pompous airheads who let their wealth do the talking. Not only was he used to them, he knew how to deal with them.

Jak decided he already hated Severn. He reminded Jak of his uncle, but instead of going for the Fortune 500 CEO look, Severn proudly displayed the King Henry VIII look. However, the electrical bolt the orb produced was intimidating. He didn't want to be at the end of it. Even more than intimidating...it was fascinating. Jak wanted to know more. How could he acquire such power?

"Do you know why you are here?" asked Severn. His jet-black goatee was cut to perfection, emphasizing his jawbone when he spoke.

"No," said Jak.

"Good," said Severn. "Then this will be all the more interesting."

"*What* will be more interesting?" asked Large Voice, remaining in his chair this time.

"He is to be placed in the Maze of Mayhem with the others," Severn answered as if he didn't believe it himself. "If he survives...well, we'll let him cross that bridge if he gets there."

"Survives!" Jak blurted. "What do you mean, survives?"

Severn looked at Orange Eye. The young warlock about Jak's age held his posture high.

"The Maze of Mayhem will test your skills, wits, and survival instincts," said Orange Eye as if he'd rehearsed the lines. "Pass and you receive the ultimate prize. Failure means one thing...death!" The young warlock's grin was broken and scarred.

"You can't do this! Do you know who I am? I'm Jak Jakobsin! My family is powerful!" Jak shouted at the ugly grin. Jak wanted to slap the grin off of Orange Eye's face. "When they find out..."

"Silence!" Severn jabbed the bottom of the staff to the floor and ripples of electricity pulsed from the orb, striking the walls around them. "No matter who your family is, or was, and no matter where you are from makes no difference to me, Jak! Your family is far from here, boy. Your only option now is to obey or die!" Severn glared at Jak. "Which one you choose makes no difference to me."

Severn's glare challenged Jak to resist or rebel. Jak's face was hot from anger, but he had no intentions of giving this dim-witted charlatan the satisfaction.

Severn leaned in and spoke something to Lonique that Jak couldn't hear. Then he turned and started walking toward a table with food and drink.

"Now leave us!" Severn ordered, waiving his hand in the air like he was swatting a fly away. "We have much to discuss."

Jak hesitated, unsure if this meant he should get up. Then Lonique gestured to the door. Jak rose and followed her. He was more than happy to leave this room and the company in it.

"See that he gets a torch," Severn called out as they reached the door. "He'll need it to get back to his tower, whence he came," he said, immensely satisfied.

Lonique escorted him out into the corridor. Jak was relieved to get away from Severn and the other maniacs.

Lonique took a torch from its sconce and handed it to Jak.

"You'll need this to find your way back," said Lonique.

"What do you mean?" asked Jak. "These bone heads know their way back," he said gesturing to the three skeletons.

"Unfortunately, you have to find the way back by yourself," said Lonique, her silver eyes studying him. The skeletons chuckled and nudged one another.

"What? There's no way!" cried Jak.

"I am sorry," said Lonique quietly and cautiously, "but those were the orders Bedlam's Keeper gave me."

"Oh, so that's what he whispered to you?" said Jak irritably. He really did hate Severn.

"Good luck." Her eyes hid any emotions she had. "You will be summoned when it is time to compete in the Maze of Mayhem."

She quickly slipped back into the room leaving Jak standing in the wide hallway with the three undead.

"Yeah, good luck," said the skeleton with the sword, and all three of them burst into laughing fits.

Jak turned and started walking in the direction they had come, leaving behind the obnoxious laughter of the undead. He stopped when he reached the first unlit corridor. The blackness choked the light from the torch. Getting back to the tower was going to be difficult. He didn't even want to think about the Maze of Mayhem.

14

DOMIC'S HAVEN

They traveled all morning and afternoon with a quickened pace. Simon liked it more when Thianna and Heaton had the lead because they moved in a steady, but manageable pace. When Sonica took the lead it seemed like they were training for an Olympic speed-walking event. Thianna reminded Sonica several times they needed to stop and rest. She was the only one who noticed Simon was growing tired. He wasn't used to walking so much.

The forest's floor was no longer flat. It rolled up and down like frozen waves in an ocean. And the shiftwood trees were larger with each passing mile, now averaging four hundred fifty feet high.

Simon didn't tire of admiring the trees. Larger than life, there was nothing frail about the trees, including their branches reaching high into the heavens, some intricately entwined with neighboring tree branches. Their leaves were as big as the hood of a car, but as light as a kite.

The marmot was also enjoying the scenery in the comfort of Simon's arms. He looked up and down each tree they passed, his whiskers twitching excitedly. Thianna and Sonica both offered to carry him, but the marmot refused to be held by anyone else.

Unfortunately, nobody's mood matched that of the scenery. Sonica wanted to reach Domic's Haven before nightfall, so she pushed the group along. Even Thianna and Heaton struggled to keep up with her by late afternoon. As the day waned so did everyone's energy and, consequently, their patience with one another.

There was grumbling about the heat, lack of water, the marmot (for sleeping and having to be carried), the lack of breaks, and everything else.

"Are we even doing the right thing, or are we just wasting our time?" said Heaton after an hour of no one talking.

"We'll get there! Just keep moving," said Sonica, clearly irritated with his comment.

"That's not what I'm talking about," Heaton grumbled.

"What are you talking about?" Thianna was already a little defensive.

"This whole guardian...thing," said Heaton. He seemed to be watching his words.

"Now is not the time."

"Yeah, it's never the time," said Heaton on edge, "but I'm pointing out the obvious! The guardians got us into this mess to begin with!"

"Heaton…" said Thianna sternly.

"What Thianna? Are you going to deny Magnanthia is in hardship? Are you going to pretend Peter and the other guardians didn't bring turmoil to our land, to our kingdom?"

"Heaton!" Thianna was angry.

"Everyone hates the guardians! Even the king hates the guardians and wants the last few dead!"

"Heaton! Enough!" Sonica turned and stomped up to Heaton. "What gives you the right to say such things?"

"Hey, watch it!" Heaton backed away and instinctively placed his hand on the hilt of his sword. "I have every right! It's my hide too!"

Sonica looked at Heaton's hand on the hilt.

"What are you going to do, attack me?" Sonica barked, not showing any sign of backing down.

"Heaton…easy," said Thianna calmly.

"No, I wasn't," said Heaton raising his hands, "it's a reaction."

The four stood glancing at one another. Everyone had something to say, but no one wanted to say it.

"Is it true?" asked Simon, the pit of his stomach twisting. "Everyone hates the guardians?" Is the guardian these three work for an awful person?

Heaton looked away from Simon. Sonica shook her head, but didn't say anything. Thianna sighed.

"No, it's not true," said Thianna glaring at Heaton who was avoiding eye contact. "Not *everyone* hates the guardians." She took a deep breath and slowly let it out. "But there are many who fear the guardians and hate what *some* of them did."

"What did they do?" asked Simon, soft spoken.

Thianna looked at Heaton disgustedly, and then to Sonica and shook her head.

"I'm sorry, Simon...we can't...now is not the time," said Thianna sympathetically. "I can see you're hurt and bothered by this, and you have every right, but we will not do justice to the cause if we try explaining it to you now."

Thianna slowly walked up to Simon. He had the urge to push her away and run from them, but he stood still as she touched his arm.

"I really am sorry," she said. "Please know there is much, much more to the story than what Heaton tells."

"Including those who still believe in the guardians," Sonica added, touching Simon's other arm.

Heaton and Simon exchanged looks.

As dusk approached, and pushed the daylight farther away, the shiftwood trees were over five hundred fifty feet tall. Two houses, side by side, could fit in the trees' trunks. Thianna lit a torch so they could see the ground better and avoid running into bark and branches. Simon marveled at the three-foot thick bark. A car could park under large pieces. Although smaller trees grew sporadically among the larger ones, the vegetation was thinning out.

"Cover," said Sonica turning around and dropping to her knee. She hid her head behind her cloak.

A series of cracks and snaps bit into the quiet evening. Simon looked around, but couldn't see anything. It sounded very close when a hand clenched his shirt and pulled him down. Heaton held up his shield as a tree-sized branch crashed to the ground twenty paces in front of them and shook the ground. An explosion of dirt, foliage, and splinters flew about, and clinked off of Heaton's shield.

"What part of 'cover' did you not understand?" Heaton stood and dusted himself off.

"What do you mean?" asked Simon.

"Sonica *said* 'cover' and then *took* cover. Pretty self-explanatory," said Heaton.

"How was I supposed to know 'cover' meant 'take cover from a falling branch the size of a tree, but stay where you are so it doesn't land on you'?"

"You shouldn't need to know," said Heaton, disappointed, "just trust us."

Simon didn't say anymore. He let it go. But ever since, he was more aware of the occasional crackling and snapping in the distance.

Dusk fell to the night. The air was unusually calm and the forest quiet. Simon's legs were burning and his feet sore with multiple blisters. He sat down on a moss-covered branch the size of a log and placed the marmot on his lap, who was frightened for a moment until he realized Simon wasn't trying to get rid of him.

"Sonica, how much farther is it?" Simon asked.

She opened her mouth to answer, but Simon put up a finger.

"AH! Don't say we're close."

"Does it matter?" Heaton cut off Sonica before she could speak. "We can still travel for a few more hours before we need to stop for the night."

"Look, I'm so tired I would be happy sleeping on this log right now," said Simon patting the fallen branch.

"You must be joking," said Heaton standing at the limit of the party's torchlight and leaning into the darkness in an attempt to keep the party moving.

"Does it look like I'm joking?" asked Simon.

"Unfortunately...no," said Heaton sarcastically. "You apparently have much to learn."

"What's that supposed to mean?" said Simon. He was fresh out of patience.

"It means you are a sloth and have nothing to offer, other than the fact you wear a Ring of Affinity!" Heaton shot back.

"I don't even know what you're talking about! Much to learn about what? Walking through a forest? Fighting off wild plants?" Simon's voice grew louder along with his anger. "What, Heaton? What do I need to learn? Huh? Tell me! I'm sure there are plenty of things *you* need to learn!"

"You want to know?" Heaton yelled. "I will tell you what you need to learn..."

"That's enough!" commanded Thianna stepping between Simon and Heaton, holding the torch high above her head so she could see both of them. "Heaton! You are stepping way beyond your boundaries! You will wait to express any concerns you may have until we are all together. We all have something to contribute to Simon's questions," Thianna turned to Simon, "which will be answered at the appropriate time as promised." Turning to Sonica, Thianna asked in a calmer tone, "How much farther *do* we have?"

Sonica went to the nearest shiftwood tree just beyond the torch's warm glow and knelt on one knee before it. Placing her hands upon one of the massive roots she spoke just above a whisper.

"It is I, Sonica Wintergreen, akin to Necodemus Wintergreen, seeking a domicile in Domic's Haven. May your spirit lighten our way to your heart. Reveal yourself to family unless hindered by foe."

In the darkness above the leaves rustled, and the still air began to stir. Leaves rolled and danced on the ground as the breeze gained strength, until the foliage was blowing by them.

The marmot took refuge under Simon's arm.

Heaton placed his hand upon his sword's hilt, but Thianna shook her head. He slowly let his hand down.

Sonica remained on her knee with both hands holding firm to the shiftwood tree's root. Her long, red hair fluttered in the breeze like a banner. The flames on the torch wavered and flickered. With a final puff of wind, and a heavy scent of spring rain, the torch went out, leaving them in silent darkness.

In the distance a large orb of brilliant light, like a chandelier, slowly descended from a shiftwood tree's branch. Rays of sea green and sky blue radiated from the orb, like light passing through moving water.

Sonica stood. "We are very, very close." She smiled triumphantly.

Simon was ashamed for acting like a buffoon and complaining.

As if she had read his thoughts, Sonica walked over to Simon. "After a long journey, home is *always* close, just within our reach, in our hearts. That is what drives us to return," she said placing a hand over Simon's heart. Her eyes twinkled with delight, and they shared a smile.

When they made it over to the orb, they all gazed up at it, studying it with eager fascination. It hung by no means the eye could see. The light hovered at least twenty-five feet above them. The nearest branch was more than thirty feet above the light.

"Is that what I think it is?" asked Thianna.

The orb was twenty feet in diameter and lit up the night like a star under the forest's thick canopy.

"Yes," said Sonica almost giggling.

"What?" Simon and Heaton both asked. "What is it?"

"A light spell," Thianna muttered.

"I thought that was a basic spell," said Heaton to Thianna. "You *can* cast one?"

Still gazing up at the majestic light Thianna said, "Of course I can...but not of that magnitude. The amount of energy it would take to suspend that amount of light for as long as it has been...cast."

The last word dropped from Thianna's lips from realization. She looked around as if expecting to see someone.

"Sonica," said Thianna, mystified by her discovery, "Did Domic cast this?"

"Yes he did," said Sonica. She couldn't smile any wider without her lips touching her ears.

"Is that Domic?" Thianna asked looking over toward the tree the orb of light came from. Simon and Heaton followed her gaze.

"No," Sonica said with a chuckle. "He has only begun to light our way. See?"

Three more orbs, identical to the one above them, hovered beneath three other shiftwood trees leading deeper into the forest.

"He is showing us the way," said Sonica as a fourth orb appeared beneath another tree. "All we have to do now is follow." Sonica walked past them toward the next orb.

As they reached the next orb, some fifty yards away, the orb behind them burst into thousands of tiny particles like diamond dust, dissipating before reaching the forest's floor.

All four of them oohed and aahed.

The display was better than any fireworks Simon had ever seen, and quieter too, no louder than a puff of air. Simon wondered if the others had ever seen fireworks. He was going to ask, but was too tired to explain if they hadn't.

A fifth orb appeared further down than the others, extending their trail of lights. They found that for each disappearing orb another one appeared further down the trail. Simon enjoyed watching each orb behind them burst into the sparkling particles and then dissipate. It was apparent he wasn't the only one. The other three stopped and watched too. It was a sight to behold, each and every time.

"Domic's Haven…is that where your family lives? Is it your home?" Simon asked Sonica, thinking of when she referred to herself as family when calling for guidance.

"No, my family does not live there," she said a little forlorn at the mention of her family. "And yes, Domic's Haven is a special part of home…a part I do not see often."

Her mood was dampened a bit, thinking of her own family.

"I'm sorry I asked," said Simon. "I can tell you're bothered by it. I miss my family too."

"No…I mean, yes! I do miss my family, but take no offense in asking me, please. It's important you are comfortable with me, and get to know me." Sonica tucked her hair behind her ear and looked at Simon.

Her gaze made him flush, and he glanced down at his feet.

"Oh, okay, thank you," he said. Grasping for something else to say he asked the next thing he thought of. "Who's Necodemus? Is he your father?"

"No, he's an ancestor." She looked at him and smiled. "But I cannot say more until the right time."

Simon smiled and shook his head.

They traveled over a mile under the guidance of the orbs. The trail was always illuminated before them and then quickly hidden under the night's black curtain, as the sparkling particles gave in to the heavy darkness behind them.

At last no more orbs appeared. As each orb disintegrated, their path was coming to an end.

When the party was halfway between the last two orbs, they exploded at the same time, their particles reaching out to one another like two massive webs. The tiny particles fell around and upon the party like twinkling snowflakes. And like snowflakes in spring, they quickly melted away leaving the party in complete darkness.

Thianna cast a light spell. The grapefruit-sized ball of light hovered two feet over her palm.

"That's so cute," said Heaton looking at the ball of light, when suddenly the area lit up like a sports arena, temporarily blinding them as their eyes adjusted.

A dozen of the massive orbs bloomed at the top of grand archways between pillars three stories high. Hundreds of smaller orbs soon appeared at the top of similar archways between the pillars, all connected together, forming a circle, or at least Simon assumed it was a circle, since much of it could not be seen behind the prodigious tree before them.

The shiftwood tree stood over six hundred feet high. The columns completely encircled the shiftwood several times. Some of the archways were a mere six feet high while others were seventy feet or more. Each archway had a glowing, glittering orb of light at its highest point.

"Whoa…. Impressive, Thianna," said Heaton with a half-cocked smile.

Thianna rolled her eyes as she canceled her light spell.

Sonica led the group, zigzagging through the pillars.

"What are these pillars made of," asked Heaton touching the one he was walking near.

"Shiftwood of course," Sonica replied, admiring them.

"They look and feel like marble," said Heaton.

Simon agreed with Heaton. The shiftwood they had seen so far looked like wood, smelled like wood, and felt like wood, and was warm to the touch. These grand archways were smooth, hard, cool, and had remarkable designs, symbols, and shapes embedded in them. Vines on many of the archways grew thick like tapestries.

"Why have we not seen shiftwoods that take on this appearance before?" Heaton asked looking up two stories above him to the glowing orb near the top of the archway.

Parting some of the vines so the others could pass through, Sonica gestured to the shiftwood's massive base before them. "Because you have never met Domic before," said Sonica.

Simon and Thianna stood on either side of Sonica craning their heads backward, sizing up the tree.

"So this is Domic's Haven," said Thianna more to herself than to anyone in particular.

Hundreds of orbs illuminated Domic in crystal green and blue rays of light, glimmering on and around his massive trunk, displaying his beauty and grandeur.

The trunk's girth was larger than any single building in Riverside. Studying the gargantuan shiftwood tree before him, Simon suddenly realized that all of the columns and arches, which resembled Roman architecture, all connected to branches high above them. They were part of the tree. Domic may be a shiftwood tree, but he reminded Simon of a Banyan tree he once saw on a visit to Florida. These formidable structures and designs were all offshoots of his branches. No ordinary Banyan tree, or any other tree for that matter, could do that.

At the base of the shiftwood's trunk was a makeshift porch with steps. The porch's structure appeared to be an extension of the tree.

Before they reached the steps, the orbs of light suddenly burst. The flickering sparks of light falling in the air.

The tiny, flickering, crystal green and blue particles fell to the ground like a winter's first snowfall. All four watched as the twinkling lights landed on their shoulders, arms, and outstretched hands. The marmot, staying close to Simon's feet, bobbed back and forth, trying to sniff the particles. Sonica was trying to catch as many as she could to see how many she could hold at once, but they all dissipated soon after landing. She admired the few she collected in her palms before they went out.

For the few seconds they were in the dark, Simon heard a distant, low rumble. He may have heard it earlier, but now it was more apparent, constant and strong.

"Does anyone else hear that?" asked Simon quietly.

"Yes," Thianna whispered. "We must be getting closer because it has been getting louder."

"That's the Great Falls of Reconciliation," said Sonica.

"Look!" Thianna pointed at a door materializing in the porch.

A light from inside shone through the four small panes in the door's window. And then, hanging next to the door, a single lantern sprang to life as if someone turned the porch light on. The lantern's flame was the only light outside. The rest of the world around them was once again lost in complete, utter darkness.

The four companions and the marmot walked up the steps and onto the porch. Simon thought it was an awfully small door in comparison to the size of the dwelling. The single door was smaller than the average door and slanted, oddly, a little to the left. Simon looked around, but there was only darkness beyond the little lantern's light.

To Simon's surprise Sonica knocked on the door. If this were her family's dwelling, why would she have to knock? Thianna and Heaton looked at each other. They seemed to be thinking the same thing.

A breeze came carrying with it a familiar scent. Simon breathed it in. It was refreshing and encouraging. It smelled of fresh lake water from Simon's home. Just as he was enjoying the familiar scent, the door opened. Simon, Heaton, and Thianna all stood behind Sonica, waiting in anticipation to see who opened the door.

"Domic," said Sonica restraining her tears. She was looking into the entryway lit by another lantern. She was focused on someone, or something, near the door. Simon, Heaton, and Thianna stared dumbfounded at an empty entryway.

"Come here young one," came a voice near the door. Simon blinked several times. Perhaps the lighting was playing tricks on him, but he saw no one.

Sonica lunged into the entryway, and holding her arms out, started crying with joy as she hugged the air.

"It has been many years," said the voice. The voice was calming, and each word spoken was direct, articulate, and rich in wisdom.

Then Simon saw him, or at least part of him. When Sonica lifted her head from what Simon could only guess was the voice's shoulder, he saw two hands, like puffs of smoke in a breeze, fall upon Sonica's cheeks. The ethereal hands vanished as quickly as they appeared.

"Please," said the humble voice, "come in. All of you."

They followed Sonica into the grand tree house. Behind Heaton the door closed and the outside lantern extinguished itself and disappeared.

"Welcome to my humble abode. My name is Domic, and this is your haven." Standing before them was an ethereal image of a tall man with a full beard.

His true form was never seen in its entirety, but appeared as translucent silver-blue particles, moving like dust in a breeze in the confines of what seemed to be his body. The rapid motion of these particles allowed Simon and the others to see this ethereal entity, to see Domic.

"We are forever grateful," said Heaton bowing his head down.

"Yes, thank you Domic," Thianna responded in kind.

Domic stepped over to Heaton and Thianna. He stood a foot taller than Heaton, who was the tallest in their party. Domic cupped Heaton and Thianna's chins in his celestial hands.

"You have no need to bow to me Master Heaton. I know your family history well. And a wonderful history it is."

He turned to Thianna. "And to you Lady Furrow, I also know your family history well, very well. You will always be welcome here." He smiled before bowing his head to Thianna and Heaton. "It is I who am honored to have you as guests in my abode."

Domic's ever-glowing body, like a small galaxy of stars, turned and moved toward Simon. It was like he was walking and gliding at the same time. Simon was glad Sonica was standing next to him. Domic was both humbling and intimidating.

Domic stood before Simon. His silver eyes studied him, reading him like an open book. Simon couldn't read Domic's expression. Was he concerned? Maybe Domic was disappointed. A faint smile escaped Domic's mouth.

"So this is Simon Whittaker...*the* Simon Whittaker," said Domic as if informing the room. "May I see your left hand?"

Simon held his hand up. The Ring of Affinity's eternal flame danced in its gem. Domic's silver eyes brightened. He marveled at the ring.

"May I?" Domic asked, extending his hand to Simon.

Simon looked at Sonica, who offered no response.

"Um...sure," said Simon not sure what Domic wanted to do.

Domic held Simon's hand in his own. The Ring of Affinity's flame turned silver-blue, the same colors as Domic. Domic's strength, power, and wisdom coursed through Simon's body. Silver and blue particles from Domic crossed onto Simon's hand and arm. The particles moved rapidly over and through Simon's skin. Simon's arm started to fade like Domic's.

Simon tried pulling his arm away, but Domic's grip was too strong. No matter how hard Simon pulled, Domic didn't budge. He stood as strong as a tree.

Simon looked over at Heaton and Thianna who both looked as frightened and confused as Simon. Sonica stood next to Domic, watching with amazement.

"Sonica?" cried Simon. "What's happening to me?"

Sonica just shook her head, not taking her eyes off of what was transpiring before her.

"Relax Simon," said Domic in the same humbling tone he had greeted them.

Simon found it very hard to relax. He was at the mercy of this ethereal being and no one was doing anything about it.

Heaton went for his sword, but before he drew it from its sheath Domic called out to Heaton without taking his eyes off of Simon, "Stay your sword master Heaton. No harm will come to our friend. You have my word, and respect."

Heaton slowly let loose his grip on his sword's hilt, but kept his hand hovering above it.

A rush of energy, both exhilarating and exhausting, coursed through Simon's arm and into his chest. He would have been knocked backward if it weren't for Domic's solid grip. Then Domic released Simon's hand. Simon felt weightless as he started to fall down. Domic's hands and arms moved like two pythons striking their prey, leaving a trail of radiant mist in their wake. Domic stood still as his hands and arms gracefully caught Simon. The others watched as his two ghostly hands lifted Simon up from under his arms and assisted him to a nearby chair against the wall.

Kneeling in front of Simon, Domic said, "Simon, you must safeguard this ring with your life. Only those who made the ring may have access to it. You and the ring are connected in a way you do not yet understand. If the ring falls into the wrong hands it will cost you your life, the lives of everyone you have ever loved, and so many others." Domic bowed his head before Simon.

"You may relax your hand master swordsman," said Domic without looking back at Heaton, who still had his hand above his sword's hilt. Heaton let his hand slowly drop to his side. "To become a team, a family, we must practice trust more than anything else. That is a commendable start swordsman.

"I will take Simon up to his room and see to his sleeping arrangements. He will need much rest," said Domic hospitably. "The three of you are welcome to join me in the kitchen and help yourselves to the warm apple cider, fresh bread, and cheese I have laid out for you."

Domic's voice was clear, but his body was like a shadow under a starry night. His silver-blue glittering hands lifted Simon up from his chair like he was a child's doll. And as the hands took Simon up to his room, another set of identical hands motioned to the others.

"Follow me," said Domic. "Someone has been waiting patiently for your arrival." His airy hands turned into an evanescent silver-blue ball of mist, like a small, lazy comet, and led Sonica, Heaton, and Thianna toward the kitchen.

Simon could feel Domic's strong arms cradling him as he was carried up a set of winding stairs. Simon was groggy and his vision was blurred, but he saw the others leaving the room with something shiny leading the way.

"Whab abut our mmmeal?" Simon managed to slur.

"Once you are well rested I will prepare you a hot meal. After you have eaten we will answer your questions, of which I am most sure you have plenty," said Domic. His voice was soothing and made Simon feel safe.

Upon reaching the top of the stairs, small light orbs, like the large ones outside, appeared one by one in rich, dark wooden sconces on either side of the hallway.

"Wow...thrr purddie," said Simon, finding it hard to speak in a sleepy haze.

He was overcome by sleep, but fought to stay awake to admire the craftsmanship. Complex designs and patterns were carved into the walls and ceiling, and each set of double doors they passed had its own scene carved into it.

One set of doors had a detailed picture of snow gently falling on a large mountain range. The snow was so real it looked like it was actually falling. Another door had a peaceful village near a river with people dancing and rejoicing with one another. He heard faint laughter and then saw a carved villager jump into the river with a small splash.

Simon didn't get to see the image on the next set of doors because sleep finally overtook him. He fell asleep in Domic's arms.

15

THE POWER IN A NAME

Jak bolted upright in the bed, startled by terrified screaming. His dark hair was wet and sticking to his forehead, sweat dripped down his ear. He frantically looked around the moonlit room, his chest heaving. The images still fresh in his mind and the echo of the screaming made him shiver uncontrollably.

He didn't know where he was or how he got here. In raw stillness he listened. He waited uncomfortably for another scream, but none came. His own heavy breathing was the only sound.

Then he recognized it. There was enough moonlight coming in the room's lone window for him to see he was back in the tower. He remained frozen in the bed to keep from breaking the silence. The dark shadows where the moonlight could not reach could be harboring anyone, or anything. Someone had screamed. He was sure of it.

Staring into the deep shadows he started to recall moments of his nightmare. The flickering light from the torch and the heat from its flame was his only comfort as he walked the cold, stony halls. And the fear…so much fear. Fear of the unknown. Fear of what was lurking around each corner. Fear of what dwelled in the long forgotten rooms. Fear of what was hiding behind the countless nooks and closed doors, waiting for someone to pass by.

He recalled the sounds beyond the reach of the torch's light. The creaking, banging and clanging, the droning and moaning, the scuttling, and hysterical laughter from a mad, twisted being. He didn't want to encounter the person, or thing, such madness came from. And then there was the agonizing screech, which stopped abruptly.

All the horrible sounds…the scuttling…the clicking…like that of an insect. Then it came to him like water overflowing the brim of a cup. He lifted up his shirt; even in the moonlight he could see the blood stain.

It wasn't a nightmare! I had been roaming those halls for… too long. I couldn't find my way back here.

✳ ✳ ✳

He remembered it all, except how he made it back to the tower. He remembered the sound of scuttling getting ever so closer, but it was difficult to tell if it was behind him or in front because it echoed off the hard stone like so many other sounds and noises. He stopped and held the torch high above his head. The scuttling stopped.

It crept slowly into the torchlight as if there were a chance it wouldn't be seen. Jak held his breath at the sight of the abnormally large, hairy spider slowly moving toward him. Its black, mirrored eyeballs were void of thought and emotion. It stopped and sank low to the ground when Jak took a step back. Its body was bulbous, resembling a large, black, hairy watermelon with a tiny head protruding from one end. The spider's hairy legs were jagged and as large as those of a king crab.

Jak froze. Holding tight every muscle in his body he prepared to dodge if the spider jumped at him. He couldn't read the spider's empty eyes so he couldn't anticipate at what angle the spider intended to attack. He slowly brought the torch down from above his head to straight out between him and the freak of nature, which emitted a series of clicks and clacks with its pinchers. The eerie sound echoed down the hollow corridor behind him.

Another series of abhorrent clicks responded from behind Jak; there were more than one. But glancing behind him, he didn't see anything. Then he heard it again and it was even closer. Glancing on either side of him, he didn't see it on the floor, but he could hear it…. The reason snapped in his mind just in time.

Spiders can climb walls!

Keeping the torch between himself and the crouching spider, Jak glanced up over his shoulder in time to see another spider making its way near him on the ceiling.

As soon as Jak spotted it, the spider sprang from the ceiling. Jak reacted. He swung and ducked at the same time connecting his forearm and torch to three of the spider's bristly legs. The large arachnid squealed like a lame rat and landed near the other spider.

The wounded spider scuttled toward Jak with vengeance; the other one followed suit. They each took to a side of the corridor as a third spider, nearly twice their size, came up the middle.

Jak yelled and flailed the torch around to scare them off, but they only hesitated. He turned and sprinted as fast as he could, burning himself several times as the torch hit his leg. He didn't slow down to look behind him; there was no need. Their legs tapping upon the stone floor and relentless clicking chatter were very close.

As he rounded a corner he saw a door at the end of the corridor. Another corridor turned left before reaching the room, but Jak wouldn't have time to try the door and then back track if the door wouldn't open. He had time to either turn the corner and keep running, or try his luck at the door. Even sprinting the spiders were gaining on him, so he decided the door was his only chance of survival.

Focused on the door Jak didn't see the long, gray arm coming around the corner from the corridor he could have turned down. The jagged claws gouged his side and the blow knocked him off his feet. Jak slammed into the stone wall, bounced off of it, and fell to the floor. His torch lay at the feet of a ghoul, a lanky creature with long arms and hands that didn't seem to fit its body.

The creature sniffed the air with its flat nose on its rotten pug face. It looked at Jak. Its eyes were black and vacant. Then it screeched, baring a mouthful of fangs. Thick saliva strands hanging from the ghoul's mouth glistened in the torchlight.

Jak's head throbbed painfully to the rhythm of his pounding heart. He pushed himself along the floor with his hands and feet in a crab walk as the ghoul took large, awkward steps toward him. Hunching, the ghoul used its long, awkward arms and hands on either wall in the small corridor to keep balance. The three spiders were coming up from behind the ghoul.

Jak glanced over his shoulder; the door was too far.

His fear ignited into fury; his face burned. He would take on whichever ugly beast reached him first. As he stood he hunched over from pain, grabbing his left side. His shirt was red and moist.

The bastard cut me open!

"Come on!" Jak yelled. "You want me! Come and get me you ugly pug! Come on! I can scratch and bite too!"

The ghoul stretched its lanky arms out like a gorilla and then eight large legs appeared from behind the oblivious ghoul. The largest of the three spiders leaped on the ghoul's back.

The ghoul spun around, but the enormous, hairy spider held on.

Repulsed by the giant arachnid, Jak had an aching desire to kill it, but had no weapon to carry out the task.

The ghoul kicked one of the smaller spiders, which had tried biting him in the leg. The spider sailed through the air like a black, hairy soccer ball with legs, hitting the wall at the other end of the corridor with a fleshy slap.

The spider bit into the ghoul's back repeatedly, and the ghoul pulled the spider's legs, tearing one off. The spider squealed and the ghoul shrieked.

Jak didn't want to hang around to see which one was going to win so he started backing away from the fray. Getting the torch meant going around the ghoul so Jak turned to go into the room…but the third spider was on the door, the same one that attacked him earlier.

In the orange glow of the torchlight, Jak saw the giant spider crouch and leap toward his head. He raised his arm in time to keep the spider from sinking its fangs into his face, but the eight legs stuck to his shirt and skin like Velcro. He pushed as hard as he could to keep the giant spider from sinking its fangs into his face, but the spider had remarkable strength. Its fangs were inches from his right eye. The acidic stench of the spider's previous meal protruded from its clenching fangs.

Shrieking and squealing, the ghoul and giant spider spun past in a frenzy of bites, rips, and tears, and then crashed into the door, spilling into the dark room.

Jak saw his chance and screamed as loud as he could. He screamed to cover up the disturbing sound of the rapidly clenching fangs just inches from him. He screamed because of the wretched smell of the digesting flesh of the last victim in the bowls of his frenzied attacker. He screamed because of the grotesque body wiggling in his hands, its brittle hair and flesh, like that of snake skin, slowly slipping from his grip. He screamed because his overwhelming fear fueled his anger, which boiled his blood. He screamed as he ran toward the only light in the dark corridor and plunged face first into it.

The spider screeched and convulsed as the torch's flame singed its backside. Jak choked from the pungent stench of burning hair and flesh. He leaped up as soon as the spider released its grip on him, and before the spider could flip over onto its legs, Jak stepped on its head. Following the crunch beneath his shoe, the eight hairy legs folded inward as Jak had seen many times spraying poison on the spiders he sought for fun in the wine cellar as a boy.

Jak threw up on the hideous corpse, twice. Then the tumultuous din from the room prompted him to pick up the torch and run. The corridor swayed back and forth. Jak fell against the stony walls several times.

He felt light-headed and nauseous so he stopped and dropped to his knees. He wasn't sure how far he had run, but he didn't hear anymore fighting. Either he was far enough away so he couldn't hear them, or one of them had finally won. He was hoping it wasn't the latter. But then he heard something that froze every muscle in his body. Scuttling. It was getting closer and closer…quickly.

He was afraid to look, but he also didn't want to be taken by surprise so he slowly turned around. A trail of blood led up to him and a small pool was forming where he was kneeling. Jak was surprised he was losing so much blood because he no longer felt any pain from his wounds.

The spider, which had been kicked against the wall, was scuttling awkwardly; one of its legs was broken, but it dragged it along in determination.

Jak turned away from the spider and began to lift himself up, but stopped. A black panther was prowling toward him. Its red eyes glared at Jak, and then it growled and crouched down, ready to pounce.

Jak looked down at his hand, wet from his own blood. He felt tired and defeated.

The panther pounced. Jak lifted the torch in a feeble attempt to gouge the panther in the head, but hit one of its paws. The panther spat in pain, and its mighty paw hit Jak's shoulder sending the torch flying out of his hand and splaying him upon the floor.

Jak struggled to get up, but collapsed under the impact of the giant spider sticking to his back. He reached for the torch, but it was too far away.

Then the inevitable happened. The spider sunk its fangs into Jak's back; the pain was sharp and hot. Jak crawled toward the torch, screaming in agony. The spider squeezed its legs around Jak and bit him over and over.

Jak tried with all his might, but couldn't go on. He slumped over the corridor's cold and unforgiving floor. Hatred, like the spider's venom, coursed through his veins. Hate for the repulsive creature biting his flesh, hate for Severn Fowl, Bedlam's *arrogant* Keeper, hate for Severn's five smug henchmen who stared and silently judged him, hate for the soul seers, the imbeciles, who dragged him to this forsaken place, hate for having no control over his fate, and hate for being born in the first place.

The dull sensation of the eight-legged abomination biting his flesh was the last thing Jak felt. The flame of the torch dying down was the last thing he saw. A low growl, squealing, and then crunching were the last he heard.

✳ ✳ ✳

Jak was perplexed. This had a dream-within-a-dream feel to it.

Am I going mad? How did I survive? How did I get back here?

Suddenly he realized he didn't feel any pain. He lifted his tattered, bloodstained shirt and looked at the spot the ghoul had punctured his side. There were no wounds, not even a scar. Reaching behind he couldn't feel any pain or marks on his back where the spider had bit him...no, more like fed on him.

Although a little stiff, he felt fine.

Jak took the kindling on the bedside stand and lit the candle. Its glow revealed the darkness's empty secret. There was no skeleton hiding near the bed. No raven perched on the windowsill. However, there was an odd shadow in front of the door. Jak slid off the side of the bed and raised the candle to get a better look.

In the shadow two red eyes glared at him. The large panther slowly rose from its disrupted slumber.

Jak stumbled back onto the bed and then stood on it.

The panther sauntered over, watching Jak's every move. Stopping at the side of the bed, it sat down on its hind legs. The red glow of its eyes dimmed and the panther grinned.

The black cat seemed to be waiting for something. But Jak couldn't take the staring and the unnatural, creepy grin.

"What?" Jak asked. "What do you want? I don't have any food."

"A simple 'Thank you' would suffice," the panther answered.

"You talk..." said Jak as more of an observation. He wasn't surprised the panther spoke, just that it could speak, but didn't right away.

"Of course I talk. I just do not make as much noise as you."

"What do you mean?"

"I mean, you made so much noise roaming the corridors I am surprised giant spiders and a ghoul were all you attracted," the panther said matter-of-factly.

"You were following me?" Jak asked. There was something familiar about the panther, but Jak couldn't place his finger on it.

"No. I was searching for you," said the panther, "and thanks to all the noise you made it did not take me long to find you. And just in time too." The panther tilted his head and grinned again.

"Oh...yeah...I suppose...." Jak felt awkward. "Umm... thank you...for your help...I...."

"That will do," said the panther. "I can tell it pains you to not only express gratitude, but to feel it." The panther moved over by the window. "Now come down from there. You look like a fool."

Jak sat down on the bed. Placing the candle back on the nightstand, Jak gazed out the window well into the starry night.

"What happened? How did I make it back here?" asked Jak. "I thought I was a dead man." Jak was trying to place what was so familiar about the panther.

"I brought you back here once I was through with the giant spider. Of course it took some time dragging you up those stairs. You are no cub," said the panther in a familiar sarcastic tone. "And you were *almost* dead."

"How did you know I was coming here?" Jak asked suspiciously.

"Because this is where I last left you," said the panther. *Last left me?*

Then it came to him. "You," said Jak studying the large panther, "you sound just like the raven that was here before..." and then another thought dawned on him. "Were you in here with us?" Jak lifted the candle and held it out to get a better look at the panther. "Why do you two sound so much alike? Are you and the raven related?"

The panther rolled his red eyes. "And how is that?" the panther mocked, "A panther related to a raven? I have no idea how it works in your world, but here it's not possible."

"Okay. So how is it you sound like the raven and claim you were here at the same time?" Jak demanded.

"For a smart one, you can be slow at times," said the panther impatiently. "I sound like the raven because I *am* the raven. As the raven I was the only one here with you, well other than the undead skeleton."

"Hey! You woke that idiot up before you, or the raven, flew off!" said Jak.

The panther grinned again. "Yes, but it was inevitable. I just got things hopping along," said the panther unconcerned.

"Yeah? Well next time a little heads up would be nice!" snapped Jak.

"Heads up? Why would we put our heads up?"

Jak shook his head. "For a smart one, you can be slow at times," said Jak mockingly. He stood up and started to pace back and forth. "Why did you attack me out there?" Jak asked gesturing to the door.

"Attack you? I have never," the panther said defensively.

"Really! Because I remember having to choose between defending myself from a mammoth panther, or a giant spider. Not a great choice, but I chose the bigger of the two. You almost took my head off!" Jak lashed out.

"I was going for the spider that had leaped at you from behind, whom by the way, I would have gotten on my first attempt had you not jabbed your torch into me." The panther was calm, making Jak's temper worse. The panther's demeanor was such that he could have just as easily been talking about the weather.

"You look fine to me," said Jak. "I don't see any burn marks."

"Only because I took the liberty of taking a sip of the healing potion before I administered it to you."

Jak looked down at his bloodstained shirt and rubbed his hand on his woundless skin.

"How else do you explain having no wounds, and most importantly overcoming the grips of death?" asked the panther. "That spider's venom was quickly overtaking you. It's a good thing it was one of the smaller spiders."

"A *smaller* spider?" Jak's voice squeaked.

"Yes. They come much larger than that. The larger they are the more venom they can inject. The larger ones can kill a man instantly," explained the panther. "I had just enough time to obtain a healing potion and get it to you. Any longer and I am afraid we would not be having this conversation."

"Where did you get such a potion?" Jak asked curiously.

"From someone who wants you to have a fair chance to compete in the trials," said the panther, "and we will leave it at that."

"Fair enough, but I don't plan on competing," said Jak.

"Refusal means imminent death," the panther explained. "It is best you try to fight for a chance to live, rather than to be executed with no chance at all. And they execute everyone who refuses."

The night sky was showing signs of giving way to dawn. The stars were disappearing in the horizon and a hint of pink and orange was peeking out.

"Well, at least I made it through the night," said Jak.

"Through *two* nights actually," said the panther. "You were out for two days and two nights." Jak stopped pacing and stared at the panther. "You were near death," the panther justified. "The deeper the wound the longer healing potions take. You were lucky it even worked with as much poison the spider had injected in you."

Jak sat back down on the bed. His stomach growled, but he wasn't sure he could eat. The reality of this place was sinking in.

"What do they want from me?" asked Jak, studying the floor.

The panther strode up to him. "We have discussed this already. The soul seers saw something the overlord wants."

"I know. You explained that, but why me? Why did they have to choose me?"

"Sometimes it is something far greater than the decisions of those around us that alter our path."

"I just want to go home," said Jak. However, the thought of home brought him no comfort.

"Get through the Maze of Mayhem, and you will have your chance," said the panther. "It will certainly place you in a better position to make it happen."

The panther went around to the other side of the bed and brought a wrapped bundle of linen to Jak, placing it on the bed next to him.

"I've been saving the rations they have been leaving outside the door for you. And since they have been rather skimpy on them I made a few extra trips myself and stole some from the kitchens," said the panther. He nudged the bundle closer to Jak.

"Do you mean the door is unlocked?" asked Jak as he opened the bundle.

There were three loaves of bread, a half a dozen dessert cakes, honey, butter, and salted pork. Jak's stomach growled in anticipation. He broke one of the loaves and ate ravenously. The panther was pleased.

"Do you plan on venturing back out into Bedlam's corridors unaccompanied?" asked the panther.

"Good point," said Jak chewing on some salted pork. Having something to eat was lifting his spirits. Looking at the door Jak saw there was no way of locking himself in; he wished there were.

"Severn's minions have been checking on you periodically to see if you made it back here. Once they saw you made it back they have been coming by with food to see if you are dead or alive. I am quite sure some will be disappointed to learn you are alive when the next set of guards return."

"Um...thanks for the food," said Jak with a mouthful of bread. After devouring the other half of the loaf, Jak looked at the food and then at the panther. "Did you want some?"

"No, but thank you. I found vittles for myself while you rested," said the panther. "I have eaten well."

Jak stopped chewing. "But then again, if I left now I *would* be accompanied, if you come with me," said Jak enthusiastically, spitting breadcrumbs as he spoke.

"Lad. We were lucky getting you out of that predicament the first time," said the panther walking back over to the window and looking outside at the dawn. "We may not have luck on our side the next time. Your only hope lies in making it through the Maze of Mayhem. Only then will you have the resources needed to make such a decision."

"Why? What do I get if I make it through the maze? I already know what happens if I don't," said Jak throwing the thought out of his mind as quickly as it came to him, but not before a spark of anger burned in the pit of his stomach from the thought of being held a prisoner and made to do something for the amusement of others.

"You get the *ultimate* prize." The panther's eyes lit up.

"If death is for losing, this ultimate prize had better be worth its weight in gold," said Jak. "So what is it?"

The panther remained silent, staring out the window. Jak thought about throwing a piece of bread at him to get his attention, but decided against it. He couldn't afford to have the panther angry with him, or worse, turn on him. Jak was about to repeat his question when the panther turned his head and spoke in a low tone, "The ultimate prize...is *power*," and then he turned back to the window.

"Power? What power? Over what, or who?" asked Jak.

"That you will discover on your own, if you make it through the maze," said the panther, his mood turning as somber and distant as his gaze. "But I assure you, it is power unlike anything you have ever known, or dreamed of." The panther looked back at Jak. "That is all I can say."

That wasn't enough. Jak wanted to know more. He still didn't know what the soul seers saw in him that was so valuable. And he wanted to know what made this power so special and unique because if it's wealth than they're in for a rude awaking. Money doesn't impress him. However...the magic Severn used, the more he thought about that kind of power the more he fantasized about all the things he could do.

After stuffing a couple of the dessert cakes down, Jak looked at the panther with a newfound interest. "So what are you?" asked Jak. "And don't say a panther because

I know that. How is it you can turn into a raven and a panther?"

The panther seemed reluctant to say. After sighing he said, "I am a changeling." He sounded sad.

"What's a changeling? And why so glum about it?" asked Jak hoping he didn't cross any boundaries with the only ally he seemed to have in this place.

"Being a changeling is a lonely existence, always feeling like an outcast wherever you go," said the panther taking refuge in staring at the skyline. "Some consider us the lowest form of life, because we have no life of our own."

Jak studied the panther. Such an odd sight. A ferocious animal with poise and confidence sat before him with a human-like sadness.

"What are you talking about?" asked Jak. "You can change into a bird and fly around, something I wish I could do, and on top of that you can turn into a bad-ass black panther and scare the bajeezus out of people whenever you want. How cool is that?"

"That is the silver lining that comes with a great price," said the panther watching the daybreak. "That price is never knowing who you are, or for that matter, what you are. I have no identity of my own."

"I don't get it," said Jak. "Everyone has an identity. What were you when you were born?"

"A changeling in the form of a raven."

"Back up just a little," said Jak trying to keep things in order. "Before you changed into the raven, what were you?"

"You are right," said the panther, "you do not get it. I was nothing before the raven. I was born a raven."

"Then that's it! Your identity is a raven that can change into a panther," said Jak as if he had just figured out the whole mystery behind changelings.

"I was born a raven on the outside, but I was, and always will be, a changeling." Before Jak could spout out another answer, the panther asked, "Have you ever found yourself amongst others like you, and yet felt different than the rest of them? Felt like you did not fit in and they did not want you around? You sit, eat, work…live among them, but you are not the same? It doesn't matter if there are tens, hundreds, or even thousands of others around you. You are still lonely."

Jak was quiet. He recalled similar moments in his past. There were so many of them.

"No one knows what a changeling looks like in their raw, natural form, not even us changelings. Many have tried, but no one has ever succeeded. A changeling does not even know it's a changeling until after its first uncontrolled change." The panther was looking long and hard at the floor. "That is the day in every changeling's life unanswered questions, like 'Why is it difficult for me to fit in?' are suddenly understood. And then, just as quickly as we have discovered what we are, we are run off, abandoned, and some are even killed, by our family, or at least what we thought was our family."

"Why?" asked Jak.

"Because we do not, and sometimes cannot, fit in. Because what we change into is unknown until it is introduced to us."

"So what!" said Jak irritably. "Many people don't FIT in. Who cares and who wants to?"

"Ah, but you are referring to being different among other humans." The panther looked at Jak. "If you were a family of ravens, would you want a panther living among you?"

"Well...um..."

"That was a rhetorical question," said the panther, "because the answer is an obvious one. But look not glum upon me. There are benefits to being a social outcast, just not too many. The trick is to use them in one's favor."

"Like what?" Jak asked curiously.

"Like...going about one's business is easier since no one takes any care as to what you are up to, and," the panther's dark red eyes narrowed and gleamed, "your foes often underestimate you, giving you the element of surprise. In a fight, the first attack can be the last attack... or the most damaging.

"With the ability to change, like so many abilities, there is a price. It is common knowledge among magic-users that changelings need to be given a name and willfully accept that name in order for us to grow and strengthen our abilities. To accept, we need only state our name. From that moment forward a named changeling is forever indebted to the one who named him."

The changeling's words echoed in Jak's head. If this was true this could be a game changer.

"What do you mean by 'forever indebted' and how does a name help you strengthen your abilities?" asked Jak with growing anticipation.

"It is not the name that gives us strength and helps us grow more powerful, it is the connection to the name giver, a gift if you will, of acceptance. Gratitude forever bonds the changeling to our name giver," explained the panther.

In other words, a servant, Jak thought.

Jak poised himself. He didn't want to sound too excited or even desperate, but he had to consciously hold back his excitement. How awesome would it be having a magical creature as a servant?

"So…do you have a name?"

The panther shook his head, but said not a word. Jak wanted to jump up and do the jig. But suspicion quickly brought his mood back down.

"Wait a minute," said Jak suspiciously. "Why are you telling me all this? You *want* me to give you a name!"

"Of course I do," said the panther. "Why would I tell you if I did not want you to?"

"What do you get out of this?" asked Jak, staring at the panther suspiciously.

"The same things you get…a friend, strength in numbers, and, as I already have told you, the ability to grow stronger *with* you. The stronger our name givers become, the stronger we become."

"So…why me? Severn and the other monkeys make better candidates, as they are clearly stronger than me. I don't know any magic…"

"Yet," the panther interrupted. "You do not know how to wield magic, *yet!* I take pride in being a good judge of character, and I take even more pride in my uncanny ability to find out secrets and privy information. And you,

Jak, are destined for greatness! You *will* know magic and you will know it well! You will be great!"

"How do you know?" asked Jak doubting the panther's intuition carried any weight.

"Because of secrets I know that my lips have untold," said the panther in a hushed tone. "Listen, and listen to me carefully. I heard with my own two ears that the Council of Wizards knows a boy has come through a portal from a strange world and he has brought a remarkable power he does not yet know he possesses. This power will become great only if those who already know the true ways of magic are able to teach the boy and are willing to give up their own lives in order for him to learn."

"And you think I'm this boy?" asked Jak unable to decide if he should be excited, or if the panther has a loose screw in his head and he shouldn't take any of what the large fur ball is saying seriously.

"Jak. You are the only boy, or person for that matter, who has come out of a portal from another world in years. You are here because two soul seers that work for the overlord saw something in you no one else can see, your soul, your inner strength. And in addition to that, Severn chose you to compete in the Maze of Mayhem without any past experience. You have not competed in any other tournaments nor have you earned your way to rightfully compete."

"You act like being thrown into this stupid maze is a good thing!"

"Because it is," said the panther. "The Maze of Mayhem is used for one purpose only, to determine who will become the next warlock and live among the elite who rule under the overlord. To be made a warlock is to have access to great power."

Jak's heart started pounding. He was more than excited. He was elated. If this was a dream he never wanted to wake up.

"But I may not even survive the maze!" said Jak.

"Destiny is calling you," the panther said cunningly. "And if I am to have a name giver, I want him to be powerful so that I too can grow strong serving him. If you are my name giver, than I will be there with you."

"You mean you can come with me in the maze?" asked Jak no longer holding back his excitement.

"If you are my name giver I have a bonded oath to serve you and protect you at all costs," said the panther. "In the maze opponents can use whatever means they have available to them to win."

This is just what he needed, an ally, or better yet a servant, who knows magic and can help him get through the maze. And if this changeling is telling the truth, then Magnanthia may not be such a bad place after all. Great power! He could live with that.

As he thought of a name to give the changeling, Jak walked over to the window and looked out for the first time at Bedlam in the light of day.

"What is that?" asked Jak gawking at the enormous structure spread out before him as far as the eye could see. Large castles and fortresses, some the size of small mountains, were intertwined by tunnels, bridges, caverns, and unusually large, black trees the size of buildings with mighty branches as wide as roads reaching out amongst the structures like claws on a dead crow. In no discernible order there were lesser structures like towers, and small forts and strongholds standing awkwardly amidst their larger counterparts.

Many of the structures resembled ruins, uncared for and forgotten. Some were simply unfinished. Yet other structures were built well, decorated with sophisticated details and designs and were heavily fortified.

Dense smog roamed ominously about the land despite the sun trying to burn its way through the low hovering clouds.

"That," said the panther, "is Bedlam, or at least part of it." Jak couldn't tell if the panther was impressed, or afraid. "An infinite labyrinth of tunnels, dungeons, corridors, and secret passageways filled with horrid creatures, the undead, magic baring beings, riches, power, and your worst nightmares searching for their next meal…. As you've discovered."

For a few minutes the two of them stared out at the enigmatic wonder.

"The warlocks rule over this?" asked Jak drinking in the majestic sight. He was taken by the pure size and wonder of it all.

"Yes…all of it," said the panther so quietly Jak almost didn't hear him. "The undead are their minions, carrying out their biddings."

"How do they control them?" Jak wanted to know more.

"Control them? There is no need to control them because the warlocks raise them. The undead are forever at the mercy of their master, for whoever raised them can destroy them by merely thinking it. And the undead know they will perish upon the death of the one who raised them. So, naturally, they will defend their master to the death for they have no other choice."

The name came to Jak.

"I'll call you Slade," said Jak looking down at the panther.

"You can call me whatever you wish, but to be my name giver I must willingly accept the name you *offer* me," said the panther.

What's the difference?

"Alright," said Jak, "I *offer* you the name Slade. Will you accept?"

The panther sat down, his tail swishing back and forth. "Slade," said the panther, trying it out. "What does it mean?"

Is he serious?

"It doesn't mean anything! It's a name!" Jak was irritated. The changeling seemed to be trying his patience. "Look! Take it or leave it! I don't want to explain myself!"

The panther was quiet and still.

Jak sighed and felt like an idiot. He may have just ruined his chance at this.

After pondering for a few moments, the panther responded. "I accept." The panther looked into Jak's eyes and said with determination, "My name is Slade! I am your humbled servant." Then Slade bowed before Jak.

Jak couldn't hold his grin back. The tides were changing and with them came power, respect, and revenge.

"WOO-HOO!" Jak yelped. Looking at Slade, he chuckled.

The door creaked open. Standing before him were the three skeletons from the other night.

"Humph," the large one grunted. "He's not dead."

"As I had said," said the rickety old skeleton. "You owe me some gold," he said to the large skeleton.

"And it looks like he has a new friend," said the skeleton with the sword teasingly.

Slade stepped forward and growled.

"Down kitty," the skeletons scoffed.

"We don't mean Jak here any harm," said the old skeleton. "We were only sent to inform him the games start tonight at sundown."

"Yeah, so he'll receive all the harm he deserves in the maze," said the sword-baring skeleton mockingly.

Then the three skeletons left the tower, leaving the door open.

16

THE TENTH OR FIRST OF THE SECOND NINE

Simon couldn't remember the last time he slept so well. A bed becomes a comfortable commodity after sleeping outside. Sitting up, he stretched and looked around the room. For a moment he had forgotten he was in a very large tree house. However, as tree houses go, this one took the grand prize. It was the granddaddy of all tree houses.

The bed he slept in was more comfortable than his bed back home. The bedding and pillows were down, and the sheets and pillowcases were silk. The room was neat and orderly. The furniture, pictures and wall hangings, along with the other décor was all thoughtfully and carefully designed and arranged. Comfort was this room's objective; it definitely was well designed. Even the fireplace responded to Simon getting out of bed. Before his feet were firmly placed on the alpaca rug, which bore an exquisite design of mountains and trees, the small flames under the mantel whooshed into a large fire as if someone turned it from low to high. The room warmed up nicely.

A fireplace? In a tree house?

Taking a closer look, Simon saw that the flames were not actually burning anything, but instead danced on the stone floor in the fireplace. And there wasn't a chimney, but there also wasn't any smoke emanating from the fire.

Simon was wearing a loose shirt and an undergarment, neither of which was his. He was unable to remember how he came to be dressed in these clothes, or how he got into the bed for that matter.

A gentle knock at the door jostled him from his thoughts.

"Yes?" asked Simon.

The door opened at what at first seemed to be on its own accord until Simon recognized the familiar evanescent hands gliding into the room and heading straight to the wardrobe.

"Good morning Master Simon. I presume you slept well. You certainly look more bright-eyed. I see you are standing on your own accord," said Domic in his polite, butler-like tone as the doors to the wardrobe swung open. "I am sure you will find something to your liking to wear." Domic's hands left a bluish-silver trail of vapors as they moved about the room laying out leather boots, fresh undergarments, and filled a pitcher with fresh water that, like a small spring, flowed from Domic's hands into the pitcher. Simon watched curiously as, what appeared to be weightless hands, poured some of the water from the pitcher into the basin beside it.

"Now that you are up and well rested," said Domic, his hands rearranging an assortment of fresh lilacs in a vase, "the other members of your party will wish to see you. I will alert them of your waking. Come downstairs when you are ready. They will meet you at the breakfast table where a meal will be ready for you.

"Is there anything else I can get for you?" Domic asked, one hand resting on the doors latch.

"Umm…no, thanks. Thank you," Simon managed to say.

"Very well sir." The door gently closed.

Simon caught his reflection in a mirror in a large, hefty frame hanging over the bureau. He looked dumbfounded.

On his way down the spiral staircase to meet the others, Simon stopped to look around. Although much care had gone into making, designing, and keeping up the tree house, nothing was gaudy. No space was wasted and everything was cared for. The wood, which was what most of the furniture and, naturally, all the walls were made of, was clean and even polished in some areas. Everything was neatly arranged.

The Keebler elves would love this place. Simon smiled and chuckled at the thought.

"It pleases me to see you smiling, Simon," said a man standing in the archway to the hallway.

The man was dressed in a loose-fitted shirt, black slacks, and black boots as high as his knees. He's the first person Simon has seen in Magnanthia who wasn't wearing any kind of armor or carrying a weapon of some kind strapped to his waist or haltered to his back. Standing firm with a casual air about him the man studied Simon as if he were comparing what he saw to notes he had taken. The man's eyes were windows into many years of studying and experience. He held his gaze as Simon walked down the stairs.

"I'm sorry," said Simon. "But, do I know you?"

"Not until this moment," said the man honestly, "but you will, and better than most people you have ever known. I am Webster Wheelock, handler and master wizard to the guardian." He extended his hand to Simon, and they shook. He was pleased to meet Simon.

"Seems like everyone here knows this guardian guy," said Simon. "Who is he?"

"That is an important question," said Wheelock, "and one we are all hoping will be answered soon." He turned around and gestured down the hall. "Come. The others are waiting for us, and Domic has prepared you a late breakfast since you missed it. A fine meal it was."

He led Simon down the narrow hall. There were no perfectly squared corners, and the walls were not flat. The wood kept its natural curves.

Domic's Haven was well lit. Magic fire was present in fireplaces, candles, lanterns, and sconces all throughout. The tree house was comfortable, cozy, practical, and most welcoming.

Wheelock led Simon into a room with many cabinets, counter tops, a food pantry, and a large wooden table. The aroma of bacon and biscuits made Simon's stomach grumble. Domic welcomed Simon to the breakfast room and immediately sat him at the table where Sonica, Heaton, and Thianna were in the middle of a discussion. They greeted Simon as Domic ushered in a plate full of bacon, biscuits, eggs, chunks of various cheeses, and fruit in front of Simon, quickly followed by a tall cup of milk and another one full of freshly squeezed orange juice.

"Will there be anything else Master Simon?" Domic asked, his folded, ethereal hands the only clearly visible part of him.

"Um...no, but thank you very much Domic," said Simon. He felt awkward being the only one with a plate full of food in front of him. At least the others were all sipping drinks of their own, but he didn't feel right eating in front of them.

"Go ahead Simon," said Wheelock patting Simon's shoulder as if he had read his thoughts. "The four of us have already indulged ourselves in Domic's triumphant breakfast. We take no offense."

"Unless you *don't* eat," said Domic playfully.

"You better get to working on that plate," Sonica teased.

Not another word had to be said. Simon was very hungry. As much food as there was in front of him, he didn't think it was going to be enough. He heartily dove into the plate. Domic brought churned butter and raw honey to the table. Simon dipped one of the warm biscuits in the honey and stuffed it in his mouth followed by a thick slice of bacon before he was done chewing the biscuit.

He was already on his third biscuit, which he covered with an egg and two slices of bacon, when he noticed the others watching him. Looks of intrigue, wonder, and concern were looking back at him. Simon stopped chewing. He wanted to say something, but his mouth was jammed with his breakfast.

"Forgive them Simon," said Domic cutting into the silence. "These have been difficult times, and this is a great moment for them...for all of us." Revealing his translucent head and upper body, Domic turned and addressed the others, "I told you to let him eat in peace. That does not entail gawking at, staring at, or studying the lad," he said with stern kindness, like a great grandfather addressing his family. The others went back to drinking, sipping, and visiting, leaving Simon the time he needed to finish his meal. Simon cleaned his plate and emptied his cups within a few minutes.

"I hope you tasted it," said Heaton.

"Manners, young master, manners," said Domic to Heaton as his silver-blue hands moved swiftly and elegantly cleaning up the table and then topping off everyone's drinks.

"Now since we have all had our breakfast and Domic has kindly filled our beverages," said Wheelock raising his cup in gratitude as he pulled up a chair and joined everyone at the table, "we have matters of great importance to discuss, including recent events the three of you have missed while getting Simon, events we cannot afford to overlook and which need to be handled with urgency."

"And what events are those?" asked Heaton.

"We will talk about these events soon, Heaton. However, we owe Simon an explanation, as we had agreed we would do when we were all together again," said Wheelock. He looked at Simon eagerly, and patiently said, "Simon, are you ready for this? Are you ready to hear our story?"

The answer to the question seemed obvious, so Simon remained silent, anticipating the explanation, but all four awaited his response.

"Yes! Yes I am," Simon said quickly before Wheelock changed his mind and moved on to a different topic.

"Very well. We will start by explaining the past few days: who, where, what, and the most compelling question…why," said Wheelock soberly.

"Unless you have any objections, I will start with where," said Wheelock as the hands of Domic set a warm cup of tea in front of Simon. Simon thanked Domic, the hands that served him, as he eagerly waited for Wheelock to continue.

"Here we gather in the kitchen of Domic's Haven, in Domic's spacious abode, a shiftwood tree, that has been gifted by Domic himself. Domic's Haven is in the oldest and largest area of Shiftwood Forrest. Many of the shiftwood trees in this area were around during the days of old, a time before the evil among us existed.

"Shiftwood Forrest is expansive. The side where we are located lies near the southeast border of Magnanthia. Of course having a border means having an end to the lands of Magnanthia and the beginning of other lands leading elsewhere.

"Beyond the kingdom's western border lies our greatest concern. It has been called the Forgotten Lands ever since evil has made its dwelling there. Most Magnanthians know little of the Forgotten Lands other than it is where the undead walk freely. Creatures with evil and wickedness flowing in their veins hide within the shadows of the Forgotten Lands.

"Magnanthia, however, is a generous land where justice was born and peace still reigns. Folks here are simple and fruitful. Love and respect have been the foundation of this kingdom since the beginning. The kings and queens of Magnanthia have always upheld this way of life and have kept peace in the kingdom. That peace has been jeopardized for the first time in centuries." Wheelock took a long sip from his cup. The room was quiet.

"Now that you have an idea where you are, it is time you start to learn what happened and who are involved," said Wheelock, his watchful eyes on Simon. "Simon? Do you know what a portal is?"

"I think so," said Simon reflecting back on fantasy books he had read and his own recent experience. "They're like a doorway to another world."

"Correct," said Wheelock. "A portal to your world was *cracked* open. This is peculiar for several reasons. First, magic-users of any kind take portals very seriously because the repercussion of opening one can be catastrophic if done improperly. Second, there are various grandmaster wizards, necromancers, and warlocks who possess items that can detect when a portal is opened and can usually tell its whereabouts. I speak for the majority when I say magic-users are enigmatic. We are most uncomfortable when others know what we are doing."

"Excuse me…what's the difference between a magic-user and wizard?" asked Simon.

"All wizards are magic-users, but not all magic-users are wizards," said Wheelock. "Anyone who has mastered the ability of wielding spells is a magic-user. The kind of spells one wields as well as how the caster uses the power determines what kind of magic-user they become." Wheelock was pleased Simon showed interest in his craft. "Warlocks are lazy. They cheat and forego the natural ways of obtaining and strengthening magic. They use whatever magic is available to them in feeding their personal fortune, and their appetites are never satisfied. Necromancers...they are in no way lazy, but they practice the darkest of all magic, and they do it not for power or riches. They do it to cause pain to others, to kill for mere pleasure, and destroy our way of life, one with love, kindness, and unity.

"The most honorable and difficult class to obtain is wizard," said Wheelock.

"Perhaps you're a *little* biased," said Heaton holding his forefinger and thumb close together.

Wheelock gave Heaton a look before Domic interjected, his voice floating in the air, "Master Wheelock is correct young swordsman. Wizards take the time to learn their spells, to know a spell personally. They draw from the manna, or inner energy, they have learned to grow and harvest over time. They use their magic to learn, and to help and protect others. And most importantly, wizards do not practice dark magic. They will have nothing to do with it. It takes great discipline and honor to *earn* one's power. Only fools *take* it.

"Taking magic power is the way of the warlock. A warlock will wield whatever magic he can find and take from others. A warlock will wield magic for any reason. Self-gain, overpowering others, humiliating others, and taking more magic from other magic-users are just a few reasons a warlock wields his magic."

Wheelock sat back in his chair, watching Simon as Domic continued, "Dark magic is mastered only by the necromancer, the only one foolish enough to delve into such evil. A warlock wants your manna and your magic. A necromancer wants your soul. Messing with your thoughts is only the beginning. Once a necromancer has tortured you, he takes pleasure in killing you. Then he raises you as an undead servant. It is his greatest thrill of all."

There was a long, solemn pause. All were lost in their own thoughts. Simon didn't know what to think. This all seemed like something out of a movie or dream.

"Third," Wheelock suddenly said breaking the silence, "the portal was *cracked* or *broken* open by an unknown source." Wheelock held up his forefinger, stopping Simon before he could speak. "Before you remind me of my own words spoken just moments ago, the answer to your question is yes. When a portal is opened there are always those who are waiting and watching. But the problem is the portal was *cracked* open."

"What difference does that make?" asked Heaton. Simon was glad he wasn't the only one that didn't understand.

"Like a door," said Wheelock addressing the entire group now, and Simon appreciated the attention wasn't all on him, "you can open it and walk through it, or you can break it and climb through the hole you made. The only reason this cracked portal was detected was because

Simon's realm has been safeguarded and under continuous observation for some time now at the University."

Wheelock spoke directly to Simon. "The University is *the* place wizards go to learn and grow. It is also the location of all chronicles pertaining to Magnanthia and discoveries within the land."

"Where is this place?" Heaton asked wryly.

Wheelock returned Heaton's wry tone with a wry smile.

"Only wizards know the whereabouts of the University," said Sonica. "However, not all wizards know. But they're tricky. All wizards lose their tongue, *whether or not* they know the whereabouts, when confronted about the University. That way, nobody can accuse a wizard of actually knowing where it is because they all act as if they don't."

"They lose their tongue?" asked Simon. He didn't know what to take literally any more. After all he was sitting in a giant tree house talking with a wizard, cleric, swordsman, and a ranger, who can talk to animals and the tree itself, or himself, whatever Domic was.

"No genius. They stop talking," said Heaton shaking his head.

"How was he supposed to know?" asked Sonica, jumping to Simon's defense.

"Because people are not walking around with their tongue falling out of their mouth…"

"Young master," said Domic, nowhere to be seen, "keep in mind, Simon is from a different world than ours. He is not accustomed to our ways, as we are not accustomed to his. We will need to help one another along. It is our duty."

Thianna and Sonica gave Heaton disapproving looks.

"Sorry…Simon," Heaton managed to force out.

"That's alright," said Simon. "I kind of figured that's what she meant, but I've seen and heard things that don't seem possible or make sense. I don't know what's real anymore and what's not."

"In time you will, Simon," said Thianna, her voice kind and caring. "And we are all here for you…to help you."

"To help me? What do I need help with?"

"In helping us," said Wheelock. "I know you have many questions. Let me finish explaining what I had started, for we have gone astray from our topic of what and who. The rest will come in time."

Simon nodded, afraid if he opened his mouth another question would come out.

"Domic?" Wheelock asked not looking at anyone in particular. "Have we learned who cracked the portal yet?"

"No Master Wheelock, but it has recently come to my attention that the overlord, or one of his warlocks, is suspected of closing it."

Wheelock returned his focus to Simon.

"We have no idea who cracked the portal open," Wheelock continued, "we only have our suspicions, as you just heard, as to who sealed it. This is troublesome because we have no way of knowing if your identity has been compromised. The timing of these events is premature. You were not supposed to have obtained the Ring of Affinity until you had received proper training. Then you were supposed to have been properly brought to Magnanthia and shown around with the support of the proper personnel and ceremonies. In short, you are not supposed to be here right now."

Simon wasn't sure how to respond. He didn't ask to come here and now he's being told he isn't supposed to be here. Heaton and Thianna's troubled expressions and Sonica's look of confusion from Wheelock's comments gave Simon the feeling he wasn't going to like the rest of Wheelock's explanation.

"Those, whose greatest concern is for Magnanthia, came together for the first time in a long while to sort out what we know and then what we need to do next," said Wheelock. "Unfortunately, time is not on our side." Wheelock took a sip of his drink.

Remembering he had a cup of tea, Simon took a sip, pulled the cup in closer like it was a long-lost friend, and wrapped both hands around it.

"This leads us to *who* is involved," said Wheelock lightly smacking his lips, savory the taste of his drink. "Since we cannot afford the time for a history lesson, I will summarize. However, this does not pardon you from your history lessons." He was serious.

"Magnanthia has always been blessed with the presence of a generous and just royal family residing in Kincape Castle, which is the heart of Magnanthia's kingdom…"

"It is so beautiful, Simon," said Sonica, "You will love it!" Sonica slouched in her chair when she realized Wheelock was looking at her, waiting for her to finish.

"Yes, Sonica," Wheelock said with a small grin hiding in the corner of his mouth, "it is very beautiful. It is referred to as Magnanthia's jewel because it is so radiant.

"For centuries Magnanthia's kings and queens have been beloved by their people because of their generosity and humble nature. Unfortunately, the love of many kindles loathing in others. Jealousy is an evil emotion that churns a person's soul, manifesting hate, disdain, and covetousness. Even the kindest of hearts can shrivel and go black if jealousy takes hold.

"In time the people, who harbored such jealousy and hate toward the royal family and Magnanthia's way of life, fled and started building a kingdom of their own. To keep paying for the construction of their kingdom they needed more gold, platinum, gems, and whatever treasure they could come by, so they allied with greedy creatures that are easily manipulated, like goblins, hobgoblins, and bugbears.

"As their wealth grew, so did their numbers and power. They soon became a threat to Magnanthia and the ideals she stands for. The people of Magnanthia, including the king, tried to ignore the darkness that grew so near to the land, but Magnanthia was eventually forced to acknowledge it and protect her borders. Kincape's army, which was once large enough to defend against any nation, was losing ground to the worst enemy the kingdom had ever been up against, its own people. These people were once helpful neighbors and concerned citizens living within the very walls they were attacking.

"The bitter Magnanthians called their new home Bedlam to spite their homeland, and were living up to its name. Some who were once wizards left the path to become warlocks, gaining more magic by stealing it and messing with powers they should have left alone. In time one of the warlocks rose up and declared himself Bedlam's overlord.

"Eventually, necromancers from other nations who have always hated Magnanthia and what she stood for offered their services to the ever-growing Bedlam and its overlord.

"Kincape's army soon found itself face to face with a new foe, the undead. For wherever there are necromancers, undead soon rise.

"To make matters worse, trolls, who had been taken over by the undead army, were brought into the war. With their brutal strength the trolls began tearing and mashing through the ranks of the royal army.

"Having lost a third of Magnanthia to Bedlam, the royal family began seeking help from any lawful nation that had not turned to look the other away, trying to ignore what was happening to Magnanthia, and could see the evil growing and wreaking havoc as it continued to pound on the door of our great nation. Thankfully, the royal family found friends in places where they thought there were none. Once enemies, the elves and dwarfs agreed to set aside their differences and they joined Magnanthia in what had become one of the greatest wars in history.

"Years turned into decades and the decades turned into nearly two centuries, and the war raged on. It had expanded to lands far beyond the travels of any Magnanthian. However, the center of the war remains here.

"Nearly fifty years ago, the eldest of the humans, elves, and dwarves met in secret in the confines of

Kincape Castle and devised a plan to end the war. Each race brought a piece of an ancient power to the meeting.

"This power is so monumental it had not been used since days of old, for reasons unknown. The people of old took this power apart and gave one piece to the elves, one piece to the dwarves, and one piece to the humans. It was understood each race was responsible for protecting its piece and the three pieces would be kept apart and never put back together again, lest it end up in the wrong hands and destroy all three races.

"That night, at the meeting of the eldest, the three pieces were once again united. The power of old was placed in nine rings. These rings have become known as Rings of Affinity.

"The nine ring-bearers were christened Guardians of Magnanthia. Each guardian was trained and educated by four handlers, referred to as a company. The guardians' companies all consisted of a master swordsman, the steel and strength of the company, a master ranger, expert in aerial combat and connecting with nature, a high cleric, the healer of the company and the undead's worst enemy, and a master wizard, the spell caster and intellect of the company. Once a guardian was united with his company he was almost invincible...almost.

"The nine guardians and their companies hunted down and destroyed most of the warlocks and necromancers, including their army of undead. The guardians' destruction caused the goblin, hobgoblin, and bugbear armies to flee in an attempt to save their own hides. The royal army, along with the elves and dwarves, caught up to them and killed so many of them they were no longer considered armies. They remain scattered among the lands. Few of the vile creatures made it back to their homelands.

"The war was so close to coming to an end! The nine guardians and the thirty-six company members reached the heart of Bedlam. For almost two hundred years various warlocks laid claim as overlord, ruler of the dark army, and each one foolishly spent their spoils and built castles, strongholds, dungeons, and caverns in an attempt to become greater than the previous ruler and to house the army of undead and their allies. This colossal structure of chaos lives up to its name. Bedlam's structure is nonsensical and the evil it houses is indefinite.

"With much of the undead army destroyed, it was not difficult for the guardians to enter Bedlam. In their last ditch effort, the overlord and his remaining warlocks and necromancers opened a portal to an underworld. In so doing the overlord unleashed an evil this world has never seen." Wheelock's voice waned. He drank from his cup, and then continued.

"Because of the cursed overlord, Bedlam was flooded with foul creatures never before seen in Magnanthia, only spoken of in tales. It was the evil unleashed that would be the end of the Guardians of Magnanthia," said Wheelock bitterly. "The four grandmaster wizards came together and banished much of the evil back to its world, but Magnanthia has never been the same since.

"Both sides had great losses so the outcome was a stalemate. Whichever side can regroup and rebuild before the other may finally win this war." Wheelock took another sip from his cup. He looked defeated, as did the others.

Simon cleared his throat. "Why don't they make more rings and train more guardians?" asked Simon meekly.

"No need to make more rings," said Domic. "Seven of the nine rings have been recovered. But it has been forbidden to train any more guardians, and when the final two rings are recovered all nine rings can, and will be, destroyed."

"What? Why is the king doing this?" Sonica asked, not holding back her anger. "The guardians are responsible for annihilating the warlocks and necromancers, *and* for defeating much of Bedlam's army!"

"Because it wasn't the overlord who defeated the guardians," said Domic solemnly. "The guardians turned on each other. Nobody knows for sure how many of the nine turned, but it is believed that at least three…maybe as many as five. And unfortunately, King Elderten is convinced Peter killed the queen before taking Princess Elleanor."

"That has never been proven!" said Thianna, uncharacteristically tense.

"It has never been disproved," Domic replied in kind, "and until it is, the king is convinced Peter betrayed him. It is unfortunate so many people believe what they hear, even with the absence of truth. This is why gossip spreads like a wildfire in dry season."

"Not everyone believes that destroying the rings is a good idea," said Wheelock.

"How come I'm just being told now about the king's decision to destroy the Rings of Affinity?" asked Heaton.

"We just found out from the Council of Wizards before your arrival," said Domic.

"What about Peter?" There was uncertainty in Heaton's tone.

"It is unlikely, highly unlikely, Peter killed the queen. There must be good reason he took the princess," said Wheelock. "The king is reacting emotionally, not rationally."

"Then we must be careful when we are around members of Kincape's army," said Thianna.

"We have few allies we can turn to," said Domic, "and fewer we can trust. A young and inspiring magic-user, Enrik, was taken just outside of the University. This has never happened before. Few know of this, and it should remain so."

Wheelock shifted uncomfortably in his chair.

"I know Enrik, and hope for his safe return," Wheelock murmured. "He is a strong supporter of the guardians and believes they were wronged."

"Do we have any good news to speak of?" sighed Heaton.

"Yes," said Wheelock. "We know where one of the two remaining rings is located."

Wheelock looked down. Simon followed his gaze, which fell upon his own two hands wrapped around his teacup. The Ring of Affinity glistened; its internal flame danced about as if it knew the story being told.

Seeing that everyone was looking at it, Simon held his hand out so everyone, including himself, could get a better look at it.

"This is one of them?" asked Simon in a hoarse voice.

"Yes," said Wheelock observing the ring with a distant look in his eyes.

"Many of our enemies have lost their lives to that ring...have they not?" asked Heaton eagerly, leaning forward to get a better look at the wonder on Simon's hand.

"Yes," said Wheelock looking somewhere deep inside the ring, "and so have many of our friends and allies protecting it. Now it is our turn.

"Only a certain kind of person can wear a Ring of Affinity and withstand its power," said Wheelock more to himself than anyone else.

When Wheelock didn't say anything, but only looked at the ring, Simon asked, "What kind?"

"Sorry?" said Wheelock looking to Simon.

"What kind of person?" Simon asked again, unsure if he wanted to know.

"It remains a mystery. Perhaps someday you will discover the answer, young Whittaker," said Wheelock looking at Simon as he did the ring moments ago. "Becoming a guardian is not a choice one can make...it is a destiny one is given."

Simon's face turned red. Everyone was looking at him and the ring as if they were on display...and then it came to him like finding the last piece of a puzzle.

"Guardian?" asked Simon in disbelief. He suddenly felt out of place and out of his league. He was in waters way too deep to be swimming in. "No...this isn't right... you have mistaken me for someone else," said Simon leaping out of his chair.

"There is no mistake young master," said Domic, two of his ethereal hands folded together at the other end of the table. "The Ring of Affinity has chosen you as a guardian of Magnanthia. The four companions before you will make up your company.

"Webster Wheelock, handler and master wizard to the guardian," said Domic as one of his evanescent hands gestured to Wheelock. Wheelock stood and bowed his head, looking Simon in the eyes with intense regard.

"Thianna Furrow, handler and high cleric to the guardian," Domic continued, gesturing to Thianna, who also stood and bowed her head, her eyes looking tenderly at Simon.

"Zacharia Heaton, handler and journeyman swordsman to the guardian." Heaton stood as Domic's blue-silver hand gestured to him. He bowed, looking Simon in the eyes. Simon couldn't tell if Heaton looked hopeful or apprehensive.

"Sonica Wintergreen, handler and journeyman ranger to the guardian." Upon Domic's introduction, Sonica smiled, stood, and bowed her head. Her eyes were still full of wonderment.

"These four have vowed to protect, train, and fight alongside the tenth guardian, which we pray will also be the first of the second nine guardians," said Domic. "They will be the tenth company."

Simon stood still, looking back at the four people standing before him. A rush of emotions hit him like a flooding river. They looked eager, confident, and dedicated. Simon wished he could reciprocate, but he was sure they were looking back at a boy full of fear, uncertainty, and confusion. He was unworthy of this position.

"I have promised to keep my vow in serving the guardians of Magnanthia," said Domic. In full ethereal form, Domic stood and then bowed his head to Simon. "This domicile is home to you, your company, and anyone you welcome into it. As for anyone who is *not* a guardian or company member who may reside within these walls, may it be known my allegiance lie only with the guardian and his company."

Simon looked at the four people and the silver-blue ethereal form of a tall, bearded man.

After a few moments, the silent attention unnerved him so he spoke. "I don't know what to say, or do," said Simon earnestly. "I don't even feel this is me, that this is my life. I'm expecting to wake any moment from this dream. I'm honored...I really am, but I don't think I can do this. I don't think I'm the one you want. It's best if I go back home." He was suddenly lost for words. "If you'll excuse me, I need...I don't know...." Simon quickly turned and left the room.

"What just happened?" asked Sonica.

"We just lost our guardian we were going to swear an oath to," Heaton muttered.

17

THE MAZE OF MAYHEM

Left alone in the rickety tower, Jak listened as Slade explained a changeling's oath to his name giver. They are bound by an ancient, magical oath; as one grows in strength and power so does the other. Jak sat on the makeshift bed eating the rest of the food as he listened with a newfound excitement.

Their magical connection will, in time, make them more powerful than they would have been individually. Their relationship is symbiotic. Jak will have more inner energy, or manna, as spell-casters call it, allowing him to cast more magic. A spell-caster's manna determines both the amount of spells he can cast and the strength of those spells before becoming exhausted.

Slade, as a named changeling, will soon be able to change into twice as many forms, from two to four.

Unfortunately, Slade has no idea when he gains this ability, or what the newly acquired forms will be. Other abilities may arise from their symbiotic connection, unique only to them, but only time will tell.

Jak was a little disappointed to learn that although Slade was bound by this ancient oath to serve him, the ancient magic did not force Slade to act unwillingly. This meant Jak could not make Slade do something that jeopardized his self-preservation. However, it is in a changeling's best interest to help his master grow and to protect him at all costs.

Jak couldn't hold back his grin. He had one heck of a bodyguard accompanying him into the Maze of Mayhem tonight.

Jak was also disappointed to find out changelings were not spell-casters. Slade was not able to assist him with learning or casting spells. Aside from a loyal bodyguard, a name giver benefited from the amount of manna he would gain from his changeling, which by nature is a magical being. This rare, symbiotic relationship gave name givers an advantage over other spell-casters who did not have someone, or something, to draw inner energy from.

Their conversation eventually shifted to the Maze of Mayhem. Slade told Jak everything he knew about the Maze of Mayhem, which, he admitted, was mostly common knowledge, but has remained consistent over the years.

The most infamous detail about the maze is that it is ever changing. No one knows what's inside of it from one trial to the next, not even Bedlam's Keeper. As the rumor goes, the maze was built with magical megaliths that shift and slide on their own accord, never allowing one single way to remain the way out.

The only way out is to successfully make it past each encounter and eliminate all competitors in the maze. If anyone succeeds at this, the maze will reveal the way out to the survivor. The survivor, by right, becomes a warlock.

Slade cautioned Jak that he has also heard that sometimes the maze itself is the encounter.

"What do you mean?" asked Jak.

"I cannot be sure," said Slade, "only that I have heard the maze, itself, has taken the lives of competitors. It is as if the maze does not want anyone to survive."

Encounters have consisted of trolls, golems, elementals, giants of all kinds, including hill giants, storm giants, and, Jak's favorite, giant spiders, a whole nest of them.

"With my luck there'll be a dragon waiting in there for me," said Jak jokingly.

"Let's hope not," said Slade. "I have never met anyone who has fought a dragon and lived to tell about it."

Jak shook his head. "This is too much! How am I going to survive this?"

"Remember, I will be with you, Master Jak," said Slade reassuringly. "If you go down, we both go down."

Master? Jak thought. *I like the sound of that!*

Jak looked the great panther over. His large paws were twice the size of a man's hand with claws like surgeon scalpels. His muscles were well defined under his black, shiny coat. And Jak recalled the panther's impulsive reflexes when he intervened and saved Jak from the giant spider.

"Perhaps we should have a plan for the trial," said Jak.

He hated saying the word…trial. The idea of being put on trial, or tested like a lab rat, didn't sit well with him. He was a brilliant kid from an extraordinarily rich family. He didn't deserve to be treated like a prisoner, and he certainly shouldn't have to prove himself. The more he thought about it the more riled he became.

"Unfortunately, I see no way of coming up with a plan for something we know very little about," said Slade.

Jak looked outside. The sun was sinking in the horizon, and twilight was coming out of the shadows far below in Bedlam.

"I have an idea that will give me an edge, but it will mean you can't be seen with me when I enter the maze," said Jak as an idea sprung to life. "You will also have to make sure you can get into the maze, which shouldn't be too difficult if the maze is, in fact, made out of megaliths."

✳ ✳ ✳

It was nighttime when the same three skeletons came to the door. Jak stood alone in the tower. From outside the window came the steady roar of a distant horde.

"I see your friend up and left ya," mocked the skeleton with the sword. His loud and fake laugh annoyed Jak, but Jak remained silent.

Slade had changed into the raven and had flown out the window about an hour ago. Jak told him to find the maze so he would know where they were taking him. The raven came back reporting there was a large ensemble of undead skeletons, gathering in an old outdoor arena encircled with megaliths. From the excessive hollering and fighting in the crowd, Slade deduced the skeletons wanted bloodshed. Although the megaliths didn't form a maze, Slade was convinced it was the location.

Jak was hoping, and anticipating, the maze was outside. This was going to make his plan easier. Just minutes before the undead skeletons came for Jak, Slade flew out the window, this time with orders from Jak to follow him to the arena, keeping his flight close enough so he could hear the signal when Jak gave it.

The three skeletons escorted Jak to a long and narrow walkway, thirty feet above the busy streets below, where four large skeletons, twice Jak's size, wearing chain mail and helmets, and armed with pikes, were waiting for him.

Jak and his seven escorts were the only ones on the walkway. Below them were thousands of undead skeletons, all shapes and sizes, scurrying to the arena, which sat at the end of the quarter-mile, cobblestone walkway. The skeletons became frenzied at the sight of Jak walking above them. They were waving up at him with their swords, clubs, torches, and anything else they were carrying. It was hard to tell if they were cheering for him or cursing him. Some threw their weapons up at the walkway. Every so often a club, blade, or torch would land on the stone path in front of them. Slade wasn't exaggerating. They really did want bloodshed.

Jak looked up into the night hoping to catch a glimpse of Slade for some reassurance, but there was no sign of him.

If that feathered feline was jerking me around I'm going to ring its neck if I ever see him again!

The arena didn't look very large from a distance. But the closer they came to its gates its true size began to show like a mountain hidden amidst fog.

Unlike most of the structures in the shadows of Bedlam, the arena was well lit with thousands of torches lining the arena's walls. Atop the outer wall stood massive stone pillars holding up large basins filled with burning oil. Black smoke billowed from the tall flames licking the starless night and shadows danced along the streets and walls from the ominous orange glow. Deep, rhythmic beating of war drums also intensified the grim walk to the arena.

There were other elevated cobblestone walkways that led to the arena. Jak assumed they were for getting the other participants safely to the event. They wouldn't want to lose their entertainment for the night now, would they?

"You should think about picking one of those up," said the rickety, old skeleton referring to the weapons they were walking over.

"Or two," the sword-bearing skeleton chuckled.

"You mean...you'll let me arm myself?" asked Jak thinking they could be setting him up, giving them a good reason to attack him.

"You don't think we're worried about it...do ya?" said the sword-bearing one, and then laughed.

Along the way Jak picked up a dagger, a short sword, which was rather heavy, and a torch. He felt a little better being armed, but only a little.

At the arena four more large and heavily armored skeleton guards were standing on either side of the tall double doors. As the group approached, the four guards turned and heaved at the two doors until they slowly groaned and creaked open. Without stopping, or saying a word to the guards, Jak and the seven undead walked through the doorway, down several different stairwells and corridors into an area resembling a dungeon, the contestants' chambers.

Chains and shackles were hanging from the walls and lying on the sand-covered floor, like dead snakes long forgotten. He wondered how many prisoners had been chained down here, stuck in this living nightmare waiting for their turn to go in the arena to fight for their lives. The rickety tower was a safe haven compared to this nightmarish scene.

Two guards stood Jak before a closed portcullis; its iron bars had bitten through the cobblestone walkway long ago. It stood just outside the reach of the light coming from the short tunnel leading into the arena. The old portcullis's rusted bars were all that separated Jak from thousands of undead skeletons. The stands were packed with skeletons of all kinds. There were little ones, large ones, skinny ones, big-boned ones, skeletons with wings, and skeletons of creatures unrecognizable to Jak. Some had no flesh at all while others still had muscle, tendons, and dead skin hanging on them like torn, ratty leather coats.

The cheering and jeering horde was silenced. Jak couldn't hear much from the pit, but he recognized Severn's condescending tone, and he was saying something about finding the next and final warlock.

"Bring out the contestants!" Severn shouted. The somber beat of war drums followed his command and the portcullis clanked as it was raised.

One of the guards jabbed the handle of his pike into Jak, causing him to stumble into the light. Jak stood for a moment under the portcullis. The crowd went wild with war cries and beat their weapons against armor and shields when they saw him. Jak wasn't expecting the coliseum to be so large, and filled. He had been to many NFL games growing up. His family could get into any game at any time. This coliseum rivaled the size of those stadiums, and the roaring crowd here meant something different to Jak. The skeleton warriors beat their shields and armor to the rhythm of the war drums. It was deafening.

"Go gett'm hero," said the skeleton with the sword. It was difficult to tell if the skeleton was being caustic or if he was actually rooting for him.

The four large guards escorted Jak to the center of the coliseum. For the first time he got a good look at the other contestants, also being escorted from their pits. There were five other contestants. Two of the contestants couldn't take their eyes off the crowd, but Jak and the other three were sizing each other up.

When the six contestants came together the guards placed them side-by-side, facing Severn up in his royal suite. The other five warlocks were nowhere to be seen. Severn looked down upon the contestants as if he knew something they didn't, which was probably the case. Then he glared at each of them, stopping at Jak. Severn's lips twisted and jerked until he was smirking at him. The pompous pig was savoring the moment.

Jak began seething. He just wanted to get on with it. The suspense might kill him before the maze had a chance.

Severn held up his hands, addressing the crowd. The drums stopped and the crowd settled. Jak had never seen so many people, for lack of a better term, so quiet. The only sound was that of a lone raven, cawing. Jak glanced up and to his relief saw Slade gliding in the airwaves above.

"You six are here today," said Severn with reverence laced with guile, "because you have been chosen! Not because of your own abilities, but because of your true potential! You each have something of value to the over-lord and our army! This is a chance for one of you to join the ranks of the warlocks, to be given power many dream of having, but few ever obtain! Tonight, you will become a part of this MAGNIFICANT army of undead," Severn shouted as he gestured to the entire arena. The undead horde roared. Severn wallowed in the cheering and battle cries before addressing the crowd.

"The time is coming when we shall take Magnanthia and build it into the most powerful empire in all the lands! Every nation that stands before us shall fall to its knees and beg for mercy...or perish FOREVER!" Severn held the Scepter of Zalaruz high for all to see.

The roaring horde was unnerving.

"Unfortunately, only one among you may join us... alive," said Severn, looking back down at the contestants. "The Maze of Mayhem will not allow more than one sur-vivor. You will have to battle to the death to earn the title of warlock!

"And if no one makes it out alive...well...I guess we won't have a new warlock, now will we?" Severn amused himself and was pleased from the chuckling and cajoling around the arena. "If there are no survivors then you will have six new undead warriors among your ranks!" The crowd roared so loud Jak's ears were ringing.

Become undead? I'll kill the idiot who raises me!

Severn raised the Scepter of Zalaruz. Red electrical strands burst from the scepter's orb, striking four nearby megaliths. The red strands danced back and forth from megalith to megalith as they rose in the air and then hovered above the contestants.

Jak was ready to jump out of the way, but the guards around them aimed their pikes at the contestants. It was apparent they weren't going to let them move from their current spot.

The four megaliths dropped down and around them, shaking the ground and knocking Jak and the other contestants over. They were boxed in.

This is their idea of a maze?

"What now?" asked a tiny, skinny kid who must have been about fourteen years old. He was the smallest of the bunch.

A rotund boy, whose muscles were hidden under his well-fed mass, and holding a short sword in each hand, grunted, "I say we give'm what they want and let the games begin," and started toward the tiny, skinny kid gripping a dagger with both of his hands. Jak figured this fight should take all of about ten seconds.

"I don't think that's what they want," said another large kid, whose muscles were not at all hidden. His physique was the most intimidating of the six. Jak figured the muscle kid was probably the oldest amongst the group, and was the first to show any sign of intelligence. "Look," he said pointing up.

Moving methodically in the flickering, orange night more megaliths shuffled their way to and fro. The ground shook and rumbled as they dropped beyond their enclosed walls.

"We're rats in a maze and this is our starting point," said Jak. They watched the megaliths fall from the sky. Soon the shaking dissipated leaving only distant rumbles.

Jak felt like a rabbit in a den full of foxes as they studied each other. His comfort lie only in knowing Slade was hiding in the shadows nearby, waiting for his command.

The other two contestants were about Jak's size and age, only not as lanky. One had short black hair. The black-haired boy was angry, like he had shown up to what he thought was a party only to find out it was a study group. The other one had long, dark brown hair. The long-haired boy was poised and disciplined. He stood out from the others.

Their silent showdown was soon interrupted by the distinct sound of rock grinding against rock. One of the megaliths rose and hovered about twelve feet off the ground revealing the beginning of the Maze of Mayhem. The megaliths were too smooth and too tall to climb.

The group looked at one another apprehensively.

There's no way I'm going first.

Finally the muscle kid stepped up and went into the maze. One by one they followed. As the last contestant past under the megalith it dropped. The ground rumbled, and silence followed.

"No turning back now," said Rotund.

"As if we had a choice," grumbled Muscles.

The group proceeded forward until they eventually came to a T in the path.

"Any ideas?" asked Muscles.

Then everything went dark. The hundreds of torches and fires around the arena went out at the same time, without the help of even the smallest of breezes. The contestants were left in the dismal glow of the two torches Jak and Long Hair carried and a few torches on the megaliths, more than likely left burning so the viewing audience could see better.

"What just happened?" asked Tiny.

"The entertainment just got more entertaining," said Black Hair.

Although the crowd disappeared in the outer darkness, Jak could feel the arena of undead watching him. A chill went down Jak's back. The moans, groans, and foul laughter from the undead onlookers became ominous and omnipresent. Severn's words echoed in Jak's head, 'If there are no survivors then we will have six new undead warriors among your ranks!'

"I say we stick together to increase our odds of getting out of here," said Muscles.

"Right...so at the end you can beat the snot out of whoever is left," said Black Hair. "I don't think so. I say we split up."

"I agree with him," said Rotund pointing to Black Hair. "I don't trust any of ya'z, so the less the better."

"I'm not going with him," said Tiny backing away from Rotund.

"Ol'right. Let the two with the torches decide which way they each want to go and then we'll decide where the rest of us go from there," said Muscles looking at Jak and Long Hair.

"Who died and made you king?" said Rotund.

Jak saw his chance to separate from Rotund, the loose cannon. "How about the three of us go this way," he said pointing his short sword at Muscles and Tiny, and then aiming the torch to the right. "Does that work for you?" Jak asked the other torchbearer, Long Hair.

Long Hair looked at Dark Hair and Rotund, and then back at Dark Hair.

"That works," said Long Hair to Jak.

"How about I hold the torch and you lead the way," said Long Hair to Rotund before the big boy could protest. Rotund threw back his shoulders and stuck out his chest.

"Yeah, works for me," Rotund grunted. "Let's get mov'n!"

And with that, the two groups parted ways.

At first Jak's party came upon obvious traps, so obvious it seemed the maze was just playing with them, or perhaps it was all part of the entertainment. On two occasions a trap door opened about five feet in front of them leaving plenty of room to walk around.

You would have to be completely daft to fall into these traps, thought Jak.

One of the pits was lined with tiny spikes and the other pit just appeared deep. Tiny kicked a stone down the one. They never heard it hit the bottom.

From time to time fire or electricity shot out of holes in the walls from a spot they just stepped away from, or burst out a few feet in front of them from a statue of various creatures and beings. Each trap brought about cackling and laughing from the unseen spectators in the dark. The ruckus from the peanut gallery annoyed Jak.

Quit playing with us and get on with it!

As if answering his request the next corridor opened into a large room. Midway into the room, a long and narrow stairway went up several stories. At the top was a faint glow coming from a torch down another corridor. After entering into the open room a megalith came down behind them, sealing the way they had come.

The three stopped for a moment and looked at each other. They had no other choice at this point so they continued on until they reached the stairway. The steps were made of stone, but they looked old and frail. There were no other torches hanging on the walls beyond the stairway where the party of three stood.

Jak was going to look behind the steps to see if anything was there, but stopped suddenly. He noticed the light from his torch didn't reveal anything behind and beyond the stairs, not even the floor or walls. Something swallowed up the torch's light.

Jak knelt down and put his torch to the ground where the darkness met the floor. His heart skipped a beat when he realized there was no floor, or walls. He was kneeling at the edge of a very deep and wide cavern. He quickly scooted back before the darkness pulled him down, or someone pushed him.

"These steps are the only way," said Jak.

"If there is nothing beyond the edge of this floor, that means there is nothing holding up these stairs," said Tiny pointing behind the stone stairs into the blackness, "and there must be over a hundred steps."

"Do you think it will hold all three of us?" asked Muscles surveying the ramshackle steps.

Cracks spread across the steps and in some areas chunks had fallen off. It was a miracle the stairway was holding itself together, or perhaps they weren't.

"If this is our only way, does it matter?" said Jak.

"Perhaps we should go lightest to heaviest, leaving you in the middle with the torch," suggested Tiny.

"Leaving me trailing with the integrity of the stairs possibly impaired," Muscles pointed out. "I don't think so!"

"If it makes any difference," said Tiny a little unnerved, "I will be the first to the top and we haven't a clue what is waiting for us up there."

Muscles thought about it, and then agreed to the plan. Tiny turned and slowly started up the stairs, testing each step before he put his full weight down. After Tiny climbed about ten steps up, Jak followed suit. Ten steps behind Jak, Muscles started up.

No matter how careful they were, parts of the stone handrails and steps crumbled, falling into the abyss below. A third of the way up, about six feet of the handrail and balusters crumbled under Jak's hand. He hadn't even put weight on it. It just broke away from under his hand.

"Careful!" Muscles yelled. "Don't wreck what I still need!"

Jak looked back to retort the obvious comment, only to see Muscles put his foot through a step and fall forward with all his weight on the stairwell. Jak froze. Muscles didn't move a single muscle.

"Tiny! Stop!" Jak yelled without moving.

First they heard them and then they saw them, a web of cracks sprout from under Muscles like he had fallen on thin ice. No one moved or took a breath; the cracking quickly stopped.

"What happened?" asked Tiny.

"What does it look like?" came Muscle's muffled response, his face pressed down on one of the steps.

"Get up very slowly," said Jak staying as still as possible so as not to provoke any further damage.

"No way!" Tiny yelled down. "He's going to cause the steps to fall apart and then we are all going to die. Stay there until we're off!"

"If you move, and I make it off this thing, I will kill you myself," said Muscles into the stone step.

Jak slowly turned to see what Tiny was going to do because if the little twerp turned and ran, the vibrations could agitate the cracks under Muscles. Jak felt he was too close to those cracks and too far from the top. The young boy looked apprehensive and unsure. After looking Jak in the eyes and surveying the situation, Tiny decided not to move.

Jak turned back to Muscles. "He's waiting," said Jak. "Go ahead."

In slow motion and with one arm at a time, Muscles lifted his upper body up off the steps, giving him a better view of his predicament, which wasn't looking too good. Then he brought one knee up under his chest, pausing for a moment to listen and look. He looked like a track runner waiting for the gunshot. Satisfied, Muscles brought his second knee forward...and then it happened.

For a moment Jak thought he was imagining it because he heard it, but couldn't see it. Following the snapping and crumbling, he saw the cracks moving again, working their way up and down the old stone stairway like thin, jagged fingers. Muscles leaped up just as the steps behind him gave way and disappeared.

"RUN!" Jak yelled as he turned and stormed the stairs two at a time. Some of the steps ahead of Jak were falling apart. He glanced back. Muscles was catching up to him. Stone crumbled beneath his feet as he sprinted up the steps toward Jak. There was a dark void behind Muscles where the old stairway was just moments ago.

Jak looked up to gauge Tiny's position. The little runt was already at the top. He was either very fast, or the sneak got a jump on them as Muscles was getting up. Jak was going to have a few choice words for short stuff when he got up there.

Tiny was at the top stomping on the brittle steps. The cracks beneath his leather boots were growing longer and spreading out like branches on a dead tree. Tiny glanced up and stomped even harder and faster when he caught

Jak's eyes. A celebratory smile spread across his freckled face as he watched the steps began to fall apart.

Jak wasn't sure if he was going to make it, especially with Tiny blocking his way...so he reacted. He cawed as loud as he could. "CAW! CAW!" he wailed nearing the top of the breaking stairway. "CAW! CAW!"

Tiny glanced at Jak curiously and then drew his dagger as he jumped up and down faster, getting excited as more pieces of stone fell from the stairway.

Jak was almost at the top. He was close enough to see the top two steps fall apart and break away, leaving just the two side stringers, which were also cracking.

Tiny braced his footing, preparing to stab Jak or push him back onto the disintegrating stairwell. Stabbed or not, Jak had to make it to the platform.

From out of the darkness a winged shadow swooped down upon Tiny's head, clawing bits of flesh from his face. The cries of the raven echoed. Surprised and bewildered, Tiny frantically swung his dagger around at his screeching attacker.

Jak attempted to jump, but his foot went through the step. His arms splayed before him sending the torch to the platform and his sword down the abyss as he fell onto the meager steps before him. For a moment he was looking straight down into the abyss through a hole in the step. His leg was stuck; he couldn't get up. Behind him a mad web of cracks chased up the stone as the stairway crumbled into pieces step by step and fell below. With only three steps remaining behind him, someone pulled him up by his shirt and tossed him over the last of the steps and partway onto the platform.

Jak landed hard on his stomach getting the air knocked out of him. A second later, Muscles landed next to him gasping for air. The two looked at each other. Then Muscles' eyes opened wide, struck with terror. At that moment Jak felt the sensation of his legs dropping. Both boys started sliding off the platform as the rest of the steps broke away and plummeted into the abyss.

Jak and Muscles held on. Their arms were out-stretched, with the edge of the platform beneath their armpits as they watched Tiny stumbling back toward them, swirling and flailing at the massive raven fluttering and screaming above him.

Tiny swung wide and missed and Slade plunged his claws into the boy's chest. Jak and Muscles watched as Tiny staggered back and fell over the edge. His scream was quickly swallowed in the abyss. The sound of flutter-ing wings followed.

The crowd cheered and hollered somewhere in the blackness surrounding Jak and Muscles.

Jak tried hoisting himself up, but his arms were too tired. Muscles lifted himself up over the edge like he'd done it a thousand times. Then he knelt down and placed his hands on Jak's shoulders, smiled, and pulled Jak up onto the platform. The crowd booed.

"Why did you do that?" asked Jak picking up the torch. "Why didn't you take the chance to eliminate me?"

"You waited for me," said Muscles earnestly between breaths, "and…it was your magic that saved us from the little deviant bastard."

"Magic?"

"I heard you call the raven," said Muscles. "It sounded funny," he said smiling, "but it was magic nonetheless. Your ways are as quizzical as your wardrobe."

Jak looked down at his blue jeans and tennis shoes. He must have looked odd to everyone else, as odd as they looked to him in their medieval sort of way.

Making their way through the maze, Jak and Muscles stopped suddenly when the crowd starting cheering again. They looked around, but didn't see anything.

"Something must have happened to the other group," said Muscles. Going by his lack of concern, Jak assumed Muscles was thinking the same thing he was, that hopefully one or more had been eliminated from the competition.

For well over an hour they ducked, dodged, and jostled their way through some difficult traps. The traps no longer appeared to be just for entertainment. The maze was out to get them.

Holding the torch, Jak convinced Muscles to take the lead since he had both hands free to defend against a possible attack. Soon after, Jak found out it was just as dangerous being in back as it was the front because some of the traps were delayed.

Jak and Muscles came to a corridor that had statues of dragon heads along the walls. Their mouths were opened wide like they were ready to bite their victim. The details on the dragon faces were realistic. Although their heads were pointing in all different directions, their eyes seemed to follow Jak and Muscles as they slowly walked down the wide hall. However, it didn't take long to discover that the dragons were not biting, they were breathing.

At the midway point the floor was made of marble with shiny black and white square tiles. There were more black tiles than white ones. After studying it, Jak pointed out to Muscles the white tiles made a path through the sea of black ones.

Muscles took out a dagger and tossed it out onto the floor. The dagger landed on one black tile and slid onto another. It was nearly struck by lightning that came out of a dragon's mouth, which blew a hole in the floor, on the first tile. Then the dagger was turned to solid ice as it slid into another black tile and was hit by a frosty ray coming from a different dragon.

"You've got to be kidding me!" said Jak staring at the frozen dagger next to the smoldering hole in the marble. The thunder from the lightning bolt was still rolling away in the night.

"Looks like you're right," said Muscles. "The white ones are a path...and we better stay on it."

With Muscles leading the way and both boys taking turns, they made their way from one white tile to the next. Some were large and others were small. At first it was a walk in the park. They stepped from one tile to the next. But the farther along they went the farther apart the white tiles were from one another, and the smaller they got.

They reached a point where the next white tile was just inside of jumping distance, but it was the smallest one yet, and the others beyond that one were even smaller. They would probably have to land on one foot to make it. However, there was a large red tile in hopping distance connecting to an easier path of white tiles, which were closer together. It could get them off the marble floor quicker.

Muscles wanted to take the red tile.

"Whadda we have to lose?" he said shrugging his shoulders.

It was a stupid question, but Jak didn't want to take the time pointing out the obvious.

The red tile just seemed too easy. It would probably incinerate a person who landed on it, or perhaps drop a ton of rock on his head.

Or maybe, just maybe, the red tile was a safe spot for the person landing on it, but lead to the destruction of everyone else on the floor, or in this case, just Jak.

What a way to go out, Jak thought, *a big buffoon jumping on a red tile.*

On the other hand the red tile could be a reward for those who made it this far. The last couple of white tiles they jumped onto were far apart; they both had to take good aim and keep their balance to land on them.

After much debate over what it could mean, who should try it, and what kind of odds they had if they kept trying to land on the ever-growing-smaller white tiles, they decided to chance it. After all, what could happen?

Muscles landed dead center on the shiny red tile. A click echoed down the hall behind them followed by a peculiar sound. A shiny red marble the size of a Ping-Pong ball rolled out of one of the dragon's nostrils.

The two boys watched the shiny red marble roll across the stone floor and onto one of the shiny white tiles at the edge of the marble floor. It rolled to a stop near a black tile. Jak and Muscles let out a sigh of relief.

"That could have been disastrous if the idiot who designed the trap did it right," said Muscles. They were so relieved they started laughing.

Another sound interrupted their celebration. Jak yelled to Muscles to move, but his voice was drowned out from the sound of a hailstorm hitting a tin roof. Hundreds of shiny red marbles sprayed out of the dragons' nostrils behind them and onto the stone floor. Jak and Muscles jumped from one white square to the next like two clumsy kangaroos. The red marbles closed in on the marble floor like a swarm of red beetles.

Behind them the red wave washed over the black and white tiles, and the fireworks began. Lightning bolts and fireballs cast from the dragons' mouths blew holes into the floor, throwing bits of black tiles and red marbles into the air. Ice rays fused handfuls of red marbles together into chunks of ice. Acid projecting out like water from a high-pressure hose made intermittent patches of fizzing bubbles, eating holes in the floor.

How they made it out alive was nothing short of a miracle. They ran out of the corridor dodging projectile marbles and dragon breath. Flaming, frozen, sizzling, exploding, and melting red marbles flew around them like mad hornets.

Aside from minor burns and nicks from debris, Jak almost escaped the exploding corridor unharmed. Bubbling with acid, a red marble hit Jak on the calf as he made his way out of the dragons-head corridor and into a smaller passage. He quickly dropped the torch and fell to the floor. With his dagger he cut off the disintegrating piece of denim. Jak flicked the smoldering denim away like it was a venomous snake, grabbed the torch, and scrambled around the corner where Muscles stood dusting himself off.

"Thanks for the helping hand back there," said Jak sarcastically.

"I owe you nothing," said Muscles indifferently. "In case you have already forgotten, let me remind you that I evened the score when I helped you up instead of shoving you down."

Neither one had any more to say. They continued wandering the maze. From the surrounding darkness came the familiar sound of rock grinding against rock as the megaliths shifted and moved around them, reshaping the maze as they moved along.

Eventually a long corridor came to a dead end.

"This can't be right!" said Muscles as if verbalizing his opinion would make the maze realize it was wrong and readjust. "Where did we go wrong?" he asked as if Jak had made the mistake.

"Nowhere," said Jak growing tired of Muscle's looking at him for the answers as if he was supposed to figure everything out for them because Muscles was the strong one.

"You made the wrong turn somewhere. Now we have to backtrack," said Muscles.

"OH...*I* made the wrong turn! Just because you can't make up your own stink'n mind doesn't mean it's *my* fault," Jak lashed out at muscle boy. "And for your information, there's a pattern in the maze, and that pattern leads to this very spot! So if you want to *backtrack* you can do so on your own because wherever the next obstacle lies, it lies somewhere beyond these walls!"

Muscles looked stunned…and ticked. He grabbed the torch from Jak and ran back down the hall.

"Hey, give me that!" Jak shouted.

Jak took off after him, but it was no use. Muscles was too fast. Jak stopped and was soon left in the dark, watching the torchlight grow smaller and smaller. Trying to catch his breath he stood still, careful not to touch anything that may set off a trap.

How am I supposed to find my way around now? Jak thought. *That idiot!*

Jak focused on the small glow from the torch down the long corridor, waiting for it to vanish around another corner. But it didn't.

The buffoon should have turned the other corner by now. Maybe something happened to him.

The thought was pleasing. He could recover the torch *and* there would be one less contestant. Jak started walking toward the torchlight, but then the torchlight started coming back to him.

What? Jak stopped.

Muscles was chugging at full speed toward Jak.

"Get out of the way!" Muscles yelled. The corridor grumbled angrily behind him.

A rusty, iron wall the entire height and width of the corridor, rumbled its way toward them bearing rusty, blood-stained spikes, hooks, and blades.

Jak turned and ran knowing full well it was a dead end.

Muscles reached the dead end first. He immediately started beating on the wall, screaming at it as if demanding it to move. When Jak came to the dead end he frantically looked around for a lever, loose stone, knob... anything.

The iron wall and its mangled weaponry closed in... fifty feet...forty feet.

"WHAT DO WE DO?" Muscles yelled staring bug-eyed at Jak.

"Give me that!"

Jak grabbed the torch from Muscles, held it high, and looked up the wall and into the dark sky. Slade flew in circles above them.

The megaliths in this area were at least twenty feet high. Slade landed on top of the dead end and looked down. There was nothing the raven could do for him but watch.

Thirty feet...twenty feet, the wall drew closer.

"There has to be a lever or switch somewhere! There must be an out!" Jak called out. At a glance he could tell the wall was moving too fast to try and climb it without getting impaled before it reached the end.

Fifteen feet...ten feet....

Jak closed his eyes and backed up against the wall.

Muscles was crying, "I don't want to be a part of this anymore! Let me out!"

Seven...six...five...four...and the rumbling stopped.

Jak slowly opened his eyes. Several spikes were inches from his head and body. The iron wall stood still like an old, grumpy sentry.

Muscles stopped yelling, his back to the spiked iron wall. Shaking and sweating, he slowly moved his head to look at Jak.

"What happened?" asked Muscles between sniffles. "Is it safe to turn around?"

The spikes and blades were not as long on Muscles' side of the wall. If the wall had not stopped, Jak would have been impaled because the spikes and blades were longer on Jak's half of the wall, but Muscles would have gone untouched. Seeing the iron contraption up close it seemed to have been designed to kill only one, leaving the other person alone, and of course horrified.

"You're okay," said Jak looking up and studying the wall. "We're going to have to climb this thing to get out. It's safe for you to turn…."

Before Jak could finish, something moved on Muscle's side. In his peripheral vision Jak saw long, thin spikes thrusting forward from the iron wall, and the sound of screechy, rusty iron followed by crunching and the distinct ting of iron slamming into rock. The invisible crowd cheered.

Jak kept looking up in the dark night above, afraid to look at what he was sure just happened. He heard himself asking, "Hey…are you okay?" His own voice sounded strange and frightening. There was no answer.

He made himself turn and look, but quickly turned away. Muscles was pinned to the dead end wall. Multiple spikes impaled his back, head, and an arm.

Frightened, Jak fought back tears and dropped into a surreal numbness.

The rumble startled him when the iron wall moved a few feet back. Not wanting to look over at Muscles, Jak looked up. The torchlight revealed his faithful companion perched above him. The raven grinned approvingly. Jak was about to say something when the floor fell from under him and he dropped into another chamber.

Jak landed hard on his back. The torch and his dagger fell next to him. This round chamber was well lit with torches lining the walls. Two others were in the room with him.

"Well, well…there's another one," said Rotund wobbling over to Jak.

Jak sprung to his feet with the dagger and torch in his hands. He wasn't going to let the big boy get too close and definitely not behind him.

"Easy there," said Rotund stopping in his place. "I just wanted to see what kind of shape you're in, that's all."

"I'm fine, thanks," Jak declared in a quiver, making it clear he did not want to be approached.

"Where are the other two?" asked Long Hair looking disheveled and tired. He was holding a torch and a sword.

Jak noticed Rotund had acquired a different weapon. He was holding a large maul in his paw. Rotund didn't look as tired as Long Hair looked or Jak felt, but he had his fair share of scrapes and cuts. Rotund seemed to be enjoying himself.

"They're dead," said Jak. The words felt foreign on his lips.

"Then I guess it's just the three of us," said Long Hair.

Jak didn't ask what had happened to Black Hair and didn't want to know.

The walls of the round room stood over fifty feet tall. Six iron double doors were evenly spaced apart on the outside wall behind the party. A small iron path, like a sidewalk, led from each door toward a round pool of lava, bubbling and gurgling in the center of the room.

A round, stone platform hovered above the lava. Staring down at the three survivors stood a creature that had the head of a bull, large, curved horns and solid red eyes. Its body resembled a man's, but with bulging muscles. The beast was decked in custom armor covering its chest and trunk; a long black cape hung from its broad shoulders. In its right hand it held the handle of a whip, which wound its way over the beast's opposite shoulder and across its midsection. In the beast's left hand was a wooden staff that looked like two tree branches twisted together.

"Great! A minotaur!" snapped Rotund under his breath. "I hate these guys!"

Jak was about to ask him why when suddenly the six double doors rumbled open and skeleton warriors streamed into the room along the outer wall until they were surrounded. The doors slammed shut behind the last undead warrior. The warriors stood against the wall, holding their swords across their long shields.

"Three of you remain," said the minotaur, his deep voice resonated, "but only one of you is allowed to leave here alive." From the surrounding darkness, the unseen crowd cheered.

"Each of you will be told a riddle. If you know the answer I will give you my staff, otherwise known as the Banishing Stick, to use against one opponent. You only need to touch your opponent and his life will be forfeit." As the minotaur spoke he continued to look at each of them. His red glare pierced through whatever confidence Jak had remaining and replaced it with fear.

"If you do not know the answer to the riddle, you will have to defeat a skeleton warrior to stay alive and in the game," the minotaur continued. "If more than one of you remains standing at the end of the three riddles, you will not only have to defeat the last contestant, but you will have to defeat either me, or the remaining skeleton warriors." The minotaur's chest heaved as he laughed. "You would be better off fighting the skeletons," said the minotaur.

Jak quickly counted. There were twenty skeleton warriors around the room. So even if he survived the war of the riddles, he was sure he would die by the blade of one of those anorexic warriors.

"Guards! Show them their place," the minotaur barked.

Three warriors stepped out of rank, marched over, and led Jak, Rotund, and Long Hair each to the end of an iron path where they were left standing in a circle of stones. Iron chains and anklets were anchored to the floor. Jak was dumbfounded when the warriors turned and marched back to their ranks, leaving the three contestants free from the chains.

The minotaur looked each of them over, but his eyes rested on Jak. Then he turned to Rotund and snarled.

Jak wondered if the minotaur heard Rotund mention that he hated minotaurs.

"You are allowed one answer only," said the minotaur to Rotund, "so answer wisely. *What is gained, but never lost? Can be shared, but never given? Cannot be held, but is carried everywhere?*"

The minotaur stood silently, staring down at Rotund.

Rotund looked like a deer in headlights. By the blank expression on his face it was obvious he didn't know the answer. He just stood there, staring into nothingness as if the answer was going to materialize before him. The minotaur didn't blink or take his eyes off of Rotund.

"Your time is running out," the minotaur grumbled.

Jak was glad this wasn't his riddle because he didn't know the answer.

"I…I don't know," said Rotund.

The minotaur lifted his gaze to one of the undead warriors behind Rotund.

"Wait!" Rotund pleaded. "Is it…WEALTH?"

The minotaur returned his gaze to Rotund. "NO," said the minotaur. He seemed pleased. "The answer is… experience." Looking at one of the warriors, the minotaur nodded and a warrior behind Rotund charged him with his shield up and sword held high.

Rotund held the minotaur's glare. The only sound in the room was the clinking of the skeleton warrior's armor fast approaching Rotund. Rotund drew a dagger from his belt, spun around, and threw the dagger, pinning it into the skeleton's forehead. The skeleton dropped to the ground in a loud clank. It didn't move.

Rotund turned and yelled at the minotaur, "Is that all you got?"

The minotaur snorted and then turned to Long Hair.

"You are allowed one answer only," said the minotaur to Long Hair, "so answer brilliantly. *Feeds, but has no mouth. Breathes, but has no lungs. Thrives at night, by killing dark. Cradle to grave in a spark.*"

The minotaur looked down at Long Hair, poised as rigid as the staff he held in his left, fury hand.

Jak was miffed this wasn't his riddle. The answer was obvious.

With little thought, Long Hair answered confidently, "Fire."

Jak was disappointed. He watched the minotaur grin, and after a dramatic pause he said, "CORRECT!"

It happened so quickly Jak didn't have time to react. He heard them before he saw them. The chains anchored to the stone floor struck quick like snakes, clasping his ankles and wrists in the shackles and causing Jak to drop his dagger. Not too far away Rotund was trying with all his might to break free from the chains, cursing them as though they had a free will. Jak tugged and kicked a few times, but gauging from the grip the chains had, he wasn't going anywhere.

The minotaur tossed the Banishing Stick to Long Hair, whose chains remained limp at his feet. Long Hair caught it in both hands, admiring it like it was adorned with rare jewels, like it was priceless. At the moment it was. He had the ability to take out one of his opponents, leaving just two to fight for the position of warlock.

"Strike ONE of your foes, and then return to your circle," said the minotaur, gripping the handle of his whip like a wild west gunslinger.

Jak felt nauseous when Long Hair turned and walked toward him instead of walking the other way around the circle toward Rotund. Maybe Rotund and Long Hair made a truce in the beginning. That would explain why only Dark Hair died in their group.

His muscles tensed and strained as he pulled on the chains with all his might like a wild animal. There was no way he was going to die by the hands of a boy that had longer hair than his sister! NO WAY!

"Yeah! Way to go! Strike that scrawny bastard down!" Rotund yelled out in an exaggerated excitement that annoyed and enraged Jak. He hated that laughing, fat, good-for-noth'n jackass. He wanted to rip him apart... "Shut UP you SPONGY SLOB!" Jak spat at Rotund, who heckled even more at Jak's pain and fear.

"Calm yourself," he heard someone say next to him. Turning away from Rotund and the boisterous laughter, he met Long Hair's gaze. "I had to take the long way around to give the crowd what they want," said Long Hair. "Besides, I can't take the chance that big mouth over there could possibly become a warlock over one of us." Long Hair smirked and then continued on toward Rotund.

Rotund's heckling quickly morphed into curses and threats when it was evident Long Hair was coming his way. "YOU'RE THE BIGGEST BACKSTABBING COWARD I HAVE EVER KNOWN!" Rotund shrieked.

Long Hair stopped just beyond Rotund's reach. "Kill me now, but I am going to come back AND KICK YOUR BUTT WHEN THEY RAISE ME!" Rotund leaned and tugged until his face was red.

"Unfortunately, it doesn't work that way...and you know it," said Long Hair calmly, and struck Rotund in the gut with the Banishing Stick. Cheering and yelling from the crowd rose like a windstorm. Rotund's stomach was glowing orange and then red. He fought the pain, clenching his teeth. The hot glow soon burst into flames, consuming Rotund from the inside-out. Rotund's scream escaped as his entire body was consumed by fire. It took just seconds for his screams to disappear and the flames to subside leaving behind ashes and bones.

The shackles on Rotund's skeleton opened, leaving the bones lying free. Jak's shackles released him and fell to his feet. Long Hair was still looking down at the bulky skeleton lying at his feet when the whip cracked through the air and wrapped several times around the Banishing Stick. With the flick of his forearm, the minotaur had the Banishing Stick out of Long Hair's hand and into his own.

"Return to your circle," he instructed Long Hair, who obligingly walked back.

As he passed Jak, Long Hair quietly said, "Unfortunately, you're next." Long Hair took his place in the stone circle standing confidently.

The minotaur turned to Jak.

"You are allowed one answer only," said the minotaur to Jak, "so answer with authority. *Hold this and you can have anything. Nations rise and fall from it. It divides kings from cowards. Hold it not, and you are nothing."*

The minotaur's red eyes glowered at Jak, but Jak looked through them and beyond. One of the lines in the riddle was familiar.

"It divides kings from cowards." Jak could hear the voice from his past.

Jak kept repeating it to himself, *It divides kings from cowards…It divides kings from cowards….*

"What is your answer?" asked the minotaur, his deep voice cutting into Jak's recollection. "Your time is running out," he warned.

"Power separates a great man from a commoner. It divides kings from cowards," said the voice from his relentless past.

"What did you say?" the minotaur asked in disbelief.

Jak was suddenly aware he was quietly saying, "Power…power…power," as if discovering the word for the first time. He articulated his answer to be sure the beast heard him well because, without a doubt, the answer was, "POWER!"

The minotaur's head flicked to the side like he had just been slapped by an invisible hand. After contemplating for a moment the minotaur reluctantly said, "Correct."

The chains around Long Hair snapped to attention, anchoring him to the stone circle. Long Hair was shocked. He was looking around the room. Jak got the feeling he was looking for plan B.

The minotaur tossed the Banishing Stick to Jak. Catching it, Jak glanced at Slade flying out of the shadows.

He looked down at the old staff that showed its age from the many nicks and scrapes in the smooth, worn wood. The tip of the Banishing Stick was a wooden knuckle.

He won! He made it through this monstrosity alive.

"Come on! What are you waiting for?" Long Hair yelled.

Oh yeah. He had to take a life in order to save his own. For a moment he was unsure of himself. But Long Hair's warning was fresh in Jak's mind, "*You're next.*"

Better him than me.

Jak walked over to Long Hair. He would touch the staff to his opponent's head quickly, like pulling off a bandage; it would be easier for both of them. Long Hair stood still. He was ready for what was coming next...and appeared unusually calm for someone who was about to die.

As Jak extended the banishing stick to touch him, the chains on Long Hair dropped freely to the ground, taking Jak by surprise. This wasn't supposed to happen! Long Hair dodged the staff with ease and kicked Jak in the chest, knocking him to the floor. The staff fell to the ground.

Jak stumbled up, gasping for air. Long Hair was going for the Banishing Stick.

Jak looked around and then remembered he had dropped his blade when the chains latched on to him. He turned to run when the whip cracked the air and he suddenly fell to the ground. The whip was wrapped around Jak's ankle and the minotaur was pulling him toward the lava pool under the hovering platform.

Jak flopped over in time to see Long Hair come down on him with the Banishing Stick. Jak tried desperately to roll out of the way, but the wooden knuckle struck him in the shoulder. He wasn't sure what happened. He was prepared for a hot, burning sensation, but instead there was nothing. Long Hair looked as surprised as Jak felt.

"FOOL!" the minotaur roared. "The charge works only for the one who correctly answers the riddle." The minotaur yanked the whip, sliding Jak a few more feet.

Jak rolled over and grabbed a chain from the stone circle Long Hair occupied moments ago.

"Use your sword!" the minotaur commanded Long Hair, and then tugged the whip, but Jak had wrapped the chain around his wrist and hand. Jak's leg was suspended in the air, and the whip was cutting into his ankle. Long Hair was going for his sword.

"Slade! The minotaur! Now!" Jak called out. The chain started slipping off his bloody wrist.

Long Hair pointed his sword at the minotaur and hollered, "Behind you!"

Slade, the raven, was swooping down behind the minotaur, wings spread and claws out. Holding the handle of the whip in one hand, the minotaur reached behind his back and drew a long sword, its polished blade gleaming in the chamber's orange glow.

The raven cawed.

Jak yelled, "Slaaaaade!"

The minotaur laughed haughtily, swinging his sword upward.

The raven changed. The panther roared!

Taken by surprise, the minotaur dropped the whip and tried moving out of the panther's way in the last seconds of his life. Slade, the panther, plowed into the minotaur, sending the horned beast and his sword plunging into the lava pool below. Catching the edge with his paws, Slade the panther leaped off the platform, landed next to Jak, and growled at Long Hair.

The undead crowd burst into wild shouting. The dark arena echoed from the din of clanking armor, weapons, and shields.

Long Hair was frozen in place at the ready with the Banishing Stick in one hand and his sword in the other. Dropping the bloody chain, Jak undid the whip around his ankle as Slade kept Long Hair at bay.

"What is this? A companion?" Long Hair spat. "That's cheating!"

Jak chuckled. If he hadn't just been kicked, jabbed, and almost dragged into a pit of lava, he would have been laughing.

"Cheating…really?" Jak shook his head and placed his hand on the panther's back. "You know what I hate more than a hypocrite?" Jak asked, watching and waiting for Long Hair to make a move. "Pretty, long-haired boys."

"You have no idea what you are doing," said Long Hair. "Bedlam will chew you up and spit you out."

"I've made it this far," said Jak, his anger burning.

"Let me live, and we can fight our way out of here! I can help you!"

"You're mad! I have no reason to trust you…or anybody," Jak hissed.

Long Hair's voice changed as did his expression. Instead of glowering he looked on Jak with sympathy. His voice was hushed, but carried sincerity. "My name is Enrik. I fight for Magnanthia!"

"I don't care who you are or who you fight for!" The hate was rancid in Jak's mouth. "I fight for Jak! And since one of us has to go...better you than me!"

"If that thing kills me you don't win! You have to kill me, or I you," said Enrik indifferently.

Jak glanced around. The skeleton warriors had not moved.

"Okay," said Jak. "Slade...fetch."

In two giant leaps the panther was on the other side of Enrik, who spun around watching the panther.

Slade crouched and then leaped high in the air toward Long Hair. Long Hair thrust his sword toward the panther, but missed his target completely. The panther had disappeared and a large raven latched onto the Banishing Stick with one claw and scratched Enrik's hand with the other causing Enrik to let go.

Swooping upward, the raven let go of the stick. It landed in Jak's hand. Enrik spun around, his sword outstretched at neck level, but Jak went low, driving the wooden staff into his gut. Enrik grimaced, as the red and orange glow in his gut grew more intense.

"You've made a big mistake..." said Enrik, sadly, and was consumed in flames.

Ashes, bones, and the sword held by the boy with long hair fell to the ground.

The raven perched on Jak's shoulder.

"Thanks Slade," said Jak exhausted and sore.

"We grow together, remember?" said Slade.

All the megaliths but the one Jak stood upon rose into the night. The coliseum lit up once again as all its torches and fire pits ignited. Tens of thousands of undead silently looked upon Jak and his raven standing in the center of the coliseum. Oddly, Jak found the silence more unnerving than the undead.

A single clapper broke the silence. Severn sat in his throne, slowly clapping.

"I give you...our seventh and final warlock!" said Severn gesturing down to Jak. The other five warlocks, on either side of Severn, began clapping. Lonique was among the shadow sentries. She looked pleased.

Then the coliseum filled with a din of banging and clashing of metal, and cheers.

Jak heard the uproar, but it sounded distant through his surreal trance. He looked at the pile of bones at his feet. How long had he been in this maze? It felt like a lifetime ago he took his first steps into Mayhem.

18

A COURTYARD ON A
BRANCH

A s soon as Simon turned his back to the five Magnanthians, he felt ashamed. Thianna called after him, but he kept going and hoped she wasn't coming for him. His mind was stuffed full of unprocessed information because emotionally he couldn't keep up. Anxiety and excitement were mixed together with plenty of fear and self-doubt, along with a heaping amount of doing the right thing with a little of doing his own thing, and adding a dash of disbelief. He needed some time alone, and he didn't stop walking until he realized he had no idea where he was.

Simon decided to keep going until he found his way back to his room. Turning this way and that way he passed by and through various rooms. Some rooms were small and cozy with a couple of chairs, or a sofa with a small coffee table and a lantern or two with just the right amount of light.

Other rooms were large. One room had two big fireplaces, puffy chairs, cozy sofas, and a reading lantern by each seat. Stuffed bookshelves lined this room's walls. Sunlight streaming through tall windows warmed and lit this room during the day. The windows were adorned with large royal red curtains that flowed elegantly from one end of the room to the next.

Simon walked over and looked out the windows. Large branches obstructed his view from the ground, but he was high enough that sunlight made its way through the forest's mighty canopy and into the library.

Another room had various supplies for making things. It was a craft room full of materials, tools, workbenches, and exotic equipment. Clothes for men, women, and children hung on racks in one of the corners.

Most of the rooms had the look and feel of a tree house, a very clean and neat tree house, with the exception of the formal dining hall. Sets of armor stood at attention against the wall donned with different weapons, halberds, swords, shields, maces, great axes, crossbows, and war hammers. The dining table ran the length of the room, adorned with fine silver and dark green vines that intertwined with the place settings in a repeating pattern up and down the table. The table could seat sixty-two comfortably. Above the table hung two chandeliers giving this room a rich glow. The chandeliers were much like the orbs in the forest that led them to Domic's Haven.

Down the hall from the formal dining room, Simon came upon a set of large, wooden double doors arched at the top and decorated with fine etchings of vines, leaves, and other plant shapes. Natural light came through arched transoms above the doors. Simon pulled on one of the big handles with both hands, but it didn't budge.

"Great...I'm locked in," he muttered and turned to leave.

A thought came to him and he stopped. Turning back around he pushed the doors and they slowly opened.

Fresh, cool air whisked by and warm sunrays fell upon him. Spread out before him was a courtyard on one of Domic's massive branches. And beyond the courtyard, a great distance away, was a magnificent sight. Shiftwood Forrest made its way down to a gully and around the base of a mountain; a hundred or more waterfalls cascaded down its rocky sides. Dozens of rainbows arched their way through the constant mist, which engulfed the base of the mountain like looming clouds. The shiftwood trees nearest the mountain were taller than Domic's Haven.

Simon walked around the courtyard, listening to the comforting rumbling and splashing in the distance and admired the systematic patterns many of the waterfalls made together, with an occasional waterfall or two breaking off the pattern. He watched, listened, and could even smell the waterfalls such a great distance away.

His stress and worries began diminishing. There, before him, was something much larger, something grand. He realized how small he was standing in a courtyard on a branch of a tree. The shiftwood trees seemed small, like blades of grass, at the foot of the mammoth mountain. The mountain, a sitting giant amongst those blades of grass, made Simon feel miniscule...and suddenly so did his own problems. He was a speck on a blade of grass. And even though his worries were real to him, there was a world full of worries out there, a world even bigger than the mammoth mountain.

A gentle voice called him. "Simon...Simon?"

Sonica stood in the door's archway. Simon looked at her, and then turned to the waterfalls. He wanted to be left alone, and yet he was glad she was there. He had acted like a fool.

"May I come out and join you?" asked Sonica. Her kindness made him feel even worse for walking out on them in the kitchen.

"Of course...it's not my place to say what you can and cannot do," said Simon trying to lose himself in the distant waterfalls, but the touch of her hand on his arm brought him back.

"I respect you," she said. "If you want to be left alone, I will respect your wish." From the corner of his eye he saw she was giving no notice to the beautiful view in front of them, but was looking at him. He wanted to look at her, but was ashamed. He could feel tears welling up.

"See how weak I am?" said Simon. "I'm crying because I'm afraid of change. I'm crying because I'm afraid of the expectations you and the others have of me, and of letting all of you down. I'm crying because I miss my father and friends back home! I'm crying, Sonica, because this place is overwhelmingly beautiful. I can actually feel the life around me!"

She moved closer to him and with her sleeve wiped his tears away.

"For the reasons you cry, confirms what Domic said… this is no mistake," she said passionately.

He looked at her, confused. Her eyes held his.

"Simon Whittaker…you are the polar opposite of weak. Your passion for life confirms this…and we *need* you. We need your help," she said placing her hand back on his arm. "Please Simon…. I promise you, your father is at peace and knows you are being cared for."

"How do you know?"

"I…I am not able to say, but please…trust me, and you will soon find out," she said. Her eyes told the truth. "And as for change and expectations, we will all help you with these issues. You have my word!" she said.

How could he say no to people who believed in him? How could he say no to such a peaceful place? How could he say no…to Sonica? She had treated him with nothing but kindness and respect.

"If your home was on the brink of destruction by the darkest evil imaginable, and I was holding in my hand the ability to help save your homeland, what would you be asking of me? What would you expect me to do?" Her eyes told him what she would do. But he didn't have to look into her eyes to know she would drop everything she deemed important to help another soul in need. Sonica had a kind heart and it showed in everything she did. From her sincere words and her empathetic response to those who were suffering, her loving nature showed in everything she did.

Simon decided then and there he owed it to her, to the others, and to himself to find out more, to see what he could do to help. Curiosity had also been sprinkled into his emotional soup.

"Okay, Sonica," he said. "I will take the next step with you…under one condition." She looked at him in anticipation of his request. "Someone explains to me why my father is at peace even though he doesn't know where I am."

A smile spread across her face. "DEAL!"

"Shall I inform the others?" said Domic behind them, his silver-blue silhouette, the tall, strong butler, appeared in the doorway.

"Yes Domic," Sonica said in her giddy state, squeezing Simon's arm, "it appears we can depart soon."

Domic turned around and walked away, vanishing from sight after a few steps.

Sonica took in the view before them. "It is called Paramount Peak. It's the largest mountain in Magnanthia, and lifeblood to all of Shiftwood Forrest and much of the kingdom. It's been said Paramount Peak is so large all the other mountains in Magnanthia could fit into it. Its falls, The Great Falls of Reconciliation, feed almost every river in the land," she said admiringly.

Simon was looking at The Great Falls of Reconciliation, but thinking of something else. "It doesn't bother you Domic was listening to our conversation?"

She looked at him like he had a banana sticking out of his ear.

"What do mean?"

"Correct me if I'm wrong," said Simon confused at her inability to see the wrong in what happened, "but it seems to me he heard everything we said. He had to have been standing in the doorway the whole time!"

"You are not wrong," she said casually. "He probably heard most of our conversation."

"This doesn't bother you?"

"Of course not." She looked concerned from Simon's discomfort. "Simon, do you know who Domic is?"

"Yeah, he's the spirit...who lives in...the tree?" The more he thought about it, Simon didn't understand who, or what, Domic was.

"Domic *is* the tree," said Sonica, giving Simon a moment to think about it. "As long as we are in, on, or around him, he is omnipresent."

Simon was trying to get a handle on this. "But he looks human."

"That is the form he has chosen, out of respect and honor, to reveal to us so we can see a part of him, and, I think," she said in a whisper, "so he can relate to us. He can no more help being with us right now as you can help being with me right now."

"He's still here?" Simon looked around.

Sonica playfully laughed at the sight of Simon looking around. "Well, you are standing on him. Look all around, Simon. Look at his many branches, his leaves, his massive trunk...all of him."

Simon began to see. "He is the *actual* tree?" Sonica nodded her head. "Wow...do all the trees have an inner spirit like Domic?"

"Yes, they all have inner spirits, but no, not like Domic's. All trees communicate to one another and to rangers, like me, who are either trained or gifted in speaking with nature. But Domic was given a gift," she said and walked over to a wood bench. It had grown up from the very branch they were walking on. "The gift is a rare and ancient magic, which allows him to sustain his life when he shares it with others. This power has become very powerful over the centuries." Sonica softly rubbed the top of the bench. "It is truly amazing what he has learned to do with his gift over time and who he has become."

"How did you discover him?" said Simon looking at the massive tree in a new light. "I mean I know you're too young to have discovered him, but how did you befriend him?"

"It was one of my ancestors, Necodemus Wintergreen, who befriended Domic. Necodemus was, and still is, known as the greatest lover of trees. He devoted his life and all of his magic to trees. Although he loved all trees, it was shiftwood trees he loved most. So he lived out here with his family.

"Necodemus knew the shiftwood trees in this area had the best chance of survival and would grow healthy and strong being so near to Paramount Peak. The shiftwoods thrive on the misty air, a constant, refreshing drink. Necodemus and his entire family dedicated their lives to protecting the trees until the shiftwoods were large enough to protect themselves.

"As Necodemus grew old and the world around him became more populated, his concern for the trees weighed heavily on his heart. He found a way, with the help of a cleric who knew the ways of the time of old, to be permitted to give a tree a small piece of his soul in order to protect Shiftwood Forrest. Before he died, Necodemus gifted the soul piece to Domic so he could be closer to the tree he so loved, and taught Domic how to use magic.

"The gift allows Domic to use the strength he gets from the sun and water to heal himself and others. This is what allows Domic to build rooms within his own body and heal what would otherwise kill many trees. The more he gives and helps others from his soul, not out of obligation or greed, the more strength he gains.

"Necodemus and his family lived their final days here, with Domic as their friend, host, and domicile. To this day, Necodemus' tomb lies somewhere within, or near, Domic's Haven."

"So the ethereal form is Necodemus?" asked Simon.

"In part...a small piece of him is part of the tree...the rest is Domic," said Sonica admiring the tree as if seeing it for the first time. "Domic wanted to honor Necodemus and allow him to be eternally remembered, so he chose to use Necodemus' form to communicate with other beings. Our family greatly appreciates it. Domic has always been so kind to us...."

Simon felt sheepish for accusing Domic of spying when really all he was doing was hearing. "Why doesn't Domic always show himself so we remember he is always here?"

"Good question," said Sonica, "one you should ask him."

"I will, as soon as he arrives with the others."

"Remember, he is there with them and here with us at the same time. Just ask," she said encouragingly.

"Right now?"

Sonica nodded.

"Okay…umm…Domic? Why not always reveal yourself to us so we know you are always here?"

"That is a great question Simon, one I am sure others have also wondered," said Domic, his silver-blue form slowly appearing close to Sonica and Simon until the image of the ancient Necodemus Wintergreen was standing in the courtyard with them on Domic's branch. "I feel it best to remain unseen to respect one's privacy the best I can.

"Perhaps it is best to think of me as a father watching over his children playing in the room. I can hear and see everything you do if I focus on you, or 'pay attention' per se; however, I choose to tune out what I can to respect your privacy. You need only to ask and like the father in the room I can 'turn the other way' to give you privacy.

"However, I am always here for you if you need me." His ethereal eyes looked upon Sonica. "I am eternally thankful to Master Necodemus Wintergreen, and I take great joy in serving his kin and their loved ones."

"I'm sorry Domic. Forgive me, please," said Simon looking down at Domic's sparkling boots. "I'm an idiot and know better than to jump to conclusions. It's a fool's way."

Domic lifted Simon's chin with a massive hand. Although Domic was celestial, his touch was very human.

"Wise words young Whittaker," said Domic lovingly in his deep, resonating voice. "You were forgiven the moment the words left your lips. It takes heart and courage to admit one's regret. An *idiot* you certainly are not." Domic smiled and patted Simon's shoulder. "The others are about to arrive," said Domic as his form started evaporating from the ground, up. "And remember Simon, I have my eyes on you," said Domic winking at him right before his neck and head evaporated, leaving Simon with a smile.

"Master Whittaker and Lady Wintergreen," said Domic at the door, his two evanescent hands properly crossing each other, "the rest of your party has arrived."

Simon waited for them to come in, but after a short wait Sonica said, "Thank you Domic. I believe Simon and I are finished...Simon?" she prompted Simon with a smile.

"Oh...yeah, I mean, yes, we are finished...thank you, Domic," Simon managed.

Sonica laughed as Domic gestured for the others to enter. Simon's face flushed.

Wheelock, Thianna, and Heaton entered the courtyard.

"I won't ask," said Wheelock lightly seeing Sonica laugh while Simon blushed.

They all gathered around a table located under a canopy of large leaves. The leaves were so large each one stretched across the width of the table. High above the canopy were leaves shaped in such a way as to capture some of the mist in the air. As the moisture gathered in the leaves, the water dripped down upon the canopy like fresh rain on a sunny day. Simon appreciated the pitter-patter of the water drops falling upon the canopy. It was comforting, and he needed all the comfort he could get right now. He was unsure of how the other three were going to respond to his abrupt departure from the kitchen.

They all sat down as Domic busied himself serving cool water, glittering vapors trailing behind his swift hands. Simon found it amusing that Domic would grab whatever item he needed from the air. It was like he had an invisible cart plumb full of…everything.

"Simon has agreed to take the next step with us," said Sonica, her enthusiasm embarrassing Simon, "but under one condition. Go ahead," she said, directing the attention to Simon. Hearing her say it like that made his proposal sound crass. Sonica seemed to think the same thing. After saying it, her smile sank.

"Look, I don't mean to come across as demanding, I just…"

"How did you mean for it to sound?" asked Heaton.

"Heaton," said Thianna. She was calm, yet stern. "Let him speak." Heaton bit his lip and took a deep breath. He was dying to say what was on his mind, but Thianna's stare held him back. "Simon, as you were saying."

"What I meant is…I didn't mean it as a demand," said Simon trying to choose his words wisely. He didn't know the others well enough to gauge their expressions and body language so he only could go by their responses. "I mean it as more of a request. I will move forward with you, but I need to know how my father is doing and how my absence has been explained to him, and to my teachers, and my friends. Although, Jessica already knows about this..." he gestured to their surroundings. "I guess I'm not sure how to handle this. You're asking me to drop my life as I know it and turn a sharp corner with my eyes closed."

No one responded, but everyone was thinking about what he said.

"My heart says I owe it to you to help in whatever way I can, but it sounds unbelievable and ludicrous to me," said Simon looking around the table at each of them. "But my heart also says I owe the people back home, in Riverside, an explanation. I want them to know I'm okay. I don't want the whole town running around posting signs up with my face on them and forming search parties, only to get fed some lame story that I was vacationing with the Wells family at Itasca State Park for... however long I'm going to be here. That wouldn't be fair to them."

Simon decided to leave it at that and wait in the silence, which he was thankful didn't last too long.

"You speak of owing us as though you are indebted to us," said Wheelock. "You owe us nothing. And you speak from your heart, for which I am pleased." Wheelock cracked his normal serious expression with a smile.

Wheelock looked to Thianna and then back to Simon. "This means, however, we are at an impasse for we hold not the knowledge you seek," said Wheelock regretfully. "Sonica is the only one that was sent to obtain you and bring you back. The extent of our knowledge of your world, including how matters are being handled there, goes only as far as Sonica's experience."

"What about the others that were with her?" asked Simon.

"The Cordon Society is a group of Magnanthians who agreed to live in your world, for reasons we know not," said Sonica disappointed with her own answer. "The Cordon Society protects a gateway connecting our two worlds. Before I arrived I was given explicit instructions not to ask questions while in the presence of the Cordon Society. Once there I was only allowed to speak to a few individuals. The Cordon Society is very secretive and offered no information to me about your homeland, outside of what I needed to know in order to accomplish my task…obtaining you. I am sorry Simon. They told me little of your family, other than your father was safe, in able hands, and everything would be all right. The only reason they told me about the Wells family is because I was about to make contact with them. As it turned out, Jessica and Randal were the only two at your location when I arrived."

Simon was disappointed. He wanted to be assured everything was going to be okay back home.

Sonica looked sorrowful. "Simon, I thought Wheelock would know more about the Cordon Society and how they were going to take care of things for you."

Sonica turned to Wheelock. "You assured me his father was not going to be harmed and would be informed of Simon's whereabouts and condition when the time was right," said Sonica holding back her frustration, "and now I am made a liar, assuring Simon his father is safe."

"I do know of the Cordon Society," said Wheelock, addressing Sonica in his usual serious tone, "and I *did* assure you. I assure you once more; Simon's father has come to no harm," looking to Simon he continued, "and this includes your home community, Riverside."

"I don't understand. How can you assure me if you can't give me the answer I am looking for?" asked Simon.

"You are correct," said Wheelock, "I cannot give you the answer you are looking for."

"But, you just said…"

"I know what I said young Whittaker," said Wheelock. "We do not know *how* the matter is being taken care of back in Riverside. However, I do know the Cordon Society is taking care of things and we need not worry about it. There are times, Simon, we need to take matters in our own hands and there are times we need to trust others to do their part in taking care of matters.

"It is my understanding that Sonica assured you your father would be taken care of before you entered the portal with her," said Wheelock, methodically stroking his goatee. "Is this correct?"

Simon thought for a moment. "Yes…yes she did," he said.

"Sonica also mentioned your friend Jessica and her brother Randal assured you they would take care of things in Riverside while you were away. Is this correct?" Simon felt he was on trial and Wheelock was the prosecuting attorney.

"Yes…they did," he admitted. Simon knew where Wheelock was going with these questions.

"Then why, Simon, is it important to you to know *how* the Cordon Society and the Wells family are taking care of the matter in Riverside when you already know that they are, indeed, taking caring of it?" asked Wheelock contemplating his own question.

Simon had to think about it; he wasn't really sure.

"You are a real conundrum," said Heaton snidely. "You are handed the greatest gift a warrior could ever ask for, and all you can do is cry over not being able to see your mommy and daddy." Pointing to Simon, Heaton addressed the rest of the party, "How is *he* going to become a guardian and help us in any way?"

"Heaton!" Thianna contested. "This is inappropriate!"

"No! I think it is very appropriate," Heaton grumbled. "Now that we are all present it is time to say what is on our minds!"

"Why is my request so unreasonable?" asked Simon.

"Because with all that is going on around here, you being homesick is *not* a priority!" Heaton barked.

"I'm not homesick. I'm concerned…"

"I know!" Heaton snapped. "You have made it clear what you are concerned about." Heaton jumped up out of his chair; Sonica flinched next to Simon. "Wheelock! It is evident our new guardian cares more for his own hide than he does for any of us! I say he gives back the ring and we move on without him!"

"That's ridiculous!" Sonica exclaimed looking to Wheelock for a response, but Wheelock said nothing.

"Here! You want your stupid ring back?" Simon stood up and tried taking off the ring. He pulled and twisted, but the ring was taught and didn't move a single centimeter. "Damn it! I order you to come off my hand!" yelled Simon slamming has hand down upon the table. "Why can't I get this thing off?" Simon tried pulling more.

"Maybe if you would actually try, instead of putting on a show," Heaton chided.

Simon pointed at Heaton. "I'm getting really tired of your accusations and your attitude!"

"Boys, this is not the way we handle ourselves," said Thianna as nicely as she could with a sense of urgency. "Time is of utmost importance and you are wasting it."

"Keep pointing at me and I will lop your ring finger off, *take* the ring back, and send you packing back to dear old mum!" Heaton threatened.

Simon's anger boiled. Simon's father taught him to respect others, speak kindly of others, do not judge, and turn the other cheek. But Simon never learned how his mother died; he knew little about her. His father would say, "Now is not the time, Simon," and quickly move on to a different subject or leave the room entirely. Simon hated not knowing what happened to her more than the empty space she left behind.

Simon anchored his stance and then straightened his finger making it clear he was not moving. Simon cocked his head to the side so he was looking at Heaton from behind his finger like he was aiming a gun at him.

Quicker than Simon had anticipated, Heaton stepped onto his chair and had his sword drawn before his foot hit the table. In two long strides Heaton made it over the table and was upon Simon. Simon shifted to the left attempting to dodge the blow, but Heaton moved swiftly.

It happened in slow motion. Heaton raised his sword and brought it down with precision, anticipating Simon's maneuver to the left. Simon saw the sword come down. In a split second Simon's brain quickly calculated the sword's striking speed and the rate at which Simon was moving and concluded he didn't have enough time to get out of the way. He instinctively braced himself for the impact…but it never came.

In the same split second everyone and everything, including sound, froze, except Simon. He continued his movement to the left, which sent him tripping over Sonica who remained stiff as stone in an awkward position.

Simon stumbled up, expecting someone to laugh, as is the tendency when someone falls down, but there was no sound. An eerie, yet familiar, silence encompassed the frozen scene before him.

Sonica was stuck in her position halfway out of her chair and reaching for the spot where Simon was standing just moments ago. She was wide-eyed and fearful. Not far from Thianna's outstretched arm and open hand was a thin chain with a lead ball on each end that had been propelling toward Heaton's ankle before it froze mid-flight, along with everything else. The trickles of water running down the sides of the leaf canopy were long icicles and the droplets splashing to the ground were diamonds sparkling in the sunlight.

The distant Great Falls of Reconciliation were still flowing, but silently, and a cluster of birds flew overhead, oblivious to Simon and his frozen comrades. Only the immediate area was affected; the rest of the world around them continued on silently.

Simon walked around the table observing the scene. He noticed Wheelock was the only one who was frozen in a comfortable position. Leaning back in his chair with his forefinger and thumb resting on his chin, he looked like a man in eternal thought. Wheelock's eyes were focused like a hawk's. He didn't seem concerned like Sonica and Thianna. If anything he seemed to be anticipating something.

Looking at this moment in time, Simon realized how passionate these people were about the guardian. Even though it was disturbing, Simon recognized Heaton's willingness to fight for the cause, even if it meant fighting Simon. And Thianna and Sonica were both looking out for Simon. He didn't see either one coming, so there was a chance Sonica would have grabbed Simon in time, or perhaps Thianna would have tripped Heaton in time. He wasn't sure why Wheelock hadn't jumped up to protect him, but the wizard didn't seem concerned.

Then a thought occurred to him…how was he going to fix this? He didn't know how time stopped, so what was he going to do to start it back up? What if they were stuck like this for life? What if *he* were the one stuck in some time warp while everyone else saw him as standing still like a statue in normal time? A sense of urgency fell upon him. He had to figure this out. He looked at the Ring of Affinity on his hand. The tiny flame within flickered wildly.

Simon recalled the waterfall he and Sonica had gone over and how he had wished there were a way to stop the situation from happening, and then just like that time froze. However, he couldn't recall what made time start up again. He just remembers he had passed out.

And then Simon felt a familiar feeling, and stumbled from a quick onset of drowsiness. He felt this way in the water before a heavy slumber overtook him and he almost drowned.

"You better sit down." Domic's voice was beside Simon.

Simon almost jumped out of his skin. Everything around him, including sound, was frozen. In the thick silence he was not expecting someone to talk.

Simon sank into the chair Domic slid behind him. He was now on the other side of the table viewing Heaton's backside and sitting in the chair Heaton was in moments ago.

"What's happening to me?" asked Simon rubbing his eyes and face to stay awake. "How come you're moving and I can hear you?"

"You are losing energy from sustaining this spell you cast from the Ring of Affinity," said Domic, one of his hands handing him Heaton's cup of cool water on the table. Simon gulped it down like a man just coming out from the desert. "And the reason I am unaffected by the spell is because my presence is both inside and outside the area of the spell...see?" he said, the floating hand pointing behind Thianna.

Behind Thianna's bellowing, long blond hair, were a pair of frozen silver-blue hands and their comet-like tails carrying a bowl of fresh fruit.

"I was able to cast a spell of time control from outside the reach of your spell, which allows me to enter the area unaffected," Domic calmly explained.

"Are you feeling tired too?" asked Simon.

"No," said Domic. "I mastered my ability to manage my inner energy many, many years ago. You will learn someday too."

"They hate me," said Simon looking at the frozen people around the table.

"No. They care a great deal about you. They have worked hard and prepared diligently for years for the chance to work as a company with a guardian...with you."

"I don't know why."

"Then perhaps it is a good idea to take time to find out."

Simon wanted to lay his head down and go to sleep. He was just thinking about it when Domic slapped him across the face.

"Ouch! What'd you do that for?"

"If you fall asleep you may never wake up," said Domic. "Wizards have died from losing too much manna trying to sustain a spell, or counter attack another spell. It is a strategy experienced wizards use to defeat enemies who are lesser than they, casting spells the lesser wizard cannot sustain."

Simon sat up.

"How do I stop the spell?" asked Simon in a tired stupor.

"Let go," said Domic.

"I'm not holding onto anything."

"I am afraid you are. You may not have consciously cast the spell, but you still cast it and are sustaining the spell nonetheless. Other than tired, how do you feel at this moment?"

Simon had to think about it, but the same answer kept coming back to him, "Scared...and safe."

"Why?"

Simon looked at the frozen four. "Can they see me, or hear me?" Simon asked.

"To them time has not stopped, so all of this will happen in a blink of an eye. When you release the spell, they will see you disappear from where you were standing and reappear in Heaton's chair."

Simon sighed. "I'm scared I'll let them down, that I'm not strong enough. I don't like to see people hurt, or hurt people. Right now, I feel safe. As long as time has stopped, I don't have to deal with it," said Simon.

"Time control is fascinating and powerful," said Domic. "When you learn to master your inner energy, you can control who is affected by the spell and even how much. A master wizard could freeze Heaton so he could not see what was happening, but just slow Sonica enough to help guide her out of the way. It is also extremely dangerous. Rapidly depleting your manna is only one of the consequences to be aware of."

Simon fell out of his chair, but Domic's hands caught him and helped him back into it.

"You are quickly losing your energy Simon. You need to release the spell…let it go."

"How?" asked Simon fighting the desire to close his eyes and sleep.

"Take control!" Domic warned. "Will it to stop! Take control of it!"

"But…"

"NOW SIMON!"

Domic's thunderous voice shook Simon's chair. Startled, Simon sat up and yelled, "STOP!" And the still scene around him came to life in a thunderous crash.

In mid yell, Heaton completed his swing and toppled over the edge of the table, hitting the wooden ground with a thud. His ankles were entangled in Thianna's bola.

Sonica's cry carried Simon's name with it far into the distance, leaving behind Thianna with her arm extended, Heaton on the ground, Sonica grabbing air, and all three discombobulated.

Wheelock stroked his goatee...and smiled.

"Simon!" said Thianna in awe, admiring the current event. "How did you do that?"

Sonica was dazzled and at a loss for words.

Wheelock turned in his chair, delightfully studying Simon.

"I don't know," said Simon in a stupor.

"And what was that all about!" said Sonica, glaring at Heaton.

Heaton tossed the bola on the table in front of Thianna. Taking his time, he picked his sword up off the ground, and glared back at Sonica. "I was shaking things up a bit...no harm done."

"No harm because Simon reacted in time!" Sonica shouted.

Heaton sheathed his sword and composed himself. He looked at Simon. "How *did* you do that?"

"I told you. I don't know."

"So *you* did nothing...it was all the ring's doing?" said Heaton throwing Sonica a dirty look.

"Not exactly, young swordsman," said Wheelock taking a sip from his cup. "You are forgetting some of the key elements in regards to a guardian and his Ring of Affinity. First, a Ring of Affinity is only as strong as its guardian. No more, no less. Second, guardians are among the few who can cast a spell using pure emotion, whether or not he knows the spell, due to the very nature of a Ring of Affinity. Third, handlers cannot inflict mortal damage upon a guardian, or have you forgotten the oath we took?"

"I have not taken an oath to protect *him*," said Heaton flicking his thumb toward Simon. "And he is no guardian."

"No matter," said Wheelock sounding like a professor with a captivated classroom. "The day we gave the oath and amalgamated our inner energy to the ring was the day you, we, committed to becoming a handler to the guardian, whoever the ring chose to bear its power. Simon and the ring have already begun the process of amalgamating, albeit, the ring is dedicated more to the process than Simon at this point," he added as he looked at Simon. "But since Simon and the ring are connected, in essence, we are connected to Simon."

"But the process is not binding at this point," said Heaton, "Is it?"

Wheelock studied Heaton the same way he had Simon, like he was disassembling him. It made Simon uncomfortable when he was on the receiving end. Heaton appeared to feel the same way, trying his best to avoid eye contact with the wizard.

"Are you willing to give up the highest honor a Magnanthian can have bestowed based on a whimsical judgment that not only carries no reason, but is just that, a judgment?" Wheelock's stare deepened. "If your tendency is one of snap judgments and emotional reactions, perhaps it is best we seek out a master swordsman who has matured and is dedicated to what he stands for. We need a swordsman who is willing to stand by his oath because his words are true and solid! We need a swordsman who has his priorities in check and places the needs of others before his own, especially those of his guardian who needs his company to guide him, teach him, and befriend him!

"Someday you will need the guardian far more than he will need you!" Wheelock's words stung their recipient. Heaton jerked his head to the side.

Wheelock neither blinked nor took his eyes off of Heaton. If looks could kill, Heaton would have dropped dead then and there. A thickening silence lingered. No one dared to say a word. It was left to either Wheelock or Heaton to speak, and after a while it was clear Wheelock was willing to wait all day.

Heaton cleared his throat and swallowed some pride. He had the look of a boy who had been scolded at the playground in front of all the other kids.

"I...meant no disrespect," said Heaton quietly, quickly glancing up at Wheelock, Thianna, and Sonica, then back to the ground. "Each member of this company has my respect, and rightfully so. And you are right master wizard. I am acting inappropriately and have dishonored the company. You have my sincerest apology," he said to the other three company members. "However, I expected more from the one the Ring of Affinity chose as a guardian," said Heaton looking away from the others. "I expected a warrior, someone worthy to fight alongside. I expected someone who was honored to be chosen to be Guardian of Magnanthia, someone who could actually use the power granted to him."

Heaton looked up at Simon without lifting his head. "I must stay my apology to you this day. I feel no remorse for my opinion of you…as selfish and whimsical the opinion may be."

Simon wanted to say something, but words eluded him. He was torn between anger and shame. He was angry because what right did Heaton have judging him? Especially with such little he knew about him. He desired to show Heaton and prove to the others what he's capable of when he dedicates to something.

In any class in school in which Simon was determined to do well, he mastered it. After hearing the Vienna Boys Choir perform in an old church during a class trip to Newport Beach, California, he decided then and there he was going to sing in choir and has ever since. He became second chair in the baritone section in school. He dedicated himself to learning how to play the guitar on his own. He won first place three times in the Riverside Talent Show strumming those strings. He was the fastest competitor on the track team. And he hasn't lost a game of chess since he was eight years old.

Determination was one of Simon's strongest traits. But the trick in using determination was to use it sparingly. Many people have weak determination because they dilute it; they are determined to do everything. People dedicate to so many causes they soon lose focus on *why* they're doing something because they're too busy thinking about *what* they're going to do next.

Simon also felt ashamed. His father taught him how important it was to help those in need. To turn your back on someone who is asking for help is turning your back on the very essence from which we were created.

Knowing he was capable of at least trying to help them, and could do well if he put his heart into it, made Simon's shame even heavier. He avoided making eye contact with the others.

"May I make a suggestion?" said Domic, his faint mirage of human form standing near Simon.

"You are as much of this company as any one of us here," said Sonica. "Speak your piece."

"That is kind of you, dear Sonica, and I wish it were so," said Domic, "but make no mistake. I will never have the burden on my mighty limbs the five of you bear on your shoulders. Together, as a team, you may fail and you may triumph. But disband and go it alone, and you all will fail.

"I suggest you each take time on the journey ahead to think about your role in this war and the impact of not only your decision, but also your actions, will have on Magnanthia, forever.

"You are to journey to Keystone Tower. There Ganlock Gammelgard awaits your arrival. This will give you until the end of the journey to make a decision. It is he who will conduct the Rite of Rings, binding you forever as guardian and company, if this is the path you choose.

As for the oath each of you took to protect the ring, unfortunately it can be broken. Integrity and righteousness are what binds you to your oath.

"The Rite of Rings is more than an oath; it is a power that connects your very existence. Only death can separate this connection. Each of you must decide on your own. For once you are bound there is no going back, no undoing it.

"However, I caution you. The reason you were chosen to be a handler in this guardian's company is not entirely known, but you were chosen. By leaving, you break your bind to the guardian and the company, forever changing the fabric of the unity. The repercussions will be felt for generations to come.

"Each of you has a demon to deal with before you can progress as guardian and company. Those who have preceded you in the roles you have been chosen to fulfill, had all faced their enemy within. Those who defeated their internal enemy went on to do great things, making Magnanthia a better place. The others were defeated.

"The warlocks will use the darkness in your hearts to turn you against one another and even yourself. Deciding to stand and fight together with all your might is not enough against this evil. You must do so with all of your heart and all of your soul."

Domic paused, allowing for questions or comments, but no one spoke.

Domic continued. "I have received urgent messages from the southwestern corner of Shiftwood Forrest. The winds in the West are foreboding, carrying with them much pain and sorrow. Death emanates from the walls of Bedlam once more. The time is coming once again when Magnanthians will have to come together to fight for the good in this world, or perish. Evil is growing strong and will strike harder than it ever has in its attempt to end this war and destroy Magnanthia. We will need heroes. Much rests upon your shoulders.

"Simon," Domic's voice softened, "I am afraid the greatest weight falls on you. You alone are given the task of becoming a Guardian of Magnanthia. You alone can wear the Ring of Affinity. The first guardians were appointed...you were chosen. The ring chose you. But you must also choose. You must choose to become what you were meant to be. It is a gift, not a command. Ganlock cannot separate the ring from you. Even a grandmaster wizard cannot take the ring from a chosen one. But you can choose to do nothing with it, and in time its power will weaken and become useless. Fundamentally destroying it.

"Heed this warning Simon," said Domic, his tone suddenly grave. "You may leave Magnanthia, but you cannot leave behind the evil haunting it. Other worlds have fallen to it. Your world is no different.

"United you are strong; however, without a guardian, there is no company."

Like vapor, Domic vanished from their sights.

"Great," Heaton sighed. "Even if I decide to stay with the company, there may not even be a company if our savior here decides he has better things to do."

Heaton turned and started for the door.

"Heaton!" Wheelock yelled, getting up from his chair.

Heaton stopped and turned. He looked tired. "What?"

"The ring did not cast the spell stopping time," said Wheelock. "Simon did."

"You are sure?" Heaton asked impatiently. He was in no mood for mind games.

"The ring knows you; it knows us all," said Wheelock making a big circle in the air with his finger, "and it will deflect *and* return the attack we intended for our guardian if Simon is unable to intercept. And remember, a Ring of Affinity is only as strong as its guardian. No more, no less."

Heaton thought about it. "What are you saying, wizard?"

"Let me show you," said Wheelock materializing a fireball between his hands. Heaton drew his sword and went for his shield. Then Wheelock turned away from Heaton and released the fireball on Simon.

Completely off guard, Simon yelled as he put his hands up to protect his face. Before impacting Simon, the flames engulfed an invisible globe around Simon followed by a gusty noise, like a large man gasping for air. The ravaging flames reunited into another ball of fire and immediately shot back at Wheelock who had just cast a shield of ice between him and Simon. The flaming ball collided with the ice, which hadn't finished forming a complete shield, and blew it apart. Wheelock was lifted off the ground and thrown onto his back. He was wet and covered in melting ice pieces.

Thianna rushed over to him. "Are you alright?"

Wheelock moaned and muttered something.

Simon laughed nervously seeing he came out of the attack completely unscathed.

"What are you doing?" Thianna asked kneeling beside Wheelock and checking for wounds.

"Making a point," he said wiping the water and ice from his face, which was marked with a smile. He seemed to have enjoyed it.

"Which is?" asked Thianna shaking her head.

"Handlers cannot kill their guardian. If Simon had not stopped time, the ring would have initiated a spell against you," said Wheelock to Heaton, "and you would have felt the repercussion of your action. I assure you."

Looking back and forth from Wheelock to Simon, Heaton sheathed his sword.

"Okay...you almost gave me a heart attack," said Simon between heavy breaths and smiling, "but...it was better than...any ride at the amusement park!"

Heaton looked at Thianna, Sonica, and Wheelock. When he looked at Simon he was about to say something, changed his mind, and turned to leave.

"Heaton...." Simon waited until Heaton turned back and looked him in the eyes. Simon could see that Heaton's hurt and sorrow outweighed his anger. "I never knew my mom."

Heaton stared into the distance, recalling a memory long forgotten. "I'm going to pack," he said in an undertone. "We have a long journey ahead of us." On his way out of the courtyard he said, "I'll be in my quarters." Then he disappeared inside the tree house.

"Do you think that will convince him to stay?" Sonica asked Wheelock as he stood and dusted ice off his clothes.

"My intentions were not to convince him, but rather show us all Simon's potential," said the wizard. Then he looked at Simon, "If we need to convince him, then it is not in his heart to do so. We would only be setting ourselves up with false hope and defeat. Like Domic said, we all have to make the choice on our own."

Heaviness bore upon Simon's shoulders.

19

BLACK TRANSFUSION

Jak was sitting at the formal dining table he had seen a few nights ago, right before his meeting with Severn and the other warlocks. For the first time since being in this wretched world, it felt a little like home. The ornate carvings and designs on the silverware and place settings, everything laid out to perfection, an abundance of food, and even the extravagant candelabras, reminded Jak of his extended visits to his grandmother's mansion.

Jak's father sent him to his grandmother's estate often when he tired of Jak or needed to go away on business. His sister, Danielle, was often allowed to stay home under the pretense that she was keeping their mother company. Jak was often alone at his grandmother's. She also wanted nothing to do with him and avoided his company. Sitting at her dining table, watching her feed her round, pudgy face, was the only time he saw her for any length of time.

Although Severn was not short and pudgy like his grandmother, Jak found himself in similar company. Severn, sitting at the other end of the long table in a high-back chair, ate his food with precision, chewing slowly and savoring every bite, much like Jak's grandmother used to do. It was common for Jak's grandmother to sit down and eat a seven-course meal for three hours... alone. He was hoping his current host didn't love food as much as his grandmother. Despite his current dining companion, Jak was happier dining in style versus locked up in a tower with stolen vittles.

"You have made quite the impression, Jak," said Severn holding up his goblet. A servant standing behind him quickly replenished the goblet and with haste returned to his place against the wall behind Severn. Jak noticed the servant was human...and alive. Severn slowly drank from his goblet.

"Would you agree, my dear Tasha?" Severn said to the beautiful woman standing against the wall toward the center of the room, while keeping his eyes on Jak.

Jak recognized her. She was one of the beautiful, dark-haired women who were in the study the night he was brought to Severn. Tasha looked a lot like Lonique. She had numerous daggers sheathed and tucked in her black leather garment covered elegantly in a black cloak.

Tasha had been watching the servants come and go from the room until Severn spoke to her. Instead of answering, Tasha examined Jak from afar and glared at him until her attention moved to another servant coming in the room. Jak didn't see Lonique.

"Well, they are not very talkative, but they have the reflexes and precision of their elven kin, and beauty that is second to none," said Severn looking at the woman, who, with her dark skin, black hair, and black leather, could easily be mistaken for a shadow if she stood still long enough.

"What do you think of Bedlam?" asked Severn as he sliced a piece of fowl from his plate, careful not to get food on the jewelry on his hands and wrists as he dipped the meat in a mint sauce. He slowly chewed it and grinned at Jak the entire time.

Jak wanted to get up and whack that stupid grin off Severn's face, but instead he stabbed a piece of fowl on his plate and devoured it. Then he lifted up his goblet, like Severn had. To his relief a servant from behind replenished it. Jak noticed it was another human.

"I could get used to it," said Jak matter-of-fact-like.

Severn wasn't impressed. His grin bent into a frown, but then contorted into a smile.

"Good," said Severn.

Jak wanted to divert the questions off of him so he changed the subject, "I was expecting your delightful skeletons to be serving us," he said stabbing a mini potato and popping it into his mouth.

"Those filthy things touching our food?" inquired Severn in disgust, "I think not. I cannot stomach my food while they are around. I will not have them *handling* my food."

"So why keep so many so close?" asked Jak.

"Because they are expendable, dear boy, and cannot harm us."

"They can't harm us?"

"Well…they can still harm *you* at this point…but that will change soon enough." Severn took another sip from his goblet, his rings sparkling in the candlelight. "I will be happy to explain later. For now, just relax and enjoy your meal. You will need your energy." Severn forced a chuckle. It was evident he knew something Jak didn't.

Jak was going to inquire as to why he would need his energy, but then decided against it. He was in no mood to play the guess-what-I-know-while-I-string-you-along game. This was his grandmother's favorite game while feeding at her trough. Jak decided relaxing would be a better choice at the moment. He and Slade only got a few hours to sleep before Jak was 'summoned' to dinner.

Jak shook his head and smiled when he realized how much Severn reminded him of his grandmother.

Then it dawned on him. Where was Slade? He had been sitting at this table alone with Severn for over a half an hour watching the pompous idiot chew his food like a cow chewing cud, and yet there has been no sign of Slade, nor mention of him.

"Where's Slade?" asked Jak trying to hide his concern.

"Who is Slade?" he asked slowly.

"Slade, the changeling," replied Jak.

Severn stopped chewing and laid down his fork. His sharply cut goatee made it difficult to tell, but he looked angry.

"You gave a changeling a name?" asked Severn even slower than his last question. Tasha flashed Jak an awkward glare, making him shuffle uneasily in his chair.

Then he remembered...Slade explained how serious receiving a name is to a changeling, how their binding relationship would make them both stronger.

"I did," said Jak keeping his composure the best he could, and then popped another mini potato in his mouth so he wouldn't have to say any more.

Across the long and cluttered table Jak could see Severn's nostrils flare. Bedlam's Keeper leaned back in his chair.

"Is he aware of the name you so kindly gave him?"

Jak knew what was bothering Severn.

"Did he *accept* it...you mean?" Jak paused assuming Severn would stew over the possibility. And then he took a long drink from his goblet. "Yes...he did," said Jak, and added, "He absolutely loves the name."

Severn slammed his fist on the table, shaking some of the dishes. The orb on Severn's staff, standing in a custom holder within Severn's reach, awakened when the table shook. Something stirred in the orb, emanating a blood red aura.

"We are THROUGH with this course!" Severn barked. "Bring in the next one!"

The servants moved in haste taking away their plates and then setting before them a platter of glazed ham with sweet carrots and greens.

Jak sat up in his chair, watching the scepter's orb. Perhaps he said too much.

"We do not care for the likes of changelings here!" Severn sneered and then suddenly gained control over his temper. An unnatural calm quickly overcame him. Looking first at Tasha and then at Jak, Severn said coldly, "The poor thing is probably dead anyway." Tasha grinned.

Jak felt the familiar dull ache of loneliness while sitting at an extravagant table for two, but this time it was accompanied with panic.

✳ ✳ ✳

Very little had been said since they left Domic's Haven after an early, yet grand breakfast of pancakes, bacon, eggs, milk, and an assortment of fresh fruit. Since then the day had grown long. The horse Simon was riding seemed to know where it was going as the group rode in single file through Shiftwood Forrest. Sensing his tension, everybody left him alone. Even the marmot rested on the tail end of the horse leaving Simon plenty of space to think things over...and over...and over again.

Heaton and Wheelock rode ahead of Simon, with Heaton in the lead, while Sonica and Thianna road behind him. Although Heaton was the only one with a long face all day, Simon felt segregated from the group as if they were all conversing with each other through telepathy and leaving him out of the talks. He knew it was his own insecurity messing with him, and not because telepathy couldn't happen because it seemed in this world anything was possible. They all had a lot to think about too.

The only one Simon felt a connection to was his furry friend, the marmot. After returning to his bedroom last night, Simon received a speech of squeaks from his little friend. Apparently the marmot wasn't pleased that Simon left him in the room all day. Somehow Simon got the idea the marmot didn't feel comfortable leaving Simon's side and wanted to be able to find him. Simon wasn't sure how he came to that conclusion since he didn't speak marmot, or squeakinese, but the brown ball of fluff had been happy ever since Simon looked him in his dark, beady eyes and said, "I'm sorry little one. It won't happen again."

Although the marmot slept most of the morning and afternoon tucked under Simon's cloak, which was kindly given to him from Domic, along with other clothes and supplies, the marmot sat on the rear of the horse the rest of the time watching Simon's back.

Among the clothes Domic gave Simon were a pair of leather gloves he was instructed to wear at all times so no one would see the Ring of Affinity. Simon needed to look as normal as possible. This included burning the clothes Simon was wearing when he came to Magnanthia. His hands were hot and sweaty. He really wanted to take the gloves off.

It wasn't until Sonica brewed some delicious tea after dinner and the party gathered around the campfire, their choppy and sporadic talk grew into a conversation. Perhaps the conversation bloomed from the sweet and amiable aroma from the tea, or maybe from contentment after eating Domic's sandwiches for dinner. It didn't matter, Simon was just glad they were all talking again and he wasn't feeling left out.

"Would you like another?" Sonica asked Simon as he emptied his cup.

"Would I? Please," said Simon, grateful for both the refill of tea, which tasted much like a dessert, and for Sonica's sincere smile.

"So, what you're saying is I'm not the only one who came through the portal?" asked Simon, returning to the conversation with his fresh cup of sweet tea and a better mood.

"Not the same portal you came through," Wheelock explained in his professor mode, "but the portal that was cracked open by an unknown source."

Although the trees were smaller around their camp than Domic's Haven and the other trees around Paramount Peak, they still dwarfed the great pines in Minnesota. The stars twinkled somewhere beyond the canopy of leaves far above.

As dusk faded into night, the campfire grew larger from the wood provided by the shiftwoods, and Simon listened and learned.

When the Cordon Society sent a party to investigate the cracked portal, the party saved a lost ranger from Magnanthia, who was being beaten by a young man. One of them knocked the young man out before he could bash the ranger in the head. Unfortunately the ranger died. His wounds were deep from passing through the cracked portal without starlight, or some other means of protection.

"What happens to a person if they pass through a portal with no protection?" asked Simon.

"They burn. Usually a body will burn down to ashes, but for reasons we don't know, his body was slowly disintegrating on the inside. He had time to speak before he died," Wheelock explained.

It wasn't long after the Cordon Society recovered the ranger that the overlord's soul seers passed through another portal Severn had opened over the cracked portal. Severn didn't even attempt to conceal the portal; as soon as it was opened the Council of Wizards, along with others, detected it.

Once the soul seers returned to Magnanthia, Severn's portal sealed the cracked portal upon closing.

Wheelock made it clear that closing a portal one did not open is no minor feat, proving Severn is getting stronger. However, Severn probably didn't crack open the first portal. When opening a portal it takes so much manna, other magic-users can easily detect it, especially the Council of Wizards.

"The Council of Wizards?" asked Simon engrossed in what he was hearing.

The Council of Wizards is comprised of four grandmaster wizards who work with the king of Magnanthia to assist in monitoring and protecting Magnanthia's borders. The four are the Ward Wizard of the North, the Ward Wizard of the South, the Ward Wizard of the East, and the Ward Wizard of the West. The grandmaster wizards oversee Magnanthia from their own towers.

"More than likely," said Wheelock, "Severn is convinced the Council of Wizards cracked the portal to get you. We have learned, however, this is not the case. The Council of Wizards suspected Severn had opened the portal. The true source remains a mystery and poses a threat to us all, especially to you," said Wheelock pointing to Simon.

"Why me?" asked Simon.

"Because someone, other than us, must have known your whereabouts," said Thianna, "and they either informed the overlord, or the overlord sent his scouts through the portal blindly. It's something we need to find out."

Sonica looked up at one of the nearby trees like she heard something. The other three stopped what they were doing and watched her.

"What is it?" asked Simon watching Sonica get up and walk over to the tree. She walked slowly; her eyes were closed. The others remained silent.

"What's going on?"

Wheelock held a hand up, signaling Simon to stop speaking.

"I cannot understand...OH," Sonica turned around. "We have company," said Sonica, "so please do not panic."

"Why..." asked Heaton, slowly standing with his hand on the handle of his sword, "should we not panic?"

A creature larger than a horse slowly emerged from the blackness behind Sonica. Its talons dug into the earth when it moved, and its keen eyes surveyed its surroundings. It had dark brown feathers on its wings and black fur on its large cat-like body. Its head was that of a bird's with a beak large enough to swallow Sonica's head in one bite.

"Sonica...behind you!" Heaton warned her, trying to remain calm so he wouldn't startle the creature. Upon drawing his sword and tossing the sheath to the ground, the creature reared up and spread its wings, its screech kin to an eagle's.

"No!" Sonica shouted, waiving Heaton down. She still hadn't looked at the creature behind her. She was more concerned with the party's reaction.

Simon had jumped up with Thianna as soon as Heaton drew his sword. Wheelock remained seated by the fire. He could have just as well been watching previews in the movie theater as he watched Sonica and the commanding beast behind her.

"He means us no harm," said Sonica, holding her hand up. "He has something to tell me." She looked at Thianna, Simon, and Heaton. "Just, stay there. You have frightened him with your abrupt reactions," she said disappointingly. Then she turned and spoke softly to the prim looking beast.

"We frightened him?" said Heaton under his breath. "A little more heads up would have been nice." Heaton sheathed his sword.

Simon couldn't hear what Sonica and the creature were discussing, but he was fascinated how the creature was attentive like a human in conversation. There was no doubt he understood Sonica. Simon could see it in his hawk-like eyes. His stance was firm and his chest was out as the prideful creature lightly squawked. Sonica listened and responded.

Simon took in the scene while Wheelock casually observed from his fireside seat, and Thianna and Heaton went on discussing other matters like this was not at all an unusual event. Several different times the creature looked at Simon.

"Simon," said Sonica looking over her shoulder. She looked stunned. "Can you come here, please?"

Simon cautiously walked over to them.

The feathers on his head were a lighter brown than the ones on his wings; they were shiny and well kept. The dark fur on his body was also shiny and clean. The creature held his head high as he looked over Simon.

"Simon. I would like to introduce you to Rahmere. He's a…"

"Griffon," Simon interjected, looking upon the beautiful creature in awe.

Heaton and Thianna quit talking behind them. Sonica's mouth hung open.

"Umm…yes," Sonica finally managed. "Rahmere is the captain…of the elite guards among the griffons," she said still looking surprised. "There is something he wanted to say to you before he left."

The griffon stood proud as Sonica relayed his message. Only a few squawks came from the griffon as Sonica spoke on his behalf.

"I have heard whispers of you among the trees," Sonica said as Rahmere looked at Simon and spoke in rhythmic squawks. "There is hope and happiness where there was once loss and pain. I wanted to see for myself the boy the trees speak of, and look into his eyes myself. If what I hear is true, that you have come to Magnanthia wearing a Ring of Affinity and will soon become a guardian, the truth will stay safe with me and you will have my allegiance forevermore."

The griffon looked at Simon's gloved left hand.

"May I?" asked Sonica, speaking for the griffon.

Simon looked at Sonica, but she looked as confused and unsure as Simon. They both turned to Wheelock.

"I know Rahmere," said Wheelock, "and the fact he is asking, and not demanding, is his means of showing respect."

Simon looked at the muscular beast. His eyes gleamed in great wonder as Simon removed the glove and the Ring of Affinity's light glistened like a small beacon.

The griffon crouched down on his front two talons, elegantly bowing before Simon.

Simon looked to Sonica for guidance when the griffon didn't rise and kept his head low. Sonica shook her head, dumbfounded. Simon shrugged his shoulders at her response. If she didn't know what to do, how was he supposed to know?

To Simon's relief, Sonica had an epiphany. Mimicking what she wanted Simon to do, Sonica spread her hand open and slowly lowered it in the air and mouthed, 'LAY YOUR HAND DOWN.'

Simon looked at Rahmere's head. Pointing at Simon was a natural, pure white V on the neatly groomed feathers. Simon cautiously lowered his hand down upon the soft feathers and touched Rahmere's head.

A sensation came over him. Simon was suddenly elated and felt a bond to the griffon. For reasons he couldn't explain, Simon trusted Rahmere and knew the griffon was not here to hurt him. He rested his hand upon the feathered head.

"Sonica tells me your name is Simon Whittaker," said a stern, kind voice. "Thank you, Simon Whittaker."

"You're welcome," said Simon, not knowing what else to say.

Even before Rahmere responded, Simon realized what happened.

"You can understand me?" asked Rahmere. The griffin looked at Simon curiously.

"You can understand him?" asked Sonica.

"Yes, I can understand him. I can understand you," said Simon looking at Rahmere, astonished. Simon heard Rahmere's words and not a series of squawks.

"You amaze me, Simon Whittaker! This is truly a great day! I believe we will see great things from you!" said Rahmere.

"*You* amaze *me*," said Simon. "You're...beautiful."

Rahmere held his head high. "I see why the ring chose you, Simon Whittaker." He looked at Sonica. "Take great care of our guardian."

"We will. I promise," she said nodding her head.

"May we cross paths again someday," he said to Simon.

Spreading his wings Rahmere leaped over Simon and Sonica, and without missing a beat, his great wings heaved him upward. Sonica's long hair whipped back, and the griffon was gone.

Sonica was amazed as she studied Simon.

"How did you know he was a griffon?" asked Heaton when Sonica and Simon returned to the fire.

"I've always enjoyed fantasy books and games back home," Simon answered, looking up toward the night sky.

"Fantasy...?" Heaton thought about it.

"What did Rahmere have to say?" Wheelock asked Sonica as he gazed into the fire.

"Another warlock has been chosen," she said solemnly.

"That makes seven…with Bedlam's Keeper," Thianna added.

"Did he find out who it was?" asked Wheelock still looking into the campfire's flames.

"The boy the soul seers brought back from Simon's world," she said, glancing at Simon. "The transfusion starts tonight," she said sadly.

"I was afraid of that," said Wheelock drifting into deeper thought somewhere amidst the flames.

✳ ✳ ✳

As elegant and delectable as it was, Jak didn't enjoy the rest of his meal. He couldn't stop thinking that they probably killed Slade and Severn had everything to do with it.

Why does he hate changelings anyway? Jak wondered.

It was his last thought as he and Severn made their way into the golden study, where Jak first met Severn. He looked for Lonique, but there was no sign of her.

The other warlocks were awaiting their arrival. They sat in their high-back chairs, which Jak now noticed resembled thrones. A sixth throne sat empty. Instead of side-by-side as they had been the first time Jak had been in this room, the thrones formed a crescent moon and were facing a six-legged platform, resembling a tiny stage. The only light in the room came from the large fireplace. The fire danced on the wood it was consuming as if it were anticipating the coming event.

"You will not need the assistance of a *changeling* after tonight," Severn scoffed as the two of them, with Tasha trailing behind, made their way to the seated warlocks. "You will be a warlock."

Tasha took out an extravagantly decorated robe from a closet and placed it over Severn's shoulders.

"Do I have a say in whether or not I become a warlock? Maybe I don't want to," said Jak regaining his confidence from his hatred toward Severn. "Maybe I just want to go back home."

"Jak, before tonight there were only six warlocks," Severn continued as Tasha secured the ceremonious robe on him, "and as powerful as we are, we will be even more powerful when there are seven. You could say that seven is our *magic* number.

"The overlord has promised us great power once our number reaches seven, a power no man has ever had before. He has handpicked each one of us to become warlocks...and placed me in charge. The overlord knows our strengths. He knows we are able to wield the power he will soon give us! We will have power even the guardians would have feared...when there *were* guardians." A horrendous smile had spread across Severn's face.

"So, you can either be given powers that go beyond the scope of your imagination, powers that will bring your enemies to their knees begging for mercy...or," for a moment Severn pretended he was thinking, "...or you can die. Which will it be?" he asked and then chortled.

"Guardians?" Jak asked. "Who are they?"

"Were, Jak...were," said Severn, looking into a mirror and admiring what he saw. "The guardians were wizards selected to fight the overlord's armies using ancient magic." There was a touch of sadness, or perhaps regret, in his tone. Severn was no longer looking at himself in the mirror; he was looking at something much farther away. "The kingdom put everything they had into the guardians. Unfortunately for them, even guardians have a weakness...and now they are no more."

"You defeated the guardians?" asked Jak.

"You ask too many questions BOY!" yelled Large Voice from his throne.

Severn waited for Jak to respond to the warlock. When Jak said nothing, he said, "Never mind him. He's been a bit under the weather since his last transfusion. And no. But I am the only one to survive the guardians' attack on Bedlam," he said boastfully. "If it were not for my wit and my ability to overcome odds, I am afraid the warlocks would be nothing but a distant memory, and who knows what would have become of Bedlam."

"What's a transfusion?" Jak didn't like how that sounded.

"Leverage, Jak...leverage over our enemies. It is the reason *we* survived and the guardians are dead," said Severn sharply, looking at Large Voice. Jak would love to have seen Large Voice's reaction to Severn's caustic tone, but the room was too dark and the warlock's hood hid his face in the flickering light.

Severn placed his hands on each side of Jak's face. His hands were cold and clammy.

433

"You will soon have more answers than you do questions," said Severn grinning, and playfully slapped the side of Jak's face several times. Jak grimaced, as each slap became harder than the next. "So no more questions and keep your mouth shut unless told otherwise!" Severn's stern voice filled the room. He took his hands off of Jak's reddening face.

"Understood?"

Jak nodded his head.

"So what will it be, Jak? Death or domination?" Severn growled.

It didn't surprise Jak that Severn actually wanted an answer to the most redundant ultimatum in all of history.

"I guess I'll go with domination," said Jak.

"Good," said Severn returning to his cordial mood. "Then follow me."

Severn walked to the platform before the seated warlocks, and stepped up onto it. Jak was about to step up with him when two hands grabbed his shoulders and pushed him down to the floor.

"On your knees," Tasha hissed.

Severn held his staff so the orb was above Jak's head. An orange glow sprang to life in the twirling mist inside it.

"From the powers bestowed to us from the ancient crypts of Bedlam..." Severn began.

✳ ✳ ✳

Sonica and Heaton were quite interested in the fantasy books and stories Simon told them about. All three of them were amazed how so many "fantasy" creatures and beings told about in books and stories existed in Magnanthia.

Simon learned many of the demihumans, like elves, dwarves, and halflings, are real in Magnanthia. He was especially delighted when they had heard of hobbits. There were no hobbits in Magnanthia, but some famous Magnanthian explorers had been to a realm that had hobbits, and they had grand stories to tell about the hairy, little beings.

The creature that held most true to the fantasy stories were dragons. Sonica and Heaton were surprised how much Simon knew about dragons coming from a land that didn't have any, at least what they consider a *real* dragon.

Dragons are the most feared of all beasts because of their intelligence, extreme wisdom from millennia of experience, brutal strength, ability to cast spells, and their uncanny faculty of breathing the element of their make-up, such as fire, ice, acid, or lightning. Dragons are also among the few ancient creatures that still inhabit Magnanthia and other realms.

Talking about things he enjoyed back home lifted Simon's spirit, but made him a little homesick at the same time. For once he didn't feel like a lost sheep.

Unfortunately, not long after Heaton inquired about Simon's knowledge of the griffon, Wheelock spoiled the ensuing connection Simon, Sonica, and Heaton were developing when he pointed out the importance of educating Simon on their recent discovery.

"What for?" asked Heaton. "He plans on going home the first chance he gets."

"The future of Simon as a guardian and the four of us as his company, has yet to be determined, and will be determined at the appropriate time," Wheelock responded in earnest. "Simon, come take a seat." Wheelock gestured to a place next to Thianna. They sat around the campfire. Wheelock sat across from them. "You may join us if you like, swordsman, but we will not sit and wait for you to decide.

"Having a superior knowledge of praying, rituals, and moral laws," Wheelock explained, sounding like a scientist speaking from a pulpit, "Thianna will explain to you what Rahmere's news means to us and all of Magnanthia."

Thianna turned her weary eyes toward Simon. Her face was pale in the flickering light. Her thoughts weighed heavy on her.

"Bedlam is home to the most nefarious creatures, beasts, and beings that thrive on an ancient evil, with an insatiable appetite for death," Thianna began, her voice matching her somber expression. "It is from this ancient evil, in the bowels of Bedlam, the warlocks draw their supernatural powers. They have been foolishly meddling with these powers for centuries; they either do not understand, or care not about the forces they have unleashed onto themselves and Magnanthia.

"The evil haunting the corridors of Bedlam has taken the lives of many Magnanthians, including our nine beloved guardians. It has even taken the lives of warlocks and their allies, the very ones who claim they control the ancient power." Thianna shook her head. "They are fools! The evil rules them.

"The process warlocks use to obtain and harness their powers is known as a black transfusion. It is crass, cruel, and against every fiber of natural law. The magic needed to perform such a heinous act is the darkest magic. Necromancers are the only ones mad enough to practice such dark magic. Even warlocks, avid dark magic practitioners, stay away from performing black transfusions. The warlocks have the necromancers perform it on them.

"The warlocks are not interested in taking time to learn magic, to study and train, to become wise with the power that comes from learning natural magic. Instead, they just take it and wield it. They take it from magic-users they kill. They have their necromancer brethren perform black transfusions to rip manna from the deceased and take it for themselves. It is unnatural." Thianna looked disgusted as if she were watching the process.

"Tell him how it is done," said Wheelock across the campfire.

"Extracting the magic from the deceased is the difficult part," said Thianna. She took a long sip of Sonica's dessert tea. After savoring it for a moment she continued.

"It entails a complex set of rituals that demand precision in order to work, rituals only master necromancers would know in great detail. I personally want nothing to do with dark magic. But there are clerics who say it is best to study it in order to defeat it." She took another sip from her cup. "I say, become better at praying. You avoid losing your soul that way.

"Once the power has been extracted, transferring it is the easy part, unless you have a weak stomach."

"Why is that?" asked Simon.

"In order to complete the transfusion, it must be consumed."

✳ ✳ ✳

Jak found the ceremony rather ridiculous, at first. Severn went on and on about a bunch of mumbo-jumbo, the warlocks ruling the lands, calling on ancient powers from below, and something about assisting the necromancers with the transfusion.

It was then, during the part about the transfusion, it happened. The room suddenly became cold and damp. Something moved among the shadows in the room. Jak grew uneasy. He had the feeling he was being preyed upon. Something tugged deep inside him, warning him, screaming for him to get up and run because whatever was out in the corridors didn't compare to the evil that had entered the room upon Severn's bidding. It was seeping into the shadows. He couldn't see it, but Jak could feel its violent presence leering at him. It was as if hate manifested itself and lurked in the dark among them.

Severn's words and tempo were cryptic. However, Jak wasn't listening to Severn's every word. He was trying to listen to the voice in his head telling him to get up and run as fast as he could until he couldn't run anymore.

Jak thought about running...but then he remembered the giant spiders and the ghoul, and how he almost died. He recalled all the unidentifiable sounds, the moans, and voices coming from the rooms up and down the corridors. Before encountering the giant spiders, he remembered there were several occasions he turned around and went another way because of the screams or screeches.

Then...Jak remembered his only friend in this dark place was gone. Slade wouldn't be there to save him in Bedlam's corridors. Where would he run? Who would he run to?

He was alone.

He thought about his choice of death or domination.

"We look to you for power and strength," the warlocks repeated in unison after Severn.

Jak wasn't going anywhere. He believed the best he could do was let time run its course and see if this ritual, this transfusion, would be all Slade said it would be, despite the nagging feeling something wasn't right.

But Jak wanted power so he wouldn't fear anymore! No more fear of his family! No more fear of this place! No more fear of the unknown! If he feared it, he wanted the power to kill it!

"We look to you for power and strength," the warlocks said, responding to Severn's requests and incantations.

The shadows around the perimeter of the room began moving and twisting together like black fog, independently from the light of the fire, which was dim as the flames cowered under the red-hot logs.

Jak looked away from the shadows and instead concentrated on the only other source of light in the room, the orb on the Scepter of Zalaruz. The glow from within was now blood red, and the smoke churned faster and faster. For just a moment Jak saw a pair of eyes in the globe staring at him, black as coal. As fast as he saw them they were gone.

The warlocks were humming to Severn's spoken incantations. Most of what Severn said Jak didn't understand because it was in a different tongue, an ancient tongue, which Severn began speaking faster and louder. Sweat trickled down the side of Severn's face. He was speaking so quickly, Severn's mouth was struggling to keep up with the words coming out.

The five warlords continued to hum in a low pitch.

A chilling draft whirled around the room, carrying with it a muffled moan, which stirred the floating shadows along the walls.

Sweat was streamlining down Severn's face and dripping down on Jak. Jak wanted to move over, but Tasha's grip on his shoulders held him down.

Severn's body swayed from side to side as his voice bellowed the ancient words. His arms began trembling. The blood-red incandescence in the orb grew more intense. Severn's arms shook uncontrollably.

In one swift movement, like two magnets, Severn's hands clasped the scepter and lifted it higher in the air. And then, with all his might Severn jabbed the staff down upon the floor. The room rumbled and shook like a heavy brass bell crashed to the floor. Jak could feel the rippling energy expelled from the staff.

The room was silent when the rumbling faded away. Breaking the silence was a metallic clank. The two massive doors leading into the inner chamber groaned as they opened, once again, on their own accord. The doors stopped when they were halfway open, parallel to one another like giant sentinels.

Severn tapped the staff to the floor three times. The fireplace burst to life, the flames lapping hungrily again at the diminishing logs. The five shadow sentries stepped up and stood behind the seated warlocks. Tasha released Jak from her grip and stood behind Severn, who remained on the platform.

Severn nodded to someone behind Jak. Then he looked down.

"Rise and turn, Jak," said Severn. "See the destiny that awaits you."

Jak slowly rose. He was afraid to turn around and look.

He shifted his eyes to the inner chamber. It contained tables full of bubbling beakers and tubes of liquids of different colors, boiling caldrons, and chains linked to the walls. It was not a cozy place, to say the least.

Jak reluctantly turned around, not sure what to expect. But he was relieved to see Lonique. Her beauty was mystifying. Like the others, she looked serious. Jak wanted to say something, anything to her, but was afraid to speak. She must have sensed his desire to speak because she gave him a quick, little, smile. That little smile was a big relief. Lonique had been the only person whose face was inviting and kind since arriving in Magnanthia.

One of the warlocks, whose face was hidden under his hood, approached Lonique. The warlock's shadow sentry approached Jak. The female sentry held a small, black and silver chest in her hands. The silver latch gleamed in the light from the fireplace.

✳ ✳ ✳

Heaton looked uncomfortable while Thianna gave a description of the ritual leading up to a black transfusion, and the unseen evil. Sonica shivered and drew closer to the campfire.

"Although I haven't witnessed the ritual, I have been told the evil they invite is so tangible and dark it gives the appearance of a black cloud," said Thianna.

"The female sentries I mentioned earlier are one quarter dark elf," Thianna continued, "and are considered a prized possession amongst the warlocks. The sentries come from an impoverished land once known for its splendor, elite warriors of elves of various kinds, forest elves, mountain elves, and of course dark elves. The dark elves were known as shadow warriors because of their uncanny ability to fight and hide in the dark.

"In return for ageless beauty, untold riches, and full protection for their dying race, a female warrior will forever be a warlock's sentry. They have come to be known as shadow sentries, as tribute to their heritage. However, when a warlock dies his shadow sentry is free to go, keeping her ageless beauty and her riches."

"How have warlocks managed to destroy and take over other lands over the centuries when they are so stupid?" asked Heaton rhetorically. "Their *shadow sentry* need only to wait for the first time they fall asleep, tip-toe into their resting chamber, and cut their throat. 'Look, I am rich and free to go,'" said Heaton mimicking his version of a shadow sentry in a high-pitched voice. Sonica smiled at his imitation, but stopped when Thianna did not reciprocate Heaton's mockery.

"They may be fools for meddling in dark magic," said Thianna soberly, "but they are not stupid. And to judge them as such, young swordsman, would be a grave mistake. Warlocks are powerful magic-users who enjoy using magic that alters, hurts, controls, or destroys their foe's mind, leaving the body alone so they can later extract any magic and raise the body as an addition to their ever-growing army.

"As for the shadow sentries, they are offered their first jeweled article at the same ritual a new warlock is made. Standing and facing one another, the soon-to-be warlock and his shadow sentry are each given a Medallion of Holding. Traditionally she wears her medallion on a circlet of silver, representing royalty, although royal they are not. Her medallion of holding contains the essence of her warlock, which is what gives her the same protection he will have against the undead."

"Which is what?" asked Simon, hanging onto Thianna's every word.

"Warlocks, like their necromantic brethren, raise the dead so as to be served by them," Thianna explained. "The undead cannot kill or harm the one who raised them. The unfortunate undead, already know this. Any attempt, and they end their own unnatural life. In addition, a warlock need only think it, and the undead he has raised are destroyed. It's called recanting. The undead spontaneously combust into ashes, never to be raised again.

"In addition to being conniving and bitter, warlocks trust no one, including their own shadow sentry, and each other. To safeguard against betrayal, and to answer your question," said Thianna raising a brow at Heaton, "the warlocks capture a piece of their shadow sentry's will and place it within a Medallion of Holding. The warlock wears this on his body at all times. The farther the female sentry is from her warlock, or at least his medallion, the weaker her protection against the undead becomes, to the point that she eventually has no protection. The undead can smell this, and they even wait for it. They know when a shadow sentry is vulnerable and has lost her warlock's protection.

"And if that is not enough to keep the shadow sentry from killing the warlock she has sworn to protect," said Thianna leaning toward Heaton, "if she willfully takes his life, she also kills her piece of will in his medallion of holding."

"What would that do?" Heaton asked, genuinely concerned.

"The piece of will the warlocks hold is their sentry's will to live," said Thianna. "If she kills her warlock, she then kills herself. If she kills a different warlock, that warlock's shadow sentry, her own kin, will kill herself."

"Of course, only a fool betrays a warlock," said Wheelock, "for they would not only kill the other shadow sentries, but such an action would bring down the wrath of the overlord's army to the dark elves' homeland."

"Sounds like slavery to me," said Sonica.

"That is essentially what they are," said Thianna. "They are bondswomen so they can have riches, luxuries, and power. It is the path they have chosen."

✴ ✴ ✴

Jak admired Lonique and her new silver circlet with the green jewel, as a similar medallion on a thick, silver and gold chain was secured around Jak's neck and tucked down his shirt. The cold metal lay against his chest.

"Now that you are united, you two will be more powerful together than either of you would be alone," said Severn on the platform. The Scepter of Zalaruz still illuminated blood red from its orb. "Lonique! Escort Jak to the inner chamber. Then join the other sentries as their equal, and stand guard." Severn commanded. Looking sternly at Lonique he added, "Remember…protect him with your life."

As Lonique escorted Jak to the large doors, Severn's previous words to Lonique echoed in Jak's head. *"And never leave his side unless otherwise instructed, and even then you are to remain nearby for your own safety."*

"Good luck," said Lonique softly, "and be strong."

She left Jak with Severn and the other warlocks standing between the two towering doors and then joined Tasha and the other shadow sentries standing in a straight line. Their backs were to the inner chamber's doors while keeping their watchful eyes on the only other door in the room, the door leading into Bedlam's corridors.

Severn led Jak and the other warlocks into the inner chamber. Rumbling, the doors started closing behind them. There were two tables next to each other in the center of the room fitted with leather straps. One table was empty; the other was occupied. Two mischievous, unpleasant looking men wearing black and red billowing robes stood near the tables, eagerly waiting. The two men reminded Jak of clergy. Only they didn't look holy.

"Enrik, meet Jak," said one of the necromancers to an inanimate skeleton laid out on one of the surgical tables.

He spoke as if introducing two guests at a dinner party but with an intentional maniacal undertone. "He's the overlord's latest addition," said the necromancer to the unresponsive skeleton, pointing at Jak. "Subsequently making you his first transfusion. All those years learning and practicing magic will be Jak's after one night."

The necromancer took notice of Jak and grinned. "Thank Enrik for all his years of studying and practicing magic you will be inheriting from him." Sarcasm dripped off every word.

Jak passed the necromancer's snide comment to the side, but the smug idiot stared at Jak, anticipating an answer. The room was silent. Severn and the other warlocks were also awaiting his response, like it was a punch line to a joke. This was all part of the process to them. One man's loss was their amusement and gain.

"Err…thanks," Jak mustered up. "I hope I can put it to good use."

"That you will, Jak," said Severn with a slight chuckle. For the first time the warlocks chuckled and chortled. Jak liked it more when they were serious. Their phony delight was annoying and creepy.

The large doors shut with a profound thud. Jak flinched as the ancient metal lock sealed them in.

Simon shivered, taking no comfort amidst the campfire's heat while Thianna told what she knew of a black transfusion, and the making of a warlock. He couldn't imagine how a process so cruel could even be devised, or what kind of person would think of something so sick, and then actually do it.

"A warlock's initial transfusion begins with the unfortunate soul who had the most manna before dying in the Maze of Mayhem," said Thianna, "which will also be the first undead he will animate, if he survives the black transfusion."

"*If* he survives?" asked Simon.

Thianna took a deep breath and exhaled. She didn't like talking about this.

"The first black transfusion can overwhelm the recipient's body, mind, and soul. Any number of things can happen," Thianna explained as if she were warning Simon. "Taking energy from the remains of a dead being is dangerous enough, but placing it in a living being can be fatal. The recipient may not be able to physically handle the transfer and may die of any type of natural death, such as a heart attack, stroke, internal bleeding, and rupturing of organs. Or the recipient could lose his mind taking it all in. Manna is not the only thing the recipient receives in a black transfusion. Within the manna are small bits and pieces of the deceased, like memories and emotions. As these pieces transfer, the recipient's mind may not be able to decipher the difference between what is real and what is...brought in.

"Think about this for a moment. Imagine pieces of your most terrible moments in life along with your best moments. Mix them up and then take in all of the emotions that came with them in a matter of a few minutes. Some of my worst moments took days and weeks to work through. Some I'm still mourning over. Some of my greatest moments I relished for hours, and even days. If the initiate snaps and loses his mind from the black transfusion, the overlord will not hesitate in having him killed, for he will be of no use to him.

"And as for the recipient's soul, the emptier it is, the better the chance he will survive. The overlord prides himself of finding souls that are bitter, hateful, and otherwise prideful because these are empty souls he can fill with what he desires. A soul full of love, empathy, kindness, and truth would reject a black transfusion and die."

"How is the essence consumed?" said Sonica with disgust.

"Experienced warlocks who have had multiple black transfusions consume small amounts of essence from their victims by means of inhaling, drinking, and eating the essence the necromancers extract," said Thianna disappointedly, "but for the first couple of times, the recipient must take it intravenously to lessen the odds of the transfusion not taking, or the recipient simply rejecting it."

"How many black transfusions does a warlock go through?" asked Simon.

"As many as he wants. With each transfusion a warlock becomes more powerful and it's less likely his body or mind will reject it. Although eventually a warlock will need black transfusions," said Thianna dismally.

✳ ✳ ✳

"This may burn a little," said the necromancer hooking Jak up to a concoction of tubes and needles. He sounded caustic, but it was hard to tell with these guys.

"A LITTLE?" Jak yelped.

The needle burned upon entry and the burning sensation spread throughout Jak's body as Enrik's essence seeped into clean branches of veins and arteries. The burning was beyond painful. It could have been sulfuric acid, or magma, scorching through his bloodstream.

Jak screamed and hollered and begged them to stop. But the louder he screamed the more they laughed and berated him.

"STOP IT! STOP IT!" Jak yelled and pleaded.

Jak was sure his insides were melting. Nothing could be this excruciating without killing someone.

He saw in his mind Enrik combusting again, the orange and red glow from the tip of the Banishing Stick spreading rapidly from his gut.

Jak became numb, and the relentless screams in the room were no longer his own. His mind and body separated for a few pain-free moments.

"Enjoying the Devil's tea?" whispered Severn into Jak's ear.

Jak didn't open his eyes to look at the madman. He clenched his teeth and eyelids, resentfully anticipating the continued onslaught of pain. Jak welcomed the numbness and prayed it would forever stay with him.

Jak shivered uncontrollably. His hair and clothes clung to his cold, clammy body.

"Wait…it's coming," Severn told Jak, tauntingly.

What? What's coming? Jak thought, but didn't ask. He didn't want to give Severn the satisfaction of knowing his questions and comments were tantalizing him. And, Jak didn't really want to know.

The answer came like a red-hot arrow into his chest. A sharp, twisting spasm ripped into his heart. The poisonous burn flashed through his body with every heartbeat.

Jak opened wide his mouth to scream from the agony. No sound came out. He opened his eyes. No light came in.

The last thing Jak heard were two people speaking in unison. "You have made a big mistake," they kept saying. One voice was his. The other voice was Enrik's.

20

THE COUNCIL OF WIZARDS

A large, round table made of solid marble rested at the center of the court among white stone pillars and archways. Green vines grew throughout the entire court. Some pillars were arrayed with mirrors of varying shapes and sizes. The court appeared extensive. Sunshine cascaded down the pillars and reflected off the mirrors keeping the white stone court well lit. A breeze wafted a sweet, green fragrance from the flowers and leaves on the vines. Two very old trees stood near to one another. A doublewide archway connected them.

Behind the two trees a sizable clay basin rested atop its thick base made of timber and rocks. Tipped slightly to one side, the basin perpetually poured water onto the doublewide archway, elegantly decorated in carvings. A curtain of water came through tiny holes in the archway. It was so calm and smooth the water reflected, like a mirror, the image of those who stood before it. The streamlet of water originating from the clay basin eventually found its way over the edge of the tower's backside.

Two life-like dragons curled restfully around the marble table, along with its wide chairs, which were all crafted from fine timber and adorned with very tall backs. Each dragon lifted its head lazily skyward, its neck forever in an elegant arc. Gold flames hurled from the open jaws of one dragon and purple flames from the other. The undying flames arched high above the marble table, intertwined, rose up like a vine, and then split off in smaller gold and purple flames, licking the sky like a tree reaching to the sun.

The court was at the top of a great, white tower stretching toward the heavens. The tower was between two majestic mountains. A vast river flowed between the mountains, split in two before reaching the tower, and reconnected upon passing the tower on the other side. The river's rapid current encased the wizard's tower.

"Welcome back to Keystone Court. It has been a long time my friends. Thank you for coming on such short notice," said one of the wizards cordially. "Each of you has come a great distance."

Five wizards sat around the marble table. Their staves lie on the table, pointing to its center forming a makeshift star. The wizard who spoke wore simple, well-aged robes. His long pointy hat slumped over near the top and had a wide brim. Like his clothes, his skin was weathered and well-seasoned.

"Ganlock, you humor us old friend," said a portly, jovial wizard with a big smile. "Your pocket guides, as you call them, make an otherwise long journey *great* indeed!" His belly and white beard shook as he laughed heartedly.

"Yesss, but are they safe?" droned a slim wizard. He was richly dressed in robes made of fine linens and jewels. His poise was stern, and his gestures controlled and calculated. He stroked his short, black beard, cut precisely to square his jaw line.

"I assure you, Warwick, the pocket guides take passages even the University will not be able to detect," said Ganlock reassuringly. "I am also confident my adaptations to Keystone will suffice *if* someone manages to follow you and your pocket guide in route."

Warwick studied the dark blue sphere no bigger than a grape floating next to him. With some reluctance he held open his robes and with a finger opened a pocket, allowing his pocket guide to jump in.

"Clever! How the guides use multiple levels of passages and pass through water," said an old wizard whose appearance was distinguished, but he displayed a modest air. His skin was pale and unblemished from the sun. He presented himself in formal, but not gaudy, burgundy robes. "Clever...very clever. You truly are a master of gateways," he said watching his royal red pocket guide leap into his pocket.

"Thank you, Ussivian. You are too kind," said Ganlock.

"I certainly hope he is not," said the fifth wizard earnestly, and then grinned. The stout wizard's long, gray beard and mane, and his weathered skin were the only characteristics revealing his age. His eyes and demeanor told a different story, one of wisdom, passion, and full of fight. He was the only wizard with a sword. "If he is too kind then you are not as great as we believe you to be." Then the wizard's sarcasm sobered. "You are *the* master of gateways in my humble opinion. And I am hoping you have a few answers pertaining to the recently cracked portal."

"My dear Boullengard, I too am hoping. I am hoping for solutions to our questions." Ganlock closed his eyes and took a moment to smell a passing breeze.

"As members of the Council of Wizards, I recognize each of you for your status and given name," said Ganlock. "Ward Wizard of the West, Warwick Darken. Your superior intellect juxtaposed with your stern and orderly ways are the reasons you are entrusted to watch over Magnanthia's westward lands. The west is Magnanthia's most difficult border. Evil spawns there as I speak. Now, more than ever, it is the frontline against Bedlam's undead army and its allies.

"Your in-depth knowledge of dark magic and your most diverse range of spell capabilities make you a valuable asset in our war against Bedlam."

Warwick held his head high.

"Ward Wizard of the East, Ussivian Seleuscius," Ganlock continued. "You are, undoubtedly, the most knowledgeable wizard of ancient magic. The University has no record of any wizard discovering, understanding, and able to use more ancient magic than you, other than the ancients themselves." Ganlock couldn't resist grinning. "Far beyond our mountain ranges to the east are undiscovered lands of old. Your uncanny ability to work in ancient spell casting makes you the ideal wizard to watch over Magnanthia's eastward lands."

Ussivian nodded in gratitude.

"The dwarves appreciate your sensitivity to their wishes to be left alone in the easternmost mountains," said Ganlock. "Their respect for you may prove to be of great value if the king calls on them to aid us in the war on Bedlam.

"Ward Wizard of the South, Abrakannezre Norresken, known simply as Abe...by choice. I will challenge anyone who denies you are the most compassionate wizard in Magnanthia. Your love and respect for trees and nature has played a major role in solidifying the kingdom's relationship with the shiftwood trees, and in kind, the wood elves, tree fairies, and other forest inhabitants. Much of Magnanthia's southlands are forested. Shiftwood Forrest covers our southern borders and beyond. The trust you have earned with the elves and shiftwood trees is vital to the war against Bedlam."

Abe cocked his head and smiled.

"And of course, Ward Wizard of the North, Boullengard, whose full name *still* remains unknown because he refuses to speak it," said Ganlock letting go a big smile after trying to be serious. "Your honor, devotion, and passion for justice long ago won the hearts of Magnanthians, and continue to do so this day. Among the elite and rare class of battle wizard, you are as deadly brandishing your sword as you are casting spells. I wish for you to watch my back, if my back ever needs watching." Another grin.

"The vast Sea of Reverie runs along Magnanthia's entire northern border. Few armies have attacked Magnanthia's northern border and none have ever succeeded. However, being near and dear to Magnanthia, King Elderten keeps you close to Kincape Castle, despite your much needed assistance at the front lines of battle.

"Kincape Castle is well fortified, resting upon the steep cliffs of Cape Kin, a great perch the Reverie carved ages ago at the mouth of Black Moon Bay, where her waters will forever cradle Kincape Castle. There is little concern for Magnanthia's northern borders." Ganlock raised his bushy eyebrows.

"Boullengard, your lifelong devotion of learning the art of war, and mastering it, says it all. Magnanthia will need your glorious skills yet again. I expect the king to disapprove of my decision, but no matter. When the time is right you will leave the king's comfort zone; you will leave Kincape Castle and Black Moon Bay. Magnanthia will need you at her front lines."

"I believe that is enough flattery for one day," said Warwick to Ganlock. "What have you called us here for? And why so secretive?"

"Oh no, no, no...flattery is gooood! Keep going!" said Abe, laughing cheerfully.

"Thank you for the recognition," said Boullengard gratefully. "But...why *are* we here? You were adamant we tell no one...including the king."

"*Especially* the king..." Ussivian pointed out.

"This is most unusual of you," Boullengard added.

"Yes, and I mean no disrespect toward King Elderten. I have served the royal family for many years and I have no intentions of ending my service." Ganlock thought carefully on his next words. "However, what I am about to propose I know the king would refuse, even if it is in his best interest. We must protect the king, even if it means protecting the king from himself. This we must do! We live in a time where the differences between good and evil are diminishing. A new kind of terror has surfaced.

"For this reason, I ask the very existence of this meeting and every word spoken here stay amongst the five of us, never to be mentioned to another soul." Ganlock made sure he had everyone's attention. "And I need it sealed with a wizard's oath."

Around the table were looks of surprise, doubt, and suspicion. Ganlock deduced this response, but was hoping for a more trusting one.

"Are you mad?" Warwick inquired.

"You do understand what you are asking us to do?" asked Abe with unduly curiosity.

"I do," said Ganlock.

"We can do no such thing," said Ussivian. "We are wards of the kingdom and have sworn our loyalty to the king. What you ask is treason. He will take every head around this table, including yours." Ussivian's long, gnarled finger pointed at Ganlock.

"This is beyond King Elderten. Or have you forgotten?" said Ganlock calmly. "The Council of Wizards was put in place long ago to protect Magnanthia. Since that time the council agreed to protect each king who rules the kingdom. Do not forget our responsibilities as grandmaster wizards. We protect the kingdom first and *then* the king."

"He's right," said Abe, his resonate voice oddly serious. "The Council of Wizards has existed long before this king. It is indeed to Magnanthia we owe our allegiance. We do not share the same loyalty as Magnanthians under the king's protection. When was the last time you needed the king's protection, Ussivian?" He laughed at his last comment.

"Preposterous! I have never needed the assistance of the king's steel!" said Ussivian.

"Precisely," said Boullengard. "It has been decided then. We place any knowledge of this meeting ever taking place under the wizard's oath."

Boullengard stood, picked up his staff, and pointed it skyward.

"Now you're talking!" Abe chuckled as he picked up his staff and stood. He touched the end of his staff to Boullengard's.

Ganlock looked at Ussivian and Warwick.

"I suppose," said Ussivian standing with his staff, "since my head isn't on the line…. What's the worst that could happen?" He touched his staff to Boullengard's and Abe's.

Warwick shook his head. "You may not lose your heads, but the king can take our wardship from the Council of Wizards. This could get messy."

"Oh, quit babbling you articulate buffoon!" Abe roared. "The Council has and always will protect Magnanthia! The king is not about to take away our territorial duties we so politely handle for him!"

Warwick sighed and then stood. "I like having a territory," he said half pouting. Then he touched his staff to the others'.

Ganlock stood, pleased with the four ward wizards.

Pointing his staff skyward, he touched it to the other four. A light shone like a star on top of a Christmas tree where the five staves met. The soft light poured over the five wizards, encased them, and then disappeared.

Taking their seats, Ganlock wasted no time.

"First, what we do know," said Ganlock. "Six of the Rings of Affinity have returned to us – "

"Wait! Only six? There should be seven!" Warwick was displeased.

Ganlock shook his head. "Peter's ring has not returned."

"Impossible! A guardian's ring returns to the Cordon Society...YOUR Cordon Society after his death! And I saw him die!" Warwick kept getting louder as he spoke.

"Be careful, Warwick," Boullengard warned. "Sounds like an accusation is formulating."

"That is not my intention. I am saying – "

"And I am saying I believe Peter never killed himself, or the princess. I was there that night too, if you recall!" Boullengard was sitting at the edge of his seat.

"They burst into a million pieces right before our eyes," said Warwick, pointing out the obvious.

"I assure you, the ring has not returned to the Cordon Society," said Ganlock. "You have my word."

"Then he must be alive," said Abe. "But where could he be?"

"Probably with the other two traitors," said Ussivian.

"I can't see Peter falling into such a trap," said Abe compassionately. "He's stronger than the other guardians. He was their leader."

"And look what happened," Ussivian quickly added.

"You blame Peter for what happened to the other guardians?" Ganlock was surprised and saddened from the thought.

"Not entirely...but he was the leader of the guardians," said Ussivian cautiously.

"As each of you watch over a fourth of Magnanthia, I watch over the Cordon Society, overseers to the guardians and their companies. If you want to place blame, then place it on me!" Ganlock's eyes narrowed.

"No one is placing blame on anyone," said Boullengard in an attempt to defuse the heating tension. "If Peter *is* alive, then he's in hiding. And the reason is obvious. He is convinced Warwick, and perhaps other members of this council, are traitors!"

Warwick shifted in his chair, uneasy. "We have spoken of the incident at Cold Hinge Mountain and further investigated his claim. Together we deduced, and ALL agreed, Peter made a mistake!"

"And we hold to our decision. However, we have not been able to explain why he was so convinced a traitor was present, so much so he was willing to risk his life, and more importantly, Elleanor's life," said Ganlock soberly. "The only way we will ever know is to find him. And hopefully alive. We must find him before the overlord and his warlocks discover he is still alive and find him first."

"*If* we find him, will we kill him for treason?" asked Warwick, displeased.

"No...we will not," said Ganlock trying hard to be considerate, "for we have no proof he has committed treason."

"No proof! One of the rogue guardians killed the queen the same night Princess Elleanor was taken. It could easily have been Peter. Besides, King Elderten not only believes Peter killed the princess when he killed himself, but holds Peter, as leader of the guardians, fully responsible for the queen's death." Warwick stiffened his already solid posture. "And I must agree!"

"The king had to bury his wife and believes his daughter has been obliterated. His grief is distorting his view, which is understandable," said Ganlock compassionately. "But his grief and anger are turning into hatred. He wants blood. Even if it is the wrong blood."

"All the more reason we must find him," said Boullengard urgently. "If Peter is innocent we need to find out what he knows. Peter was not nearly as angry as he was hurt the night he and the princess *disappeared!*" Boullengard calmed himself with a long breath. "Peter has always loved the princess…" he said sadly, "he would never harm her."

"Where do you suggest we start looking?" asked Ussivian. "If he's hiding beyond the borders of Magnanthia we may never find him."

"A guardian can find him," said Ganlock reluctantly.

"Now I *know* you are crazy," said Warwick. "Those two guardians betrayed the king. They betrayed us all! What makes you think they will help us?"

"Or we would want their help?" said Ussivian.

"They will not help us," said Ganlock regretfully, "…and the moment they betrayed the king, they no longer were guardians," Ganlock looked worn out and burdened. "They have joined the overlord's ranks…they are warlocks."

"And you want to create another one? For what purpose! So he too can go mad and kill more Magnanthians?" Warwick's face was red and his eyes darkened. "The first nine guardians were a mistake! They were given too much power! And worse, the men given these powers were too weak! I will have nothing to do with creating another one! I say we find Peter, kill him, and then kill the other two for good measure!"

"Calm yourself, Warwick," said Ussivian. "You are a ward wizard. Act like one."

Warwick glanced at Ussivian, and after a second thought he started calming down.

"We have a choice to use a guardian to find Peter," said Ganlock pausing to search for the right words and to get a read on the four wizards before him. Boullengard, as he was hoping, was eagerly awaiting a plan. Abe was actively listening to both sides, seeming to be in favor of finding Peter, and not killing him. Ussivian seemed distracted, or perhaps distant, as if he had something else on his mind. And Warwick, with no surprise, was furious…. "However, we do not have the choice whether or not we create another guardian…because one already exists."

All eyes fell on Ganlock.

"How can this be?" asked Ussivian. "You have neither the authority, nor the ability to do this! It takes all three of the ancient pieces to make another ring. Once the dwarves and elves find out what happened to our Guardians of Magnanthia, they will have nothing to do with making more!"

"You are correct. I have neither authority, nor ability," said Ganlock. "But he was not created...he was chosen."

"Chosen?"

"How?"

"By whom?"

"Impossible!"

"Who is he?"

Ganlock put his hands up to quiet everyone. He understood it is rare for any magical item to choose, or summon, a particular person, but the University has it on record that it has been done before.

"I, and the Cordon Society, know who the ring chose, but it is still unclear where, or from whom, it came. Whether the power within the ring, a spiritual realm, or a person chose him is unclear. But he was chosen nonetheless." Ganlock placed his hands on the table.

"Since you know who he is we should inform the king immediately and have him brought in," said Warwick, his animated excitement uncharacteristic.

"This is precisely why I am not revealing his name to the council...at this time," said Ganlock keeping a watchful eye on each wizard.

"This is an OUTRAGE!" burst Warwick. "If you do not inform the king...then I must!"

"Then the king shall remain uninformed of the chosen guardian, and left befuddled when the Ward Wizard of the West falls dead at his feet," Boullengard intensely cautioned.

Warwick was at a loss for words and unease lined his features.

"Did you forget we are under a wizard's oath?" said Boullengard impatiently, leaning into the table. "You will drop dead before completing any sentence with intent of telling someone what we spoke of here!"

Warwick's lips became paper-thin.

"*How* did it happen? Which ring chose him?" asked Ussivian.

After a long pause Ganlock answered. "It is best, for now, I do not reveal how it happened...until we can all see eye-to-eye."

"Perhaps Warwick is right," said Ussivian sharply. "You are asking us to act on trust, and yet you offer none in return. Perhaps it is best letting the king handle this his way."

"A Ring of Affinity is very powerful and contains ancient magic few understand," said Ganlock. "Warwick is right. It is too powerful to place in the hands of someone too weak. We did our best in helping to choose nine men to become guardians, and we took great care in making nine Rings of Affinity.

"This time there are two distinct differences. First, we did not choose this guardian to have a ring; the ring chose the guardian. A rare occurrence in itself. Second, and most important, this Ring of Affinity was not crafted by mere man. This ring is ancient and was crafted by a much higher power. It is the tenth Ring of Affinity."

The five wizards were silent, looking around the table at one another.

"So you have seen the ring?" asked Boullengard.

"I have."

"Can you reveal where the ring is at this moment?" Boullengard asked hesitantly.

"Yes," said Ganlock. "And this takes us back to the cracked portal. The individual the ring chose was not in Magnanthia, but in a different realm. He needed the ring to pass through the portal."

"He already donned the ring?" Abe choked on his own words.

"Yes, so he could enter a portal into Magnanthia," said Ganlock matter-of-factly.

"He is not of this world...most unusual," said Ussivian intrigued.

"The most mysterious aspect of these events is not that the ring chose the guardian, or that the guardian came from another realm, as peculiar as they seem," Ganlock lowered his voice as if someone outside of the meeting might hear. "No...the most mysterious and, I fear, most concerning aspect of all is the portal was not cracked open in Magnanthia...it was cracked from the other side."

The five wizards sat around the table in silence. For several long moments the only sound was the water flowing from the clay basin, over the doublewide archway, and onto the stone floor.

"But, we know the overlord opened the portal, took a boy, and made him a warlock," Abe explained unconvincingly.

"He *reopened* the cracked portal," said Ganlock, "but he did not crack it the first time. Someone, or something, in the guardian's realm did."

"What now?" Boullengard eagerly awaited Ganlock's reply.

B. R. MAUL

"First," Ganlock cautioned as he stood and picked up his staff, "Be mindful. Take great care considering what we discussed here today. As for what we need to do...we need to remember why our forefathers put in place the Council of Wizards. As wizards we have devoted our lives to learn of powers, good and evil, unseen by the human eye. It is a wizard's responsibility to use this knowledge, wisdom, and power to protect the people of the land against such revolting evil. Magnanthia comes first! The king and the royal family are second, regardless of promises of riches, land, and positions the king has made.

"Second, there's a chance that Peter and the princess are out there," he said looking out to the mountains, "and the best chance in finding Peter is with the help of the chosen guardian, whether we like it or not," he added looking at Warwick and Ussivian. "And we must keep the chosen guardian, and the knowledge that Peter and the princess may still be alive, from Bedlam's overlord *and* King Elderten. Until we can find a way for the king to trust the chosen guardian it is best we treat the royal army as much as a threat to him as the undead army.

"Third, the two Rings of Affinity the former guardians still have in their possession, need to be recovered and brought back to the Cordon Society," Ganlock continued. "This shall not be a task to take lightly. However, I'm quite sure King Elderten will have no quarrels giving us what manpower he can spare to assist us.

"And finally, we need to find out why the overlord is still alive. Nobody knows how the overlord survived Peter's spell at the Battle of Barren Hill. Few know of the spell, and even fewer know how to counter it. I suspect he received help."

Ganlock knelt down. Cupping his hands he took several drinks from the streamlet.

"Any questions?" he asked.

"What of the chosen guardian? Where will he dwell? Does he have a company?" Warwick sounded concerned on the surface, but his anger still shown through.

"Let me worry about the guardian," said Ganlock. His tactful nature was second to none.

Addressing all four, Ganlock continued. "Upon returning to your towers moments from now, no one will even know you had left. Return to your work as usual, but begin gathering whatever information you can. And remember to be mindful. The king must not learn of the chosen guardian."

The four pocket guides rose from the wizards' pockets.

"As you know, your pocket guide is the only way back to your tower. Do not stray from the guide's path or you could be forever lost. Once your pocket guide returns you to your tower, then and only then, is this meeting adjourned and the wizard's oath completed."

After their farewells, the four ward wizards followed their pocket guides under the double archway, disappearing in the calm waters.

Ganlock closed his eyes and took a moment to smell a passing breeze. He took his time admiring some of the vines and leaves as he made his way to a pillar. The pillar was adorned with several long mirrors, a few were framed in marble and a few were framed in timber.

"My, my, my," he said looking at his reflection. "I am beginning to look old." He chuckled and smiled, and then sat down on a nearby bench.

"This certainly is not my tower," a voice guffawed beside the bench.

"Perhaps you took a wrong turn," said Ganlock grinning at Boullengard, whose green pocket guide floated in front of him.

"Perhaps your pocket guide has spent too much time hanging around in pockets." Boullengard returned a grin. "However, I suspect this was no accident."

"I needed to speak to you alone my old friend, without the ears of the other council members." Ganlock rose from his bench. Together they walked back to the great marble table, but remained standing.

"We have a traitor among us," said Ganlock, "and I want someone else to know of this; someone I trust."

"When you say 'among us' are you referring to the kingdom? Because if you are this is old news my friend. Or are you referring to the council?" Boullengard watched Ganlock attentively.

"The latter, I'm afraid. As I pointed out earlier, there are few wizards who know of the spell Peter used against the overlord, and even fewer who would know the counter spell. I informed the council that Peter was taught the spell and was going to use it against the overlord in battle." Ganlock's disheartened face shook.

"Are you sure it's one of us? We are not the only wizards who know of the spell," said Boullengard.

"No...I am not sure...but there are few who knew Peter was planning on casting it against the overlord. His company, notable board members at the University, and the Council of Wizards are the only ones who knew," said Ganlock in his renowned calmness.

"Only two of his company members are still alive," Boullengard thought aloud.

"And one is the wizard," Ganlock added to his thought.

One of Boullengard's eyebrows arched up. "There you have it. The guardian's wizard would have the least to lose and most to gain. Any wizard who is on the University's board would be insane to gamble a prestigious position with such influence. And as for the Council of Wizards, we too share a comparable risk, and I dare say with higher influence."

"I hear you old friend, but it is too simple. And I know this wizard well. It doesn't add up." Ganlock's face grew long at the idea.

"I will not claim to know him as well as you do, but I do know him. Wheelock is a great man, and an even greater wizard, but I would not put it past him...or anyone for that matter."

"Yes, I suppose you are right," said Ganlock. "The most important thing is that I shared my suspicions with you, and now we can put our heads together." Ganlock smiled at Boullengard. "You had better be off my good friend," he said leading Boullengard back to the watering archway.

Boullengard's green pocket guide waited near the curtain of glossy water.

"How do you know it wasn't me? Maybe I wanted to help the overlord. Maybe I will tell every one of my allies and they will hunt you down," said Boullengard, his one eyebrow arching high.

"I do not know," said Ganlock patting his old friend's shoulder, "but I am willing to put my life on it you are not the one. Oh, and you are still under the wizard's oath. You would drop dead before the thought left your lips," he casually added.

Boullengard thought about it, and laughed. "You are tricky...very tricky my friend!"

The two old wizards shook hands, and Boullengard turned and followed his pocket guide through the passage.

Ganlock closed his eyes and took a moment to smell another passing breeze.

AUTHOR BIOGRAPHY

B. R. Maul grew up in Moorhead, Minnesota. Having studied creative writing and secondary English education in college, he planned to teach high school before embarking on a writing career. A sudden turn of events, however, compelled Maul to begin writing immediately. This, combined with his lifelong love of fantasy fiction, resulted in his debut novel, *Portals, Passages & Pathways*.

Maul currently lives in Fargo, North Dakota, with his wife and three daughters.

NOV 06 2015

Made in the USA
Lexington, KY
21 October 2015